IT'S A
LEARNING
CURVE

A NOVEL

IT'S A
LEARNING
CURVE
A NOVEL

GILA ARNOLD

MENUCHA PUBLISHERS

Menucha Publishers, Inc.

© 2018 by Gila Arnold

Typeset and designed by Rivkah Lewis

ISBN 978-1-61465-655-5
Library of Congress Control Number: 2018930947

Published and distributed by:
Menucha Publishers, Inc.
1235 38th Street
Brooklyn, NY 11218
Tel/Fax: 718-232-0856
www.menuchapublishers.com

Printed in Israel

To my parents,

Who have given me everything, from the
gift of life to the gift of believing in myself.

And to my grandparents,

Who have always been my
most loyal and ardent fans.

ACKNOWLEDGMENTS

WHEN IS A writing career launched? The first time someone reads your work and says, "Hey, kid, you have talent"? That first breathtaking time that your name appears in print?

There are so many who have given me boosts along my career path, but several who deserve special mention: my Great-Aunt Irene Klass, *a"h*, and, *ybc"l*, my cousin Naomi Mauer, publishers of the *Jewish Press*, for being the first to print my work and even ask for more, back when I was a teenager; Ruchama Feuerman, whose writing workshop in Passaic and individual guidance as she helped me prepare my first novella for print in her book *Everyone's Got a Story* gave me the confidence I needed to start my writing career; and Leah Kotkes, who read my first short story and didn't rest until she'd connected me with *Mishpacha* magazine and ensured it would be published.

I owe a huge debt of gratitude to the supremely talented and even more supremely *menschlich* editors at *Mishpacha* for investing in me over the years—particularly to Bassi Gruen and Avigail Sharer, whose amazing literary brilliance is topped only by their amazing ability to overlook my occasional (or frequent) difficulty with deadlines, and whose guidance played a large role in shaping *It's a Learning Curve* over the year it was serialized in *Family First*.

Thank you as well to Rav Chaim Zev Malinowitz for his rabbinic guidance, to Dr. David Blass for his psychiatric guidance (about my characters, not me, though there were times I might have needed it as well), and to Harry Katz, Esq., for his advice about legal matters in the storyline.

It has always been one of my life's dreams to publish a book. The fact that you are holding this dream in your hands right now is thanks to Esther Heller, editor-in-chief at Menucha Publishers, for offering to publish my serial, and to Chaya Silverstone, whose talented copyediting and great eye for detail polished this work to a sheen.

To my husband, Meir—my supporter, advisor, and confidant—for every *berachah* you've brought into my life, and particularly for the seven most wonderful *berachos* in the world: Yitzchak Aryeh, Moshe, Tzvi, Shuli, Mordechai, Tova Bracha, and Aharon. Thank you to my children for putting up with an *ima* who's sometimes too distracted and often on the computer too much, and thank you for somehow, miraculously, turning out so unbelievably awesome despite me!

To the Rosenthal, Arnold, Hertzberg, Friedman, Frank, and Aharon clans: Whether close by or across the ocean, there's nothing like family. And I won the jackpot with mine—both my own and my in-law family.

And, above all, to the Source of all of these *berachos*, and of every other blessing in my life. There are no human words adequate enough to express all I owe to Hashem, for every second of my existence, but, as in everything else in my life, I can only use the tools that He gave me. For giving me that tool—the gift of words—on top of everything else: Thank You.

PROLOGUE

THE UNIVERSITY LECTURE hall was packed, and as Aviva walked down the aisle to find a seat, she felt a funny sense of time folding in on itself. Last time she was on this campus, she'd been twenty-three and pregnant with her second. Uncanny how it all came back to her; she rarely spent time looking back on the past. All those late nights studying for finals while nursing Chavi, her oldest. Her very first client ever, a seven-year-old girl with a minor lisp and a major case of ADHD, who ran up and down the university clinic each session, with a mortified Aviva in hot pursuit. Missing her graduation because she was in the hospital giving birth.

Aviva settled down in her seat, front row and center, and took out her laptop.

"Well, if it isn't Aviva Heyman! How *are* you?"

Aviva looked up. Dr. Samuels, her old professor for articulation disorders, had stepped up to the lectern and was now beaming down at her. Aviva didn't question how her professor still remembered her name twelve years down the line. It was just one of those things that she took for granted in life, that she made a lasting impression wherever she went.

"Thank G-d, I'm doing well. It's so wonderful to be back here. As soon as I saw that you'd be presenting this apraxia workshop, I knew I just had to come."

Dr. Samuels nodded appreciatively. "Tell me, what are you up to these days? A top student like you, I'm sure you're excelling at whatever you're doing."

Aviva was conscious of a funny squirming inside, and her voice had an unusual falter as she replied, "Oh, I'm still working for the Board of Ed. Great benefits, you know."

"Certainly… Well, good for you." Was that a hint of disappointment in the professor's voice? "And your family? You had two babies, I remember, while you were in the program. I still remember how you sat an exam a week after giving birth." She shook her head. "Those babies must be all grown up now!"

Aviva smiled. "My girls are already getting to be teenagers," she said. She decided not to add that there were six more under them.

"Teenagers! Well, good luck with that!" Dr. Samuels gave her a wink as she turned away to set up her PowerPoint.

Aviva chuckled in response, but, for the second time in the conversation, she felt uneasy. How had it happened that she, the graduate that every teacher had assured would make her mark on the world, was now reduced to platitudinal quips about raising children?

SURI SPOTTED AVIVA as soon as she walked into the lecture

hall, but she decided not to approach her until the break. She knew that otherwise, Aviva would've expected her to sit in the empty spot to her right, and, from long-ingrained habit, Suri was not interested in sitting all the way at the front of the room. Nor was she interested in seeing Aviva's smirk as she told her this. Even back when they'd roomed in seminary together, Aviva had teased her about her need to stay buried in the safe middle of the classroom ("your compulsion to hide," Aviva had called it).

So Suri chose her own seat, quietly taking notes during the first half of the seminar (Aviva, as she'd expected, was the star questioner of the group), and when the break was announced, she got up and walked over to the front, pretending that she hadn't noticed her friend until well into the lecture.

"Suri!" Aviva brushed her sheitel out of her eye as she stood up. Suri always felt dwarfed by Aviva when they stood next to each other. Even when Aviva didn't wear heels, she was a head taller than Suri. And Aviva always wore heels.

"I didn't know you were planning on coming!" Aviva said as she patted her arm. "Too bad, I could've given you a ride."

Considering the two lived in the same neighborhood, and were both speech therapists working for the local Board of Education, it was surprising how little their lives intersected with each other on a daily basis. They were the kinds of friends who invited each other to their *simchah*s and called to wish a good *yom tov*.

"*Nu*," said Aviva. "You brought something to eat? Good, let's go outside and catch up." She led the way out of the hall, Suri following.

It took five minutes of Suri trotting to keep up with Aviva's determined pace, and another five standing by awkwardly as Aviva was hailed by an old professor coming out of his office (*No*, she had to remind herself, as unbidden seminary memories suddenly rose, *this professor is* supposed *to ignore you, standing quietly next to Aviva—he doesn't know you!*), but finally they stepped out into the spring sunshine.

"Gosh," Aviva said as they walked through the campus to find a shady bench. "I remember my total culture shock the first time I stepped foot in this place. Little Bais Yaakov girl meets the big bad secular world."

Suri glanced around. She'd gotten her degree through an on-line master's program geared for *frum* women. Even now, she couldn't imagine going to school every day on a college campus like this one. But Aviva, of course, was a different story.

"I'm sure you handled yourself just fine," she said as the two sat down.

"Hmm?" Aviva's mind had clearly jumped to a different subject. After opening up her Tupperware container and taking a bite of her avocado salad (Suri felt so humdrum with her tuna sandwich), Aviva burst out with, "Do you ever feel like you're stagnating?"

Suri blinked. "Stagnating?"

"As in not moving anywhere."

Suri removed her glasses and wiped them with a cloth. "I know what stagnating means. Are you talking life circumstances? Personal growth?" She treaded delicately.

Aviva plucked a fallen leaf out of her salad and threw it on the grass. "I'm talking about the fact that we're still at the same boring old job, doing the same boring old thing, as every other speech therapist who graduated with us. Don't you ever feel the urge to do something...bigger?"

Suri looked at her warily. "The urge? Honestly, no." But she hesitated, as she twirled her glasses between her fingers, and Aviva pounced on her hesitation.

"What? You have an idea, don't you? Tell me!"

Suri didn't look up. "It's really just a dream. But I've been thinking for a while how nice it would be to open my own speech center. You know, a local clinic, where the *frum* families in our neighborhood could come for therapy rather than driving forty-five minutes to the clinic in Huntington, or begging the Board of Ed for the services that they should be getting in the yeshivos, but that never seem to materialize." She shrugged as she met Aviva's eyes.

They were alight with excitement. "Suri!" she cried. "I love it!"

Suri gave a little shake of her head. "Aviva, I told you, it's just a dream. An impractical one."

"Why?" Aviva demanded, leaning closer.

Suri noticed some college boys throwing a football in the distance. "Well, for one thing, you need a lot of money to start a business like this, and the stomach to weather the beginning until it succeeds. *If* it succeeds."

Aviva waved her hand. "Of course it will succeed." With Aviva, everything succeeded. "And we'll find the money. Listen," she said, her voice taking on an urgency that surprised Suri. "I've been looking for a while now to do something more with my life. I think…this is exactly what I need right now. I want to throw myself into a business, spend every waking second on it, and watch it grow into something wildly successful." She gripped Suri's elbow. "We can do it, Suri. We really can!"

Suri chewed slowly on her tuna, not saying anything. This was so Aviva—impulsive, energetic, and so irritatingly assured. How in the world could Suri give up her good, steady income, to pursue this fantasy? She was not the daring type; she never had been. She was quiet, reliable Suri, a safe, middle-of-the-classroom type of girl.

Your compulsion to hide.

Suri stared at Aviva, so confident in her belief that all the world was hers, if only she reached out her hand to grasp it. And suddenly, Suri felt a wild something bubbling up inside, felt an urge to throw back her head and laugh at the wind, and heard a voice that couldn't have been her own saying, "Aviva, if you find us the funding, then I'm in."

—

SURI'S ONLY COMFORT over the next few days, when contemplating her moment of utter rashness, was that there was no way Aviva would actually find the money. So she went about her job, not even mentioning the conversation to Shaul. And then, exactly one week later, Aviva called her.

"We're good to go!" she said breathlessly. "I found our investor!"

"Whaaat?" Suri dropped the chicken she was in the middle of cleaning and sat down. "So soon?"

"Of course," Aviva said proudly. "I told you I'd take care of it, didn't I? I spent hours and hours on the phone this past week contacting foundations and *askanim*, and, finally, I hit gold. Zalman Jeren—you know, as in *the* Jeren, whose name is on half the yeshivah buildings in this state. Well, he was interested in our idea, and willing to provide funding."

"No way," whispered Suri.

"Absolutely," Aviva assured her. "Basically, Mr. Jeren has a daughter-in-law who's an occupational therapist. She's still young, but he's sure she's got what it takes to excel. So if we manage to jump through all the right hoops on the planning stages, he'd want us to offer her a job. But with a caveat—he doesn't want her to know it's coming from him."

"So we'd be getting involved in family intrigue," Suri said drily.

"For the amount of money he's offering, I'll get involved in as much intrigue as he wants," Aviva shot back.

"So you said..."

"What do you think I said?" Aviva laughed. "So we'll be three instead of two!"

"Crazy," murmured Suri.

"Not crazy. *Hashgachah*. Pure *hashgachah*. So *nu*, you know what this means?"

Suri closed her eyes as she heard Aviva's gleeful voice.

"We're in business!"

CHAPTER 1

ONE HUNDRED PEOPLE.

Aviva glanced at the mirror as she put on her sheitel. Shirel had kindly responded to her emergency call and blown it for her last night, not even once questioning why Aviva had insisted on wearing the sheitel outside when every single forecast had predicted heavy rain, all day. That's why Aviva loved her *sheitel macher.*

One hundred people times five dollars equals enough money to finally send in that order for more therapy games.

She dabbed on some lipstick.

Or—if Suri is in a really good mood—to buy those animal-shaped chairs I found that would be the perfect accent to the waiting room/ play area.

Of course, Suri would tell her they should use the money to pay the electric bill.

Five hundred dollars. That is, assuming they got one hundred women to their event that night—*and* that all of them paid. Suri, being Suri, had estimated closer to fifty, and had also wanted to charge more per person. But it was Yael Jeren who'd insisted the merely symbolic fee would draw more people, and also send the message that they're an organization that services the whole community, rich or poor.

For once, Aviva had to agree with Yael's assessment. But…five hundred dollars? For all this effort?

She sighed as she clasped on her necklace. Unreal how much money went into running a business.

Aviva glanced once more at her reflection. The emerald-colored stones, trendy but not large enough to be clunky, went perfectly with her silk shirt. She gave a nod at herself, standing straight and confident, everything in place. Perfect.

Then she froze.

I forgot to do something.

She mentally raced through everything on her checklist as she gathered her things. She—they—had been planning this lecture for weeks. Though their clinic had officially been in operation already for almost a year, getting the word out to the community took time and patience, and the very small initial trickle of clients—mostly friends and family—was finally, finally starting to pick up. And now, at last, their spanking-new premises—thanks to Zalman Jeren—were ready.

It was time to introduce themselves to the wider community.

They'd already done the official opening ceremony, honoring Mr. Jeren and plastering the local paper with photos of him and the mayor cutting the ribbon. But this was something else—it was reaching out on a more personal level, positioning themselves as the neighborhood experts parents could turn to for advice. The idea for this informational evening for mothers—"How to Foster Your Child's Development"—was Aviva's, and it was she who'd masterminded the event, arranging every last detail. For weeks now she'd been thinking of little else. So what had she forgotten?

It was only as she stood by her front door, car keys ringed around her finger as she balanced several platters of home-baked health bars ("brain boosting," she would label them, as she'd tell the mothers the ingredients in the power recipe she'd concocted), that she realized her omission.

That was when fourteen-year-old Chavi came bounding down the stairs, saw her mother, and came to a blazing halt.

"Are you going *out* tonight?" Her eldest's eyes were shooting sparks. "Am I babysitting *again*?"

Oops.

Aviva rallied quickly. After all, if Chavi had been just the slightest bit less absorbed in her own teenage world, she would have remembered that tonight was the big night.

"Yes, I need you to babysit," Aviva said calmly. "Dinner's warming in the oven. Chaim should be home soon from *Masmidim*. And…" She hesitated. "If you really want, you can skip baths tonight. Though I'd rather you didn't," she added.

Chavi's mouth was open in outraged protest. "I told Hindy I'd study with her tonight. You never said *anything* about babysitting! And this is the third time this week!"

The platters were getting quite heavy. Aviva shifted her arm and managed to glance at her watch.

"Listen, honey, I'm sorry, but I need to go. Tell Hindy to come here to study, after you get the kids to sleep." In the distance, she heard high-pitched shouts coming from the basement, and she knew if she didn't exit soon, she would soon become embroiled in whatever argument was going on down there.

"I have to go," she said again, and, with a wave at her mutinous-looking daughter, left.

THE SIGN ABOVE the front door winked cheerily: "Big Bounce Child Therapy Center." All along the large picture windows were brightly colored paintings of children jumping, leaping, and twirling. Aviva gazed proudly at the storefront before heading in. They'd sat for a while with Yissachar, a brand and marketing expert, talking out different names. Suri had favored the straightforward: Children's Therapy Center. Aviva had wanted something ambitious, like Aim High Therapy. It was Yael who'd come up with the bounce concept, and though Aviva had thought it too whimsical, Yissachar had liked it. So Big Bounce it was.

Aviva set the trays down on the folding tables they'd set up earlier. She had to admit, over the months, the name had grown on her, especially when the interior decorator she'd hired had filled the waiting play area with mini trampolines and colorful bouncy balls. Hopping bunnies, kangaroos, and other smiling animals adorned the walls, window dressings, and light fixtures. Suri had frowned at the extravagance—*An interior designer? Really?*—but Aviva's insistence had won the day.

She looked around the room with satisfaction. Maybe she could convince Suri about those animal chairs as well.

"Oh, good, you're here." Suri came hurrying out of the office. "I was just working on our expense list. The accountant said he needs it next week."

Aviva nodded, not really listening. Accounting details were not what interested her, and she was grateful that Suri had taken on that responsibility. The three partners had never outright discussed it, but, early on, each had naturally assumed the role that fit her most. Aviva was the big concept, publicity person. Suri took care of administrative duties. And Yael…

Aviva frowned. Just what did Yael do exactly? Stand around making comments? And where was she, anyway?

She spread out the lace tablecloth that she'd brought from home, smoothing out creases. She'd considered candles, but thought it might be too much. Instead, she arranged small flower bouquets along the buffet. The bakery had already delivered the pastries she'd ordered, and their platters needed just a tiny bit of rearranging.

Suri whistled as she walked over. "Are we making a bar mitzvah?"

Aviva rolled her eyes. Suri's idea of high decorating was using matching plastic tablecloths and plates. "I think we need more chairs," Aviva said.

"There are more stacked inside the office. I didn't want there to be too many empty places."

Aviva looked up from her flowers. "You have no confidence," she admonished. "I'm betting we get over a hundred tonight. We've advertised this all over the place!"

Suri just shook her head. "Since you probably don't want my help here, I'll go back to my expense sheets."

Aviva looked around suspiciously. "Why isn't Yael here?"

Suri shrugged. "I guess she'll come soon. Meanwhile, we better hurry up. People should be arriving in ten minutes."

Aviva waved her hand. "Jewish time, my dear. I'm not expecting anyone for at least half an hour."

"Yeah, but—"

Suri stopped as the front door opened. A lady in slacks and sunglasses peeked in.

"Hello, is this the lecture on child development? Oh, am I early?" She walked inside and sat down on one of the folding chairs.

We didn't only advertise in the frum community. Aviva silently finished Suri's remark as, cheeks burning, she made a bold note on her mental checklist to be ready much earlier next time.

YAEL GRIPPED THE steering wheel, willing her car to go faster. Why was she forever leaving her house five minutes late? Ephraim, her husband, was such a punctual person, he didn't get her struggles in this area.

"What's so complicated?" he would ask. "It takes you twenty minutes to get somewhere, you leave the house twenty minutes in advance. Simple math."

Simple, indeed. But it didn't take into account all the million things she was trying to get done before leaving, or the other million things that somehow came up just when she was really, truly, ready to walk out the door.

And it also didn't take into account, Yael thought grimly as she turned the corner onto the block of their clinic, having to deal with a severe case of chickening out.

Earlier that afternoon, she had actually been tempted. It would've been so easy to call up Suri—not Aviva, she couldn't have said this to Aviva—and told her she had a family emergency, or a sudden stomach virus, and, so sorry, but she just wouldn't be able to make it tonight. They could've carried on perfectly well without her. Aviva was a natural speaker; she could hold a crowd for an hour's lecture easily. There was really no need to end off the evening with Yael's awkward, stuttered, reading-off-the-paper occupational therapy contribution.

How she'd gotten roped into this public speaking gig, she had no idea. True, she'd supported Aviva's idea for this community evening. But she'd assumed Aviva would be doing all the talking.

Yael scanned the block. All the parking spots were taken. And on the next street, and the next as well. Her heart started pounding. How many people *were* there sitting in that room? And just where was she supposed to find parking?

She finally left her car in the small lot behind the pizza place, praying it wouldn't get towed. Her eyes widened as she approached the clinic. Through the windows, she could see that the place was absolutely packed. There were even women standing in the back.

And she was going to get up in front of all of them?

She walked inside as inconspicuously as possible. The crowd, she saw, was rapt, as Aviva, together with a volunteer from the audience, demonstrated games to encourage language development. Yael gulped. How would she follow such an act? The five pages of text sitting in her purse that she'd been checking compulsively every five minutes to make sure they hadn't disappeared, suddenly struck her as having all the panache of a fifth-grade oral presentation.

Resolutely, she put one foot in front of the other as she made her way to the front of the room, and even remembered to smile at some of the women in the crowd. She couldn't get over the turnout. There must've been at least two hundred women packed into that room. Suri, sitting off to the side, gave her a warm smile, eyebrows raised to indicate her disbelief over the size of the audience. Yael leaned her back against the wall, trying to calm her racing heart.

Aviva finished her speech, to lively applause, and turned to introduce her colleague. Yael slowly stood up, walking to the podium.

She placed her sheets on the lectern, faced the vast crowd, and panicked. "Hi, my name is Yael." Her voice sounded young and squeaky. *I can't do this.*

She willed herself to go on. "I'm the clinic's occupational therapist, and my job is to help develop fine motor skills in children."

She felt like she was gasping for air. She forged on through another few paragraphs, not quite aware of what she was saying, but steadily making progress toward her goal of being able to finally finish.

And then it happened. Someone asked a question. "My five-year-old is still not able to button. Based on what you just said, should I be getting her evaluated for fine motor deficit?"

Yael coughed. She sputtered. She mumbled an answer as best as she could and then, flustered, it took her several moments until she found her place in the prepared speech text.

When she finally finished, the applause was certainly nowhere near as exuberant as it had been for Aviva. But at least it was over. She walked away from the lectern, relieved.

Until she caught Aviva's eye.

It was shooting daggers.

CHAPTER 2

BIG BOUNCE THERAPY Center, how can I help you?"

Suri cradled the phone on her shoulder as she held her fingers poised over the keyboard.

"Speech therapy for your son," she repeated as she typed *Moishe Ginzberg, five years old.*

"We'll need a copy of his evaluation faxed to us, and then we'll give you a call when a slot opens up."

Aviva walked into the office at that moment, and Suri winked at her. "No, the wait time isn't very long at the moment. Something should become available within the next few weeks."

Aviva smirked. It had taken them ten long months of desperately seeking clients to reach this point where they could now boast a waiting list. The success of their evening event had done wonders toward publicizing their clinic.

Suri hung up the phone as Aviva rifled through the cabinet with client files. "Have you seen Mayerfeld's file around?" she asked. "I know I put it back here last week."

Suri got up and walked over to the cabinet. She reached up to the OT shelf and pulled out the file.

"Yael is also working with Donny Mayerfeld," she said.

Aviva blew her a kiss. "What would we do without you?" she asked as she hurriedly scanned her notes from last session.

Suri sat back down at the desk and glanced at the computer screen. "Aviva, when do you think you'll have another opening?"

Aviva shrugged. "Don't know. No time soon. My kids are complaining as it is about how much I'm out of the house." She said it nonchalantly, but Suri caught a dark flash in her eyes. "What about you? Your schedule isn't full, is it? I must be seeing double the amount of kids you are."

Suri clicked the hole puncher open and shut, willing herself to respond calmly.

"Well, there's a reason for that."

Aviva was still perusing her file. "Is there? Things extra busy at home?"

Suri looked up sharply. Was that sarcastic? No, it couldn't be. Even outspoken Aviva wouldn't be so cruel as to intentionally imply a comparison between her own large, hectic family and Suri's small one.

Still…

"If you haven't noticed," Suri said, an unbidden edge in her voice, "I've been working two jobs here. I'm a part-time therapist, and full-time secretary!" Her voice crept up a notch. "And you think my schedule isn't full? So heartwarming to know how much my hard work is appreciated!"

Aviva looked at her, startled. Her eyes narrowed. "Of course it's appreciated! But this is what we signed up for. There's no way our clinic will succeed without hard work. We're all putting in the hours. You think I'm not working hard?"

Suri slumped back in her seat, suddenly feeling childish. Of course Aviva worked hard—she put in longer hours than any of them.

Feeling sulky, she punched several buttons on the keyboard, lips pursed. Aviva was on her way out of the office when Suri finally spoke up. "You know, it's not even good business practice."

Aviva's head swiveled. "What isn't?"

Suri swept her arm around the office. "Me doing all the administrative work. We could make more profit by hiring a secretary, and clearing up my time to see more clients."

Grudgingly, Aviva nodded. "You have a point, I guess," she said slowly.

Suri peered at Aviva. She'd gotten to know her friend well over the past year, much better, in many respects, than she had all those months rooming together in seminary. And now, in a flash, she got her partner's hesitation.

"Aviva," she said. "We don't have to do it alone. It's okay to say we need to hire outside help. It's a sign of growth, you know."

Aviva shrugged, rocked back and forth on her heels, and finally said, with an exasperated shake of her sheitel, "If you *really* think you can't handle it…I'll start looking for a secretary."

—

YAEL TRIED TO look comfortable as she sipped some Chardonnay. The crystal glasses always made her nervous. Truthfully, she was more of a cola drinker, but her father-in-law, a self-proclaimed wine connoisseur, insisted on personally filling everyone's glass at these monthly *melaveh malkah*s for all the Jeren children and children-in-law. To refuse the drink would be awkward—and make her sisters-in-law start to wonder whether she was expecting.

But why, oh why, couldn't they at least use plastic cups?

Yael had to smile at the image of her mother-in-law, sitting complacently next to her husband, with her makeup and elegant jewelry, serving anything on plastic. But at every single family gathering, Yael had nightmares about dropping one of those ridiculously heavy goblets, and hearing the clan's collective gasp as it shattered. Luckily, in the four years that she'd been part of the family, it hadn't yet happened.

She *had* broken a china plate, though.

It was soon after they'd gotten engaged, and Yael, in her eagerness to help, had jumped up from the table to clear, and the plate had slipped from her sweaty hands. The mistake had been all the more embarrassing because, as she was later to find out, nobody cleared in the Jeren family. They had housekeepers for that.

Her mother-in-law had shown admirable restraint, pursing her lips for only a moment before smiling kindly and calling for Maria to come clean up. Embarrassed, Yael had joked about not being able to trust the family china with her. But no one at the table had smiled.

She'd also had yet to find out that her in-laws did not have a sense of humor.

They were good, generous people, and she'd certainly come to admire their many positive qualities over the years. Still, even four years later, she looked around family gatherings like this one and couldn't help but wonder what in the world she was doing there.

Ephraim was telling over a *dvar Torah* to his father. As the only boy in the family, he was the undisputed crown prince, and his mother was also listening eagerly as he spoke.

On the other side of the table, Rina, her sister-in-law, was talking loudly about her retail clothing business.

"It's been so busy at the store lately, it's not even normal. I've had to hire two extra girls to work in the afternoon hours. It's that pre-summer shopping season—you know, everyone needs to stock up before they go up to the country, or to camp, or on their European vacations."

She said the last two words nonchalantly, but Yael knew what was coming next.

"Speaking of, did I tell you all where Shloimy and I are going this summer? We finally decided on the trip to Bulgaria. Shloimy really wanted Switzerland, but I told him, we've done that so much, Bulgaria at least will be something different."

Nods all around the female side of the table.

"That sounds interesting," said Chayale. "I wish I could convince Yudi to go to Europe, but he hates traveling. So we just stay in our summer home. Hey, Yudi," she said, turning to her husband. "What do you say about going to Bulgaria this summer?"

"What?" Her husband, who'd been listening to Ephraim's *dvar Torah*, turned to her and blinked. "What did you say? Bulgaria?"

"Yeah!" Chayale smiled brightly. "Rina and Shloimy are going. Wanna join them?"

Yudi shrugged. "You can go if you want. I'm happy staying in the bungalow."

He winked at Ephraim, who was sitting opposite him, as if at a kindred spirit. Everyone knew that, of the siblings, Rina and Zahava went on annual exotic vacations, while Chayale and Ephraim stayed local. They all assumed that Ephraim, like Yudi, was not into traveling. What they didn't know was that it was because of Yael that they stayed put at home. The thought of cruises and luxury hotels and buying the wardrobes to match just made her cringe. Not to mention what *her* siblings would say, if she were to announce such a trip.

"Anyway," continued Rina, "I felt so relieved once we booked the tickets. I've been working just nonstop this entire year, and I really need a vacation."

Her father turned to her at those words. "Business is booming, eh?" he asked, obvious pride in his voice.

"Totally, Tatty. We've become really trendy among the fashionable set."

Was it Yael's imagination, or did her sister-in-law's eyes briefly rest on her as she said that?

Rina continued, "I'm even thinking about expanding. I just found out that the bedding store next door is closing down."

Zalman beamed. "Grab it! I'll put up the funds if you need."

Rina smiled. "Thank you, Tatty," she said, inclining her head.

Zahava piped up. "I'm also looking forward to our cruise. Ever since I became manager, I feel like the firm has taken over my life."

She said it like she was complaining, but Yael knew that it was really a boast. In the Jeren family, hard work and business success were of supreme value.

Then Ephraim spoke up. "You should see how hard Yael's been working for her new clinic."

Yael blushed, as her father-in-law turned in her direction. "How's my newest investment coming along?"

"*Baruch Hashem*," she said, trying to muster up a self-confident ring. "The new center looks so beautiful after all our renovations." And, for what had to be the hundredth time, she added, "Thanks so much, Tatty, for the donation. Without that, it would've taken us years till we could afford such a nice place."

Zalman waved his hand, looking pleased. "When I saw how hard you're working to make this a success, I decided to help out a bit, that's all."

"More than a bit." She laughed. "Amazing, how this job just fell into my lap, isn't it? I mean, to think *they* called me, said they were looking for an OT to partner with, and someone had recommended me..." Aviva had told her it was a former client, but she still, after all this time, couldn't imagine who that could be.

Zalman was shifting uncomfortably, and Yael was content to let the topic die there, but Ephraim continued on. "The clinic's been doing phenomenally. Yael is busy all the time, she has all these clients, and she's always over there working. And just recently they ran a huge event—they advertised it all over the city—and about half the community came out. Yael was the keynote speaker!"

Yael looked at her husband sharply. Half the community? Keynote speaker? Just what was he doing, exactly?

"Is that so?" Her father-in-law was looking at her with more interest than he'd ever shown before.

"I never pictured you as a businesswoman," added Rina, with just a touch of...was that jealousy?

And then Yael caught the expression on her husband's face. It was nothing short of smug. That's when she understood.

Ephraim finally had something about her that he could be proud of.

CHAPTER 3

"**D**ELICIOUS!" ZEVI SMILED at Aviva across their dining room table. "Too bad birthdays only come out once a year."

It had taken quite an effort to get the special dinner ready and kids to bed so that Aviva and her husband could enjoy this rare time alone. She'd almost been tempted to buy a cake at the bakery, but she just couldn't bring herself to do it. Birthday cakes were meant to be lovingly baked.

Zevi wiped his mouth with the linen napkin. "How did things go at the clinic today?"

"Great!" Aviva put down her fork—her small portion of steak was mostly uneaten—and sat up straight. "I have this kid who I've been working with a few weeks already. He does this crazy thing with his tongue when he's trying to make the *S* sound, and no matter how much I've tried, I could not get him to say it the right way. Finally, today, I had an idea for a new approach, and I told the mom we were not leaving that room until he got it." She took a sip of water, then smiled. "Well, we went a half hour overtime, but by the end, he did it. It was such an amazing feeling—he felt great, I felt great, the mom felt great. There was such energy in the room!"

Zevi looked a bit wistful as he said, "Must be so nice to know you're improving people's lives."

Aviva bit her lip. *You mean, as opposed to sitting in an office all day playing Sudoku?*

But she held herself back from saying it. Good wives were supposed to give their husbands emotional support.

Besides, it was his birthday.

A sudden flash from the past: She was at her *vort*, accepting mazel tovs from all the guests, eager for the compliments about her *chasan*.

"Such a mensch!"

"A real tzaddik, wonderful *middos*! Always ready to help another bachur!"

"A real *bren* for life! Always *besimchah*!"

She'd smiled and glowed, but deep down, she'd felt uneasy. Where were the comments about his *hasmadah*? About his brilliance in learning? Just a few days earlier, her friend Toby had gotten engaged to one of the top bachurim in Lakewood, and everyone was falling over their feet in praises. And her Zevi—he was fun, he was charming, he made her feel all warm and relaxed—but she couldn't help asking herself how it could have happened that she, the all-perfect Aviva Feld who excelled at everything, could have ended up with a less than top-grade *chasan*.

Zevi had stopped chewing, and was looking at her curiously. "What big ideas are you contemplating?"

She shook her head. "Nothing. Tell me about *your* day, birthday boy."

He shrugged. "Same as usual."

Of course, the little prick of self-doubt had gone away quickly, in the excitement of the engagement, the wedding, *shanah rishonah*. But then had come the bombshell: Her husband had announced that he wanted to leave *kollel*.

"It's just not for me, the full-time learning," he'd pleaded, seeing the look on her face.

Aviva had convinced him to stick it out for another year. It wasn't just to save face to her family, though, she had to admit, picturing her sisters' reactions hadn't been fun. But it was mostly that Aviva had always imagined herself as the self-sacrificing supporter of a learning husband.

After one more bench-warming year, it was clear to them both that Zevi had to leave. And suddenly, after receiving her reluctant go-ahead, he was back to his old self—the person she remembered from their dating days, when she'd giggle for hours as he related his hilarious *bein hazmanim* adventures. Now, that Zevi was back, exuberant and alive with his plans to start his own printing business.

"So many of my friends are looking for a place to print their *chiddushei Torah* cheap. I'm telling you, this'll be great!"

You were supposed to be the one writing the chiddushim.

But, nevertheless, Aviva had pitched in to help him start the business, and Heyman Printing was born. (He'd wanted to call it *Hey, man!* Printing, but she'd nixed it.)

She swallowed, watching as he shot a quick glance at the refrigerator. *He wants ketchup for the rosemary baby potatoes, but he's too scared to ask.* Shaking her head, she asked, "Anything new at work?"

Zevi gave a lopsided smile. "Well, I finally beat my Sudoku record."

Birthday or no, Aviva refused to smile back.

Over a decade later, Heyman Printing was still around, but it wasn't exactly the rousing success her husband had planned. He had clients here and there, but spent a lot of time hocking with the guys in the rented offices next to his own. She'd repeatedly given suggestions for how to drum up business, offered to run marketing campaigns, but he'd always brushed her off. Aviva could never understand it: Did Zevi actually *enjoy* running a lackluster business? But over time, she'd learned to just leave him alone.

The room had gone uncomfortably silent. Changing the topic, she said, "Guess what the latest is at the clinic. We're looking to hire a secretary."

"Already?"

She sighed. "Yeah, that's what I said. I mean, it's not as if we've turned the corner yet; we're still not making any profit. We're barely breaking even, and that's only because Zalman Jeren's footing so much of the bill."

"So whose idea is this?"

"Suri's. She's been doing most of the administrative work, and she says it's eating up too much of her time. She could be seeing more clients if we had a secretary."

"She has a point," Zevi said slowly.

Aviva raked a hand through her sheitel. "Of *course* she has a point. But who am I going to find who will work for us at minimum wage, because that's all we can afford to pay?"

Zevi put down his fork. "I…uh…have an idea for you."

She looked at him questioningly. "Who?"

His mouth stretched into a broad smile. "Me."

SURI LOVED HER house. Small, neat, and cozy, it was exactly the kind of place she wanted to come home to at the end of a long day of work. She'd always been a homebody; she remembered all those times as a girl when her mother would push her to go play with some friends, and she insisted she was perfectly happy curling up with a book.

But that was only half of it, she reminded herself, as she set down her purse on the side table in the hall and headed for the kitchen. The other half was that she didn't really have close friends to play with. Not until she was older, already a teenager, when having friends suddenly became a vital need. And that's when she'd discovered the secret to making friends: Find a girl with a dominant personality who's looking for a loyal sidekick.

Using the same tried and true method, she went through several profitable friendships throughout her high school years, proving her value as a friend in the way that she knew best: by being a good listener and steadfast companion. As soon as she'd met Aviva, that first day of seminary, she knew that she'd found yet another such personality to latch on to. And that was exactly what had happened, Aviva graciously allowing her to ride the wave of her own popularity.

Suri cut herself a slice of the cake left from Shabbos as she put up some coffee.

Was this what was happening again?

She shook her head at the decorative fruit tile above the counter. She had to stop thinking this way. Not everything was about Aviva. She was a good therapist in her own right.

Right?

Suri sighed and kicked off her shoes. Aah, did it feel good to relax. Sometimes the stresses of running the business could get to her. Shaul had noticed—not that she'd complained; she rarely complained. She was not the complaining type.

Even if I complained, who would listen?

She pressed her hands against her head, willing the cynical voices to stop. No, she hadn't said a word because, all things considered, she felt very fortunate to be where she was. After all, just a year ago, this whole thing had been a pipe dream, a mere fantasy about what she would do if she were someone other than quiet Suri Taub. And now, here she was, actually fulfilling her dream, accomplishing, making a difference in the world. Who would have believed?

All thanks to Aviva.

Quiet! she silently bellowed. The coffee was ready. She got up and poured herself a cup. Hearing the door open, she took out a second cup as well.

"Hi, Mommy! Wow, coffee and cake! Thanks!"

Miri threw her knapsack on the floor and sank down in a kitchen chair. "I took the biology test today. Waaaayyy harder than I expected, but I think I did okay. And they had production tryouts this afternoon. That's why I'm home early."

Suri raised her eyebrows. "You mean you didn't try out?" It wasn't really a question.

Her daughter, so like Suri herself at that age, shrugged. "Who wants to have all the headaches of rehearsals, and then have to go up on stage, in front of everyone?"

Suri briefly closed her eyes, hearing her mother's voice in her head. *Go out and play with some friends!* She smiled at her daughter.

"If that's what you really want."

Miri grinned back, relieved. She took a sip of her coffee and sighed contentedly.

"Hey, Mommy, someone mentioned you today."

Suri looked at her in surprise. "Mentioned me?"

"Yeah. It was a girl in my class, Bracha Mayerfeld. She said that her little brother's getting speech at your clinic, and that her mother keeps going on about the amazing speech therapist. Course, I proudly told her that it's my mother! You treat him, right?"

Suri felt a tightening inside. *No.* "I can't tell you that, sweetie. Confidentiality laws."

But there it was again, that obnoxious voice.

Aviva, Aviva, Aviva!

CHAPTER 4

FOR ONCE, AVIVA could barely keep her mind on her work.

Her husband wanted to become...her secretary? Every little rational and irrational part of her brain was screaming, *Baaaad idea.* Okay, so maybe he did have the extra time on his hands. Why couldn't he invest it in actually working to grow his business? Rather than spending half his day being somebody's secretary? Worse, *her* secretary!

The idea was so absurd that she'd chosen to pretend it hadn't been said. And that was the end of that...or, at least, it should have been. But, somehow, the look on his face kept elbowing itself inside her thoughts, at the most inconvenient times.

Such as in the middle of therapy sessions.

"Mrs. Heyman, it's your turn!"

She gave a little start as she looked down at the girl sitting next to her at the small table.

"Sorry, Rivky, I lost track. Where's the dice?" She rolled and moved her piece around the board.

"Hmm, it says I have to close my mouth tight for three seconds. Let's do that together."

Lip closure...sure getting a lot of practice in that *nowadays.*

"You did great!" Aviva smiled at the end of the session as she held out the prize box for Rivky to choose from. She turned to Rivky's mother. "Have her practice sitting with her mouth closed a few times a day. Try it while she's chewing as well. It'll be hard for her, but the more she works those muscles, the better. It will also help curb the drooling. Next time we'll start on the speech sounds."

She tousled Rivky's hair as she and her mother exited, then sat back down at the table to write up her session notes.

Zevi wanted to become...

Her brooding was interrupted by her phone ringing.

Aviva glanced at the number. *No. Not Naama. Not now.*

But avoiding her sister was just plain childish. And childish was something that Aviva, as the certified baby of the family, had worked her whole life to overcome.

"Hello, Naama. How are you?"

"Super." Her sister was never anything but super. Not now, not as a kid, when she was the big sister Aviva looked up to and had to live up to. One of the three big sisters, that is.

"How are things going by you?" Naama asked. "How's Zevi? The kids?"

Zevi wants to spend his days playing Sudoku on our clinic's computer. Chavi has officially gone on strike in protest of the one too many times I've asked her to help. And the rest of the kids are acting more and more like vilde chayahs every day.

"Things are great," she said brightly. "*Baruch Hashem*. Everyone's doing wonderfully."

"Glad to hear. I'm calling to tell you about Nossi's *upsherin*. We're doing it next Sunday at two."

Nossi was Naama's first boy, after six girls. Knowing her sister, Aviva could only imagine what the *upsherin* would look like.

"So exciting! What can I bring?"

Naama had her list ready. She wanted tzitzis and *kippah* cookies, frosted in colors that matched her scheme, and a roasted-veggie salad.

Aviva felt her already taut insides stretched to snapping point by the time she hung up. It would take her hours to frost every single cookie to perfection. Just when was she supposed to do that? During her dinner prep time? Instead of reading a bedtime story to her kids? In lieu of laundry?

Every voice of sanity inside was screaming in protest, but she knew just when she would end up making those cookies. In the wee hours of the morning, in between dealing with Kayla's nightmares and Binny's bedwetting. And somehow, somehow, she would manage to produce confections worthy of a Feld girl's *upsherin* party. Everyone would be admiring, raving, shaking their heads in wonder.

Because Aviva—she could do it all.

⟋

YAEL FINISHED PUTTING away the last of her therapy toys and picked up her purse in relief. Time to go home, at last. It was nice feeling so accomplished at the end of her day—but, she had to admit, it was even nicer to head home to her yummy little children.

Walking down the hall, she heard voices coming from one of the rooms and peeked in. Aviva and Suri were sitting at the table, talking. Yael instantly felt a jab of insecurity. The two of them were always having business conferences together, and, somehow, never thought to include her. Not that she really felt a right to have a say in the decision making. Her two partners had a good six years' experience on her, but in self-confidence they were decades ahead. With Aviva, especially, she felt she couldn't even open her mouth without sounding like a foolish little neophyte.

Yael hesitated by the doorway. Maybe it was partly her fault? Maybe if she just believed in herself more, then her partners would value her more as well.

Just do it. She propelled her feet forward into the room.

"Hey, guys! Okay if I join the secret powwow?"

Aviva raised her eyebrows coolly—she always gave off the feeling of being slightly irritated by Yael's presence—but Suri smiled pleasantly.

"I was just talking about a kid I'm working with," Suri said. "I'd be happy to get your input as well."

Yeah, right, Yael's inner critic snorted, but nevertheless felt buoyant as she sat down cross-legged on an exercise mat.

"It's an apraxia case," Suri continued. "And the mom's frustrated about the lack of progress. I've explained that in apraxia, progress is really slow, but she doesn't want to listen."

Aviva shook her head darkly. "This is her oldest, right? Mom's part of the iPhone generation. Instant gratification."

Though Aviva's eyes only grazed Yael for the briefest of moments, still, she squirmed on her mat. She often wondered just how old they thought she was. True, her oldest was only three—but then, she'd gotten married at twenty-four.

"That's the other thing," Suri went on. "I've told her again and again how important the practice at home is, especially for apraxia, but each session she has a different excuse for why she couldn't do it. Now, it's not for me to judge, but you can't complain about lack of progress and then—"

"Oh, stop being so nice!" said Aviva. "Give me a break. What, exactly, is she so busy with that she can't take out five minutes a day to practice with her son?"

Yael shifted her position on the mat. She could picture plenty of days where those five minutes would be hard to come by.

"I don't know if that's fair," she said softly. "A mother with two or three little kids at home can have a lot on her plate. Factor in working full-time to support her *kollel* husband—I don't know if this one is, but so many are—and I think they deserve a round of applause just for making it to the therapy appointment!" She grinned. "Double round if they make it on time!"

Suri nodded approvingly. "Well said, Yael."

"Yes, very." They both looked up apprehensively at the sarcasm in Aviva's voice. "It's so nice to sound all generous and understanding when you have no idea what it's really like to support a husband when you don't have a rich father-in-law, or to juggle a large family with all their needs." Her knuckles that clutched her pen were white as she snapped, "Don't talk to *me* about being fair."

Yael sucked in her breath. Wasn't hard to figure out who the "rich father-in-law" jab was directed to. Still, whatever Aviva may think, Yael could picture *exactly* what that life looked like.

After all, that was the way she herself had grown up.

Aviva was watching her, and Yael, feeling a sudden surge of empathy, said, "Sorry, Aviva. I know I don't need to lecture you about how hard it is to raise a large family and work full-time."

Apparently she'd said the wrong thing. Aviva stood up, with an imperial sweep of her sheitel, and said, "You are completely wrong. It's not *hard*. It's a *privilege*. I've always been thrilled to work to help support my family *and* be a good mother at the same time. When my Chaim needed extra help with *kriah*, I sat with him a half hour every single night until he caught up. And these mothers can't even find the five minutes to do speech exercises?"

She bit her lip, as if holding something back, and stalked out of the room.

"Why do I always say the wrong things around her?" Yael murmured as she rolled a therapy ball back and forth on the mat. Sighing, she turned to Suri. "A half hour every night... Is she, like, human?"

Suri just shook her head. "Welcome to the world of Aviva Heyman," she said.

CHAPTER 5

AVIVA HUNG UP the phone, and felt her hand—the one that was holding the carefully cut tzitzis-shaped fondant—quivering. "Zevi!"

Her husband came rushing into the kitchen. "Everything okay?"

Ever since their birthday conversation that Aviva had been pretending hadn't happened, Zevi had been cautiously polite around her.

She gestured to the phone. "Mommy just called."

"How nice."

"She wants to come for Shabbos."

"How nice."

Aviva closed her eyes. "*This* Shabbos."

Pause. "How n—"

"Oh, be quiet!" The fondant was mushing itself into a ball in her hand and, irritated, she threw it on the counter. "Since they're making the trip in for Naama's *upsherin*, she and Tatty decided to make a long weekend of it and come here for Shabbos."

"Okay." Zevi looked at her curiously. "So what's the problem? Is it me you're worried about? Don't worry, I'll be a good boy. I won't make any big bad remarks about helping out your clinic by becoming the secretary."

Aviva rolled her eyes and ignored this, just as she'd been ignoring every other little reference he'd tried to plug into their conversations over the past week. Did he honestly think she was interested in speaking about the topic?

"I'm worried," she said as she rolled out the fondant ball and started recutting the tzitzis shape, "about where in the world I'm going to find the time in my life to get this house ready and cook for my parents."

Zevi didn't say anything. She knew he wanted so badly to say that it didn't matter, that her usual Shabbos menu was fabulous, that the house was always kept in a guest-worthy state.

But they'd been married too many years for him not to understand what it meant that her mother was coming for Shabbos.

SURI PUSHED OPEN the door to the clinic and raced for the office. She'd planned on leaving fifteen minutes earlier this morning, but Miri had wanted to discuss something with her, and if her teenage daughter wanted her advice, well, the rest of the world would have to wait. But now she had a client arriving any moment and she still had to...

What in the world? She skidded to a stop.

There were people in her office. Three girls, looking not much older than Miri. Who'd given them permission to just walk in?

She put on her toughest professional voice. "Can I help you?"

The girl who'd been sitting in Suri's office chair quickly stood up.

"Uh, yes…we're, uh, here for the observation."

"Observation?" What was that supposed to mean? For a second, her heart started hammering. Were they being inspected by some state agency? Did the government overseers do that to businesses without advance notice?

And even if they did, would they really send three frum teenage girls to do it? Suri, get a grip.

She got a grip.

"Observation?" she asked again. "I'm sorry, but I don't—"

She was interrupted by a whirlwind of Aviva, flying into the office. "Oh, good, you're here." Was she talking to Suri or to these mystery girls?

"Welcome, glad you got here on time. What are your names?"

The girls—all of whom were dressed almost identically in cardigans, pencil skirts, and designer clutch bags—responded in chorus.

"Esti."

"Gitty."

"Fraidy."

"Lovely to meet you." Aviva shook hands all around. "Yes, well, I'm Aviva, speech therapist, and this is Suri, also a speech therapist. And, I believe one of you is OT—ah, yes, er…"

"Fraidy," the girl supplied.

"Of course." Aviva smiled vaguely, but Suri had the impression that she wasn't even paying attention. "Well, you'll be paired up with Yael, then, she's our occupational therapist. She should be here any second. Shall we get started?"

She flashed a brilliant smile around the room, which landed on Suri.

Started?

"Aviva," Suri said calmly. "A word first, please?"

They stepped into the supply closet.

"Explain." Suri leaned back against the shelf of articulation cards, arms folded.

Aviva looked at her, wide-eyed. "I didn't tell you? I'm sure I mentioned it a few weeks ago, when they first contacted me."

"Who first contacted you?"

"Their school. The Gelbman program. You know, the *frum* graduate school for the therapies. They called a few weeks ago about placing some of their girls here to do their observation hours. They pay us for it—sounded like a win-win opportunity."

Suri tried not to let her annoyance come out in her words. "So you said yes without checking with me or Yael?"

"I *did* check!" Aviva said. "I'm almost positive I did!" She rubbed her temple. "At least, I think I did."

Suri suddenly noticed how white her friend's face was. "Aviva? Is everything all right?"

Aviva's eyes flew open. "Of course. Why would you think it wasn't? My parents are coming for Shabbos, that's all. I've been up late every night, cooking and cleaning." She sighed. "Listen, I'm sorry this was sprung on you. I guess I was so busy with planning the mothers event, I just forgot to tell you about this. But, now they're here, and I can't very well tell them to go home. Do you mind just making the best of it for a semester? After that we can reevaluate."

Suri knew apologies didn't come easily to Aviva. And, under the circumstances, there was really nothing to do but accept this one gracefully…and go out to shake hands with Gitty, the cardigan who would be her personal shadow once a week for an entire semester.

—

YAEL WANDERED INTO work, her head still very much at home. *What had Ephraim meant?* she asked herself for the hundredth time. First, there was the incident at his family's *melaveh malkah*, where he told his father some fantasy story about Yael being the keynote speaker. Like it was something to brag about, making an utter fool of yourself in front of hundreds of women, and having your coworker scathingly remark afterward about schoolgirl performances that bring into question the entire professional reputation of their center. It wasn't like he didn't know. She'd come home crying afterward, and relayed the whole miserable tale.

And now, this morning. Simi had been up half the night, poor thing. Teething, Ephraim had dismissed it, but Yael was sure there must be something wrong. She was all prepared to cancel her clients and stay home with her baby, but Ephraim wouldn't hear of it.

"How can I send her to the babysitter in this state?" she'd asked.

"Call up that Russian lady who lives down the street and ask her to come over today," her ever-practical husband had immediately responded. "It's a mitzvah to give her the *parnasah*, anyway."

Yael had hesitated. True, Helena was a sweet old lady, but Yael had her doubts about whether she was a match for her toddler. Still, she supposed Simi would be sleeping most of the day…

And boy would it be nice for Yael to get some sleep, as well.

"But I'm her mother. If she's not feeling well, shouldn't that come before my job?" She'd looked beseechingly at Ephraim.

"Yael, you're a successful business lady. The clinic needs you. All your clients need you. It's a waste of your precious time, staying home with a napping child."

There was such pride in his voice that without further argument she'd called up Helena and prepared to go to work. But it only hit her on the way, in between her yawns, the implication of his words.

A waste of her precious time? Staying home with her child? But—wasn't that exactly what she'd been doing, with just a few hours' break for her part-time job, up until this year?

By the time she stumbled into the clinic, her eyes were half-closed. *Coffee!* her brain screamed, and she forged her way toward the coffee corner in the office.

"Yael. Finally!" Aviva stepped out of the supply closet, her arms laden with toys.

If she gives me mussar about coming late, I'm going to snap.

But Aviva was waving her in the direction of her therapy room. "There's someone in there for you to meet. Her name is Fraidy, and she's an OT student at Gelbman who will be doing her observation hours here this semester. I told her she could look around our therapy room until you get here."

Yael's mouth opened and closed several times as a line of protests fought their way to her lips, but in the end, she opted for a meek nod. You couldn't fight with Aviva. Resigned, she walked toward her therapy room.

"Hello, Fraidy? I'm Yael. Nice to meet you."

The girl in the brown cardigan jumped up. "Hi, Yael. I'm so glad to meet you. I'm really looking forward to our time together. I have so many questions about therapy practice, and though of course I ask my teachers, there's nothing like seeing it in real life, you know? I hope it's okay that I'm gonna ask, like, a million questions!" A little giggle broke through her flow of words. "I was so excited when I found out you were the OT I'd be observing," she went on. "Someone that I know!"

Yael, who'd been feeling increasingly uneasy—and wanting, more than anything, to sit down and drink the coffee now burning her hand—looked at her in surprise.

"Do I know you?"

Fraidy giggled again. "Well, not *personally*, I guess. But I feel like I do. You're Mrs. Savetsky's daughter, aren't you? I went to Machon Bayla for high school, and everyone knew about the principal's daughter who married into the famous Jeren family. I was so excited to meet you! I mean, Mrs. Savetsky literally changed my life with her weekly *shmuesses* to the school and her twelfth-grade *hashkafah* class. Literally! And now, to be working under her daughter!"

The girl grinned. "It's like a dream!"

CHAPTER 6

EXHAUSTED.

Aviva glanced at the living room couch.

She was utterly, completely drained.

What if she sat down for just a minute?

With a shake of her head, she pulled herself away from the living room, back into the kitchen. At 2 a.m. on Thursday night—after a way-too-long week—if she sat down on the couch, she would not get back up. And she still had a full night's work ahead of her.

An hour ago, Zevi had popped up sleepily from where he'd dozed off at the kitchen table (he seemed to think his duty as a husband compelled him to join her, in spirit at least, in her madness), and mumbled, "Donja think is time tagoda sleep?"

She'd looked at him, big, red watch-shaped indentation on his forehead from resting his head on his arm, and told him to go to bed. After all, it wasn't as if he could help her with the mushroom crepes.

She rubbed her eyes, stopping when she realized she was getting dough in her eyelashes. Her fridge was packed with gourmet dishes; her house was sparkling like Pesach. And she was a miserable, wrung-out wreck.

Is this really worth it? She could hear Zevi's voice—or was it her own?—bouncing off the silent walls. *Will Mommy really care if I serve brownies for dessert instead of crème brulee?*

No...and yes. Her mother had somehow managed to pull off gourmet Shabbos meals and a sparkling-like-Pesach home every single week. So what was wrong with her, that the effort was turning her into a rag doll?

A rag doll with a nasty temper.

She winced as she thought back to the scene earlier that evening. Chavi had come into the dining room, where Aviva was elbow deep in silver polish.

"Hey!" her daughter exclaimed. "Didn't I just polish those candlesticks yesterday?"

Aviva mumbled something about spots that she'd missed.

Chavi looked like she wanted to say more, but instead shrugged. "If it makes you happy." Teenage eye roll. "Anyway, Ma, when will you have time to help me with my *Navi* project? It's due tomorrow."

Aviva looked up, wide-eyed. "Tomorrow? And you're just now—"

"—and I've been asking you all week to help me," Chavi cut in. "And every single time you told me to ask you later!" She sounded near tears.

Aviva's shoulders tightened. "For your information, young lady, your grandparents are coming for Shabbos, and I've been extremely busy getting ready. It would be nice, of course, to have some help—" She quickly bit her tongue, but not soon enough. That was not fair of her, and even she knew it.

Chavi, of course, pounced. "Help? I've been helping every single stupid day! You'd think the president of the United States is coming to visit, for goodness sakes! And now you can't even help *me* one little bit for this project, and I'm gonna get, like, a zero on it!" The tears were coming out now.

And that's when Aviva had snapped. "Don't go blaming this on me! You are fourteen years old, and you still need your mother to do your homework for you? Go do it yourself, and stop making me feel guilty!"

Chavi had stalked out, tears gushing, and Aviva was left to feel like the worst mother in the world.

Now, as she wearily folded one more crepe, she wondered what was different. She'd hosted her parents many times before, and never had she felt like she was about to splinter into a million little shards.

"YOU LOOK LIKE you shouldn't be here."

Through her pounding headache, Aviva squinted at Suri. "Huh?"

Suri patted her on the arm as she brushed past on her way into a therapy session. "You look awful. Go home and go to bed. We can survive here one day without you."

Instead of replying, Aviva just laughed, as if the suggestion was clearly a joke—but then winced from the pain in her forehead.

She'd even considered wearing glasses today instead of contacts. But she just couldn't bring herself to do it.

"I'll do an early night tonight," she told Suri. "That's all I need. And after this weekend, I deserve it!"

"Right! How'd the visit go?"

"*Baruch Hashem*, I pulled it off." Mommy had been impressed with her food, her kids had behaved, and at the *upsherin* yesterday, everyone had complimented her cookies. Now she just had to get through the day somehow.

"Not surprising, but glad to hear." Suri smiled, then glanced at her watch. "Steinberg's late again." She turned back to Aviva.

"Listen, not to add to your headache, but have you made any progress in finding a secretary? Because the work, it's getting too much to handle. I almost double-booked Yael this afternoon; I'd somehow forgotten to enter the first kid in the computer."

Pound, pound. Aviva put a hand to her head. "Sure, if you want to hire my husband."

Suri stared. "Your husband?"

Aviva hadn't really meant to say that. "Uh, just joking."

"Oh. Well, ha, ha, then." Suri looked at her curiously.

She sighed. "I mean, he did offer, but it's a totally ridiculous idea. Forget I said anything."

If she hadn't been feeling so awful, she would have given Suri one of her looks to show that the topic was really closed, and that would've been the end of it. But all she could do was rub her temple pathetically as Suri asked, "Why is it so ridiculous?"

YAEL SAT AT the little therapy table, helping five-year-old Ruchie slowly cut around the line of a large circle. *Glad it's not Tuesday*, she thought. She'd been appreciating the day of the week every day since last Tuesday's introduction to Fraidy, the grad student with the endless supply of questions. "Why are you holding his wrist this way?" "Why did you choose this approach and not a different one?" Even, for crying out loud, "Why did you decide to play Connect Four and not dominoes?"

It was enough to drive anyone insane, and make Yael fervently grateful for Wednesday, Thursday, Friday, and Monday.

Only problem was, tomorrow was Tuesday once again.

Ruchie's mother cleared her throat and, with a start, Yael quickly reached out a hand to position Ruchie's fingers better. Had Mrs. Fried realized she'd been daydreaming? She and Fraidy could've been sisters; the two had the same unnerving habit of watching everything Yael did like a hawk. Most mothers passed the time talking on their cell phones. But Ruchie's mother leaned forward attentively, watching every movement.

Yael shifted uneasily. It was the type of situation Aviva could handle without being fazed a bit, and even Suri could go on working with her quiet confidence. But Yael tended to fall apart under scrutiny.

The session ended, and as Yael stood up to escort them out the door, Mrs. Fried held up a hand, motioning for her to sit back down.

"A moment, please. I want to talk to you about something."

Yael nodded. "Sure, what's up?" She hoped her voice didn't sound as fluttery as her stomach felt.

Mrs. Fried placed her hands flat on the table and leaned forward. "This is already Ruchie's sixth session by you and, frankly, I haven't been seeing any improvement."

"Oh," Yael squeaked. "Well…uh…it takes time, you know, until you start seeing…um…change, it doesn't happen overnight. Improving fine motor functioning is a process." She was glad she finally hit upon that last line. It had a nice, professional ring.

Mrs. Fried was tapping her fingers impatiently. "Listen, I didn't expect anything to happen in the first week or two. I did give it time, and we've been doing the homework every day, yet after six weeks, Ruchie's still having the same struggles with buttoning, and cutting and drawing, and her kindergarten teacher tells me that her frustration levels have hit a new low." She tilted her head to the side. "Something here just doesn't seem to be working."

A huge weight of dread settled in Yael's stomach. She desperately tried to think of something to say in her defense. "I...I'm sorry, it really does take time, you know, even six weeks isn't a whole lot of time..."

Mrs. Fried cut her off. "I think you should know that I consulted with a different OT, someone a friend of mine recommended. This woman, as soon as she heard me describe Ruchie, said right away, 'It sounds like she has serious sensory issues. I hope she's getting intense sensory therapy, like massages, brushing, and swinging.'"

She stopped, and the look she gave Yael made her squirm as nervously as if she was sitting in the principal's office. "So then I told this woman that my therapist hasn't mentioned *anything* about sensory therapy. And do you know what she told me?"

Yael really didn't want to know.

"She said, 'Well, I think it might be time to find a new therapist.'"

CHAPTER 7

THE OFFICE PHONE and her cell phone rang simultaneously. Suri's hand wavered between the two. A glance at her cell phone screen told her it was her father's aide. The office phone might be a new client.

The client always comes first, she thought ironically as she snatched at the landline before it stopped its pealing.

"Big Bounce Therapy, how can I help you?" She typed in the details of the new client, while at the same time reading the text that Jackie, the aide, had just sent.

Couldn't rch you by phone. Dad's refusing to eat again. Plz call.

Suri dug her fingernails into her hand. She and her siblings had all agreed that assisted living would be the best move for Tatty. He needed social stimulation and an accessible minyan. With Mommy gone, he had just been sitting at home, depressed, not even interested in going to their houses for Shabbos. All in all, the move had been a good one…except when he had his fits of—well, she hated to say it, but—childish stubbornness.

And in such circumstances, she, the youngest, the daddy's girl ever since she was a kid, was the only one he would listen to.

She sighed. She'd have to make the trip into Brooklyn after work, there was no choice.

Yael walked in as Suri was texting Jackie to expect her within the next few hours.

"How'd your day go?" she asked, watching Yael put her files away. She always felt a little sorry for the younger woman; it was easy to get bulldozed by Aviva if you didn't know how to stand up for yourself, and Yael always seemed to cower whenever Aviva looked her way.

Yael shrugged. "Okay." She looked like she wanted to say more, but instead went back to her files.

"We just got a call for a new OT case," Suri continued. "What's your schedule like?"

Yael was still facing the file cabinet. "Just had a spot open up," she murmured.

"Yeah?" Suri clicked on the schedule screen. "Who finished?"

"Fried."

"Already? Didn't they just start a few weeks ago?"

Yael took a moment to answer. "She...uh...said she wants to end it."

"Oh," said Suri uncomfortably. She tapped on the keyboard. Should she ask? "Did she say why?"

"Of course." Yael turned in her direction. "Because her daughter is miraculously cured of all fine motor deficits. She wants to nominate me OT of the Century."

Suri gave an uncertain smile. Was that sarcasm? She didn't know Yael well enough to tell.

Yael sighed. "The dark and ugly truth? She says I messed up

big time in my diagnosis and she wants to go find an OT who knows what she's doing. What do you say—should I quit?"

Suri blinked. "That's quite a jump." *Good thing Aviva's not here.* She stood up and walked over. "But I do think you should go out and treat yourself to a nice, big ice coffee. With caramel and a scoop of ice cream. It's what I always do to get over rejection." Well, actually, what she did was curl up in her bed, head buried under her pillow.

A slow smile spread across Yael's dejected face. "You're trying to say this happens even to therapists who know what they're doing?" She gave a little laugh. "That idea actually sounds amazing. Wanna join me in celebrating my first major mess-up?"

Suri found herself really wishing she could take her up on it. But the bridge traffic into Brooklyn beckoned. "I'm sorry, I need to go somewhere else right now."

She put a hand on Yael's shoulder. "But how about tomorrow?"

AT THE SOUND of the buzzer, Aviva pushed open the glass door and stepped inside the large room. It had been years since she'd visited Zevi's office—she'd had to check up the address before coming. The space seemed smaller than last time she'd been there, but that was probably because more cubicles had been added to the office floor since then. From the hum of activity going on, this freelancer's hub seemed a happening, exciting place to be. Most people were busy working at their desks. Some were standing in small groups, impromptu business consultations.

Zevi, she suspected, would probably be by the water cooler.

Sure enough, she found her husband standing outside his cubicle with two other men, coffee cup in hand, cracking jokes.

"…and then the *shver* says—Aviva! What are you doing here?"

There was a brief pause as his two friends looked at him, confused, apparently thinking that was part of the joke. Then they followed the direction of his wide eyes, saw Aviva standing there, and, with a slap on his back, melted away.

"Hi, Zevi. Sorry to disturb you at work." She tried very hard to keep any sarcasm out of her voice.

But Zevi didn't seem to be on the lookout for sarcasm. "Wow, what an honor!" he exclaimed, breaking into a huge grin. "Can I make you a cup of coffee? Or…" He looked around his office space helplessly, and finally lit upon a box of Mike and Ikes. "Jelly bean? Any color but red. Those are all gone."

Despite herself, Aviva found her lips twitching. "No thank you." She sat down on Zevi's swivel chair, as he leaned against the cubicle wall, looking at her.

"Is everything okay?" he asked. "I know the weekend took a lot out of you."

She quickly nodded. "I'm fine. Just needed a good night's sleep. I woke up this morning feeling much better." She paused, as he waited.

"I came by because we need an ad printed up, and I figured it would be better if we work on it together in person."

Zevi raised his eyebrows. In the past, when the clinic needed ads or flyers printed, Aviva would just e-mail him the information and he would bring the flyers home with him.

"Haven't been satisfied with my graphic designer?" he asked, lightly enough that she could sense the hurt.

"No, not at all. I just thought…" She stopped because she didn't really know why she'd come down in person. "Anyway," she finished lamely, "I'm here, so if you have the time right now…"

Zevi rolled his eyes. "I have the time right now. Show me what you want and I'll see if Shimmy's available."

Shimmy Rubin was a graphic designer that worked down the row from Zevi. They often worked together on projects. Aviva sometimes wondered if Shimmy was any more successful in bringing in clients than Zevi was.

Aviva showed Shimmy the wording she'd written up. "It's for the local directory. We opened up too late to put in an ad last year. This year I want a big full page."

Zevi scanned the paper. "I'd change some of this if I were you. You're making the center sound as fun as preparing for a Shabbos with the in-laws." He winked.

Aviva laughed. Zevi was the only person in the world that she could take criticism from. Somehow, he knew exactly the right spots to hit, and the right way to hit them.

"So how would you write it, then?" she challenged.

He grabbed a chair from the cubicle next door, pulled it up to the desk, and sat down. "What makes it fun to come to therapy? Think from the perspective of a child."

"From the perspective of a child? How am I supposed to do that?"

Zevi leaned back in his chair and pushed his glasses down on his nose. "Your problem," he observed, putting on a European accent, "eez that you are not in touch with your inner child."

He sat up and tossed Aviva the jelly bean box. "I zink you need more of these and less crème brulees in your life."

She caught the box, and suddenly she started to giggle. So hard that tears streamed out of her eyes, and the guy from the cubicle next door stuck his head in to make sure everything was okay.

"Zevi," Aviva finally said, after catching her breath, "you know what? I think I should come by here every day after work."

"You can do even better," he said, his face suddenly turning serious. "You can have me *at* work every day."

Aviva blinked—she had not intended to start up that conversation again. Not now, when she was more relaxed than she'd been in weeks. Or months.

Then again, Suri had thought it was a good idea. And Aviva was getting pretty desperate to find someone.

She looked at her husband, rocking back and forth on his chair as he scribbled something on her page. Why, exactly, had she been so opposed to this idea? Right now, she couldn't remember.

Aviva straightened her shoulders. "Okay." She held up a finger. "But only temporarily, until we find someone full-time."

CHAPTER 8

I
T HAD BEEN one of those mornings. Aviva had started off behind because she'd fallen asleep too early the night before and hadn't prepared the kids' lunches. That was already a recipe for disaster in the morning, and it didn't help when Kayla stalked into the kitchen and asked for a smoothie for breakfast. And then Chaim wanted an omelet. And Tzippy needed fifty dollars for a class trip—and a signed note because she'd lost the permission slip.

Then Chaim remembered that he hadn't done his math homework, and Goldy came downstairs crying because she had no more clean uniform shirts ("Tzippy keeps stealing mine, just because we're the same size!"). And Chavi, of course, was still glowering at her from yesterday, when she'd come home from school in a huff and slammed a paper down on the table: her *Navi* report, with a big red D written across it.

If someone gave marks for mothering, Aviva was sure her grade wouldn't be any better than Chavi's.

Feeling like a total failure, she slipped out of the bedlam of her house, leaving Zevi to do car pools and pick up everyone's mood (how *could* he bounce in from shul with a perky "Great morning, *chevrah*!" with all the shouting and crying going on?). But not before she heard his cheery "See you soon!" wafting out the door along with her.

As if she needed reminding.

She'd had plenty of time to regret whatever had possessed her to allow Zevi to take the secretarial position. What had she been thinking? And what, for that matter, was Zevi thinking, wanting to spend half his day playing receptionist? The more she thought about it, the less sense it made. Yet Zevi seemed to be looking forward to this as if it were his ticket to financial success.

Not that he had spent his working career up until then pretending that mattered.

Aviva entered the clinic still carrying the weight of her morning fiasco. Didn't help that the moment she stepped inside, she was greeted by Esti, her grad student shadow. Aviva stopped. No. It wasn't Tuesday. It definitely wasn't Tuesday. Why was she there?

"Hi, Aviva!" Esti bounded over. "I switched my day this week, remember?"

"Oh, that's right." Just what she needed.

Even though it had been her idea to bring in these students, Aviva was starting to realize she hadn't properly thought the thing through. There was something about having an overeager girl sticking to you like gum on your shoe that was profoundly irritating.

"What's on the schedule today?" Esti hopped alongside Aviva as she gathered up her materials. "Do we have that stuttering case again? Yay! I love stuttering!"

She loves stuttering.

"Personally, I think voice disorders are better." Aviva turned to see Yael walking behind them, grinning. "Vocal nodules, they're just the greatest!"

Esti gave Yael an uncertain smile, clearly not getting it. Aviva tried not to laugh. Feeling her mood suddenly lighten, Aviva gave a friendly, "How are you, Yael?"

Yael glowed in surprise. "Fine, thanks!"

Aviva's mood continued to brighten as the morning wore on; the clinic was without a doubt her milieu. She loved the mental challenge and creativity involved in coming up with just the right therapy game plan, and she thrived in the role of clinic hostess, making regular forays into the waiting area to meet and greet the parents. Even Esti's dogged shadowing ("Where're you going now, Aviva? Ooooh, washing for lunch? Hold on, I'm coming too!") didn't drag her down too much.

Until she stepped out into the reception area, Esti on her heels, and was greeted by a well-known, booming voice.

"Welcome to Big Bounce Therapy Center! Hey, lady, you look familiar! Have we met?"

The parents sitting in the waiting area gave her curious glances and behind her, Esti giggled. "Is that the new receptionist?" she asked. "Funny that it's a man—I always thought they were girls. Have you really met before?"

Aviva knew that her cheeks must be a deep, fiery red. She had intended to keep the fact of their relationship quiet, not quite hiding it, but not advertising it unnecessarily. Instead, the first second into his new job, Zevi had made sure to announce it to the world. Count on him to make such a hoopla over everything.

She turned to Esti and mumbled, "Yes, we've met before. He's my husband."

─

YAEL CAME HOME completely wiped. Ever since the Ruchie Fried disaster, her confidence had been ebbing drastically, and she'd been having one bad therapy session after another. Today, it was with Leahleh Steinman. Mrs. Steinman had asked Yael a reasonable enough question: What causes organizational issues in children? And instead of reciting the textbook answer she'd learned in grad school, Yael had hemmed and hawed and floundered her way through some disjointed statements, finally emerging with the conclusion that she didn't know.

She wouldn't be surprised if, next week, Mrs. Steinman asked to terminate therapy.

"Mommy!! Mommy home!" She barely had time to put down her bags before a pair of little hands wrapped themselves around her leg. She lifted her little son high in the air.

"How's my Sruli?" Hugging him tight, Yael sat down on the couch, feeling her work tension dissipate. Aah, the joy of a chubby three-year-old cheek pressed into your own.

"Tammy take me park! And Simi fall down! And Simi cry! And I not cry!" Sruli was squirming from her grip in his exuberance to tell her about his day.

Yael gasped dramatically. "Simi fell down! Where did she fall?"

"Here." He pointed solemnly to his knee. "And Simi cry a *lot*!"

Tammy, the babysitter, came walking into the living room holding eighteen-month-old Simi. "Hi, Yael. The kids had such a great time at the park. Simi just got a little scrape, that's all."

Yael nodded, smiling at her. "Of course, I wasn't worried." She was not one of those over-anxious mothers. Caring for her own seven younger siblings had taught her a lot.

Simi joined her on the couch and, as Tammy waved good-bye and slipped out the door, Yael sank back in contentment, snuggling with her kids. It was so good to be home.

Three hours later, she was sitting in Sruli's bed reading him his third bedtime story when she heard the front door open. Ephraim was home from *kollel*.

She said Shema and kissed Sruli good night, then walked quietly downstairs. Ephraim was sitting at the kitchen table, clearly ready for supper. "How was your day?" she asked.

Ephraim looked up and shrugged. "Fine. Busy. I learned through lunch." He said the last part hopefully, and Yael took the cue.

"You must be starving. Here, it's spaghetti and meatballs tonight."

Her cooking skills, trained in her mother's home, tended toward the simple, yummy, and filling. This had been one of her many anxieties during their engagement period, when she'd first started discovering the vast cultural chasms between their worlds. Ephraim's dinners growing up had been cooked by housekeepers or bought at local restaurants, and included ingredients that would have eaten up a full monthly salary in the Savetsky home. Yael had made a valiant attempt when they were first married to cook some unpronounceable French dishes she'd dug up in a cookbook—only to discover, to her relief, that Ephraim's years away in yeshivah had trained him to prefer the *heimishe* to the haute cuisine.

Ephraim ate silently for several minutes. When he paused for a refill, he asked, "And how was your day?"

"Okay." Yael said it hesitantly.

"Things getting busier?" he asked. "Are you getting more clients?"

"Yeah, I guess." *Ask me,* she silently begged. *Ask me if I feel things are going well. Ask me if I'm enjoying it.*

"Well, that's great," he said as he took another mouthful of meatball. "You know, when I spoke with Tatty today, he specifically asked me about you. How the clinic is going. He said he's impressed with the way you're handling things. That you're realizing the potential he could tell you had from when he first met you."

Yael swallowed. "Wow. Realizing my potential. That's…quite a compliment." From her father-in-law, it was huge.

Ephraim seemed as pleased with himself as if he'd just handed her an expensive present. "Yup. You can tell he's really into it. And I told him how much you're enjoying the work. I mean, you are, right?" He was still looking at his fork. The question was clearly rhetorical.

Yael took a breath. "Sure am," she said.

CHAPTER 9

SURI WALKED INSIDE the clinic, nodding at the parents sitting in the waiting area as she passed (she saved the small talk for Aviva). She glanced at the receptionist's desk as she headed inside the office. It was sure nice not having to deal with the administrative hassles anymore...or, at least, to anticipate not having to deal with them.

She was still spending time teaching Zevi Heyman the ropes; their new receptionist and very first employee (could you call your partner's husband an employee?) was high on enthusiasm, but lower on recall of details. Even after a week, he still kept asking her how to use the computer system; she hadn't even approached the topic of filing insurance claims. Yet he did a great job answering the phones and schmoozing up the clients and she supposed that, in any business, client rapport was what counted most.

Unfortunately for her.

Files in hand, Suri entered her therapy room. Today she'd be starting treatment with the son of a friend of hers, and she wasn't sure how she felt about that. Tzippora Benjamin davened in her shul and volunteered for the Drive-a-Bubby rides that Suri coordinated for the elderly in their community. On the one hand, it was nice dealing with someone she knew. On the other hand... well, she was dealing with someone she knew.

"Hi, Suri! This is so cute!" Tzippora came into the room, a young boy in tow. "Ezzie, say hi to Morah Suri. She's Mommy's friend, and she's going to play with you."

Ezzie paid zero attention to Suri; he zoomed straight for the cars in the corner of the room.

Tzippora chuckled. "Ezzie loves cars. He can sit all day lining them up in a row." She sat down in one of the kiddy chairs next to the table. "How fun! I feel like I'm in kindergarten again!"

"There's an adult chair next to the door."

Tzippora waved her off. "No, I'm serious, this is fun." She put her purse down. "Oh, by the way, I meant to tell you about the ride the other day for Mrs. Hershkowitz. Such a sweet lady, but you can tell she's lonely. She invited me out for lunch after I drove her home from the doctor. She'd be a good candidate for your social groups."

Suri nodded, wavering between wanting to jot down the information—after all, she was looking to beef up attendance at the monthly social events for the elderly she'd started organizing as an offshoot of Drive-a-Bubby—and striving to keep this meeting strictly professional.

With a brief nod, she said, "Great. Now, tell me about Ezzie."

Tzippora sat up straighter. "Well, I brought him in because he's almost three and still not speaking much. He's my oldest, so I don't really have what to compare him to, but his playgroup teacher recommended I check this out."

"I see." Suri glanced at Ezzie. He was busily lining up each car perfectly straight, oblivious to their conversation. "What types of things does he like to play with?"

As Tzippora spoke, Suri felt a growing unease. She took notes, asked questions, and at last said brightly, "Now it's time to play, Ezzie!"

Ezzie didn't look up.

"He can be shy among strangers," Tzippora murmured.

Suri sat down on the floor next to the boy. "Ezzie, I see you're playing with cars."

"Cars," Ezzie repeated, still focused on aligning them against the wall.

She pulled a red car out of the line and pushed it toward him. "The car is driving."

Ezzie caught the car and, still without glancing at her, put it back in its place. "Car," he said.

"See, that's the problem," Tzippora commented. "He only speaks in single words like that."

"Mm-hmm." Suri's eyebrows furrowed. She took out a small doll. "Look, Ezzie, the dolly is riding on the car. She's driving to Mommy." She started moving the car in Tzippora's direction.

With a howl, Ezzie jumped up, grabbed the car away from her, and planted himself again in the corner, back turned to both women.

"He, uh, likes to play by himself," Tzippora said uncomfortably. "Don't take it personally. I'm sure he'll warm up to you with time."

But Suri wasn't so sure at all.

"AUTISM." SHE SPOKE the word aloud into the silent office as, across from her, Aviva flinched. "What a terrible word to suggest to a mother."

Aviva was sitting at her husband's vacated desk chair. The two of them were the only ones in the clinic; Yael always ran out as soon as she finished with her last client, to get home to her kids. Aviva never failed to make a resentful comment about this, but Suri understood the urge to race home. If she had young children waiting for her, she would do the same.

If... But she quickly slammed the door on that thought before it had a chance to escape. *Baruch Hashem* for the three wonderful children that she had.

Anyway, right now, it was someone else's child she was worried about.

Aviva was holding up a cautionary hand. "Suri, you realize that you're not mentioning the word 'autism' to anyone, right? Only a qualified medical professional can make that diagnosis."

Suri blinked. "Of course, of course. But, I mean, to suggest that she take him for a psychoneuro eval—I have to give her some reason for it, don't I?"

She paced back and forth across the office, stopped next to Aviva, and pounded a hand on the desk.

"The worst thing is that I know her! I run into her all the time! Imagine—she'll always associate *me* as the one who first broke the news!"

Aviva stood up. "No, no, no! Suri, you're not breaking any news to anyone! You don't *know*. You're just suggesting an evaluation— that's all."

Suri was silent as Aviva went on. "Listen, Suri, you have no choice and you know it. It would be much, much worse if she always associated you as the one who missed the signs, or who was too scared to tell her that she suspected something, and pushed off a diagnosis for another year or two because of that."

Suri picked up a big smiley-face stress ball Zevi had sitting on his desk. She stared at it for a moment, then gave it a giant squeeze. "This wouldn't bother you at all?" she asked.

"Sure it would." The answer came out so quickly, Suri wondered if Aviva was offended by the question. Or lying.

It was so hard to know what was going on inside Aviva.

"But I would do it anyway, because I know it's what's best for the child, and that it's my job as a professional."

Suri found herself straightening up at the words. Best for the child. Professional duty. Of course.

She wondered what it was like, living with inborn clarity and confidence. In the absence of her own, it sure felt nice borrowing some from Aviva.

"You're right," she said.

"Of course I am." It didn't even sound arrogant—just natural. "So here's what you should say to her—"

The office door opened. Zevi poked his head inside.

"Hi, ladies. Am I interrupting something top secret?"

"What are you doing here?"

Suri was surprised to hear how sharply Aviva said it.

"Going out to *minchah* and realized I left my hat," he said, snatching the item up from on top of the filing cabinet. Stuffing it on his head, he turned to Aviva. "Madam, may I offer you a ride?"

"Thanks," she said drily, "but it might be hard fitting my car into your trunk."

He grinned. "Yeah, it might. Well, will I at least see you at home soon?"

"Soon."

With a wave, he left, leaving Aviva to scowl at the door. "Left his hat here… Give me a break. He came back to check up on me."

Suri cleared her throat uncomfortably, and Aviva blushed. "Forgot you were here," she mumbled.

Then she sighed. "He thinks I work too hard. He always did, but because I was stupid enough to make one little comment the other day… Aren't I entitled to say I'm exhausted without being subjected to this babying?"

"You're also entitled to a vacation if you're that exhausted."

Aviva glared at her. "I'm not *that* exhausted. Just a little tired." She picked up Zevi's stress ball and started rolling it back and forth on the desk. "I don't know what's wrong with me. I've always been able to do everything well without falling apart, and lately everything's—"

She stopped abruptly. The ball rolled off the desk and bounced across the floor.

"Yes?"

"Never mind… Things are fine. Maybe I should go to a doctor. I bet I'm low on iron."

I've always been able to do everything well. Suri's eyes narrowed as something snapped inside.

"Oh, please. You don't need a doctor; you need rest. Even you have your limits. Why is it so hard for you to admit that?"

CHAPTER 10

TZIPPORA WAS JUST as cheery this week as last.

"Hi, Morah Suri! Here we are!" Her pocketbook swung from her arm as she bounced in, pulling Ezzie along with her.

I'm about to wipe that smile right off your face. The thought made Suri squirm in her seat.

Ezzie headed straight for the cars in the corner, without a glance at Suri.

She cleared her throat. "Ezzie, come sit over here."

He didn't even look up at his name.

"He can be stubborn," Tzippora said with an indulgent smile. "He does what he wants, this kiddo. His playgroup teacher says the same… Oh, were you able to reach her?"

Last week, Suri had asked her permission to speak to Ezzie's teacher. Their conversation had only strengthened her suspicions.

"Let me play a bit with Ezzie and then we'll talk at the end."

Tzippora's eyebrows shot up at Suri's tone. "Oh! Uh, sure."

Today's session was no different than last week's. Suri pulled out all the stops—puppets, bubbles, balloons, a veritable sound and light show, but Ezzie just stared blankly at a spot on the purple wall behind Suri's ear, not even cracking a smile. Tzippora's eyes furrowed as she interjected a running mix of excuses and encouragement ("He went to sleep late last night." "Ezzie, come on, look at the pretty bubbles!").

After one last fruitless attempt, Suri sat back down opposite Tzippora. "His teacher told me that in playgroup he tends to play on his own, rather than with the other kids."

Tzippora nodded. "She told me that too. You think...maybe he has, I don't know, ADHD? Should I get that checked?"

Suri clenched her hand hidden in her lap. She wished she had Zevi's stress ball.

"I think getting him checked out would be a good idea," she said slowly.

Tzippora blinked. "Okay. If you say so. Where do I go to test for ADHD?"

Suri took a breath. Clench, unclench. "I didn't say ADHD. But I think it's worth it to have him evaluated by a developmental pediatrician. Or a psychologist."

Tzippora had already begun typing the information into her phone. Now she paused, fingers suspended over the screen. "Not ADHD? You suspect something else?" Her childlike eyes narrowed. "What?"

Suri kept her voice low, measured. "I'm not a doctor. I really can't say. But I do see some signs that are worrying me a bit, and—"

"Signs? What signs?" Tzippora's voice rose higher.

Suri glanced at Ezzie, still planted in his corner with the cars. "The fact that he doesn't seek out interaction with other people, not children or adults, is worrying. That he doesn't even seem to attend to what's going on around him—as if he's in his own world."

Tzippora's face was white. Suri couldn't go on.

"Wait a second. It sounds like—are you talking about…" She closed her eyes and whispered, "…autism?"

The look on the young mother's face made Suri want to cry. "I'm not saying anything. I'm not qualified to diagnose. I'm just saying…if it was my child…well, you should check it out."

Tzippora didn't even seem to hear her. "Autism. My G-d." She looked over at her son, stunned.

She's never going to see him the same way again. You've just ruined her life.

Suri bit her lip. *No,* she told herself, hearing Aviva's voice inside her head. *You did what needed to be done.*

"I'm so sorry," Suri said. "I know it's a terrible thing to contemplate."

Tzippora shook her head as she stood up. She swayed in place for a few moments, as if finding her balance, then abruptly walked over to Suri, bent down, and gave her a hug. "Suri, thank you." She straightened up, and Suri could see the wetness in her eyes. "It must've been so hard for you to mention this."

Tzippora walked over to Ezzie, gently pulled him up, and started walking with him out of the room. At the door, she turned back.

"Thank you for caring."

YAEL CAUGHT UP to Suri as she was heading out to her car. "Hey, how'd your day go?"

Suri slowed down her stride to smile at Yael. "*Baruch Hashem*, great. Really great. Yours?"

"Fine." All her therapy sessions had gone off without a hitch, she'd had no complaints from anyone—she supposed that was as fine as it gets.

Would she ever reach the point in her career where she could say "really great" with as much shining satisfaction as Suri had?

They both turned at a voice from behind. "Does that mean the Big Conversation went well?"

Suri grinned at Aviva, who walked up next to them. "It went fabulously. Difficult, but the mother was really appreciative. I felt like I'd done something good for the kid, by leading them on the right path to help."

Aviva nodded. "That's our profession at its best, right?"

"Well, it was all thanks to your good advice."

Yael's head swiveled back and forth, feeling like an increasingly irrelevant participant in this heartwarming paean to their vocation. Whatever this big advice was that Suri had sought, she obviously had not gone seeking by Yael. Maybe it was speech specific, she tried telling herself.

Ah, come on. You also would've chosen Aviva over yourself, hands down.

She cleared her throat. "I know it's good *tikkun* for the ego, feeling clueless every now and then, but, well, care to let me in on the secret?"

Suri giggled uncomfortably. "Sorry about that. I suspected something about one of my clients, and didn't know how to tell the mother, and Aviva helped me out. That's all."

Nice and vague. Yael nodded wisely. "Ah, I see."

Suri lifted her eyes over Yael's head, back to Aviva. "What are you doing leaving so early? Taking your husband's advice?"

Aviva glowered at her, but it was a friendly glower. "I'm actually taking my own advice, for your information. I have a doctor's appointment."

Once again, Yael felt like the odd one out. "Oh, are you feeling okay?" she asked.

Aviva shrugged, looking straight ahead. "I'm fine," she said curtly. She stopped next to her car and took out her keys. "Well, see you two tomorrow."

Suri waved brightly. Yael's was halfhearted.

Why, with her two partners, did she always have the funny sense that she was back in junior high?

***

AVIVA CAME HOME from work the next day and, discovering the house surprisingly quiet, quickly snuck up to her bedroom. She kicked off her heels, took off her sheitel, and lay down.

Where everyone was, she didn't want to think about. Maybe Chavi had had a spurt of big-sisterly devotion and decided to take them all out to the park? Maybe Zevi had sprung for a spontaneous pizza night?

Right now, she didn't care. All she wanted was to get in a quick nap before the troops came home. Maybe, then, she'd have enough energy to actually mother them, rather than simply marshaling them through dinner and bedtime as fast as she could.

She rested her head on her pillow and closed her eyes. Tried to allow herself to drift off.

The house is a wreck. I should really take advantage of the quiet to clean up.

She shut her eyes more firmly. No, she needed sleep.

And the laundry. I really must throw in a load. By the time she'd come home from the doctor yesterday, she hadn't had a chance to do her regular nightly housekeeping chores.

It would take her just a minute to get the machine going.

But she needed to rest. Dr. Stein had been firm in her advice: "You're working yourself too hard. You're not twenty years old anymore. Respect your body's needs. You have to cut back on something."

She'd been annoyed by her words. What, at thirty-six she had to start acting like a creaky old lady? The doctor was talking as if she was practically ready for an old-age home, for goodness sakes.

Aviva tried to relax, but somehow, the thought of rest was just making her tense. How could she rest when she had so much to do? Cut back? She'd practically laughed aloud, right there on the examination table. Where, exactly, could she cut back? Hire a housekeeper with money that she didn't have? Cut back on her work hours when the family's primary *parnasah* came from her income? Give up some of her kids for adoption?

Sighing, she picked herself up from the bed. Just one load, she promised herself, and then she'd really go to sleep.

The phone rang on her way to the laundry room. She raced to grab it.

"Hello?"

It was the doctor's office. Yesterday's blood test results had come back.

"And?" she prodded. "Low iron?"

"No, it's not that." The doctor's voice was cheery—too cheery.

Aviva braced herself.

"Mrs. Heyman, there's a very clear reason for your exhaustion." She gave a slight laugh.

"You're expecting."

CHAPTER 11

AVIVA STOOD MOTIONLESS in the hall outside her laundry room, phone still in her hand from the doctor's call that had taken place—when? A minute ago? An hour ago? All she knew was that the doctor's words were still reverberating through her head in a thousand echoing blasts: "You're expecting! Expecting! Expecting!"

She held herself straight and still, squeezing every muscle into place. Like a general surveying his troops. Head high...neck, still working. Shoulders doing their job. Knees locked in place. She took a deep, steadying breath.

Breathe in, breathe out. In control.

She could handle this. She could handle anything.

She could handle another baby. On top of the eight children that she was already...not handling.

Aviva's breathing started speeding up. She put a hand to her chest.

Breathe in, breathe out. Staccato beats.

She was.

Not handling.

Anything.

In her life.

In, out. Ragged breaths. *Beep, beep, beep.*

She turned, startled. What was beeping? She looked down at her hand, found she hadn't hung up the phone. Quickly, she pressed the off button.

In her room, she buried her head in her pillow. Silence—she needed the world to be silent right now, to let her think, to let her pull herself together.

And, suddenly, from the depths of the silence, she heard a conversation. A conversation that had been buried deep in her head for decades.

It was a conversation she should never have overheard. Standing outside her parents' room—how old could she have been? Five? Six? Young enough to still be seeking her mother's comfort from a bad dream. (The mocking "You're too old to be crying from nightmares!" would come later—words that would keep her rooted and shivering in bed, words that always carried her mother's strident voice, though they had never, to her memory, been uttered by her mother, but rather by Aviva herself.)

That night, Aviva had stood outside the bedroom, clutching her blanket, about to knock, when she'd heard the startling pronouncement from inside:

"I lost the baby."

Aviva had stopped her fist midair. Lost the baby? What was her mother talking about? They didn't have any babies. Had her mother been watching someone else's baby?

"I'm so sorry." That was Tatty, and he was whispering.

"My fourth time."

Even from the other side of the door, Mommy's voice sounded so sad, and Aviva began to back away, frightened. Mommy lost *four* babies? How could that be? In their home, she was always the one who found the lost things.

"This must be so hard for you." Tatty was speaking so low, Aviva had to listen really hard to hear him. But Mommy's voice was, as usual, strong and sure.

"Hard? There's no such thing as hard when you're talking about Hashem's will."

From the distance of decades, Aviva now heard those words once more, heard the steely conviction which had inexplicably sent her scampering back to her bed in fright, and a deep shudder went through her.

There's no such thing as hard when you're talking about Hashem's will.

This wasn't even hard. This was another baby. Another gift from Hashem. Her mother had lost four, and now she was expecting yet another one. Life wasn't hard; life was great. Great, great!

From far across the house, she heard a door slam. The kids. They were home.

And she was expecting another one. Ribbono Shel Olam.

She squeezed her eyes shut.

Ingrate.

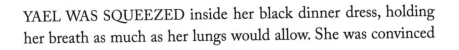

YAEL WAS SQUEEZED inside her black dinner dress, holding her breath as much as her lungs would allow. She was convinced that one great whoosh of an exhale was all it would take to blast the overworked buttons clear across the room. Served her right for not updating her dress wardrobe after Simi was born. When had Tatty and Mommy Jeren gone more than a year without being honored at some organizational event?

"And you remember my daughter-in-law, Yael, of course. Yael, Mrs. Smithereen."

Yael nodded politely at the woman as jewelry laden as her mother-in-law, who was now grasping her hand enthusiastically to demonstrate just how fondly she remembered Yael. Her name, of course, was not Smithereen. That was the generic name she'd privately assigned to all her mother-in-law's high-fashion friends. She'd learned the hard way, after her first year of trying all sorts of mnemonics to keep the people straight in her mind. She would recite lists of names before each event, certain her worth as a Jeren daughter-in-law depended on it. She eventually realized the hopelessness of her attempt at ingratiation, when she'd eagerly greeted Mrs. Warenburg at a Jeren corporate luncheon, only to have a mortified mother-in-law hiss that this was Mrs. Goldberg.

After that, they all became Smithereen.

Ephraim had laughed hard when she'd confided this to him, a rare case of him appreciating her irreverence for anything Jeren related. He walked up to her now, together with his father, the big showman's smile on her father-in-law's face that Yael had come to associate with public events. A third man strode beside them, distinguished looking and bareheaded.

Next to her, Mrs. Smithereen gasped. "Isn't that…?"

"Senator Pearl, I'd like you to meet my wife, Esther." Her father-in-law had stepped neatly up to their group, a hand on the senator's arm.

Her mother-in-law glowed. "Senator, it's such an honor to have you here tonight."

His answer was as smooth as his smile. "For a couple who devotes themselves to the public welfare as much as you and your husband do? Believe me, the honor is all mine."

Tatty Jeren was in his element. "And this is my daughter-in-law, Yael. You may be interested to know, Senator, that she recently opened a children's clinic, to service the community children for all their speech and occupational therapy needs."

Yael cringed. Why did her father-in-law feel the need to introduce her this way to every person he met, like he was her publicity agent?

The senator's "How wonderful" sounded as fake as Mrs. Smithereen's insistence that she remembered Yael perfectly, and Yael didn't think there was any need for more than a polite nod in return.

But her father-in-law didn't let a subject go so easily. That, she reflected, was what made him such a successful businessman.

And her such a lousy one.

"Yael, I have an idea for you," he said a short while later, when they were all seated at the front table reserved for the family. "Pearl has made his political career positioning himself as the champion of children's causes. I'll bet if you invite him to visit your clinic, he won't be able to refuse."

Yael swallowed her salmon fillet. "Visit the clinic? Why?"

Apparently, it was a really dumb question. Ephraim quickly jumped in, as if to cover up for her unworldliness. "Tatty, what a great idea! Imagine all the publicity they'd get!"

Publicity. Ahhh.

"Oh, yes," Yael chimed in. "Great idea."

Zalman Jeren pointed a finger at her. "Go ask him now."

"Now?" This was the kind of conversation that required at least a week of rehearsing and priming for.

"Of course. In a few minutes they're going to start the program, he'll get up to speak, and after that he'll be out the door. If you don't catch him now, you'll lose your chance."

Gulp. With the eyes of the entire clan upon her, she had no choice but to put down her napkin, brush the crumbs off her dress, and make her way to the dais where the senator was seated with the heads of the organization. How did such a task land in her lap? This was the sort of thing Aviva should be doing.

Aviva. Imagine her reaction when she found out they'd be receiving an official visit from a state dignitary. And that it was all thanks to Yael's efforts.

Somehow, the thought propelled her forward, and even gave her the confidence to croak out, "Excuse me, Senator? Do you have a minute?"

He did have a minute. And merely five minutes later, she found herself floating back to the Jeren family table, grinning ear to ear.

"He said yes!" Yael knew she was shrieking, but she couldn't help it. She felt this was a triumph on the magnitude of her father-in-law's billion-dollar business deals—and the best part was that it had taken place in front of every single member of Ephraim's family.

For the first time she could remember, she was looking forward to work Monday morning.

CHAPTER 12

SURI WAS JUST leaving her house for work when she got the call from Aviva.

"I won't be able to make it today. Can you please call my clients to cancel?"

It was as if Aviva had just announced that a meteor had struck her house. It took Suri a moment to respond.

"Is everything okay?"

"Everything's fine." The answer was quick, emphatic, and clear as day: everything is *not* fine, thank you very much, and no more questions.

"If there's any way I can help…"

"Yes, by calling my clients as soon as possible. It'll look really bad if they come all the way out to the clinic before they get the message."

The clinic felt different that day without Aviva's presence—subdued, somehow, as if, in the absence of Aviva's dynamism, it had taken on Suri's persona instead. She'd hoped things would liven up when Zevi arrived in the afternoon (according to their part-time arrangement, he worked for them during the busy after-school hours), but, to her consternation, he too did not seem his usual self.

Suri was very tempted to ask Zevi if everything was well at home—something told her he would be more forthcoming with information than Aviva—but she held herself back. She'd realized, from the moment they'd decided to hire Zevi Heyman, that working with her friend's husband was a sticky proposition, which could only work if firm boundaries were drawn. Asking him to reveal personal information about his wife probably crossed those boundaries.

But the next day, when Aviva again called in sick, Suri started to get seriously alarmed, enough to question Zevi. "This is really not like her," she explained.

Zevi's quick smile calmed her down. "*Baruch Hashem*, Aviva's well. There's nothing wrong with her. It's just a…personal issue."

Suri knew she'd have to be satisfied with that, though she was burning to know what kind of personal issue could keep Aviva home from work for two whole days.

Reassured at least that it wasn't any of the worst-case scenarios she'd been fearing, she walked back to her therapy room, mind still full of the mystery.

"Everything okay?" Gitty, her grad student shadow, was sitting at the therapy table, writing up some notes.

Suri liked Gitty a lot—she was quiet, sensible and responsible, and she reminded her of her own Miri.

"Yeah, fine. Just trying to pick up the slack for one of my partners, who's been out sick." Or whatever.

Gitty nodded. "Oh, that's why things are so much quieter around here. I was trying to put my finger on it. Usually when I walk in, I feel like I've come to such a fun, happening place. Today it was more like a doctor's waiting room."

Suri stared at her. Gitty had hit on the problem exactly. And if Aviva's "personal issue," whatever it was, were to drag on longer... she had a funny feeling that their Big Bounce Therapy Center would become more like a halfhearted amble.

Suri took a breath. Could this possibly be a moment of *"be-makom she'ein anashim"*? Was it all up to her to keep up their center's happening reputation? Was Suri about to make the breakthrough of her life, revealing heretofore unknown social talents?

She glanced at her watch. Her next client wasn't due for another twenty minutes. She'd been planning on sitting in her room, catching up on session notes...

"Hi, Mrs. Levy, how are you?" She pushed her way into the waiting room/play area, where several mothers were leafing through magazines.

Mrs. Levy looked up and smiled. "Fine, and you?"

Suri's mind froze. What now? Should she try to make conversation, when she had absolutely nothing to talk about? The Levys weren't even her clients! Or leave it at that and move on?

Aviva wouldn't leave it at that. But Aviva always knew what to say. Suri coughed. "Um, how's the weather out right now? Getting hotter?"

Getting hotter? Her cheeks flushed. *Gee, Suri, let's not over-whelm them with your scintillating conversational skills.*

Mrs. Levy nodded politely. "Sure is." She went back to her magazine.

Suri ran away, before she could make any other stupid attempts at socializing.

Face it, honey. Aviva you're not.

$$\sim$$

YAEL HAD HER usual Tuesday headache. She'd thought that, with time, her grad student's steady flow of questions would have to slow down—after all, how many questions could one person possibly have? But she'd been wrong.

"So I've finally decided on my topic for our research paper," Fraidy announced over lunch. "How to diagnose and treat sensory processing disorder. What do you think? I thought it was a really important topic, because so many of our kids present with sensory issues, and if we miss those signs, well, then, we've missed the boat, right?"

Yael could feel her face reddening, as she kept her head steadily trained on her yogurt. "Sounds like a good idea," she managed.

"Yeah, I thought so. But I'll need loads of help, you know, not just research that I can do on my own, but real-life case studies. Like, what tips you off about a client? How do you know it's not ADHD, or some other disorder? Or maybe it's both? What kinds of treatments have you found most helpful? Have you had any exciting breakthrough stories?"

Yael pursed her lips. She felt like walking out of the room. Or punching Fraidy in the nose.

Come on, there's no way for her to know that she's hit your very weakest spot. Luckily her disastrous missed-all-the-sensory-disorder-signs client had not been on a Fraidy day.

She took a breath. She could not rudely leave. Or start a brawl. So she reverted to her only other option.

"Any friends get engaged this week?"

Without stopping for breath, Fraidy changed course mid-sentence. "Yes! Chana Rivka! I was so shocked! She hadn't said a word!"

Yael settled back, pleased with herself. *Shidduchim* and clothing were her two no-fail topics to get Fraidy off her case.

Just then, Suri poked her head in the room. "How's it going, Yael?"

Yael jumped up. "Suri! I wanted to speak to you about something." She'd purposely delayed telling her news about Senator Pearl's visit, hoping that Aviva would be back and she could make the proud announcement to the two of them together. But, as things stood now, she realized they couldn't wait forever to start making plans.

With a quick apology to Fraidy, she pulled Suri into an empty therapy room and told her about the visit she'd arranged.

Suri's eyes were wide, and for a moment she didn't say anything. Yael began to worry that she was upset.

"Maybe I should've consulted with you guys first," she said. "But this was just such a great opportunity, and my father-in-law said I had to ask him right away, and I was so sure you two would be happy..."

Suri smiled. "Of course I'm happy. It's a fabulous opportunity, and I'm glad you took the initiative."

Yael's shoulders relaxed.

Suri continued. "I'm thinking of Aviva, that's all. This is the type of thing she should be organizing. And I just don't know what's happening with her right now."

Yael sucked in her breath. "I thought she just had a virus or something. Are you saying there's something really wrong with her?"

Suri snorted. "Aviva doesn't take off of work for a virus." And suddenly, all of her nagging worries poured out. "She's not talking, her husband's not talking, nobody's saying anything. But if you ask me, there's something really strange going on."

AVIVA LAY IN bed, the room dark, feeling waves of nausea overtake her. Morning sickness had hit sudden and hard, and she couldn't even muster the energy to get dressed.

"What is happening to me?" she murmured aloud. She'd never had this before. Well, morning sickness she'd had. But she'd always pulled through it, kept on with her life anyway, and somehow, it became bearable. She remembered Mommy's admonitions, back when she was expecting Chavi, not to let the pregnancy take over her life. "If you act like you're sick and weak, then you'll feel sick and weak." To Mommy, weakness was the worst state in the world.

Aviva brushed a sweaty strand of hair out of her eyes. What would Mommy say if she would see her now? And why, oh why, was she having such a hard time pulling herself together?

It was almost a week now since she'd gone into work. Everyone was getting really worried, Zevi told her. He wasn't on her case, though. He believed in people taking care of themselves, and thought pregnancy deserved pampering. Ever since they were married, he'd been after her to relax.

A knock on her door. "Mommy?" It was Chavi. With Aviva out of commission, much of the household tasks had fallen to her eldest daughter, who had quite begrudgingly stepped up to the plate. Her frequent exasperated noises were loud enough to reach Aviva's bedroom.

"Mommy, Bubby just called."

The words made Aviva sit up in alarm. "Bubby? Bring the phone to me, please."

Chavi stepped into the room. "She hung up. I told her that you weren't feeling well."

Aviva's heart hammered, as Chavi continued. "I told her that you haven't been feeling well *all week*, and that I've been doing all the work around here."

CHAPTER 13

AVIVA HAD BEEN expecting a nervous phone call from her mother ever since Chavi had announced to her, in grand Chavi fashion, Aviva's total incapacitation. So she was surprised when the day went by without hearing from her. (Suri had called, again. And, again, Aviva had put on a cheery voice and assured her that everything was fine, that she was just taking care of some urgent personal business. Even though they both knew that with each passing day, the lie was becoming more and more obvious.)

By the next day, Aviva was beginning to wonder if maybe the phone lines were down. In the entire country. Or, more likely, she suspected that Zevi was screening her calls. Still, Zevi wasn't home all of the time (though he'd been allowing himself frequent breaks from his printing work to run home and check up on her).

She shifted in her bed, rolling from one side to the other. Tomorrow was Friday, and she'd have to somehow put Shabbos together. How would she manage to do that, if she could barely stand on her feet? She had some friends who confessed that there were some weeks that they only made chicken soup and cholent. She'd always scoffed at such laziness.

Nine more months of this, sweetheart. And then you'll be making Shabbos with a newborn, and then with a toddler... At the rate you're going now, you could be doing a soup-and-cholent Shabbos for years!

She pulled the blanket up around her head.

And then heard the doorbell.

It was a sharp peal, and she wondered who it could be. Her kids' friends always tapped shyly at the door.

She heard the stampede of little feet, the heavy door slamming open, and then—

"Bubby! We didn't know you were coming!"

Aviva sat up so fast in bed, she thought she might faint.

Her mother. Here in her house. This. Can't. Be. Happening.

She should have realized, when Mommy didn't call. Why hadn't she thought of this possibility? Why hadn't she done something to prepare, just in case?

The place was a wreck. She was a wreck.

Could this be just a really bad dream?

Aviva closed her eyes. Opened them again. Wiped the sweat off her forehead. No, this was really happening, and she had just seconds to prepare, before her mother saw her in this state.

She jumped up, ignoring the sudden wave of nausea, and quickly opened the blinds, made her bed, and, running to the bathroom, splashed some water on her face. She winced at the mirror. She looked so washed-out. Makeup. That's what she needed. Blush. Lipstick.

Someone was knocking on her bedroom door. Biting back the panic, she called out, "Come in," as she quickly settled herself back down on her bed in what she hoped was a perfectly-in-control pose.

"Mommy! What a surprise! What are you doing here?"

Her mother's quick eye took in every corner of the room before settling on Aviva.

"Chavi told me you've been sick for a week. I assumed something was terribly wrong that you were choosing to hold back from me. Since your father couldn't take off of work, I got on a train and came myself."

"Oh, wow. Such a long trip." Aviva couldn't think of anything more to say.

Her mother came closer to her bed and peered at her face. "So what's the matter?"

Aviva put on the biggest smile she could muster. "Nothing, really. I'm fine. Just under the weather."

Her mother snorted. "Don't 'under the weather' me. Look at you. Lying in bed for a week. Letting the house fall apart. The kids running around wild like I saw when I walked in. No, this isn't like you. There's something seriously wrong and you're afraid to tell me. But I can handle it; I'd rather *know*."

Her mother had seated herself at the foot of Aviva's bed, and was already squeezing her eyes shut as if bracing herself for the news. Aviva sighed. Though it was still quite early in the pregnancy, she saw she had no choice but to tell her.

"Mommy, it's nothing terrible at all, *chas veshalom*. In fact, it's good news." *So good you've been throwing yourself a week-long pity party.* She tried to shout down that voice with over-enthusiasm. "I'm expecting, *be'ezras Hashem*! Isn't that wonderful? I've just been having a severe case of morning sickness, that's all."

"Expecting?" Her mother's features softened for an instant, as a smile just edged its way onto her lips. Then she frowned again. "*This* is why you've let yourself fall apart? For a little nausea?"

She stood up briskly, and Aviva scrambled up as well.

"No, no, lie back down." Her mother put out a commanding hand. "Since you're not well enough to take care of your regular responsibilities, I'll do them for you. Just tell me where the cleaning supplies are."

Aviva felt herself quivering inside. "Mommy, please. I can do it. You rest from your trip."

Her mother was already out the door. "I wouldn't think of it. I came to be helpful. You continue lying down, I'll get the house in shape and make dinner. You probably need grocery shopping as well. And ironing. I saw the way the boys' shirts looked." She shook her head. "It's a good thing I brought some extra clothing, just in case. Looks like you can use my help for another few days at least."

She closed the door firmly behind her.

SURI GOT THE text during work. Sylvia, the social group facilitator that she'd hired to run Drive-a-Bubby's social events for the elderly, had a stomach virus. Ah, that was too bad. The women looked forward all month to this event, and she hated canceling on them last minute.

Feel better, she wrote back. *Know anyone who can sub?*

The answer came back quickly. *Why don't u do it urslf? I'll snd u the materials.*

Suri read that and immediately shook her head. No. No, no. She was not cut out as a social group facilitator. She looked out of the office window, where she could see the parents sitting in the waiting area. Over the course of the week, she'd made several more attempts at schmoozing with the parents, at pretending to be Aviva, sometimes with more success, sometimes with less, but each time it was a huge, forced production, requiring a good twenty minutes' recuperation alone in her room afterward.

She could just picture what it would be like, leading a group of women who are all looking toward her for the express purpose of helping them make conversation. It would be the biggest joke of the century.

It was still weighing on her later that day, when she came home from work. With a sigh, she scrolled through her contacts. No, there was no choice; she'd just have to cancel.

"Hello, Mrs. Fishman? It's Suri Taub calling. I'm so sorry, but we're going to have to cancel the get-together tonight. Sylvia's sick."

Suri's heart sank as Mrs. Fishman expressed her disappointment. For so many of these women, she knew, this was their primary social event of the month. That's why she'd started the gathering in the first place. If she had the funds and the time, she'd organize it every week.

Shaul walked through the door just as she hung up with Mrs. Fishman. "Why the long face?" he greeted her, eyebrows crinkling in concern. "Bad news?"

He probably thought it was about her father. That was where much of her stress came from nowadays.

"It's the elderly social group. Sylvia canceled, and I know the women will be so disappointed."

He hung up his hat and jacket, then turned to her and said, "Why don't you do it, then?"

Suri frowned. "You're the second person to suggest that. But you know I'm no good at these types of things."

Shaul peered at her. "What types of things? Connecting with elderly women? Showing your concern and care for others? Helping people with communication problems?"

He was smiling just a bit too smugly, and Suri glared at him. "You know what I mean." She waved her hand vaguely. "Leading groups. Speaking in public."

He raised an eyebrow at that. Even she had to admit that it sounded pathetic, calling a group of fifteen or so friendly senior citizens speaking in public.

She took a breath, as the mantra kept running through her head: *You're no Aviva, you're no Aviva, you're no Aviva...*

Shaul was still staring at her, and, suddenly, the realization hit her, loud and clear.

You're not Aviva, no. But you're Suri. And as Suri, you can do this.

With a big, bold smile, she raised her head. "Okay. I'm on."

And she picked up the phone to call Mrs. Fishman back.

CHAPTER 14

SURI MOVED THROUGH her Shabbos preparations with her usual efficiency, but with an extra bounce. The glow from last night's event was still with her. The women had been so appreciative, so welcoming, and she'd found, to her surprise, that running a social group was actually fun—at least, for women of this age group, who had no expectations of bells and whistles, and were not stingy on the compliments.

She was still repeating them to herself as she mixed the potato kugel. "We had such an enjoyable time." "You have a beautiful way of making everyone feel comfortable." And, especially, "You should lead these groups every month!"

That one kept tickling her brain, because, really, why shouldn't she? If only to save the organization the money they were paying Sylvia. *But Sylvia's a professional facilitator. She knows how to anticipate what each woman really needs, how to handle problems that may arise. And I'm just...playing at this. Pretending.*

Enjoying the feeling of, once in her life, being the center of attention.

Her lips curled up as she shook her head at herself, but later that afternoon, when she repeated some of her thoughts to Shaul, he brushed her hesitations aside.

"You already know what I'm going to tell you."

Suri shrugged, and didn't reply. Yes, she knew—but sometimes, she needed to hear it anyway.

"You know where this is coming from, and it's not about you not being qualified."

Miri was in the next room, setting the dining room table, and Suri noticed her ears perk up. Uncomfortably, she said to Shaul, "Maybe we should discuss this another time?"

"What's there to even discuss? This is a *chesed* you're good at, you have the time for it, and it would be beneficial for both them and you. Just because of your lack of self-confidence—"

A clatter came from the dining room. Miri had dropped a spoon, which showed just how intently she'd been listening. Suri turned away.

"Later, please," she hissed. The last thing she needed was for Miri to hear she lacked self-confidence, when she was forever giving her daughter pep talks about boosting her own.

Shaul went back to brushing his Shabbos hat, but something else was niggling at Suri. What was it?

A few minutes later, her cookies were out of the oven. She'd made them for a neighbor's *shalom zachar. Just chocolate chip*, she always felt the need to apologize, knowing that someone like Aviva would've brought over a tray of frosted baby bottles or something...

Aviva. That was it.

Chesed. Lack of self-confidence.

And one really bad friend.

She was on the phone with Yael a moment later.

"Hi, sorry to bother you, I'm sure it must be hectic." Suri paused, hearing the crying going on in the background. She'd forgotten what Friday afternoon was like with babies. She shouldn't have called, it wasn't considerate.

"Hey, Suri! How are you?" Yael's voice sounded cheery enough. "I don't have much time—I'm in the middle of baths, and still need to mop the floors, but what's up?"

"Mop the floors?" Suri blurted. "You don't have...?" She stopped herself, horrified. What business was it of hers whether Yael had a full-time housekeeper like she'd always imagined?

"...time for all that, do you?" she finally finished lamely.

Yael laughed. "Of course I don't have time. But that's never stopped me before."

Suri wrinkled her brow. She liked Yael a lot, but she still felt there was something missing, something she didn't understand about her.

"Fine, I'll make it quick. I'm planning on visiting Aviva on Sunday, to see how she's feeling. Wanna come along?"

There was quiet on the other end. Finally, Yael said, "Aviva's okay with that?"

"Aviva doesn't know. If I asked her, she'd say no, everything's fine, just like she has this entire week. But things are obviously not fine, and even if she doesn't want to talk about it, as her friends, we should be showing her that we care."

The pause was even longer this time. Suri thought she caught Yael whispering the word "friends" and something else she couldn't make out, and she wondered if she'd been wrong for asking her.

But, at last, Yael said, "Sure, sounds like a good idea. I'm happy to come along."

IT WAS LATE Sunday morning, and Aviva sat down to a cup of coffee and a huge, delicious sigh of relief. She had just escorted her mother out the door; Zevi was personally delivering her to the train station.

She'd had a bit of a scare when, after closing the door on the two of them, Zevi had run back inside moments later. Had Mommy decided to stay, even after an entire Shabbos's worth of effort convincing her that Aviva was really, truly handling things on her own?

Shabbos had been a ridiculous game of one-upmanship. Aviva's mother, determined to show just how necessary her presence was, had cleaned and cooked up a storm, and Aviva, equally determined to show that she was doing just fine, had cooked up her own storm, with the result being enough food to cater a bar mitzvah, none of which Aviva had been able to force down her throat.

But her efforts had done the trick. It had taken only a little persuasion to convince her mother that she could take the Sunday train home. When Zevi had walked back in, she'd nearly had a heart attack. But her husband, bless him, had run into the kitchen without a word and a minute later emerged with a steaming mug of coffee.

"Enjoy." He'd winked, placing it down on the glass coffee table. (Without a coaster; he never remembered the coaster. But, considering the circumstance, she forgave him.)

He ran out once more and as she took a sip, she felt a glow of warmth that was only partially due to the drink. For the past few days, she hadn't been allowed to touch coffee. She'd tried once, only to be treated to a hissed, "Caffeine? In *your* state?" from her mother.

She took another sip and closed her eyes. What a wonderful husband she had. She didn't appreciate him nearly enough.

Zevi had not yet come back from the train station when the doorbell pealed. Aviva sat up, surprised. From somewhere upstairs, she heard Chavi's voice screaming, "Door!" Whom she was expecting to respond to her command Aviva didn't know, but assuming it was one of Chavi's friends, she slowly lifted herself from the couch and opened the door.

"Surprise!"

Stunned, Aviva saw Suri and Yael standing in the doorway.

"My goodness! What are you doing here?"

They both had determined grins on their faces.

"Okay if we come in?" Suri asked. She was carrying a covered plate in her hands.

Aviva quickly stepped aside, waving them inside. Bewildered, all she could think was, *Thank G-d Mommy was just here.* Imagine the horror if her two partners had chosen to come for a surprise visit last week, when the house was in a state of chaos.

They all sat down on the couch. Yael gazed around the room; Suri looked straight at Aviva.

"You do look fine," she conceded.

Aviva gave a short laugh. Of course she looked fine. With Mommy here, it was back to the sheitel and makeup. (Imagine if they'd come last week, when she was in her old ratty snood!)

"I told you everything's okay," she said tightly. Why had they come? When all she wanted to do was relax after the weekend's ordeal.

There was a short pause, then Suri seemed to remember she was holding something.

"For you." She held out the plate, covered with a white napkin. She shrugged apologetically. "It's just chocolate chip cookies, nothing fancy, but I wanted to bring you something."

Aviva lifted up the napkin, saw the big, chocolaty cookies, and, inexplicably, felt tears well up in her eyes. With a much softened expression, she grinned at Suri. "Thank you. These smell heavenly. I'm going to taste one right now!"

She took a small bite, and discovered that for the first time in a week, she had an appetite. "Delicious!" she declared, offering the plate to both women.

Yael had been shifting uncomfortably in her seat. Now, taking a cookie, she gestured with her head to a picture on the wall and said, "That's cute."

It was a large photo of her children. Aviva nodded graciously. "Yeah, they're a cute bunch."

"No, I mean the fact that their outfits are color coordinated to match your living room decor. Did you do that on purpose?"

Aviva looked at Yael in surprise, and burst out laughing. "Yes, actually, I did. And you're the first person who's ever asked me that!"

Yael seemed pleased and, as if having gathered courage, she leaned forward and said, "We came to tell you that we miss you and can't wait for you to come back."

Suri nodded. "The whole atmosphere in the clinic is different without you."

"Totally dead," Yael agreed solemnly.

Aviva felt the same warmth as before slowly spread over her— even without the coffee. "Thanks, guys. I miss it too. Don't worry,

I'm planning on coming back soon." She paused, and then, realizing she could do it, added, "Tomorrow, actually."

"Wonderful!" Yael exclaimed. "Because we have a big event coming up, and we can't plan it without you."

CHAPTER 15

A MAN WEARING A pink Bina's Bakery hat and balancing six trays of cupcakes staggered through the door of the center.

"Who's in charge here?" he called out from behind the trays.

Zevi was up on a ladder hanging a banner proclaiming "Big Bounce Therapy Center Welcomes Senator Pearl!" He nodded toward Aviva, who had just run in from the other room. "Catch her if you can."

Aviva paused by the long buffet table, where Suri's daughter, Miri, was arranging an elaborate candy platter. "I think it would look better if you stand up the lollipops in the center and scatter jelly beans around," she said.

Miri nodded and without a word started rearranging her design. Aviva watched her for a moment, a funny look on her face. She caught Zevi's eye, who motioned to the man by the door.

"Ah, the cupcakes arrived. Good." She pointed to the empty section of the table. "Careful with that tray—I don't want the icing on the American flags to get smooshed... Ah, Yael, you're here."

She turned away from the cupcakes to greet a breathless Yael running through the door.

"Sorry I'm late, I just—"

Aviva waved her hand. "Doesn't matter." She really didn't need to hear yet another one of Yael's excuses. The girl had a punctuality problem, plain and simple. "The pictures need to be hung up in the therapy room."

Yael nodded and ran off. Aviva stood still a moment, swiped the sweat off her forehead, and looked around. Things were coming together nicely. It was a good idea she'd had, making the senator's visit into a children's extravaganza. They'd invited all the children and parents to a party at the clinic. They'd hired a magician for entertainment, and Yael would be running arts and crafts projects. When the senator came, he'd see a fun, happening center, and they'd have a large, excited crowd to greet him.

As she swiveled around the room, a chair suddenly materialized behind her. With a slight frown, she sat down. Counted one, two, three. Sure enough, within five seconds a drink of water had arrived as well, presented with a flourish by her husband.

"Zevi," she said with a sigh. "You made me rest and take a drink just fifteen minutes ago."

"So that means you've been running around fifteen minutes too long. Should I bring you a stool to lift up your feet?"

Aviva clenched her teeth. Planning this event had definitely been the magic pill that broke her out of her self-pitying mode and got her to move past her morning sickness. (As always, her mother had been right.) In the thrill of the bustle and activity, she could almost forget she was pregnant…if not for Zevi, dogging her every move and making her feel like an invalid.

Worse…like a child.

She spoke softly so that no one else would hear. "What would you like me to do? Stay at home for nine months kicking back my feet?"

"Why not?" he said agreeably. "Work is highly overrated anyway."

He gave a short laugh and Aviva's eyes narrowed. "That's your motto, huh?"

"You bet," he said quickly. Too quickly, and his eyes shifted away from her. "One of us at least has to have some sense in life." He shrugged as he said it, sounding oh so flippantly boyish. Yet something in his tone was off, though Aviva didn't register it until a few seconds later, when he abruptly got up and walked away, murmuring something about insurance filings. That's when she sat upright, eyes wide.

Oh. *Oh.* Zevi—easygoing, unflappable Zevi—was hurt.

She leaned back heavily in the chair he'd brought her, and groaned. She should get up and apologize.

Here? In front of everyone? Besides, what exactly had she said that was so bad? She'd been teasing him about his work ethic since they were married.

"Teasing" might not be the right word, my dear. Still, for him to suddenly get all sensitive on her ten minutes before the children were supposed to arrive, an hour before Senator Pearl and all the local media…

Aviva stood up so fast, she had to steady herself from the

sudden dizziness. Ten minutes! She would have to deal with Zevi later. There was too much to do.

She raced into the OT room to see how Yael was faring. As the largest of the rooms, this was where they would be running the art activity. In the past week, they'd run a picture drawing contest for the children, and now had a supply of nearly a hundred variations of "We Love Therapy!" pictures.

Yael waved as Aviva entered. She was up on a step stool, and a roll of masking tape hung from her wrist. She hopped down, asking, "How's it look?"

Aviva opened her mouth and closed it again. This was not at all what she'd had in mind. She'd pictured the artwork arranged in orderly rows on the wall opposite the door, to instantly impress a person walking in. Instead, Yael had clustered them in odd-shaped formations around the room. She supposed it was more artistic Yael's way, but artsy was not the effect they were going for here. Aviva quickly calculated in her mind—would they have time now to change it?

Yael was looking up at her eagerly, and something in her expression reminded her of Zevi. What was it? She pressed her fingers to her eyes, trying to focus, to name the something that was rising up uncomfortably in her throat.

An eagerness to please…to be accepted by her.

Yael's expression had turned to concern. "Are you okay? Can I bring you a cup of water? Knowing you, you probably haven't drunk all day."

Aviva managed a smile, though she had a sudden urge to sit down and put up her feet. Or better yet, to crawl into bed for a week, where she could reflect on people's vulnerabilities, most of all her own.

"Thank you. I drank a few minutes ago. It was just a passing headache. Oh, and Yael? The picture arrangement looks beautiful. Really artistic."

Yael beamed.

SURI STOOD IN the crowd, clapping as the senator arrived. He'd brought with him a small entourage of aides and, together with the journalists and cameramen snapping pictures, she had to admit it made for an impressive display for the clinic. She was so pleased, especially for Yael, who was standing at the head of the reception committee, right next to her father-in-law, and bouncing up and down from excitement. Or maybe it was nerves. To Suri's surprise, Aviva had told Yael that she should be the one to officially welcome the senator to their clinic, while Aviva would perform the grand tour.

Suri wondered afterward why she was surprised by that—after all, it was the gracious thing to offer, considering this had all been done on Yael's initiative, and Aviva could hardly be called ungracious. Yet even Suri, if she closed her eyes, could still see the vision of Yael bumbling through her speech at the lecture for parents a few months back—and she was the more impressed by Aviva's gesture.

Suri held her breath as Yael got up, casting an apprehensive glance at her father-in-law, and smiled brightly at the crowd. She spoke briefly but clearly: "It gives us great honor to welcome Senator Pearl today..." Suri could tell she'd memorized the speech word for word, but her poise and confidence as she spoke were such a far cry from that last attempt that when she'd finished, Suri felt like running over and giving her a hug.

Instead, she hung back to mingle with the parents, which she knew was her job. Not far from her, Zevi had a small group of fathers gathered around him, and they were all cracking up over something he'd said.

"Suri? Do you have a minute?" Mrs. Gibber, a mother of one of her clients, stepped up next to her. From the corner of her eye, she saw Aviva talking to Senator Pearl as she led him toward the therapy rooms.

She turned to Mrs. Gibber. "Sure. What's up?"

She was prepared for a discussion related to her son's treatment. She was not prepared for what followed.

"What's going on with your insurance payments?" The woman's lips were pursed, as she spoke distinctly enough to be heard above the background noise. "I was told that you're covered by Aetna."

Suri raised her eyebrows. "With Aetna, you'd be reimbursed for out-of-network services," she explained. "You have to fill out the paperwork yourself, but we're happy to provide you with any documentation you need."

Mrs. Gibber was shaking her head vehemently. "That is *not* what I was told when I first started therapy here. You told me that you were providers with Aetna, and I said, 'You mean in-network?' and you said yes. And now, lo and behold, I get a bill from you for the full cost of the sessions! What's going on here?"

Suri felt like something was caught in her throat. "Hold on a second. *I* told you this?"

The lady waved her hand impatiently. "Okay, not you." She gestured to Zevi, standing and schmoozing a few feet away from them. "Your secretary."

CHAPTER 16

BIG BOUNCE THERAPY, please hold." Zevi kept the phone by his ear as he turned his attention to the client standing on the other side of his desk. "Hey, it's Shwekey! Shwekey's here! You gonna sing for me like last time?"

The young boy was grinning from ear to ear. "I-I-I don't kn-n-now," he stuttered, giggling.

His mother beamed. "Leiby, sing Mr. Heyman the song you learned yesterday. Leiby told me he was going to sing it for you."

The boy was red-faced and squirming with excitement, but he shook his head shyly.

Zevi reached across the desk to tousle his hair. "No problem, kiddo. First go into Mrs. Heyman and practice real good, and then you can come out and give me a whole performance."

Leiby's mother hesitated by the desk. "Uh, I'm really sorry, but I forgot to bring the payment again. Can it wait until next week?"

"Sure, sure, no problem." Zevi waved them on. "Work hard, Shwekey!"

Suri, watching this exchange as she wrote up some session notes in a corner of the office, frowned. As Zevi, with a lingering smile, went back to his computer screen, completely oblivious to the phone still in his hand, she cleared her throat.

"Don't you have someone on hold?"

He looked up, startled. "Oh, man, I forgot." He pressed a button. "Hung up. Ah, well, they'll call back." He threw the phone down on the desk.

Suri shifted uneasily. "I hope so. I wouldn't want to lose a new client."

Zevi raised his eyebrows. "Like we have to worry. Ever since that big media event, the phone has been ringing nonstop. At this rate, you guys are soon gonna have enough to retire!"

Suri pursed her lips. *Not if you keep letting people in without paying*, she thought. She debated whether she should remind him that just yesterday they had discussed this exact issue, and told him that a client more than two weeks in arrears should not be allowed into therapy.

Zevi was humming a Shwekey song as he worked, and Suri decided against it. Besides, it wasn't really what she wanted to say. What she really wanted to ask him about was the whole insurance issue that Mrs. Gibber had brought up at the event last week. She just hadn't determined the best way to raise it.

She scratched her nail against the rough surface of the desk, as the debate which had been raging inside her head struck up once more. Who to confront? Should she ask Zevi directly, casually mention the conversation with Mrs. Gibber? Or bring it up to Aviva, and let her work it out with her husband?

As she'd told Shaul, it seemed more *tzanua* to go through Aviva—but what if it led to *shalom bayis* problems? Did she want that on her head? And yet—looking at Zevi, who was now taking hoop shots with his smiley-face stress ball into the wastepaper basket—she couldn't help but think that Aviva would be better able to understand the severity of the issue, if indeed it was an issue.

"Ouch!" A splinter had stuck into her nail. Zevi looked up. "You okay?"

Suri nodded and stood up. Aviva had brought this on herself, she decided, when she'd brought Zevi in as secretary. She had to have known what kind of awkward situations she'd be getting herself into. This was business, wasn't it?

She gathered up the files, still hesitant. What if it turned out to be true, what Mrs. Gibber had said? That Zevi had been giving their clients the wrong insurance information? How would Aviva react?

She didn't even want to think about it.

Slowly, she walked out of the office. *You know what Aviva herself would do in your situation. She would immediately head to the person most capable of dealing with the problem, and make sure it gets sorted out as soon as possible. Business is business, she'd say.*

Suri took off her glasses and wiped her eyes. Yeah, but nobody had warned her that this would be part of the business.

AVIVA WAITED FOR the door to close behind her client, and then lifted her feet up onto the second chair. She'd gone back to her old, packed schedule, and, while she would never admit it, least of all to Zevi, she did feel worn-out at the end of the day.

Ha! She could just picture what Zevi would do if he got wind that she was actually tired. Probably schlep in a cot and force her to conduct her therapy sessions while lying down.

She shifted uneasily in her chair. He was a good man, her husband, and he certainly cared a lot about her. She knew she had no reason to complain. Even if he could be a bit overprotective when it came to her. (But only when it came to her. That was the strange thing. In every other way, he was Mr. Laid-Back.)

She had still never apologized for her remark about his lack of work ethic. She had thought to do so several times, but never found the moment when it felt right, and then, she'd gotten annoyed after hearing him tell Suri how impressed he was with her daughter's helpfulness at the event, and go on to joke about his own teenage daughter never agreeing in a million years to give up her afternoon like that. Why, she'd demanded furiously, did he need to air their dirty laundry in public? It was bad enough that she had a selfish teenager on her hands—did her partners need to know about it?

She'd restrained herself, with great effort, from actually saying this to him. There were some things that just weren't in Zevi's nature to understand.

Aviva leaned her head back against the wall, as the thought occurred that it was *davka* this in his nature that attracted her.

She swung her feet down at the knock on the door. "Mind if I come in?"

Suri looked like she'd just swallowed a hot pepper whole—her face was red and her eyes watery. She sat down opposite Aviva. "I have something I need to discuss with you."

"What's up?"

Suri took a breath. "It's like this." As she related the conversation with Mrs. Gibber, Aviva felt a growing dread settling in her stomach.

Suri put her hands on the table. "Maybe it was a one-time thing," she said carefully. "And maybe Mrs. Gibber even misunderstood. But, you understand, if, uh, *someone's* been giving our clients wrong information about what insurance networks we're part of—not intentionally, of course, but, maybe, just out of a bit of, um, sloppiness..." She hesitated, and Aviva finished the sentence for her.

"It would cause a total financial disaster."

Suri nodded grimly.

Aviva's head was reeling. The implications! Insurances reimbursed only a fraction of the cost for out-of-network providers... If parents had mistakenly thought they'd be getting higher coverage, the clinic would have to swallow the difference. Not to mention the PR disaster, with furious parents wanting to know how they could have made such an irresponsible mistake...

Irresponsible. Anger welled up inside. Suri might be trying for tact, but Aviva had no doubt who was behind this, or that Zevi was, indeed, capable of such a major flub, of casually giving out information without taking the time to check that it was accurate. How could he! It was one thing if he cared so little about his own printing business that he let it go to the dogs, but to take her precious clinic that she'd worked so hard to build up and carelessly destroy it? She felt like storming over to him right now and...

And?

She squeezed her eyes shut.

Her husband. Oh, her husband.

Aviva lifted her head and squared her shoulders. Looking Suri directly in the eye, she said, "It was me. I think it was me. I gave

Mrs. Gibber the wrong information. One day when I was sitting in the office and you weren't there, I couldn't check, so I just told her what I thought was accurate."

Suri was staring at her incredulously. "Oh. Um…oh," she finally managed.

"Really." Aviva's voice got stronger, with the pride of her self-sacrifice, of finally doing something for her husband. "Don't worry. I'll straighten everything out."

CHAPTER 17

YAEL STOOD OUTSIDE Rina's Racks, her sister-in-law's clothing store that she had somehow never mustered up the guts to step foot into. Until today.

The craziest part was, she was entering these hallowed precincts of the uber-sophisticated by actual invitation of the proprietress. It had happened just after the Senator Pearl event. The entire Jeren clan had shown up—she assumed by her father-in-law's orders. Still, she'd been touched by this unexpected show of support. And, when the big miracle had happened (*no, not miracle*, she reminded herself, because Ephraim hated when she put herself down; *the anticipated outcome of an insane amount of practice*) and she'd actually done a decent job welcoming the senator, her sisters-in-law had approached her one by one and warmly congratulated her. It was the first time that Yael had felt accepted.

It was in the context of this sisterly spirit that Rina had looked her outfit up and down—and Yael had dressed with as much care as she possibly could on that day—and kindly offered to take Yael shopping at her boutique.

This was exactly the kind of offer that would've sent her scampering back home a year earlier—or even a day earlier. But somehow, flying high on her success, she decided to fling self-dignity to the wind and say, "Sure, thanks!"

And thus she found herself inside the chicly decorated boutique, arrived at the moment of truth. Looking around, she saw a few ladies she vaguely recognized from her in-laws' social circles. Women her own age were browsing through racks while chatting, and Yael couldn't help but feel that they were staring at her, wondering how an imposter like her had dared to enter their upper-crust store.

Stop it! she told herself firmly. *Of course you belong here! You're a Jeren!* The argument wasn't such a good one, because she felt like an imposter Jeren as well. But today, after her success, after her father-in-law's beaming congratulations and—especially—after Ephraim's glowing look of pride, today she finally felt capable of assuming the Jeren badge. She stared back calmly at the women, and couldn't help but gloat at their expressions as Rina spotted her and came running forward.

"Yael! So lovely you came!" She gave her a hug (Rina did hugs?), loudly declaring to the women near her, "My sister-in-law. This is my brother's wife, Yael." She grabbed Yael's arm, as if taking ownership, and was already steering her over to a rack of clothes on the side of the store.

"My newest collection, just arrived, I thought of you immediately." She was still talking in her gushy showman's tone, and for the first time Yael was struck by how similar Rina was to her father; they both seemed to come alive with their work.

Over the next hour, in between helping customers, Rina

selected and measured and rejected outfit after outfit, until, at the end, Yael found herself with a whole new wardrobe. It was clear that Rina had decided to take Yael on as a project.

"Now you're not just a success—you're dressed for it as well!"

AVIVA RUBBED HER eyes and glanced at her watch. It was 10 p.m. She'd never stayed at the clinic so late before. Zevi was undoubtedly worried, even though she'd told him she had work to do. She took another sip of coffee and looked once more at the computer file.

She had almost reached the bottom of their client list. Just two more calls—two more humiliating conversations—and then she would have all the information she needed to tally up the numbers and see just how much Zevi's mistake had cost them.

Next was Ziskin. She checked the phone number and dialed. Even after several straight hours of these calls, she still had to work up her courage.

"Hello, Mrs. Ziskin, this is Aviva calling from Big Bounce Therapy Center. I'm sorry to bother you at such a late hour, but it just came to our attention that there's been an error in the insurance information that was given out to the parents. Please tell me, do you pay through a health insurance or privately?"

A minute later she hung up, making a mark next to the Ziskins' name. They were okay; they paid privately anyway. And the Zuckerbergs, the last name on her list, used an insurance that they were in-network providers for. Aviva stood up and stretched her arms. Well, she'd done the hard part, and done it all on her own. She hadn't even mentioned a word to her husband about the issue.

You deserve the Best Wife of the Year award, she told herself, grinning, as she walked up and down the room to muster up energy for the task ahead. It hadn't affected everyone, but there were enough clients who'd been told the wrong insurance names, enough angry and sometimes hysterical clients who'd declared that they'd never heard of anything so un-businesslike, and were just barely mollified by her assurances that the clinic would cover the difference themselves.

"But what about from now on?" they demanded, and she had to admit that, from here on, if they wanted reimbursement for their sessions, it would be at an out-of-network rate, and they would have to fill out the paperwork themselves. Everyone grumbled, and more than a few threatened to leave the clinic altogether.

And now, it was time to assess the grand total. She unwrapped the chocolate bar that she'd bought herself for dinner and took a large, fortifying bite. Math had never been her thing and these numbers were dizzying. She wished she could ask Suri to do this for her, but she did not want to involve her at all. She'd said she would take care of it herself, and she was determined to see it through to the bitter end. All on her own.

She set her teeth and began attacking the billing lists. A half hour later, the sudden creak of a door made her jump. Hand on her heart, she turned, alarmed.

"I thought some kidnappers must have been holding you hostage here, and I came to rescue you."

Aviva's heart sank. "Hi, Zevi. So you didn't leave your hat this time?"

He walked into the room, and she hurriedly averted the computer screen away from him.

"You weren't answering your phone, and I got worried. What in the world are you doing here so late?"

Her eyes narrowed. *Bailing you out*, she wanted to say, as anger rose inside. "Zevi, I'm not a child. If I told you I had work to do, why can't you just accept that and trust that I'll come home when I'm ready?"

Zevi shrugged. "Don't know," he said. "Maybe it's because, ever since I've known you, you've taken care of everyone other than yourself. I don't trust that you'll stop before you run yourself ragged."

She stared at him. He was so infuriating, her husband, and yet, for some crazy reason, she felt something wet pricking inside her eyes, which irritated her even more. Slamming her hand on the desk to try to stop the ridiculous tears—had she been this hormonal in her other pregnancies?—she glared at him. "I just have one more thing that needs doing here, and then I can go home."

"Anything I can help with?" He sat down next to her and, before she could stop him, pulled the screen over to face him. "Billing?" He looked at her quizzically. "Isn't that my job?"

Aviva shrugged, biting her lip. She wished she could come up with some plausible lie, but nothing was coming to mind at this time of night. Besides, a part of her was almost happy for Zevi to realize what she'd been doing for him all night.

Zevi was examining the screen more closely. "What is this? Are these people who haven't paid?"

"Whose insurances haven't paid."

He caught the cold note in her voice, and stiffened. "Wait a second. Did I mess up with something? Forget to bill someone?"

Now that he was asking her outright, she didn't know quite what to answer. He was looking at her with his innocent, boyish eyes, and yet, after all, how *could* he have made such a mistake, such a ridiculous, expensive mistake, just because he'd been too lazy—yes, that was it, pure laziness!—to look up their list of insurances?

Suddenly, all her resentments and disgrace from the entire night rushed up and, before she could stop herself, she said, "Oh, it's much worse than that. So far, you've cost us"— she looked at the computer screen—"over ten thousand dollars. And I'm not even halfway through."

CHAPTER 18

ZEVI STOOD ABSOLUTELY still, staring at her. "Ten thousand dollars? You're joking."

Aviva shook her head grimly. "Probably be closer to fifteen by the time I'm done."

Her husband's face turned white. "But, I don't understand—what did I do?"

She told him about the insurance mix-up. He sank down in a chair.

"I'm an idiot." He looked dazed. "A total, complete idiot."

Aviva's lips tightened. "Why did you give them information without looking it up?"

Zevi shook his head. "I don't know. I don't even remember. Maybe I figured I would just answer them quickly, and then check it up later?" He shrugged miserably.

Though Aviva had just spent the past day playing the martyr for his sake, inexplicably, seeing Zevi in this weakened state aroused all her frustration.

"I'm sorry, but that was rather—"

"—idiotic. Yeah, I already said that." Zevi slumped back in his chair and closed his eyes. "Who discovered this?"

"Suri."

He nodded. After a few moments, he opened one eye and asked casually, "So, you guys ready to fire me?"

Aviva stopped short at that. Fire him? How could she fire her husband?

Suri could, though. For a moment, the idea was even tempting. Tell Suri to let him go, and Aviva would no longer have all the headaches of having Zevi around.

She glanced at him out of the corner of her eye. No, Suri couldn't do that either, not without creating a major rift. She let out a loud breath. Why had she ever given in to the idea of Zevi coming to work for them? If anyone was an idiot here, it was her.

Zevi was actually waiting for an answer, she realized. "Of course not," she said with a weak laugh. "I…I actually took the blame for it myself. Suri doesn't realize it was you." She paused, waiting for his thanks for her sacrifice. But he remained silent, though his eyebrows popped up. She continued awkwardly, "But we do have to make sure this never happens again."

"Sure, of course." It was scary how relieved he looked, and her annoyance crept up once more. *Why should he care so much about keeping a dinky secretarial position? Doesn't he realize how beneath him this is?*

"You do remember, though, that this job was only meant to be temporary, right? Until we expand to the point that we need someone full-time, and then we hire someone else."

"Uh, yeah, that's right." He seemed startled.

She chewed her lip. Her husband was supposed to be a partner in a law firm, or a CEO, or...

Don't go there.

Zevi had picked up a pen and was doodling on a paper. "I'll borrow the money from a *gemach*."

"What?"

He looked at her. "Fifteen thousand dollars."

She made a face. "From a *gemach*? Don't be ridiculous. How will we pay that back?"

"Not we. Me. This was my fault. I'll"—he waved his hands in the air—"I'll work harder. Make a bigger effort to get printing jobs."

Aviva snorted, then immediately regretted it when she saw the hurt on Zevi's face.

Zevi leaned forward. "You don't believe me, huh? You don't believe I can do it?"

She didn't answer. He lowered his eyes.

Abruptly, he stood up. "It's late. I'm going home."

At the door, he paused. "Thanks for picking up the slack for me. But I never asked for that, and, frankly, I would've rather taken the heat for my own mistake. I'm a big boy."

He closed the door behind him.

—

UNDER HER IN-LAWS' long dining room table, Yael slipped off her shoes and stretched out her legs. This was their first *melaveh malkah* in a while; they had adjourned to accommodate summer vacations.

"So today was the Cooper bar mitzvah, and you should've seen the setup they had for the kiddush."

As always, Rina was the one dominating the conversation.

"And the food! Sushi! Crepes! Carving stations! It was like a wedding."

"The Coopers have always enjoyed raising the bar on *simchah*s," her mother said, pursing her lips.

"Well, listen to this one, Mommy! Guess what Libby Cooper was wearing at this over-the-top bash?"

"It couldn't have been a Rina's Racks exclusive, could it?" asked Zahava.

Yael shifted in her seat self-consciously. She had debated beforehand whether or not to wear one of the outfits Rina had given her. (She'd offered to pay—though she'd gaped at the price tags—but Rina had waved her away with a gracious, "Not for family.")

She'd made the mistake of including Ephraim in her internal debate. "I don't understand," he'd said. "When she was so nice to you? Why wouldn't you?"

"Because…because…it just seems so…" There was no way to express such a nebulous feeling, especially not to a man, and the word she ended up with—"nebbish"—just sealed her losing argument.

So here she sat, a walking advertisement for Rina's Racks, as Rina answered brightly, "You bet it was. And everyone knew it as well."

"How did everyone know?" Yael asked.

Rina, Zahava, and Chayale all burst out laughing. "*Everyone* knows what Libby Cooper is wearing," Chayale said.

"Oh." Yael looked down at her plate.

"Anyway," Rina continued. "That reminds me that I have news to share."

Everyone perked up at her words, including Rina's husband, sitting next to Ephraim.

Yael's mother-in-law was beaming, and it was clear she was already anticipating an upcoming *simchah* where she could show the Coopers just what it meant to raise the bar.

But Rina looked directly at her father. "I've decided the time has come to take my business to a new level. I've started developing a line of my own clothing—the first designs have just come out."

Across the table there were gasps and whistles.

"Your own designs?" cried her mother. Your very own?"

Apparently, this was very impressive news, though, call her ignorant, but Yael failed to see why.

"Wait a second," cried Zahava, holding up her hand amidst the tumult. "Do you mean to say that you've hired a designer to design clothing exclusively for you, or that you're actually designing them yourself?"

"Myself." Rina smiled proudly, and gave another glance at her father.

"You've always been so artistic," her mother murmured. "But to have kept this from us until now! This must have taken ages to put together!"

"It did," Rina agreed. "It was a lot of hard work. But I didn't want to say anything until…that is, just in case…"

Yael finished her sentence. In case it didn't work out. No Jeren wanted to admit of failure.

"Anyway, I took classes at night at a fashion institute, and learned all about clothing design. It was a lot of fun!"

"When did you have the time?" marveled Chayale.

Rina gave a little laugh. "Well, I was barely home. Good thing we have such a treasure of a nanny and a housekeeper. Right, Shloimy?"

Yael looked over at Rina's husband. Though he quickly assented, it seemed to her that he didn't think it was such a good thing at all.

"Anyway, it was worth the time investment. Now this moves me from being just a higher-line retailer, to a real creative force in the *frum* world. I can *create* the styles, not just sell them!"

Zalman cleared his throat. "Well done, Rina," he declared, and, at his official stamp of approval, Rina's face shone. "I'm looking forward to seeing some of your new designs."

"But, Tatty, you're seeing it right now!" She grinned. "On my very first model!"

And, to Yael's horror, Rina flung an arm straight in her direction.

———

"THERE YOU GO."

Suri stood in the office, mouth opened in shock, as Zevi handed her a check for fifteen thousand dollars.

"But…that's a lot of money," she said weakly. "I can't just take this from you."

"Why not? It was my mess-up. I want to pay back the clinic."

Suri stood holding the check—the biggest check she'd ever held in her life, probably—and didn't know what to do. On the one hand, he was right, and business sense dictated that she take it. On the other…

"Listen, I know that *I* certainly couldn't afford to pay out fifteen thousand dollars just like that. I feel terrible taking this from you and your family. Maybe we can work out some other way." She fished around in her mind for some other payment method that didn't involve actual money.

Oy, she was so not a businesswoman. What would Aviva say? That is, she caught herself, if it were involving someone other than her own husband.

Her eyes suddenly narrowed shrewdly. "Does Aviva know about this?"

Zevi looked away. "Yeah…uh, kind of. But if it's okay, I'll ask you not to talk to her about it."

Now Suri felt really uncomfortable. "Listen," she said, holding out the check. "Please take it back. Really."

Zevi waved his hand. "No, it's the clinic's. I just meant that this topic…uh…stresses her out, and more stress is the last thing she needs right now, especially in her condition."

Suri raised her eyebrows. "Her condition?"

But Zevi had clamped a hand on his mouth, looking like a boy who'd just thrown a ball through a glass window. "Nothing. No condition. I did not say a word."

CHAPTER 19

AVIVA WAITED UNTIL Rikki and her mother were safely out of the therapy room, then picked up the rag doll Rikki had just been playing with and hurled it clear across the room. It slammed into the wall opposite her with a dull thud and fell down on the floor.

There. That felt better.

She let out her breath. It wasn't really about Rikki, and the fact that she had been acting with all the brattiness that a four-year-old is capable of. Goodness knows, she'd encountered enough of that in her professional career. No, it was that Rikki had to go and choose *this* morning to plant herself on the floor with the doll and refuse to cooperate in any activity, right after Aviva's stormy scene at home with Chavi over her unilateral decision to drop out of honors math (it was laziness, pure laziness). To make it worse, Zevi had supported Chavi on this—but that was no surprise.

Of course, all this was on the heels of several very frosty days between her and Zevi—the worst she could remember in all their years of marriage. She didn't even understand what she'd done wrong this time. She'd been so proud of herself for jumping to take all the blame on herself, to save her husband's face. How could he not appreciate that?

She stood up to pick up the rag doll. When was the last time she'd thrown something like that? She ran a hand through her sheitel. Coffee. She needed coffee, badly.

She stalked out of the room and headed toward the office.

"…yeah, we also have a son with learning issues. We've gotten him special tutors, and my wife's worked with him a lot, but still, you know, you have to adjust your expectations. I don't expect him to become a *rosh yeshivah*, huh?"

Aviva's face was livid as she walked behind Zevi's desk, where he was busy talking to a parent. After the mother and son walked away, Aviva took a seat next to Zevi and hissed, "Is there a reason why you feel the need to air all our family secrets to the world?"

Zevi raised an eyebrow. "I didn't realize Chaim's learning disability was a secret. It helps parents when they hear they're not the only one dealing with these issues."

Aviva glared. It wasn't that she was ashamed of Chaim. But to go shout to the world that their son is *learning disabled*? For what purpose? Just so that others could whisper about them, say, "You know, the Heymans, they have a son with *issues*"?

She was all the more frustrated because she knew she couldn't even try to articulate this; Zevi didn't understand this type of reasoning. Instead, she said, somewhat petulantly, "Why don't you just share all our private information while you're at it? Before I know it, you'll be telling all the parents here that I'm expecting."

Zevi shifted in his seat, and her heart plummeted as she recognized the guilty look on his face.

"Well, now that you mention it, I did have a slip of the tongue the other day…"

—

SURI WALKED INTO the doctor's waiting room and scanned the area for an empty seat. Her breath suddenly caught in her throat. Aviva! She was there too!

Aviva had spotted her and, face slightly red, motioned for her to come sit down.

Wouldn't you know it? My once-in-three-years checkup, and look who I meet.

She'd been avoiding Aviva for the past few days. The fifteen-thousand-dollar *gemach* check weighed very heavily in her purse, and she still hadn't decided what to do with it. She wished she could consult Aviva about it, but, of course, she was the last person Suri could ask.

Aviva's face had turned redder. "So, um, you're here for a—"

"Checkup," Suri answered hastily. "My routine checkup."

Aviva nodded. "Wow, I haven't gone to one of those in years." She laughed, while Suri stared at her.

"Be grateful for that," she said darkly.

Aviva looked surprised. "I meant—it's just so like you, to make sure you get to your regularly scheduled checkups. Responsible, and all that."

Suri squirmed. How could she expect Aviva to know this was a touchy subject? "Oh. Right."

They sat next to each other in silence. Suri wondered whether she was supposed to say anything, whether Aviva knew that she knew why Aviva was there.

At last, she said cautiously, "So, uh, how're you feeling?"

"Fine."

Aviva drummed her fingers on the arm of her chair. "Zevi told you my news."

Suri gave a half smile. "*Beshaah tovah.*" She swallowed. She still found conversations about pregnancy painful, even after having reconciled herself to her beautiful three-child family.

"So, uh, has it been hard, coming to work and all in your condition?"

Aviva shook her head. "No, it's fine." Suri nodded, but Aviva seemed like she was deliberating about something.

At last, she burst out, "Actually, no, it hasn't been fine! It's been really rough, forcing myself to come to work when I'm all nauseous, and keeping up my house when I'm exhausted all the time. I've just been pushing myself along, day by day, holding on until I start to feel more like myself. Whenever *that* will be."

Aviva stopped and took a breath. Suri watched her, transfixed. She had never heard Aviva admit to weakness before, not in all the years she'd known her. She knew she should empathize, express something to the effect of how hard it must be, maybe even give her a hug to show her that she cares.

But she just couldn't. Not about this. Not after hearing Aviva kvetching about the fact that she was expecting.

"So sorry for you," she replied stonily, and picked up a magazine.

IT WAS YAEL who suggested they ask a *rav*. "We should really have one anyway. A *posek* just for our clinic. Issues can come up, and we need someone familiar enough with all the ins and outs of the business."

Suri agreed, but felt who to choose was a decision the three of them should make together. In the meantime, Yael offered to consult with her father.

"Your father?" Suri asked curiously. She had never heard anything about Yael's family before. Everything was always about her in-laws.

"Sure, didn't you know? My father's a *rosh kollel*. He's pretty well-known, actually. People come to him all the time for *shailos* and *eitzos*."

"Really? No, I hadn't known at all!" Suri noted the unconcealed pride in Yael's voice, the way she glowed as she spoke about her father. It was a marked contrast to her usual squirms of discomfort whenever anything Jeren related came up.

Yael and Suri walked out during lunch to make the call from Yael's car. Suri resisted commenting about the luxury vehicle—she sensed that Yael would not appreciate her even noticing.

Odd... she couldn't help but think, contemplating her friend. And then, *I wonder...if it were me...*

It was an interesting thought (interesting, and purely speculative; the rate she and Shaul were going, they wouldn't have to worry about hiding luxury cars anytime soon).

But she put it aside to philosophize upon at some later point. In the meantime, they had a phone call to make, and as Yael dialed, Suri kept peering out the window nervously, in case Aviva took it into her head to go out for a walk or something.

Yael's father was thorough in asking for details, but his *psak* was decisive. They did not need to have any qualms about taking the money. Zevi's negligence had caused damage to their business.

After they hung up, Yael turned to Suri brightly and said, "Well, that's that, then."

Suri nodded slowly. It was nice to have the confidence now that she wasn't being a terrible person by taking the money.

But, somehow, she still felt like a terrible person. For the second time, the thought flitted through her brain: *What if it were me?* What if Shaul borrowed fifteen thousand dollars without telling her? True, that wouldn't happen in a million years. Steady, straight, dependable Shaul would never just rashly borrow money like that. He also wouldn't have gotten himself into such a mess to begin with.

And if he had? How would you react?

Yael was watching her. "Suri," she said. "This is not your problem. Aviva and her husband are going to have to work it out by themselves. And, you think, if it wasn't this money thing, it wouldn't be something else? Every marriage has its"—she hesitated, looked away for a second—"issues." She took a breath. "Right?"

CHAPTER 20

YAEL LEANED BACK in the well-worn dining room chair, soaking in the Shabbos atmosphere of her parents' home. She hadn't felt this relaxed in ages. It had been way too long since they'd come for Shabbos.

That realization had hit her earlier that week, when she and Suri had spoken to her father. It was so nice to hear his wise, reassuring voice! And then, she'd come home that day, and Ephraim mentioned that his parents had asked about their Shabbos plans. They hadn't been to them for a Shabbos in a while, he said. And suddenly, she'd snapped. A while? They were there at least once a month for the *melaveh malkah*s, and very often more than that. How much did his parents want from them? Whereas her family... She couldn't even remember the last time she'd been to their house.

People had warned her about this, she remembered. When she first got engaged, friends half-jokingly told her that when you marry into a rich family, they expect more than their share of face time in exchange for more than their share of support. Yael had dismissed this; she was so close to her family! Besides, everyone knew that it was the girl's family that got to spend the most time with grandchildren.

And yet, somehow, her friends' warnings had borne out. Partially because coming to her parents meant squeezing their whole family into a cramped room, and displacing some of her siblings in the process. And partially because she felt bad putting the burden of hosting them on her mother, who worked full-time and then some—whereas her mother-in-law had a live-in house-keeper and a whole wing of the house to offer their family.

Still, when Ephraim had relayed the invitation, she'd put her foot down and insisted it was high time they visited *her* family for a change. He'd looked surprised by her vehemence, and she had to admit, her husband had never expressed any hesitations at all about spending time with her family. It was just...well...her in-laws just always seemed to be such a strong ever-lurking presence in their lives.

Yael closed her eyes for a moment, basking in the lively chatter among her siblings, at all her sisters fawning over Sruli and Simi, at the way Ephraim slid so easily into the Torah discussion taking place among her father and brothers. She glanced over at him, and saw the enjoyment on his face. He, too, was glad to be there, she realized.

She questioned why she was so surprised by that. After all, she remembered, back when they were engaged, he'd been delighted at marrying into her family.

"You don't know how lucky you are," he'd told her. "Growing up in such a special family, with such a *chashuve* father. When you walk into your house, you just breathe the Torah in the air!"

She'd glowed from that comment, because up until then she'd

been feeling very unequal in their relationship. Why had the great Jeren family been interested in her, was the question that had gnawed at her throughout their dating. Even more so because, at twenty-three, she was already approaching the age where potential *shidduchim* would start to question why she wasn't already married. And so when she'd heard that the Jerens wanted her for their only son, she'd been astounded. She was a good girl, she knew, but there was nothing particularly special about her, nothing to make her stand out in a crowd.

Nothing, that is, except her family. And clearly, Ephraim saw this as a major bonus, as something that she was bringing into the *shidduch* to counterbalance all his parents' money. At the time, she'd felt proud and relieved.

Of course, looking back on it now, Yael realized that the fact that Ephraim and his family had been impressed with her *rosh kollel* father and Bais Yaakov principal mother had nothing to do with her, really. She had never been part of the equation at all.

Yael felt tears suddenly pricking her eyes, and she blinked hastily. Her family was so different from her in-laws in every respect… How could she not have realized what a culture shock it would be, marrying into the Jeren family? More to the point, how could her parents not have realized? Ever since her marriage, she'd felt a barrier erect between her and her sisters—the have versus the have-nots. She sometimes felt like screaming at them that she didn't even need any of the fancy clothing and gifts and homes and vacations thrown her way. It was the warmth of family and acceptance that she needed.

"Hey, Yael," her sister Raizy suddenly said. "I love your outfit. Is that new? It looks really expensive!"

Yael shifted in her seat. "I got it as a gift. From my sister-in-law." She paused. "It's part of her new clothing line that she's developing. An accomplishment to be proud of, huh?" The last words came out sarcastically, and she rolled her eyes, as if to indicate, yeah, exciting for those who are shallow enough to care about such things.

Ephraim was looking at her, she realized, and his eyebrows were raised. But she didn't care. She wanted so badly to show her family that she hadn't changed, that she was the same non-materialistic big sister they'd always known.

There was a short pause at the female side of the table, and then her mother said, "How lovely. Your sister-in-law is so talented."

"Her own fashion line?" squealed Chanie, Yael's fifteen-year-old sister. "That is sooo cool!"

"Do we, like, get discounts for being family?" asked Raizy.

Startled, Yael said, "I-I don't know. I mean, maybe, I can ask. But really, calm down, it's not *that* exciting. It's just clothing."

Chanie shook her head in disbelief at such a statement as, down the table, Ephraim briefly caught Yael's eye—and then looked away.

―

"YOU HATE MY family."

Yael's eyes widened as she rocked Simi's Pack 'n Play in an effort to get her to sleep. "*Chas veshalom!*"

"My sister, then."

Yael shook her head, heart thumping inside. "No, of course not. What has she ever done to me?"

Ephraim shrugged. His mouth was set in a hard line. "That's what I want to know. She's always been very good to you. She even gave you all this clothing for free. So why would you speak that way about her to your family?"

Yael looked down at Simi, rolling and squirming inside the Pack'n Play and not looking remotely ready for bed. What could she answer? She didn't even know herself. Rina, like the rest of her family, had never been unkind to Yael. Still, there was always something there unspoken. She thought about the countless little looks, insinuations about her clothing, her sense of style, her knowledge of high society.

It was always there in the background—the fact that Yael was an outsider.

Out of the corner of her eye, she glanced at her husband. And did he think so too? Did he ask himself, the way she still did every now and then, why he had married her?

Yael hung her head. "I'm sorry, I shouldn't have spoken the way I did. It was pure *lashon hara.*"

"You bet it was." Ephraim wasn't letting her off the hook so easily. Apparently, an insult to his family was a personal insult, even when it was said by his wife.

She sighed. "I said I'm sorry. What more do you want?"

He turned away. "It wouldn't hurt you to make more of an effort to be close with my family," he muttered. "Rina's a great person, you know. Smart, hardworking. The type of person it's *kedai* to be close to."

"So that maybe she'll rub off on me, huh?" Yael shot back before she could stop herself. "Admit it—you wish I could be more like her."

Ephraim looked startled, but didn't say a word.

———

MONDAY MORNING. SURI covered her mouth with the files

she was carrying to hide her yawn. No matter how much she tried to get a good night's sleep Sunday night, Monday morning was always a killer.

The phone rang. Though she was already late for her client, no one else was in the office right now, and she quickly answered it.

"Hi, this is Nechi Goldfeder speaking. I'm calling about getting speech therapy for my son, Avi."

Suri sat down at the computer. "Sure. Do you have an evaluation already, or would you like us to do that?"

"I'd like you to take care of that." The mother on the other end paused as Suri typed. "Oh, and please make sure he gets Aviva Heyman. I've heard she's the best."

Suri felt her insides turn to glue. "Uh…I don't think she has any available slots right now," she stammered.

"Well, can't you free one up?" Mrs. Goldfeder demanded. This was clearly a woman used to getting what she wanted. "My son is already being treated at your clinic for OT; I should think we deserve special treatment."

Suri cleared her throat, clenching the cordless. "I'm sorry, but she doesn't have anything available. You can either wait a few months, or you can book an appointment with—" She stopped for a moment, realizing the lady thought she was the secretary. Probably better that way. "With our other speech therapist."

"Is she any good?"

Suri felt her breath catching in her throat, as she squeezed out an answer. "Yeah, she's also good."

CHAPTER 21

SURI GOT OFF the phone and slammed it down a bit too hard on the kitchen table.

Miri looked up from her math homework. "Frustrating phone call?" she asked.

Suri shrugged at her daughter. "That was Mr. Berger from the shul. There's some kind of sewage problem in the basement."

Miri nodded slowly. "And they called you because…"

"Because we're supposed to have our senior social group tonight, and now our meeting room's out of commission." She sat down at the table. "I *hate* disappointing them."

"Why don't you just do it somewhere else?"

"Last minute?"

Miri smiled at her. "What about our house? I'll help you get ready."

Suri shook her head. "Thanks, sweetie, but this isn't like hosting a *Neshei shiur*. Some of these women are in wheelchairs. The venue needs to be accessible."

"Oh." Miri went back to her math, while Suri started chopping vegetables for a salad. She'd have to call everyone soon.

"Ma, I have it!"

Suri looked up.

"The clinic! There are no steps to get in, and nobody's there right now!"

Suri considered. A grin slowly broke out on her face. "How lucky am I to have such a brilliant daughter?" she said. "That's a great idea!"

AVIVA HAD FELT herself simmering inside all afternoon. She'd come home to find the living room a royal mess: Kayla had invited friends over to do a *Chumash* project, and somehow this project involved spreading poster board, markers, and glitter glue all over the living room carpet.

"Um, basement?" Aviva had asked, as she'd taken in the scene.

"Chaim's there, playing with friends," Kayla said.

"Your bedroom, then?"

"Chavi's in there, on some *important* phone conversation, and she wouldn't let us in." Kayla glared.

"What about the kitchen table, at least?"

Kayla threw back her hair as her eyes opened wide. "What, and get your kitchen all dirty?"

At that point, Aviva had admitted defeat. At least they'd spread newspaper over the carpet.

Besides, she thought, as she switched her heels for Crocs and headed to the kitchen, she didn't really want a bunch of ten-year-old girls around as she prepared dinner. But she stopped short as she entered the kitchen. Instead of fifth graders, she found two-year-old Kivi sitting on the counter, spreading a mixture of corn-flakes, ketchup, and dish soap, while five-year-old Tova cheered him on.

Aviva's mouth opened in horror. "No! Kivi, *No!* Mommy does *not* let!" She scooped Kivi off the counter, holding him at arm's length to keep her work outfit clean. "Zevi!" she called as she carried Kivi to the bathtub. "Where are you?" Furiously, she stripped off her toddler's clothes. Wasn't Zevi—who'd left the clinic a whole hour earlier than she had—supposed to be in charge here?

Chavi emerged from her room. "Tatty's not here," she said.

"What? Where is he?"

Chavi shrugged elaborately. "Don't know. I think he said something about meeting with a client."

Aviva's hands stopped in the middle of their struggle to pull Kivi's shirt over his wriggling head. "A client? Are you sure?" She immediately bit her lip. Why shouldn't Zevi have clients to meet? He did run a printing business, after all.

Chavi nodded sagely. "Yeah, weird, huh? Tatty never seemed to care about his business before, and now all of a sudden I hear him on the phone asking people if they know people who need printing services."

Aviva's eyes narrowed. It *was* weird. Almost as if...

"It must be because of the money he owes," Chavi continued.

Aviva looked up sharply. "What are you talking about?"

Chavi sighed, her long brown hair swinging back and forth. "Come on, Mommy, you don't have to keep pretending that I'm a baby. I know what's going on around here. Tatty borrowed a whole lot of money from a *gemach* to pay someone back for something. I heard him talking about it on the phone."

Money from a gemach? To pay back someone? Chavi heard him talking about it?

Why was her teenage daughter more in the know than she was?

Lips pressed, Aviva slid Kivi into the bath and began soaping him vigorously. Back turned to Chavi, she said, "Very nice that you know how to eavesdrop, but the mitzvah of *kibbud av ve'eim* still exists. Don't go bragging about Tatty's personal secrets that you managed to overhear."

Would I ever—ever—have thought to approach Mommy and ask her about the lost babies? No, even at age five I knew enough not to.

Aviva didn't turn around, but she heard Chavi stomping away. *Slam.* Now she was sulking in her bedroom. *Good. Let her think about the proper way to speak to her mother.*

Anyway, she could not possibly be angrier than Aviva herself.

Borrowing money? What was Zevi thinking? When she'd told him not to! When she'd pointed out that he had no way of paying it back! The clinic was hers, after all—why couldn't he trust her to make that call, to figure out, together with their accountant, how the business could recoup the money? Whatever he advised would certainly be better than taking on fifteen thousand dollars of personal debt!

But no. Zevi had to be rash, impetuous Zevi, acting without thinking, doing according to the whim of the moment. And now look where they were…

Her eyes were starting to sting, and she hurriedly scooped Kivi out of his bath, dried and dressed him, and deposited him in his crib. She ignored his protests—bedtime needed to be *now*.

Her breath was starting to catch in her throat, and her simmering temper was threatening to spill over. She ran downstairs and grabbed her purse.

"Mommy!" Kayla cried from the living room. "Where are you going? We wanted your help!"

"Out," Aviva gasped. "I need to go out."

"What about dinner?"

"Tell Tatty to make something."

"What should I make?"

Aviva's head swiveled. There was Zevi, standing by the front door. His face was wan, but his expression was just as jaunty as ever.

She felt like hurling something at him.

"Oh, anything you want," she said tightly. "I just spent the past hour cleaning up all the messes here because you went and left without leaving anyone in charge."

Zevi's lips curled. "Whoa." He leaned his head against the doorframe. "Thought you'd be happy that I was finally working. Isn't that what you kept saying you wanted?"

The words burst through her lips in a strangled cry. "I wanted you home!" And then, dimly knowing that she wasn't making sense, and that she wasn't at all managing to express her hurt, her anger, her betrayal, she muttered, "Oh, never mind," and brushed past him.

"Where are you going?" he asked.

"To the clinic." It was the first thing that popped into her mind.

He raised his eyebrows. "Didn't you just come from there?"

Aviva didn't have a good answer. All she knew was that the clinic was the place where she felt good, competent, and in control. "I need to go back," she said.

EVEN BEFORE SHE entered the clinic, Aviva's senses told her that something was wrong. The lights were on, for one thing.

As she opened the door, she heard voices coming from one of the therapy rooms. A lot of voices.

Feeling a sense of rising disquietude, she tiptoed down the hall. What was going on?

The voices were coming from the OT room. She walked over to the one-way observation window—allowing parents to observe therapy sessions without distracting the children inside—and peered in. Her mouth opened in shock.

Suri was sitting in the middle of a circle, talking animatedly to a bunch of senior citizen ladies. Aviva couldn't tell what Suri was saying—the microphone wasn't on—but she could see that the women were all listening avidly, nodding and smiling. Now a conversation had broken out among some of the women. Suri sat back, and Aviva couldn't help but notice how at peace she looked. She seemed to be really enjoying herself with these old ladies, whoever they were.

And suddenly, she didn't know why, but the anger and hurt and betrayal that had been simmering inside all evening, all at once spilled over. Tears poured out of her eyes, and, glancing around to assure herself no one was watching, she sat down in the hall to get a hold of herself.

She sat still for quite some time, with tear-stained cheeks, continuing to watch the group through the window. It seemed like this gathering was over, because the elderly women were standing up. Now they all gathered around Suri, giving her glowing thanks, some even hugging her. Aviva's eyes narrowed as she watched. *Look at Suri. Everyone loves her. She has perfect children, a perfect family, she's never ruffled or overwhelmed. Why can't I have that peace in my life? What's wrong with me?*

The tears were threatening to start up again, and Aviva bit her lip hard, jumping to the side just as the door opened and women started pouring out. As she waited for Suri, she felt herself getting more and more agitated, until all the force of her pain seemed to burst forth as Suri walked out the door.

"Suri."

Suri literally jumped at the sight of Aviva.

"Aviva! You scared me! What are you doing here?"

Some of the older women had stopped to look curiously at her.

Aviva's eyes narrowed. "I might ask you the same thing. How could you bring an outside group here into our clinic without permission?"

Suri seemed taken aback. "Permission? I didn't think I needed to ask permission."

"That's because you didn't think!" Now that she had an excuse for her anger, the feeling was intoxicating. "What would have happened if one of these women had fallen, or gotten hurt? Would our insurance cover it, for an illegal gathering?"

"Illegal?"

Aviva waved her hand. "Not permitted on our premises. Non-business related. Did you stop to think about that? Huh?" She paused, feeling a distinct pleasure in watching Suri squirm.

"I didn't think so."

CHAPTER 22

SURI DROVE SLOWLY up to the entrance of Miri's high school, scanning the crowd for her daughter. Each week, she tried to take a different kid with her to go visit her father, and today was Miri's turn. After the day she'd just had—she couldn't remember the atmosphere in the clinic ever being this frosty—all she really wanted to do was go home and curl up in bed. Sitting two hours in rush hour traffic was on the very bottom of her wish list right now. But she couldn't disappoint her father; she knew how much he thrived on these visits.

Couldn't disappoint. Not her father, not the elderly ladies. And look where that got her: Aviva's embarrassing accusations of irresponsibility. Shooting daggers in her direction whenever they crossed paths today. Aviva was taking this whole thing really personally, and it was making Suri quite uncomfortable.

Well, that's no shocker, after what she's just been through with her husband's financial blooper. No wonder she was so sensitive about this. And why weren't you?

Because she just couldn't handle disappointing other people, even at her own expense.

She rubbed her shoulder as she spotted Miri, and waved at her. A hot bath. That was what she needed. *Would it have been so terrible to make this visit tomorrow? Even if Tatty would yell about it?*

Miri slid into the car. "Hi, Mommy, how was your day?"

Suri gave a half smile. "Isn't that supposed to be *my* question?"

It never ceased to amaze her how similar her eldest daughter was to her. The teenaged Suri, too, had never liked talking about herself, had always preferred deflecting attention to others. Come to think of it, she still did that.

Miri turned the CD player on. "Hey," she said brightly, "How'd your social group go last night? Did it work out at the clinic?"

Suri hesitated. Her daughter had been so proud of her suggestion, and it wasn't her fault that Suri had failed to think of the insurance implications, or that Aviva had chosen to get so upset about it.

"Yeah, sweetie, the meeting was great. Super idea!"

"Well, I got it from that day I was there helping out, to set up for the senator's visit. I remembered there were a few kids in wheelchairs there."

Suri nodded. "You were a really big help that day. Yael's still talking about how impressed she is with your maturity." She stole a fond sideways glance at her daughter.

Miri glowed at the compliment, but her brow instantly furrowed. "Mommy," she said slowly. "That reminds me. There was something I'd meant to tell you from that day...but from all the excitement I forgot about it. Something I overheard."

"Oh?" Suri's heart started beating faster. What now?

"About Yael." Miri paused for a moment, and Suri raised her eyebrows at her.

"Yes?"

Miri fiddled with her bracelet. "I hope it's not *lashon hara*... I mean, I think, since it's about your business, you should probably know, right?"

Suri nodded, waiting.

Miri took a breath. "So it's like this. There were a bunch of mothers standing around talking to each other that day, and they were all saying how..." She paused, and then rushed forward. "How they're disappointed with the level of the occupational therapy at the clinic. And then one woman says, 'It's common knowledge that if you're looking for OT, you're better off going elsewhere.'"

IF SURI HAD felt the fifteen-thousand-dollar check a leaden weight in her purse, she now felt like she was carrying around a ticking bomb. What, oh what, should she do with this information? Run with it to Aviva? That seemed the obvious step, but she was scared of what she might set in motion. Aviva had never particularly liked Yael; that much was clear. And if she thought Yael was crippling their clinic's success...

But she is! Miri heard it straight out! Why should Aviva be more concerned about our success than you are? You're equal partners here!

Suri didn't have to search far for the answer. It was because, whatever Yael might be professionally, Suri really liked her as a person. And even beyond liking her, there was something more...

She felt sorry for her.

Suri didn't know why, exactly. After all, Yael was richer than Suri could ever hope to be in a thousand lifetimes. On the outside, there was certainly nothing to pity. And yet, somehow, for some reason, she did pity her. Beneath the surface, there seemed something so vulnerable.

Suri rubbed her snood vigorously. She'd meant to consult with Shaul last night, but by the time she'd returned from her father's, Shaul was on his way out to shul, and she'd had to muster all her energy to put seven-year-old Ari to bed, and make an attempt at conversation with twelve-year-old Baruch, before collapsing.

And now here she was, in the clinic, with Aviva in the room to her right, and Yael in the room to her left.

Caught in the middle. How appropriate.

What. Should. She. Do.

Ask a *rav*? *Oh, hey, why don't you call Yael's father again? Excuse me, Rav Whatever the Name Was (had Yael even mentioned it?), but can you please tell me if I'm allowed to pass on lashon hara about your daughter?*

Suri started as the door suddenly swung open, and Aviva stuck her head inside.

"Hi, Suri." Her tone was wooden, and Suri understood that Aviva had still not forgiven her for her unauthorized use of the clinic. "Message from my husband. Your next client just called to cancel."

"Oh. Thanks." Probably better, anyway. Her next client was a fourteen-year-old with problems with executive function and decision making. She felt in no position to help anyone else with decision making right now.

Aviva was still lingering by the door. Suri felt herself shriveling up in the face of Aviva's coolness. Why was she so angry? It had been an innocent mistake, after all. Nothing to warrant Aviva's taking this as a personal insult.

Aviva swiveled around to exit the room, and Suri found herself desperately calling out, "Aviva! Wait a minute!"

Aviva turned back, eyebrows raised. "Yes?"

Suri felt like crying. She couldn't take this coldness, couldn't stand having Aviva angry with her, and suddenly she was back in seminary, apologizing again and again for having complained about the noise level from Aviva and her crowd while Suri was trying to study.

Aviva was tapping her foot impatiently in the doorway.

What Suri wanted to say, like a little girl, was, "Don't be mad at me." But what came out of her mouth, without stopping to consider, because she knew exactly what reaction she would get, was:

"I've got something really important to tell you. But come inside and close the door—this information cannot leave the room."

<hr />

SHE'D PREDICTED AVIVA'S response perfectly. All animosity instantly melted away as Aviva leaned forward, eager to hear the news. And suddenly, they were friends again, best buddies, co-conspirators.

All because she'd chosen to throw Yael to the wolves.

Aviva's eyes were dangerously narrowed. "Tell me everything again. The entire conversation, word for word."

Suri hesitated, already feeling sick to her stomach. "I can't tell it to you word for word. I told you, I didn't hear it myself; Miri did. Which probably makes a difference in terms of whether we're allowed to believe it," she added, though she actually had no idea if that was true. Shaul had made an attempt a few years earlier to learn *Sefer Chafetz Chaim* at the Shabbos table, but, somehow, it had fizzled out.

Aviva brushed this aside. "When we're talking about something that can cause you potential damage, you're allowed to take precautions even if you can't one hundred percent believe it."

Suri blinked. Would Aviva never cease to amaze her? "Ah…I didn't realize I was dealing with an expert in *shemiras halashon* here."

Aviva shrugged. "You learned it in seminary just like me."

Do not be jealous. Do not be—

"Anyway," Aviva continued. "The question is, what are we going to do about this?" Her hand was clenched. Suddenly, she slammed it down on the table. "I knew from the beginning," she said softly. "Right from that first speech, when she stuttered her way through it, like a little kid, I could tell she wasn't the right caliber." She raked a hand through her sheitel.

"You don't have to say it, Suri. I know you're thinking it. It's been one stupid decision after another. Taking on a partner without researching her first. Bringing in those irritating grad students. Hiring my—" She stopped abruptly, and shook her head.

"But don't worry. We're going to get to the bottom of this. We'll just have to figure out how."

CHAPTER 23

"GOOD MORNING, SURI!"

Suri looked up at Yael's bright, cheerful face, and forced an answering smile onto her own. *Hypocrite. Hypo-crite. Here you go smiling at her as if you're friends, while really you're plotting her destruction behind her back.*

She pushed open the door to her therapy room. Okay, she allowed herself. Destruction was probably pushing it. They weren't even talking about the possibility of letting her go.

"It's tricky," Aviva had said, drumming her fingers on the table, in yet another one of their intense strategizing sessions. "I mean, we owe all our start-up money, and all the funding for this building, to her father-in-law."

"And hiring her was one of the conditions," Suri had reminded her, for the umpteenth time.

Aviva grimaced. "I know, I know. It was a stupid, blind mistake, agreeing to that condition without checking into her first."

Suri had shaken her head. That wasn't what she'd meant.

Problem was, she didn't know what she'd meant, other than that she was feeling crazy guilty for setting the ball rolling in the first place by relaying the conversation to Aviva, and that she knew she would feel awful if it led to Yael's losing her job. Other than that, she didn't know what to feel.

Especially because a tiny, honest part of her was whispering that Aviva was right. They shouldn't have agreed to take on Yael without investigating her first, no matter how much money was involved. And, though she hated to admit it, Yael did not seem up to snuff professionally.

She let out her breath with a huge, exasperated whoosh, as she readied her room for the next client. Avi Goldfeder would be coming for the first time, and Suri was secretly dreading meeting this mother who'd been so insistent that she must have Aviva as a therapist.

She scanned his file as she waited for him to arrive. He was already being treated by Yael, for sensory issues, it said, and Suri found herself reading Yael's session notes more carefully than she'd ever bothered reading them before, to try to find some hint, some proof of competence.

Avi wasn't behaving well today, and I had him go on the bouncy ball to try and calm himself down.

Suri winced at the childish way of writing, and slammed the file shut just as she heard the knock on the door.

"Come in!" Suri blinked at the woman who swept in the door.

Nechi Goldfeder wore designer sunglasses perched on top of her custom sheitel, and was outfitted in a slightly more sophisticated version of the trendy styles that Miri's friends were wearing. On most women, attempting to dress like a teenybopper would look ridiculous, but this lady managed to carry it off.

Behind her trailed an eleven-year-old boy, obviously reluctant to be there by the way his mother kept prodding him through the door.

Finally, she sat herself and her son down. "Nechi Goldfeder," she announced, leaning across the table and holding out her fingers. Suri wondered if she was supposed to kiss them. Instead, she grazed them in a light handshake, as she said, "Suri Taub. I'm looking forward to working with Avi."

Avi was scowling, and did not look remotely pleased to be sitting there. His mother nodded vigorously, as if to compensate for his lack of response. "We're looking forward as well. My husband and I, we're not sure exactly what the problem is, but there's definitely something wrong." She smoothed down her blouse as she looked at her son.

"So you came because you noticed something lacking in his language skills?" Suri prompted.

Nechi shrugged. "We came at the…um…recommendation of his rebbe." She shifted in her seat as she glanced around the room, and then suddenly burst out with, "Do you really work with kids who have trouble learning in school? Because the rebbe said we needed to get him checked out by a speech therapist, but my husband couldn't understand why. He said speech therapists were for lisps and things."

Suri raised her eyebrows at that but responded calmly, "There's a very wide range of issues that speech therapy covers. Yes, we treat lisps and articulation disorders, but we also deal with language issues, stuttering, oral motor weakness, voice disorders like hoarseness, and language pragmatics. And that's not even counting things we don't treat in our clinic, like swallowing disorders."

Nechi blinked. "What was that last thing you said? Pragmatics?

What's that?"

Suri wondered whether this was the woman's way of avoiding discussing her son's language problem. With a small sigh, she said, "It's the social context of language—you know, picking up non-verbal cues, understanding social context, things like that. Now, regarding Avi—"

"So you mean, say a girl doesn't really have friends, and is speaking inappropriately...there's a way to treat that?"

Suri began to perceive that she was going somewhere with these questions.

"Yes, absolutely."

The woman's face brightened. "Oh, because my daughter's been going through some kind of rough social time, and my husband thought it was just normal teenage stuff..."

That was the third time she'd quoted her husband, Suri noted.

"...but I wasn't sure about that."

"You can certainly bring her in for an initial consult," she said.

"And would that be with Aviva Heyman?"

Annoyance flickered inside. "*No.* That is, it's up to you, but you can bring her to me as well. Now, getting back to Avi—can you give me an idea of what the rebbe feels are his problem areas?"

Nechi settled back. "I know he says Avi has trouble under-standing what's going on in class. Though his OT thinks it might be a concentration issue."

Suri's pulse quickened. "You mean Yael?"

Nechi nodded. "Yeah. She's working with him on exercises that can improve his focus."

Don't ask. It's not fair of you. Don't— But the opportunity was too good. "Tell me," Suri said slowly. "Have you found his focus to be improving from the therapy?"

Nechi Goldfeder pursed her lips. "Frankly? Not at all."

⟍

AVIVA AND SURI sat across from Moshe Hirth, a business coach that Zevi knew. Aviva didn't automatically trust Zevi's opinion when he claimed, "This guy's tops, the real deal!" But she'd done her own research, and found that he was, indeed, good at what he did.

Now, he was listening intently as she told him about the Yael saga, from the beginning to the most recent developments. Suri was sitting silently next to her, letting her do the talking.

"We're in a tricky position, you understand," she concluded. "We can't outright fire her—"

Hirth held up a hand. "Let's not jump ahead. Who said anything about firing her? Just because of one overheard conversation? Of a certain sense that you have, when you're not even occupational therapists yourselves?"

Aviva felt herself growing defensive. "Listen, I don't need to be an OT to notice when someone is not doing her job properly. I'm not saying she's awful or incompetent," she added fairly. "But she's not exceptional. And, for our clinic to succeed, we need it to maintain its reputation for outstanding professional standards. Are we wrong for wanting that?"

Next to her, Suri was squirming, and Aviva felt a trace of annoyance. She knew Suri felt uncomfortable about the whole thing, that she felt sorry for Yael. Well, did she think Aviva had no feelings either? Of course she pitied the girl...but pity had no place when you were talking about the success of your business.

Hirth was scratching something on a notepad. "You're right, Mrs. Heyman," he said. "If she is really dragging down the clinic's reputation, then obviously you need to do something about it." He turned the notepad toward them. "But you don't know that for sure. So here's my idea. How about you write up a survey—of customer satisfaction—to send out to all current and former clients of your clinic? Include a whole bunch of questions, like the ambience of the clinic, the level of cleanliness, the wait time—the whole shebang. I've written up some sample questions here. And, among the questions, you'll ask about their level of satisfaction with the therapy services."

He paused, tapping his pen on the pad, as Aviva slowly broke into a smile. "That way, you'll get a real read on what clients are thinking, and we can decide how to proceed from there."

CHAPTER 24

FRAIDY WAS ALREADY parked at the therapy table when Yael walked through the door. She was bent over a laptop, looking way too intense for Yael's liking. For the past several weeks, Fraidy had been going on and on about her master's thesis, asking Yael a million and one questions, insisting on reading entire sections aloud and getting Yael's critique on them ("I don't know, maybe I should've included more examples here. I know I already have five, but maybe they're not good enough? And the research section—is it too short? Do you think I should use that journal article I told you about? I mean, I *could* get the Finnish translated if I need to.").

Yael's own thesis paper was a chapter of her life she generally tried hard to forget about. Researching, writing, organizing her time… None of these was her forte. The irony of a grad student looking to her for advice would be quite humorous if not for the fact that she was actually expected to answer her questions—week after excruciating week.

Bracing herself, she gave a quiet "Hello, Fraidy," as she put her bags down. Fraidy looked up, beaming.

"Yael! I'm so glad you're here! I wanted to ask… Whoa! Where'd you get that awesome outfit?"

Yael blinked at her sudden change of direction. Then she looked down at her clothing. Of course. Today she was wearing a Rina's Racks exclusive.

Silently blessing her fashionista sister-in-law for the first time, Yael put a big, sparkly grin on her face—big enough, she hoped, to make Fraidy forget about this week's burning questions, and said, "So glad you like it! I got it at my sister-in-law's store. You know Rina's Racks? On the Avenue?"

Fraidy's eyes were bugging out further and further. "*Rina's* your sister-in-law?"

Yael nodded eagerly. "She designed this herself."

"No way!" Fraidy said, awed. "Tell me your secret—how do you get a sister-in-law like that?"

Yael smiled. "By marrying her brother."

Fraidy giggled, that look of awe still in her eyes. Yael turned away, suddenly uncomfortable. She started setting up her equipment while Fraidy, after a moment, went back to her laptop. Suddenly, she said, "Hey, I forgot to mention—impressive survey you guys put together."

Yael looked at her blankly. "Survey?"

"Yeah, that customer satisfaction survey you mailed to your clients. My little brother came here for therapy a while back, so my mom got a copy to fill out. Real thorough job. Speaking as someone who's been spending the past billion hours making up research surveys for this thesis paper, I must say, I was impressed."

Yael didn't know what to say. She couldn't well admit that she had no idea what the girl was talking about. Settling on an uncertain "Uh, thanks," she went back to her equipment, her mind racing fast. What in the world was this about? And, more to the point—if the clinic was sending out a survey, why didn't she know about it?

YAEL HUNG AROUND the office, hoping for Aviva to leave so she could catch Suri alone. Fat chance, she realized, as Aviva stayed on, moving industriously from one task to another. Just how much work could one person possibly have to do? Every now and then, Aviva shot her curious glances, as if wondering what Yael was still doing there—she, who usually ran out the minute she finished with her last client.

Suri, too, was in the office typing something up, but now she'd finished and was starting to pack up her things. Realizing the question would just have to be asked in front of Aviva, Yael stood up and said, as casually as possible, "So, guys, what's this survey I've been hearing about?"

Suri gave a visible start, and quickly turned her head away. Aviva, shooting Suri a dirty look, said calmly, "I met with a business coach recently and he suggested we send out a customer satisfaction survey to all our current and past clients. A way to keep our fingers on the pulse of what our clients think about us, and figure out what areas we need to work on developing. He said it's a healthy thing for every growing business to do."

Sounded innocuous enough, but Yael couldn't restrain the choking feeling she had inside. If it was such a standard business move, why was Suri looking so guilty? And why hadn't they told her about it?

She traced the outline of her purse clasp as she said, "I was just surprised when someone mentioned it today, and I didn't know what they were talking about."

Now Suri was quite obviously avoiding eye contact, as she began restacking the files that she had already stacked a minute ago. Once again, it was Aviva who answered.

"You didn't?" she asked smoothly. "So sorry—we didn't mean to keep you in the dark. I was just all excited about this idea after my meeting with this guy, Hirth, and, well, you know me, once I get it in my head to do something, I like to jump in and do it right away. Guess in my excitement I forgot to mention it to you. Here," she added, opening a drawer of the desk and pulling out a sheaf of papers. "This is a copy of the survey. Standard questions, nothing exciting."

Feeling silly, as if she was back in junior high and was receiving a last-minute pity invitation to the popular girl's birthday party, Yael stepped forward to take the copy, and stuffed it in her purse without looking at it. She didn't know what to say. That, despite Aviva's reasonable explanations, she was still hurt that they hadn't told her about this? That the fact that Suri still hadn't said a word made her suspect something more was going on?

Stiffly, she picked up her purse, preparing to leave.

"Yael?"

She swiveled toward Aviva.

"We were just talking, Suri and I, about some upcoming continuing ed classes that we wanted to attend. And I was wondering"—now it was Aviva who was adopting the overly casual voice—"what classes you've been taking in your field. It's so important to update our knowledge."

Yael's eyes narrowed. What was she trying to tell her? "Of

course I take classes. I have to, to maintain my license." No point mentioning that she usually opted for the easiest online courses available, no matter the topic.

Aviva nodded. "Sure, naturally. Just thought I'd mention—in case you ever want to take off a day of work to attend a workshop or something. We'd be happy for you to do it—if you feel it will advance you in your profession."

Confused, Yael looked toward Suri as if for an explanation of what Aviva was really trying to say, but Suri was still focused on those files.

With a shrug, Yael said, "Yeah, I'll keep that in mind."

HER MIND WAS still in a whirl from the day when Yael sat down to supper that night. The minute she'd gotten through the door, she'd read through the entire survey with a fine-toothed comb. At last, she'd had to agree with Aviva that the questions did seem to be standard fare. True, the one about satisfaction with OT services made her gulp, but there was also one about speech, as well as a question asking what additional services they would like to see the clinic provide. All reasonable and professional.

So why did she have this sense of impending doom?

Ephraim, too, was unusually quiet at dinner. In an effort to lighten the mood, Yael said, with forced cheer, "Tell Rina I got a compliment on her clothing today. My grad student couldn't stop raving." Ever since her disastrous comment at her parents' house, Yael had been going out of her way to praise Rina.

Ephraim nodded, with a small smile. "I'll pass it on. Tatty will love to hear it. It's been all about Rina lately, in every conversation." He paused, as Yael lifted her eyebrows at his gloomy tone.

"You spoke to Tatty today?" she asked.

He grunted as he scooped up some mashed potatoes. "Uh-huh. He was asking me about my learning, how it's going, am I seeing success. His buzzword. I said yeah, I am, but I—you know, Tatty's idea of success in learning is different than mine. He expects me to be on the *rosh yeshivah* track, if I was really successful. And if not…" He looked up at Yael. "He mentioned today that the position at his company is waiting for me, whenever I'm ready. No pressure."

Yael furrowed her eyebrows. "But you're not ready."

"Of course I'm not. I'm having real *geshmak* in my learning. Besides," he added, his voice lowering to a mutter, "once I enter the business world, the competition's on. Which sibling is most successful. No way I can compete with Rina—I never could."

He scraped his fork around his plate, then looked up suddenly, his face brightening. "You know I actually overheard Tatty bragging about you to a friend of his the other day. Not Rina—you!" He shook his head slowly, a grin spreading on his face.

"My wife, outdoing my big sister. Imagine that!"

CHAPTER 25

THE MEETING IN Hirth's office was set for Sunday, 10 a.m. Aviva had spent much of the past week reviewing and tabulating the results of the completed surveys. She was gratified by how many people had actually taken the time to fill them in—and even to write something complimentary in the comments section.

"It's a sign of how much our clients value what we do," she'd told Zevi, as she'd sat up yet another late night in the office. When he'd shown up with takeout and an offer to keep her company, for once she'd been nothing but grateful. It was his way, she knew, of trying to thaw things out. He hadn't actually said anything about the fifteen-thousand-dollar loan, nor had she outright apologized for her cutting remarks. But as soon as he'd appeared, with an anxious smile, she'd felt a twenty-pound load she hadn't even realized she'd been carrying melt off her shoulders.

If he had been the first to reach out, she felt he deserved a gesture in return, and so she asked him to join them at their meeting on Sunday. To show how much she valued his opinion at such a crucial juncture. It was a completely spontaneous move, and as thought out as spontaneous moves usually are. Which is why she wasn't prepared for the look Suri gave her as the two made their way into Hirth's office, where Suri was already waiting.

"Oh. I hadn't realized..." Suri began frostily, eyebrows raised, but she quickly stopped herself from explaining what she hadn't realized. Too awkward, apparently, in present company. Aviva twitched her eyebrows back at her, trying to figure out why Suri would be upset over the fact that she'd brought her husband along. With a shrug, she sat down in one of the plush office chairs.

"So," Hirth began, rubbing his hands together. "We're back. You have results for us?"

Aviva nodded, then realized Hirth was not looking at her but at Zevi. Feeling a twinge of annoyance, she cleared her throat as she pulled some papers out of her folder.

"Yes, I do," she said pointedly, handing a copy to everyone. "I've charted the results, including the comments. Overall, I was very pleased. Parents seemed to have a very positive impression of us." She paused, giving the others time to look at their charts, before adding, "With one notable exception."

Suri, sitting next to her, paled as she read the results. "Oh no," she said softly.

Aviva nodded grimly. "Turns out it wasn't just that small group of mothers who had complaints."

Hirth was reading the paper carefully. "Fifty-five percent satisfaction rate with OT services... Hmm..."

"Hey, it's more than half," Zevi said with a short laugh.

Hirth looked at him. "I'm sure you agree that your business can't survive if only fifty-five percent of customers are happy."

Once more, Aviva felt the stab of annoyance. *His* business? Did this Hirth assume, just because Zevi was a man, that he was the one in charge here?

Zevi seemed to guess her feelings, because he quickly held up his hands and said, "It ain't my business. I'm just the secretary."

Somehow, having her husband admit to this successful business coach that he was only a secretary irritated Aviva even more. Slapping her paper down on the desk, she said, "Obviously we can't continue with such poor OT services. The question is, what are we going to do about it?"

To her left, Suri was staring at the floor. To her right, Zevi was whistling under his breath. She rolled her eyes. *Honestly!* Why were they being such wimps? Was she the only one with the guts to run a business?

Clenching her teeth, she looked up at Hirth. At least he seemed sympathetic to her predicament.

"Well," he said slowly. "You have two options. The first one, of course, is to let her go."

Suri wrenched her eyes away from the fascinating floor tiles. "No!" she cried. "We can't do that! It would kill her, absolutely kill her."

Aviva's face reddened. "Listen, I feel as bad as you do about firing someone, but let's be realistic here. We're the ones who need this business to succeed. Not Ms. Made in the Shade Jeren. I don't know if she took this on as a cute little hobby job or what, but you can be sure it's not what's putting food on their table."

Suri squirmed. "There are more things to a person than just money. You have no clue why she took this job."

"And you do?"

Suri shrugged silently. "All I'm saying is firing someone is not so black and white."

"I never said it was!" Aviva pursed her lips. Suri was making her out into some kind of monster! "So what's your solution? Continue keeping her on until our whole clinic goes down the tubes? Just as long as her self-esteem remains intact?"

Here Zevi interrupted. "Listen, Aviva's right, we can't just let this situation continue the way it is." Aviva shot him a gratified glance. "And," he continued, "Mrs. Taub's right as well. It's not so *pashut* to simply fire her. Especially because, legally, she's one of the partners, no?"

Aviva felt a sudden swelling of pride inside. This was her husband—sounding oh so smart, fair, and sensible—talking. "Yeah, that's true," she said. "And, in any case, we can't afford to alienate Zalman Jeren's deep pockets."

Zevi turned to Hirth. "You said you had a second option?"

Hirth rubbed his nose. "Simple, really. You keep Mrs. Jeren on—and hire someone else as well."

Zevi's eyes widened, as Suri said doubtfully, "Do we have enough of a demand for two therapists?"

But Aviva was nodding her head vigorously. "Yes! Yes, we do! Or, that is, we will, once we get the word out that the clinic has hired Ms. Razzle Dazzle occupational therapist. We'll make sure to get a top-notch name, and do a whole advertising blitz…" She could already feel her heart beating with the thrill of the challenge. She grinned. "It's a brilliant idea!"

YAEL OPENED AND closed the clasp of her Hermes bag—a present from her mother-in-law—compulsively as she sank down in her seat, fervently hoping the lecturer wouldn't notice her. With the sensation of being back in graduate school hovering strongly over her, she stole glances at the people sitting around her, all anxiously waving their hands. Well, if there were so many people ready to volunteer to try out this therapy demonstration, what were the chances he'd call on her? Slowly allowing herself to breathe again, she sat back up in her seat as the lecturer called on the woman with her hand highest in the air—a woman who reminded her irresistibly of Aviva.

Yael went back to doodling in her notebook, her old standby in graduate school as well, when the lectures were either too over her head or just plain boring. Why, exactly, had she gone into this field? She groped back in her memory, trying to find that glimmer of interest, that aha moment that made her decide this would be her lifelong profession.

But all she could muster up was a memory of sitting at her parents' dining room table with a pen and paper, writing out the pros and cons of OT, speech, and special ed. "You've always been good with your hands," her mother had pointed out. And so OT had won the day.

It hadn't taken long for her to realize that occupational therapy was much less about the arts and crafts projects she loved and much more about anatomy and physiology. But she'd stuck with it, earning her degree, in preparation for the day she'd have the honor of supporting a *kollel* husband, just like her mother.

Who could've imagined she'd marry a husband that needed no supporting?

She scratched her pen back and forth on the smooth paper, shading in the young girl she'd been drawing, as she tried to bring her focus back to the lecture. The DIR Floortime therapy was actually something she was interested in learning, but that's not really why she was attending this workshop. It was because Aviva's pointed advice to become better educated in her field kept nagging at her inside her head. But it wasn't for Aviva that she was spending the entire day inside this stifling lecture hall. It was for Ephraim. Because she so desperately wanted to make him proud of her.

And becoming the most successful OT she could be was the only way she knew how.

CHAPTER 26

"WAIT!"

Zevi, on his way out to *maariv*, stopped at the door and turned at Aviva's voice. She hurried over to him. "Just want to check that you're coming right home after davening. I'm expecting—"

"Oh, are you? I couldn't tell at all."

She made a face at him. "I'm expecting someone to come over for an interview, and I'd appreciate if you could be here to keep the kids quiet."

He twirled his hat around in his hand. "You know I don't like this idea. I still think you're making a mistake."

She glared at him. She didn't need to hear yet another *mussar shmuess* about her decision to keep this hiring process a secret from Yael. To her, it was an obvious decision—imagine how awkward it would be, interviewing new occupational therapists in the office, right under Yael's nose! And then, of course, out of common courtesy she would have to be made a part of this process, which was the last thing Aviva wanted. No, she had made a mistake once already in not checking out Yael's professional credentials well enough; she was determined to do *teshuvah* for that this time around.

"I didn't ask your opinion," Aviva said coldly. "It's my business, and this decision is on my *achrayus*, okay?"

Zevi blinked from her harsh words, as if stung. But he just shrugged, and gave a small wave as he slipped out the door.

SURI DUMPED THE laundry basket on her bed and started folding towels, as she contemplated the events of the past week. Aviva, with her usual headstrong determination, seemed well on the way to making a new hire. And what would that mean for Yael?

"Why the frown?"

Suri looked up as Shaul entered the bedroom. Shaking her head, she said, "I'm still thinking about this Yael thing."

"Whether you're doing the right thing, keeping this a secret from her?"

Suri's eyes widened. "I meant worrying about how she's going to react eventually. But…yeah, that too. It doesn't seem right, hiring a new therapist behind her back."

"That's because it's *not* right," her husband said calmly.

She looked at him. How did he manage to see things with such a clear perspective of right and wrong, when, to her, it was all muddled inside?

"But Aviva said…"

He waved his hand dismissively. "She has her own reasons for doing things. What do *you* think?"

Suri's eyes narrowed as she placed a neatly folded towel on top of the pile. If she were in Yael's place, would she rather enjoy blissful ignorance as long as she could?

She sighed. "Okay, yes, I would want to be told. But what can I do? This is Aviva's decision."

"Why? Aren't you an equal partner here?"

The simple question brought her up short. Yes, she was supposedly an equal partner in this clinic, wasn't she? So why was it that she always had the sense Aviva was in charge, that she was expected to defer to Aviva's judgment? Seeing Aviva's husband at the meeting the other day had just brought it home starkly—in this business, the Heymans got a double share of voting rights.

Suri bit her lip. "You think I should insist to Aviva that we tell Yael what's going on?" she asked doubtfully. The idea of insisting anything to Aviva didn't sit very well.

Shaul tilted his head to the side. "Why not? And if she doesn't listen, you can always just tell Yael yourself. Isn't that what you would want your friend to do?"

SURI CORNERED AVIVA the next morning. Yael hadn't arrived at work yet; it was just the two of them in the office.

"Listen," she began, heart beating fast. Her words came out in a rush. "I was thinking about it, and it feels like we're making a mistake, not being up front with Yael about the new hire. However awkward it might be for her, it will be much worse if we keep it a secret and just spring it on her. That'll make her suspicious of our true intent."

Aviva was staring at her. "Depends what our true intent is," she said.

Suri blinked. "What do you mean?"

Aviva shrugged, but didn't answer. Plowing on, Suri continued, "So whaddaya say? Are you up for telling her right now?"

Aviva didn't even pause to think. "Absolutely not," she said. "We made a decision and we can't be constantly second-guessing ourselves. It's not healthy."

Suri took a step backward. "Oh," she said uncertainly. Maybe Aviva was right? Suri certainly didn't feel she was in a healthy place as far as decision making went. Was it better to adopt Aviva's policy of making a firm decision and not looking back?

"Anyway," Aviva continued. "It's a moot point because as it happens, I've already found a new OT."

Suri's eyebrows shot up, and she felt a sinking feeling inside. "Really?"

Aviva looked pleased with herself. "I interviewed her last night. This time I did a lot of research into her first, and she seems exactly what we're looking for. If, uh, you agree after meeting her, then I say we go for it."

Suri stared at her. *If you agree*—as if Aviva had any doubts whatsoever. Suddenly, she felt a burning inside. Once again, this was Aviva doing what Aviva wants, expecting Suri to just meekly go along. Well, what if she *didn't* agree? Or—thinking of Shaul—insisted Yael meet her first? Her blood started pounding. Could she do it? She raised her eyes to meet Aviva's.

"I...uh..."

Just then, a client walked up to the office window.

"Mrs. Silver!" Aviva moved toward the door. She turned back to Suri. "I told her to come Monday morning to meet you. If you like her, she'll start immediately."

And she was gone—together with Suri's big moment.

—

THE SCHEDULE SAID Goldfeder was scheduled to come this morning. Not Avi; Dini, the seventeen-year-old sister with social skills problems that his mother had mentioned at their first meeting. And, Suri remembered well, had wanted treated by Aviva. Suri wondered what she had done to merit having another Goldfeder in her second-rate care. Zevi Heyman had told her that the mom had specifically requested her when she'd called, had said something about the social groups that she runs for the elderly. Odd that Mrs. Goldfeder had known about that—not too many people did. Still, it seemed farfetched to jump from a *bubbies'* get-together to helping a teenager with social skills. More likely it was Aviva's long wait-list that made the decision.

Whatever the case, here Dini was, knocking on the door. "Come in!"

Suri wasn't sure what she'd been expecting—probably a teenage version of her mother, who tended to dress like a teenager herself. But Dini walked in with a very short haircut, a denim skirt and a T-shirt, and a nose ring.

Suri blinked several times. Somehow, this didn't fit her picture of a teen with social problems. Of a teen with a different type of problem, yes.

Nechi was following close behind her daughter. "Hello, Mrs. Goldfeder," Suri said brightly. "And you must be Dini. So nice to meet you!"

Once again, the girl surprised her. Suri, had she thought about it, would've expected a scowl or a growl. But Dini returned her bright smile and even stuck out her hand. "Nice to meet you, Mrs. Taub. Thanks for agreeing to see me."

Well, one point for good introductory social skills. She asked Dini to sit down next to her.

"So, Dini, tell me about yourself..."

There followed a ten-minute discussion about Dini's life as a senior in high school, her family life and social life, which to Suri's ear sounded quite normal. If anything, a lot more normal than Suri herself at that age. Dini was answering questions appropriately, making normal eye contact, and doing a decent job keeping up her end of the conversation, considering the natural awkwardness of the situation. Suri shot a questioning look at the mother. Where, exactly, was the problem?

That is, aside from the nose ring.

Finally, Nechi turned to her daughter and asked her to step out for a minute. "Can you please run out to the car? I think I left my cell phone there and I need it."

It was a lame excuse even to Suri's ears.

"I get it; you want to speak to Mrs. Taub alone," Dini said, eyes narrowed. But she left the room.

As soon as the door closed behind her, Nechi leaned forward urgently. "The nose ring—that just happened last week. And the haircut was the week before. And the crazy thing is, she didn't seem to be doing it to make a statement, like I'm sure you're thinking. She didn't seem to even be aware that there was a problem with it. She just walked out of the house one morning, and came back after midnight, with that ridiculous thing in her nose. And showed up at school with it the next day.

"I ask you...this girl doesn't have a problem with social awareness?"

CHAPTER 27

THE SHABBOS MEAL was already cleared and Suri had just sunk down on the couch with a book she'd been looking forward to starting all week when Shaul brought up the topic she'd been dreading.

"So, how'd the big conversation go?"

Suri took her time responding. "Conversation?" she said finally, stupidly. "Which one?"

Shaul never let her get away with such ploys. "The one where you were going to stand up to your coworker and do what's right."

"Oh. That one." Why did she have the unnerving feeling that she was back in elementary school admitting to a teacher that she hadn't done her homework? "I tried, I really did. But just as I was about to get firm on the subject, Aviva's client came, and there was no chance to bring it up after that."

She looked at her husband, scared of his disapproval, and pleaded again, "I really did try."

Shaul's expression was gentle as he said his next words, but they still slapped her in the jaw. "I'm sure you did. But will the fact that you tried make any difference in the end to Yael?"

Suri sucked in her breath. How had she reached this point? How had she become such a weak person? Hadn't she always prided herself on her integrity, on sticking to her values no matter what? She leaned back on the armrest and closed her eyes. Had it always been like this? Nice, high-note principles that crumbled with the wind at the first sign of confrontation?

Eyes still closed, she murmured, "I'm such a coward. What was I scared of, anyway? That Aviva would yell at me? Not want to be partners anymore?" *Not want to be friends anymore.*

"You're not a coward," Shaul said. "You're a peacemaker."

Suri made a face. "Polite way of saying coward." But she laughed, and sat up straighter, as something inside her shifted slightly.

Peacemaker? Yeah, there was something to that...

"I'll speak to Yael after Shabbos," she said.

YAEL GAZED AROUND the large, elegant dining room, the curtained picture windows, the rows upon rows of tables. Her eyes lighted upon a family a few tables away; the teenage girl reminded her of her sister Chanie. What would they all say, she wondered, if they knew she was sitting here in a hotel, in Florida, whisked away...

Someone nearby cleared his throat loudly. "Um, Yael? You want to order?"

Yael tore her eyes away from the Chanie look-alike. A waiter was standing nearby, eyebrows raised. Blushing, she took the menu from Ephraim's outstretched hand.

"Uh…I'll have…uh, the chicken," she said, eye alighting on the first recognizable item.

Ephraim ordered the mishy-morshy, or something that sounded like that. After the waiter swept away with their menus, Yael leaned forward and smiled. "Still can't believe we're here. It's like a dream!"

He smiled back. "Happy birthday."

She giggled. "Just no singing waiters, okay?"

He pretended to look disappointed. "And here I'd been practicing the harmony."

Yael leaned back in her seat. She couldn't remember the last time she'd been this relaxed. It was as if she and Ephraim were dating again.

"Why do you think your parents decided to surprise us like this? They've never given me such an extravagant birthday present before."

Ephraim's eyes twinkled. "They like you a lot, you know."

Yael blushed. She couldn't really say if that were true. "You think they got mixed up with the year? Thought it was my thirtieth, instead of twenty-ninth?"

He shrugged. "Yeah, I thought of that. But it's just not like them to not keep track."

Yael nodded. True, it wasn't.

"I think it was just their way of saying they appreciate how hard you've been working, and they thought you deserved a rest. I know they've done this for my sisters in the past." A fleeting frown passed over his face, which he quickly pulled back up into a smile. "I'm lucky I'm married to you, I suppose. I would never rate a surprise weekend getaway on my own."

Yael grinned as she said with a wink, "Uh, mister, I think I only rated this because I'm married to you!"

They both laughed hard at that, until finally Yael leaned back in her seat and sighed, contented. "I could stay here forever. You think Mommy and Tatty would be willing to take the kids for another month or so?"

"Sounds good to me." Ephraim leaned back in his chair as well. "But the kids would probably miss you."

She cocked an eyebrow. "Ya think? Your mother does a much better job spoiling them than I do."

"And the clinic would miss you too."

Yael's face darkened, as a heaviness suddenly settled on her. Why had he brought that up?

"Nah," she said, as lightly as possible. "They can get on fine without me."

He gave a short laugh. "What are you talking about? There's no OT services without you."

She shrugged. "Yeah, well." She wanted so badly to tell him of her suspicions, of her fears that something was brewing, how Aviva was acting so cold recently, and Suri—even Suri!—so strange. That she didn't know what it meant, but something whispered that it wasn't good.

It was much better for her to stay hidden in this Florida getaway, where she didn't have to think of such things.

Yael looked at Ephraim. "Let's make a deal," she said softly. "No more mention of the clinic until we come home Monday morning."

AVIVA WALKED INTO the doctor's office and went up to the desk. "I'm here for my twenty-week ultrasound," she said, hating the fact that her voice shook slightly. Every single pregnancy, this anatomical scan was always the most nerve-wracking part for her—even more, in a certain way, than the birth itself. She remembered back to when she'd been pregnant with Chavi, how Zevi had accompanied her, stood next to her in the room as they both gazed at the screen, and how his infectious excitement at seeing every little baby organ had calmed her down and pulled her mind away from the fear that maybe one organ wouldn't be there like it should.

But that was ages ago, and they'd long passed the cute young couple stage where Zevi joined her at every doctor's visit. Zevi was home with the kids, enjoying his Sunday time with them, and she—for goodness sake—what was she doing, trembling like a two-year-old when this was her ninth time going through this?

"How are you today, Mrs. Heyman?"

Aviva murmured a reply as she lay down on the table, eyes screwed onto the screen in front of her. Ultrasound technology had sure changed in the past fifteen years. The image was so much more vivid and real than she remembered.

She closed her eyes. *Think of something else. Think of what you need to do when you get home.* She opened her eyes. No, all pregnancy she'd been doing that, focusing on anything but the little life inside her, as if by ignoring it she could pretend…

What?

She didn't want to finish the sentence.

Look at the screen, she commanded herself. *See your baby, this baby that's really, truly growing inside you. It's not the baby's fault that—*

She stopped herself again.

The technician was calling out names as she scanned. Heart. Spine. Liver. Kidney. With each matter-of-fact label, Aviva felt her shoulders relaxing. *It will be okay. It will be okay. You will deal with this baby, and love it, just like you've loved every single one before.*

Brain.

There was a pause, a way-too-long pause, and Aviva lifted her head up, heart thumping. "Is there a problem?" she croaked.

The technician blinked at her, as she slowly continued her scan. "Not sure," she said at last, in a not very reassuring voice.

Aviva felt a fog cover her brain. She squeezed her eyes shut. "Oh, please, Hashem. Please, please, please, please..."

After what seemed like ages, the scan was over, and she had lifted herself up into a sitting position. The technician was fiddling with her computer, taking a long time to type. Meanwhile, Aviva's lungs were about to burst.

"Well?" she said at last.

The technician looked up and handed her some papers. "I recommend you do an amnio," she said. "I saw some markers, some signs... I think you should get this baby checked out."

CHAPTER 28

AVIVA WALKED INTO her house with a big smile pasted on her face. She was assaulted at once by her entire clan. "Mommy! You're home!"

"What's for dinner?"

"How'd it go?"

The last one was from Zevi, asked quietly, and Aviva gave him a brief, private nod. "It was fine," she said, though her heart squeezed hard inside her at the lie. Now, in front of the kids, was not the time to talk.

He smiled, that easy, reassured smile, and she felt like screaming. *No! It's not fine at all! The entire world is tumbling down!* But she had to get a grip on herself, because she was the mother here, and she had to be strong, she could not let her children see how terrified she was inside, how she was carrying a baby who might be all wrong, all wrong…

She shook her head, struggling to place her anxiety inside a box and shut the cover firmly. Later, after she'd made dinner and put her kids to bed, after Zevi had left for shul in blissful ignorance, she would sit by the computer and research brain disorders and amniocentesis and every little bit of information the technician had thrown her way, after insisting that she must speak to her OB to get actual medical guidance. Aviva had sat rigidly across from the lady, knuckles whitening as they gripped the desk, and must have frightened her enough that she put her hand on Aviva's arm and said, "Don't worry, honey, it might not be anything at all. Either way, you'll have a beautiful baby, and that's all that counts, right?"

Aviva had not even bothered to reply to such an inane comment. That's all that counts? To give birth to a baby with who knows what kind of disorder, defect, syndrome from the wide list of medical problems out there in the world? But she'd steeled herself, straightened her shoulders, and, with a tight smile, stood up and said, "Thank you so much. I'll be in touch with Dr. Resnik, then."

And now she was home, and going to spend the next few hours feeding and caring for her family, and not think about anything else. She walked through the house in a fog, willing herself to keep moving, to do what she needed to do. Chavi, she noticed, was sitting at the dining room table, head bent over a notebook. *Chavi.* With a pang of guilt, Aviva realized how much she'd been neglecting her relationship with her eldest lately. She walked over to her, put her hand on her shoulder, and said, "What's that you're working on?"

Chavi looked up. "*Chumash.* I have a big report due tomorrow." She looked wary as Aviva sat down next to her.

Aviva swallowed and made her voice gentle as she asked, "Need any help?"

Chavi gave her a slow smile. "Yeah, I'd love some."

That sweet, trusting smile was making Aviva feel all shaky inside. She stood up. "Let me just put some dinner up, and then I'm all yours." She was trembling as she headed into the kitchen. *Oh, Hashem, what if there's something seriously wrong with my baby? And what if I deserve that, because I've been such a terrible mother to my other children? And what if...*

Zevi met her in the kitchen, holding out a mug. "Hot chocolate. With a marshmallow. For the soon-to-be new mommy."

Aviva's eyes widened. And then she burst out in sobs.

—

SURI ARRIVED AT the office Monday morning bright and early, with a distinct feeling of dread. She had tried all weekend to reach Yael, unsuccessfully. And now the big day had arrived, the new occupational therapist would be starting to work, and the most Suri could hope to do in terms of damage control was to head Yael off at the door, to give her a few minutes' advance warning.

It wasn't much. Not much at all. And, as she pictured the highly uncomfortable conversation in her mind, she couldn't help but feel anger as well. Why should she get stuck with this job? Aviva should be doing it!

She paced back and forth nervously, as Shaul's words ran through her mind. *You're a peacemaker.* Yes, she knew why she needed to do this task, unfair as it was. Because she would do it well, and Aviva wouldn't.

The realization put an invigorating bounce in her pacing.

She came to a halt at the sound of the door opening. Aviva walked in, followed by a tall woman wearing a neat sheitel, well-cut jacket, and businesslike heels.

"Ah, Suri, you're here already." Aviva gave her a smooth smile that looked strangely put on. "Meet Naomi, our new OT. We're really lucky to have her; she left a cushy job in the famous White Cliff rehab center to come work for us."

Naomi smiled. "Nice to work closer to home for a change," she said as she held out her hand to shake Suri's.

Suri, of course, had read her impressive resume, but seeing her now she understood immediately why Aviva had liked her. The two were practically clones, the way they dressed, the way they presented themselves, even their mannerisms. From the firmness of Naomi's handshake, Suri knew that this was a lady who valued professionalism.

She sighed inwardly. Poor Yael. Next to this powerhouse, she wouldn't stand a chance.

"Welcome." Suri shook her hand awkwardly, not knowing quite what else to say. As self-conscious as she often felt with Aviva, at least she had nearly two decades of friendship to give her confidence; how was she supposed to make conversation with a stranger who stood so straight and dignified before her, and swept her eyes around the office as if she owned it?

Aviva saved the moment by clapping her hands and saying, "Well, shall we get started? Let me give you the grand tour." She continued talking as she led her away. "I didn't schedule your first client until eleven; that should give you enough time to get familiar with the place. You'll be working in this room down the hall. Sorry it's a bit underequipped—we're working on purchasing more OT equipment now that there are two of you…" Her voice trailed off as they walked down the hall, two sets of heels clicking away.

Suri shook her head grimly as she glanced at her watch. Her first client would be coming in a half hour; she hoped Yael would make an appearance soon.

But a half hour later, there was still no Yael, and with a sinking heart and a vague worry whether everything was well with her friend, she headed toward her therapy room.

YAEL'S SPIRITS WERE higher than usual as she got out of her car and headed for the clinic. The weekend away had done her a world of good. The vacation was exactly what she'd needed, and she patted herself on the back for the decision to make it a real vacation, by not doing anything work related. Suri, she'd seen, had tried to call her several times but, as she'd told Ephraim defiantly, whatever it was could wait until Monday. She was entitled to a break.

On the early-morning plane ride back, she'd come to a decision. She would make this work. She would do whatever it takes, going to courses, researching therapy approaches, preparing fun games at home. She owed it to Ephraim, to her in-laws who believed in her, and to herself, to prove that she was no less capable than her colleagues if she set her mind and heart to it.

She pushed open the door, grinning at the parents sitting in the reception area. She realized she'd forgotten to let Suri and Aviva know that she'd be late this morning; it had been such a last-minute thing, and she'd barely had time to call up her first two clients to cancel. She hoped her partners hadn't been wondering where she was, or thinking she was irresponsible.

She quickly scooped up her files and headed down the hall to her therapy room. Five-year-old Henny Wolf was her first patient, and she'd already planned out the paper dolls they would draw and cut out; Henny would love that. As she approached her room, she noticed that the light was on in the small room across the hall. Strange; that room was almost always vacant. Who could be in it? Curious, she put her things down in her own room and walked over to see.

The curtain over the window was drawn, but standing to the extreme side, she could peep through the crack enough to see an unfamiliar woman sitting at a table reading through some files. Yael frowned. Who was this woman? She glanced around, wanting to ask Suri or even Aviva, but neither was in sight. At last, she gave a brief tap on the door.

"Come in!"

Yael walked inside the room. Her cheeks reddened as she hesitated, not exactly sure how to put the question. The older woman looked up questioningly. "Hello. Uh…I'm Yael, the occupational therapist here. Can I ask who you are?"

The other woman stood up and, striding over, she stuck out her hand. "Oh, so you're the other one. I'm Naomi, the new OT. Very nice to meet you."

CHAPTER 29

YAEL NEVER KNEW what reply she made, but somehow, she made some response to Naomi's introduction and then speedily backed out of the room. She raced into her own therapy room, locked the door, and then sank into a chair, putting her head down on the table.

What did this mean? What did this mean?

Her head was pounding, and she didn't even know what to think. A new OT? But why? Thoughts swirled inside her head until she felt dizzy. She lifted her head and squared her shoulders, trying to force herself to stay logical. *Okay, they're allowed to hire a second OT in the clinic. After all, they have two speech therapists. No one ever said that it would be only me forever.*

But why didn't they tell me?

Yael stood up, began pacing. Maybe they thought she'd take it the wrong way? *Gimme a break. And this I wouldn't take the wrong way?* She shook her head. A mistake. An oversight. That was all.

She took a breath.

Right?

Yael picked up the file of her first client. She was coming in ten minutes. *Focus. Plan out your session. Remember, you said starting today, you would try to do your hardest, give it your all…*

Tears suddenly pricked her eyes. She slammed the folder down on the table. She needed to speak with Suri.

Yael walked down the hall, pausing by Suri's therapy room. The curtain was drawn over the window, and she put an ear to the door to hear if Suri was with a client.

"Aviva, it's not right! She'll be devastated when she finds out!"

Yael's eyes opened wide, and she pressed her ear harder to the door.

"I thought you were going to tell her over the weekend."

"I tried, but I couldn't reach her. And then I thought I'd head her off this morning, but she still hasn't come to work."

Aviva snorted. "How responsible."

Outside, Yael's eyes narrowed, as she heard Suri murmur, "She must've had a reason."

"Anyway," Aviva continued, "I'm sure she'll understand that we felt it was time to expand."

"But you and I both know—and she probably does too—that we don't have the caseload to support two OTs."

Yael gasped. Her heart was thudding so loudly that she didn't hear the footsteps until Suri's next client had walked up right behind her. Blushing at how she must look, eavesdropping like a little kid, she jumped back from the door, retreating just in time as the kid knocked on the door and walked inside.

Blood pounding, Yael walked into her own room, grabbed her purse, and walked rapidly out of the clinic.

AVIVA SAT IN Zevi's swivel office chair, staring at the computer. She'd just finished with her last client, and decided to take advantage of the quiet office to do some research. She glanced at the clock. Zevi was out at *minchah*—she only had a few minutes.

She bit her lip as she did a search for fetal brain development disorders, even as she berated herself for being ridiculous. Trying to research such a broad topic was beyond futile. She had a doctor's appointment scheduled for the next day; the sensible thing to do was to push the whole thing firmly out of her mind until then.

But that was asking the impossible.

Her brain whirled as she saw results about genetic disorders, cephalic disorders, brain malformation... Feeling mild panic set in, she clicked on one page and began to read.

"Fetal alcohol syndrome?" Aviva whirled around as Zevi walked up behind her. "Is this for one of your clients?"

Aviva gave a noncommittal shrug. Her throat was too constricted to answer.

He glanced at the website, which showed a picture of a baby affected by FAS. "*Nebach*," he said, shaking his head. "To have to suffer his whole life because his mother couldn't control herself."

"What if I drank too much wine at Kiddush, right at the beginning...?" The words came out in a whisper; Aviva hadn't intended to say them aloud.

Zevi looked at her in surprise, and began to laugh. "Aviva, you aren't seriously trying to say you're worried about our baby having fetal alcohol syndrome?" He laughed some more.

She blinked hard. She hadn't had a chance to tell him about the ultrasound yesterday—or, more to the point, she hadn't been able to muster up the courage. Somehow, saying the words aloud—*our baby may have a serious problem*—made it much more real and frightening.

Now she squeezed out a tiny smile. "No, I don't really. But... but..." She wanted so badly to tell him, to share her terrible fears, but she didn't know how to say the words, and did she really want to say it right here, right now, in the middle of the clinic office, where anyone could walk in?

Zevi was staring at her pale face in consternation. "Aviva, you look terrible. You know there's no reason to worry, right? *Baruch Hashem*, you've already given birth to eight healthy babies, and there's no reason to think this time will be different. Everything will be fine, got it?" He bent his head to catch her averted gaze. "Hey, more than fine—fabulous!"

Aviva shook her head mutely. This was too much—way too much. She blinked rapidly, swallowing hard, but she couldn't stop herself. For the second time in two days, she felt the tears gushing out. She covered her face as she swiped for the tissue box.

Zevi waited silently for a few moments, and then said quietly, "Aviva? Please tell me what's going on. Another old neighbor passed away?"

The last line was said sarcastically, and Aviva couldn't blame him. Yesterday, when he'd questioned her about her sudden burst of sobbing, she'd made up a lame excuse about old Mrs. Schwartzberger, her parents' former next-door neighbor, passing away in her nursing home. It had sounded unbelievable even to her own ears. Mrs. Schwartzberger had passed away five years ago, and Aviva hadn't shed a tear at the time.

Aviva hiccupped and blew her nose, as the tears began to subside. As hard as this was, she had to tell him. Bracing herself, she said, "Zevi, I need to tell you something. About the baby. Something that came up yesterday at the ultrasound."

She watched her husband's face pale, and she closed her eyes, pushing herself to continue, to verbalize it. "The technician didn't say what, just something about the brain. No," she corrected herself, remembering. "She didn't say that either, but she spent a crazy amount of time looking at the brain, and you could tell that's what was concerning her. She told me to get it checked out, to do an amnio." Aviva paused, as Zevi slowly nodded. "I have an appointment with my doctor tomorrow."

The anxiety on her husband's face was a mirror of her own, she knew. But, unexpectedly, she felt a slight lightening as she watched him absorbing this, sharing her fear. He opened his mouth to say something—and suddenly the office door opened.

"Well, I'm finished for the day."

Aviva and Zevi swiveled around.

"Ah, Naomi," Aviva said, putting on a bright smile as she tried to refocus. "How did it go?"

Naomi gave a brief, satisfied nod. "Very good. You have a nice clientele here."

Aviva's smile turned a little more genuine. "Yes, we really do. The parents are very interested in being involved in the therapy process. Well, I'm so glad you enjoyed your first day. You had a chance to look around, get to know the place?"

"Oh yes," Naomi said, as she smoothly put her files and materials away as if she'd been there months already. "And the other therapists seem lovely."

Aviva paused. "Thera*pists*?" she asked. As far as she knew, it had only been her and Suri today.

"Yes." Naomi looked at her in surprise. "Suri, the one you

introduced me to this morning. And that other woman, the other OT—Yael, I think her name is? I saw her briefly this morning as well."

"Oh—ah, of course." Aviva didn't know what to think. She hadn't seen Yael all day, and had assumed she hadn't shown at all. But now...

"I'll see you tomorrow, then," said Naomi, giving a wave as she walked out.

Aviva gripped the desk, trying to steady her thoughts. How much could she deal with in one day?

Zevi was watching her, she knew, and she was ashamed to look at him. "Maybe she wasn't feeling well, and went home," she said, hopefully.

But her husband was shaking his head, and she knew that if Yael had been there and gone home so quickly, it did not bode well at all.

And her heart actually quailed as she realized: She would have to tell Suri.

CHAPTER 30

YAEL HAD SPENT much of the day huddled in bed, the words *failure, failure, failure* running through her head like a mantra. It was only when her babysitter went home that Yael roused herself, as Sruli came clambering onto her bed, Simi running after her big brother as fast as her chubby little legs allowed her. As Yael lost herself in a big, delicious cuddle, she realized it was the first time she'd smiled all day.

"Boy is Mommy glad to see her two favorite little people in the world!" she said, squeezing one yummy cheek against each of her own.

"Mommy sandwich!" shrieked Sruli gleefully, while Simi giggled.

It was exactly what she'd needed to get through the rest of the day. By the time she'd put them to bed and come down to eat dinner with Ephraim, she was in a much calmer state of mind than she'd been in earlier that morning, when she'd run out of the clinic like a madwoman, with no thought or plan other than the instinct to flee.

Facing Ephraim was a whole other story. Yael didn't know quite how to tell him what had happened. After their wonderful weekend together, she'd felt their relationship was finally getting back on track—and now this? How would he react if she walked into the kitchen and told him, "Today my partners decided to push me out of the business by hiring someone to replace me"?

True, they hadn't actually said that; but anyone with half a brain could see it was the bald truth. The fact that they obviously thought Yael wouldn't catch on showed just how little they thought of her intelligence.

She sighed as she dished out minestrone soup to Ephraim.

"How was your day?" she asked quickly as she sat down, hoping to beat him to it.

"*Gevaldig*," he said, beaming. "My learning was so much more *geshmak* today after our getaway." He took a spoonful of soup. "But I want to hear about you! How's the star OT doing?"

She'd confided in him, on the flight home, about her resolution to become the best therapist she could be, and Ephraim, naturally, had applauded this wholeheartedly. Now the whole thing seemed like one big, not very funny joke.

Yael squirmed in her seat as she answered, "Fine."

"Just fine? How'd all your sessions go? You told me you had these great ideas for today."

Yael kept her eyes trained on her bowl. Why did Ephraim always interrogate her about her work? Why couldn't he ever think to ask about the kids, how her outing to the park had gone, what kind of drawings she'd made with them? It was always the clinic, as if that was the only thing worth anything in her life.

She decided she couldn't completely lie. "I...uh...didn't end up seeing any clients today," she said. "I came home early. Wasn't feeling well." She mumbled the last line, though really, she told herself, it was the absolute truth. She couldn't remember feeling this lousy in a long time.

"Sorry to hear that." He looked concerned, which made her feel even worse. "Maybe the weekend away tired you out. We should've come home yesterday instead of this morning."

"No, we shouldn't have," she said emphatically. "We both needed this vacation. There's nothing wrong with taking off a day of work every now and then."

From the way Ephraim raised his eyebrows, Yael could tell she'd said something shocking. Well, in his family's worldview, it was.

She squeezed her fingers around her spoon. Should she tell him about Naomi? About Suri admitting that they didn't have enough of a caseload to support two of them?

The fact that she'd proven a failure as an OT?

She watched him calmly eating, trying to imagine his reaction if she were to tell him all this. Deep down, she feared that it would completely ruin their marriage. That he would no longer respect her.

She gave a little shake of her head. No, she decided, it just wasn't worth the risk. She took a breath.

"You wanna hear the cutest story about Simi?"

SURI LOOKED OUT the window with interest as Aviva brought the car to a slow stop next to the curb.

"You're sure this is it?"

"It's 36 Harrington Boulevard. That's what you told me, right?"

Suri had pulled Yael's address off of their office computer. Now, as she looked around at the sprawling, spread-out houses, separated by well-kept, generous lawns, she began to realize how little she knew about Yael's life.

"I've never even *been* to this side of town," she murmured.

Aviva curled her lips. "Surprised? Where did you expect a Jeren to live?"

Suri didn't answer. She supposed she shouldn't have been surprised, but still…this house didn't seem to fit Yael at all.

"I bet you a butler answers the door," Aviva smirked. And then, after a pause, "*Now* do you believe me when I told you she doesn't need this job?"

At that, Suri pursed her lips. She'd been absolutely beside herself when, last night, Aviva had broken the news about Yael meeting Naomi and then running off. "I *told* you this would happen! I *told* you!" she'd actually shrieked into the phone, and must have so startled Aviva that, when Suri demanded they go out to Yael's home to apologize, Aviva hadn't even protested. She'd agreed that if Yael didn't show up the next day, they'd head out during their lunch break to see her.

Now, as they stood outside the polished wooden door, Suri felt her palms go sweaty. Maybe they should've called in advance. How would Yael react when she saw them?

Aviva had already rung the doorbell, and within a few minutes, the door opened—not by a butler, but by Yael herself. And her eyes opened wide.

"Oh," she said. "Oh…" She didn't seem to know what else to say, and Aviva helped her out.

"Can we come in?"

Yael nodded, and the two women followed her inside, both looking around as they walked.

"What a beautiful home," said Aviva, in a hearty voice that told Suri she was feeling uncomfortable. "It's decorated with such taste."

"It was my mother-in-law's interior decorator," Yael said in a low voice, as she led them into the living room. Aviva and Suri both sat down on the leather couch, while Yael sat in the armchair opposite them.

Feeling awkward, Suri added to Aviva's chorus by saying, "What beautiful paintings!" The walls were filled with oil-painted scenes.

Yael's thanks seemed more genuine this time, as she added, "I painted them myself."

"Did you?" Suri's mouth opened in shock, and Aviva looked impressed as well. "I never knew you were so talented."

Yael shrugged. She sat back in her chair, eyeing them silently. Suri saw she was not planning on making this easy for them.

With a glance at Aviva, Suri began. "Listen, I'm sure you know why we're here. Naomi, the new OT. We realize that you met her yesterday, and were probably really confused, and we came to apologize for causing that."

She paused, as Yael crinkled her nose. "I don't understand. What exactly are you apologizing for? Confusing me?"

Suri raised her eyebrows, as Aviva spoke up. "No, we're apologizing, of course, for not having told you in advance about the new hire. We should have... We meant to..." Suri glanced at Aviva in surprise, but she seemed quietly unabashed by the blatant untruth. "But, somehow, things happened so fast, I heard about this woman and wanted to grab her before someone else did... She's a real gem."

Suri added, "I meant to tell you over the weekend, and I tried several times but you didn't pick up your phone."

Yael nodded. That sounded legit. And she knew for a fact that Suri *had* tried calling, and she'd decided not to answer.

"We felt it was time to move forward," Aviva added, and Suri noticed, to her shock, that Aviva was playing with her rings, and seemed unnerved by Yael's continued silence. "You know, bring in new blood to our staff. We were sure you would agree as well, knowing how much you care about the clinic's success…"

Here Yael gave a loud sigh, and Suri could tell she wasn't buying this spiel one bit.

"Listen," Yael interrupted, laying a hand on her glass-topped coffee table. Suri noticed the hand was trembling. "Please don't insult my intelligence. We all know there isn't enough work right now to fill two caseloads. Maybe in the future, but not for a while."

She leaned forward, and now Suri could see her whole body was shaking.

"So I'd appreciate you be straight with me and tell me the real reason you're here."

Next to Suri, Aviva's mouth dropped, as she stared at Yael as if seeing her for the first time. Suri shifted in her seat, feeling suddenly apprehensive. Neither of them said anything.

Yael gave a small, twisted smile. "How about this, then? Let me save you the trouble…" She looked them both in the eye, first Aviva, then Suri. "I quit."

CHAPTER 31

SURI AND AVIVA spent most of the ride back to the clinic in shell-shocked silence. Suri kept glancing at Aviva, wishing she would start up the conversation, but her friend's eyes were glued determinedly to the road, lips pursed tightly.

Finally, as they pulled up to the clinic, Suri spoke up. "We need to talk about this."

Aviva nodded. "I didn't see it coming, Suri. I admit—I totally didn't see it coming." And, with a soft sigh, she added, "Poor Yael."

Suri picked up her purse. "We both have clients now, but this needs to be discussed ASAP. Meet after work?"

Aviva quickly shook her head, cheeks reddening. "Uh, no, I can't. Doctor appointment."

"Oh," Suri said awkwardly. Why oh why was she still feeling that surge of jealousy every time Aviva mentioned anything pregnancy related? "Um…okay, tonight, then?"

Aviva hesitated. "Not sure. I might not be up to it, after the appointment," she mumbled.

Suri raised her eyebrows at that. True, it had been many years, but from what she remembered, prenatal checkups were hardly exhausting. Sounded to her like Aviva was trying to avoid discussing the unpleasant topic of Yael's quitting.

"Aviva, this is urgent. We've clearly hurt Yael terribly, and we need to figure out what to do about it."

Aviva twisted her ring around her finger. "I know, I know. How about tomorrow morning? We'll come an hour early, the office should be quiet."

Suri grudgingly nodded. She didn't like pushing this off until tomorrow—her instinct was to turn right around this instant, burst into Yael's house, and beg her to come back to work. But faced with no other choice, she opened the car door and switched her brain back to work mode.

Dini Goldfeder was her next client. The girl was still a mystery to her. The mother kept insisting she had social awareness problems, and had her stories to prove it: one week, Dini had been sent home from school for mouthing off to her teacher; another time, she'd instigated a fight over nothing with her longtime best friend, and actually laughed when she'd declared to her mother that the friendship was over.

But every time Suri spoke with Dini, she had the impression of a poised, articulate, reasonably mature teenager who did not exhibit any of the classic signs of difficulty with social pragmatics. It seemed clear, based on her mother's anecdotes and also Dini's ever-evolving appearance, that something was going on here. But that something, Suri was increasingly starting to feel, seemed out of her purview as a speech therapist.

She'd tried hinting as much to Nechi Goldfeder, but the woman didn't want to hear it.

"A friend of mine, her daughter went through exactly the same thing. The school was on the verge of kicking her out, and then someone suggested that she just wasn't picking up on—what do you call them—social cues. After a few sessions, my friend says she was a different person!"

Nechi's eyes were wide as she'd told her this, almost pleading, as if begging Suri to work the same magic with her own daughter.

Now, as Suri hunched over her therapy table, squinting at Dini's file as if hoping it would reveal the key to unlocking this mystery, she wondered what more she could possibly try.

The minutes ticked by, and still, the Goldfeders didn't appear. She glanced at her watch, wondering if everything was okay; they were usually punctual. Just as she was about to call, the door opened, and mother and daughter trooped in. Nechi came first, dressed to the nines as usual, though her face looked wan. But Suri's mouth dropped open as she saw Dini, trailing after her. She was wearing a ratty sweatshirt, her hair hung loosely around her face, and her eyes had deep, droopy bags under them.

"Have you been ill?" she blurted.

Nechi glanced at her daughter who was staring at the floor, her face a mask. Nechi gave a slight shrug. "You could say that," she said, her mouth twisted. "She's been lying in bed for the past three days, refused to come out for anything. It was quite a fight to get her to come here today."

She glared at Dini, who was still staring down, not responding.

"You could have canceled if she was that sick!" Suri said.

Nechi shook her head, eyes narrowed as she lowered her voice and came closer to Suri. "She's not sick, believe me. Just pure teen-age stubbornness. She'd been kicked out of school once again for chutzpah—this time to the principal, of all the stupid things—and so she goes and puts on a big show of depression."

She rolled her eyes, but something that she said struck a light in Suri's head.

"How do you know it's just a show?" she asked.

FOR THE FIRST time in fifteen years, Aviva asked Zevi to come with her to a doctor's appointment.

She wasn't going to, at first. She'd told herself she would handle this alone, and only break the news to Zevi gently afterward. That this was what a good wife would do, and she owed it to her wonderful husband to be a good wife.

But as soon as she'd stepped into the office after their disastrous meeting with Yael, and Zevi had beckoned her over and handed her a bag with a sandwich and a muffin ("I picked up some lunch for you since I kind of figured you'd forget to eat otherwise, and I don't want you fainting at the doctor"), her resolution totally crumbled.

"Zevi," she said, in a small, childlike voice that didn't sound like her own at all, "do you think you can come with me to this appointment? I'd really feel better if you were there."

To her surprise, Zevi's face broke out into the widest grin she could remember seeing.

"Of course! I'm so happy you asked!"

Aviva was taken aback by his enthusiasm, and the sudden realization struck her with force; she'd thought she was doing him a favor by sparing him this anxiety, but in reality, there was nothing he wanted more than to share it with her.

And so the two headed together to the doctor's office later that afternoon, and sat with clenched teeth and squeezed fists as the doctor reviewed the ultrasound results.

"It's something with the brain, right?" Aviva said desperately as Dr. Resnik sat silently scanning the images. *Just tell me already!* Her nerves were stretched as thin as they could go.

The doctor looked up. Her usually smiling face was serious, and though she spoke with a light tone, Aviva could tell she was weighing each word carefully. "Not the brain exactly. There were some indications from the ultrasound—markers, we call them— certain unusual anatomical signs which can be correlated with Down syndrome."

Aviva dug her fingernails sharply into her palms as, beside her, Zevi sucked in his breath.

"Down syndrome?" he croaked.

Dr. Resnik quickly added, "As I said, these are merely indications. They could be nothing at all. The most effective way to diagnose Down syndrome prenatally is through an amniocentesis. I would certainly recommend you undergo this exam—that is, if the two of you are interested in knowing with certainty one way or the other."

Aviva glanced at Zevi, as the silence hung thick in the office. *If they were interested…* How would it feel, knowing the little baby she was carrying inside was disordered, that all she had to look forward to after enduring several more months of pregnancy was an abnormal baby, who would need to be cared for for the rest of his or her life? She shook her head. Zevi was staring at her, and she was sure her face must be deathly pale, because her heart seemed to have come to a painful standstill.

They both seemed to be waiting for her to say something, but couldn't they see she was incapable of speech right now? At last, Zevi spoke.

"Thank you very much, Doctor. We'll need to discuss this, and consult with our rabbi. We'll let you know when we decide what to do."

CHAPTER 32

ZEVI HAD INSISTED on taking Aviva out for a coffee, even though the last thing in the world she wanted to do right now was eat. The ride from the doctor's office had been completely silent, with Aviva struggling the entire time not to cry. She'd done too much of that in the past few days.

Once she was ensconced in a cushioned bench at a corner table at Coffee 'n Cream, the new café that had opened downtown, Aviva had to admit that Zevi had used smart strategy. Here in public, there was no way she would dissolve into tears. They would have a calm, logical conversation, weighing their options, discussing the what-ifs, the repercussions, all with cool, controlled emotion.

She sucked in her breath, as Zevi studied the menu. Her baby might have Down syndrome! No, she was going to cry, burst into tears right here in the middle of everyone, and there was one of her clients who just sat down three tables away, and she couldn't do this, could not, needed to get out of here *now*...

Zevi looked up at that moment. "Split an appetizer?" he asked.

Aviva's mouth dropped open. How could he be thinking about something so ridiculously inane when their world was about to fall apart? She quickly lifted a menu up to her face, to hide the tears spilling out, pretending to be intensely interested in which stupid appetizer her husband wanted to split—as if that was the biggest issue they had to think about right now.

Suddenly, tears dissolved into fury. She slammed down the menu.

"How can you think about food at a time like this? Don't you… don't you even *care* about what the doctor said? Doesn't it mean anything to you, that our baby might have…might be…" She bit her lip, unable to continue.

Zevi sighed. "Of course I care. It's…it's…" He waved his hand around, for once at a loss for words. "Well, terrifying to think of what might be." He paused for a moment. "But I don't see what we can do about it right now, other than daven that things should turn out all right." He picked up his menu once again. "And I happen to be hungry. Is that allowed, ma'am? Or do I have to go on a starvation diet until you give birth?"

Zevi's smile was so disarming that, despite herself, Aviva found her lips twitching through her tears. How did he always manage to hit just the right spot?

"No, you don't have to starve," she murmured with a half smile. "Go ahead and order something for me, too, and then you can eat both."

"Oh, I get it. Instead of you eating for two, I'm eating for three." He grinned. "I can get used to that."

Aviva shook her head, wondering how Zevi could so calmly give the waiter their orders while her insides were boiling into a churning, melting mass of goo.

When the waiter left, Zevi looked at her, his face suddenly turned serious. "Aviva, I've already made an appointment with Rav Biederman. You can decide whether you want to come along. We'll see what he says about doing the amnio." He picked at a slice of bread, crumbling it onto the table. "But, personally, I'm going to work under the assumption that our baby is perfectly healthy—until proven otherwise."

Aviva raised an eyebrow. *Just like that? He's decided that the baby is healthy, the fears unfounded, he'll play "let's pretend" for the next four months, and woo-hoo, things will be just grand?*

She frowned. *That's not the way it works, Zevi*, she wanted to say. *That's not the way I work.* But then she realized, *No, but that's the way he works. Isn't that the way he lives his life, the way he runs his printing business, the way he deals with responsibility? Smile, close your eyes, and hope that everything will work itself out?*

She clenched her fist around her water glass as she took a deep breath. She'd been wrong about taking the blame for his billing mess-up; wrong when she'd thought she should spare him facing the doctor. But this time she thought she got it. *Here's to being a good wife, Aviva.*

"Be'ezras Hashem," she said with a big, fake smile, even as her molten insides burned a hole through her heart.

FOR THE SECOND night in a row, Yael dreaded dinner with her husband. If last night she'd gotten away with being evasive, what in the world could she hope to say now? *"How was work, honey?" "Great! Fine! I quit! Have some meatloaf?"*

Her heart was thudding so painfully as Ephraim's return from *kollel* approached, that she couldn't help but ask herself why. Why should she be so nervous about sharing this with her husband? Wasn't he supposed to be on her team here? Support, encouragement, and all that? What, exactly, was she so worried about?

But the anxiety bubbles inside her stomach grew to full-blown hot air balloons by the time Ephraim had sat down at the table and thanked her for the French onion soup ("Wow! My favorite!"—as if she didn't know). She decided not to wait for his usual question, but just get it out before her stomach burst.

"Wanna know how my day was?" she asked, stirring croutons furiously around her soup bowl.

He looked up. "So, how was your day?" He smiled, and added, "Was just talking to Tatty today about you. Seems Chayale's Dovy needs OT, and Tatty was insisting she drive him out to your clinic, because you're the best." He winked.

Yael blanched. Treating her nephew would be so not good, on way too many levels to count. "He wants Chayale to make the trip here from Flatbush? But that's insane! And what in the world makes him think I'm the best?"

"Ah, you know Tatty's feeling about supporting family. I also told him that's ridiculous, but apparently he's really pressing the point with Chayale."

Yael took a breath. Here goes. "Well, tell him not to bother, because as of today I'm no longer working there."

Ephraim's soup spoon clattered onto the floor. He blinked several times rapidly, his hand still arrested on its way to his mouth.

"*Excuse* me?"

"You heard me right." Now that the words had been released, Yael felt her anxiety replaced with a sort of manic hysteria. "Ephraim, I had no choice, they hired someone new, didn't even tell me, it was so obvious they were trying to replace me, I wasn't going to wait around for them to fire me, better to keep my dignity and just leave, and so I did, this afternoon, and I don't regret it one bit! So far, at least."

Ephraim's body was still rigid as he stared at her, trying to absorb her fast flow of words.

"Slow down," he said, frowning. "You're not making any sense. Why in the world would they want to fire you?"

She felt tears prick her eyes as she said, "Isn't it obvious? It's because I'm just no good as an OT!"

"Why would you say something so crazy? You're an awesome therapist!"

"I'm not, I'm substandard!"

"Don't put yourself down! You're way above average!"

Yael felt her hysteria mounting. Why was he insisting on something he had no clue about? "How can you know that? You have no idea, you never did!"

But he refused to listen. It was as if he had to convince himself. Ephraim's face had gone from white to red, and he was now ranting at Aviva and Suri's gall in accepting her resignation.

"They're nuts! *Mamesh meshugeh!* Just wait till Tatty finds out! After everything he did for them! He's going to pull their funding, they know it, how could they have forgotten the condition—"
He stopped abruptly.

Yael stared. "Condition?"

Ephraim squirmed, eyes averted. "Nothing, wrong word. Just meant..."

But something shifted in Yael's brain, something that had never quite made sense to her...until now.

"So that's why they offered me the position in the first place?" she whispered. "Because Tatty made it a condition of his funding?"

Ephraim didn't answer. There was utter silence in the room for several moments, as Yael processed this—processed that everything she'd believed up till now about herself had been a total lie.

Finally Ephraim said, in a choked voice, "Yael, I don't think you've ever fully appreciated how fundamental your business success is to the way my parents view you…to the way they view *me*."

He paused. "One thing's for sure; whatever you do, you cannot let on a word about this to Tatty and Mommy."

CHAPTER 33

AVIVA DID NOT look herself. That was the first thing that Suri noticed, when she walked in for their early-morning meeting about the Yael fiasco. Aviva's eyes were red and puffy, and her skin pasty as if she hadn't slept all night.

"You look awful," Suri blurted. "Are you okay?"

Aviva gave her a curt nod. "I'm fine. Just out a bit too early for my taste. I had to ask Chavi for help getting everyone out of the house, and she did not appreciate it." Aviva bit her lip, as if she hadn't intended to say that last part, and then tried to laugh it off. "Teenage girls—you know how they are."

Suri laughed along, even though she felt she was doing a disservice to her Miri, who was always happy to help out. Then again, how much help did she need—her boys were already old enough to be self-sufficient.

It was time for a change of subject.

"So," she said, locking the office door and sinking down in a chair. "Yael. What do we do?" She'd decided last night that she would be careful not to assign blame. She wanted this meeting to be productive.

Aviva rubbed her temple. Despite her excuse, she still looked awful.

"Way I see it," she said, closing her eyes, "there are three issues at hand here. One, do we want to accept her resignation or insist she come back? Two, if she resigns, what does that do to us financially? And three"—she opened her eyes—"how are you such a *tzaddeikes* not to scream 'I told you so' when this was totally my fault?"

Suri's face grew warm. "Thanks," she murmured.

Aviva cleared her throat. "Starting with that second topic… Don't mean to be crude, but we do need to think about the monetary implications of her leaving. Up till now, we've had a real bonanza with Mr. Jeren backing us. We could never have built our building—never even gotten started—without his donations. So obviously if she leaves, that dries up. And that's not *pashut*."

"He even made it a condition of the donation," Suri added.

Aviva waved her hand. "That has no legal standing, I checked."

"What about *menschlichkeit?*"

Aviva narrowed her eyes. "Let's please remember here that we didn't fire her; she quit. How can he have *tainos* on us?"

Suri raised an eyebrow, and Aviva gave a short laugh. "Okay, so he *will* have *tainos* on us, of course." She sighed. "The real question is, how much do we try to bring back a therapist that isn't really up to snuff, just in order to get access to Daddy-in-law's cash?"

Suri rubbed her shoe against the floor, silent. The way Aviva put it, it seemed so clear what the ethical decision was. She sighed.

"I don't know. It still feels...how can we just accept her resignation like that? After all we've been through together? This clinic is hers as much as it is ours!"

Aviva raised her eyebrows. "In hard cash, it's a lot more hers. But in everything else? We both know whose soul and sweat has gone into building this, and it's not hers. In fact," she mused after a pause, in which Suri was forced to acknowledge the truth of her words, "I've often wondered how invested she really was in the clinic. How much she really wanted to be. She always came in just for her sessions and left right after, she never seemed interested in taking responsibility for any of the management or decisions, and even the one big event that she initiated—Senator Pearl—I was the one who actually coordinated it."

Aviva rubbed her forehead tiredly, and then said softly, "I'm not trying to be snotty here, honest. But, the truth—do you think, deep down, Yael might be happy about this excuse to pull out?"

꠹

THE FLOWERS WERE Aviva's idea. A classy way of saying thank you for everything. Suri still had misgivings about letting it go at that, at not pressing their point harder with Yael.

They'd tried. At the meeting, they'd decided to give Yael a chance to come back, to send her an e-mail telling her how much the clinic would miss her, how it wouldn't be the same, she belonged there, and so on. Suri had advocated for doing it in person, but Aviva thought making two house calls within two days was bordering on the ridiculous. A nicely worded e-mail was just the thing, she'd declared—and Aviva did it well.

Nevertheless, within a half hour, Yael's response had shot back, brief and sharp. *Thanks but no thanks. We all know you're better off without me.* As if she'd seen right through them.

Maybe they should've gone in person. Or maybe Aviva was really right about Yael. Deep down, Suri thought she might be.

It was all too confusing.

So they'd decided on flowers, a bursting, vivid bouquet, with a flowery thank-you note attached. But Suri couldn't help feeling that it was far too final a gesture, far too soon.

WHEN AVIVA STUCK her head into the office during her late lunch break, she saw Zevi had not yet arrived.

He'd been coming later and later in the past month; she knew he'd been putting in more effort than ever before on seeking out clients for his printing business—not just because he'd stopped making wisecracks about work being way overrated and was instead looking as overworked as Aviva herself, but because she'd come across a stack of receipts from the loan *gemach*, attesting to the fact that Zevi had been steadily making payments, chipping away at their fifteen-thousand-dollar debt.

Aviva had swelled with pride at the sight.

But, as Suri had hesitantly brought up just last week, before the whole Yael fiasco turned everything on its head, they'd reached the point where they needed a secretary to be adding hours, not cutting back. She appreciated so much how Zevi had jumped in when they needed it most, but perhaps it was time…

Aviva had heartily agreed. She'd long felt it was time for Zevi to go back to where he belonged, running his own business. And yet, now, walking into the empty office, she had to admit…she'd really been looking forward to seeing his grinning face.

At that moment, the door burst open and Zevi rushed in,

hand held protectively on his hat. His face lit up when he saw her. "Sorry I'm late. I was meeting with…" he lowered his voice, "the *rav*."

"Ahh." Heart hammering, Aviva asked, "And?"

Zevi hung up his coat. "I told him everything. And he said not to do any tests."

"Ah," she said again. No tests. No knowing.

Just this morning, Aviva had decided she would rather not know anyway. But now, suddenly, she had a desperate desire to *know*, to research, to prepare herself as much as she could.

Zevi seemed to read her mind. "This doesn't mean you can't learn whatever you want about Downs, just in case. All it means is that there's no *toeles* in our finding out for sure in advance—and, of course, nothing's ever for sure."

He sat down at the desk and turned to the computer, as if the conversation were closed. Aviva stared, wondering at his calmness…when she anticipated another four months of being a nervous wreck.

━

YAEL FELT LIKE she was moving through the world in a fog. Ephraim had still looked glum when he'd left for *kollel* that morning. He was certainly taking this even worse than she was, as if it had been he who'd been pushed out of his job. As he left, he reminded Yael yet again, "Remember, if my parents call—not a word."

As if she could forget.

And now she was faced with a whole day at home with her kids, which is what she'd been dreaming of for quite some time— and all she could think about was what a failure she was.

To think—the only reason she'd gotten the job in the first place was because her father-in-law forced them to hire her.

The only reason the Jerens wanted her for a daughter-in-law was because of her *chashuve* father.

She herself was…nothing.

The e-mail from Aviva and Suri came in the morning; she dismissed it immediately. They'd needed to assuage their guilty consciences, that was all. Of course they didn't really want her back.

As the day wore on, she grew more and more listless. The babysitter had come as usual; she didn't even have her children to distract her. It was just her own miserable self…

It was in the afternoon that the flower delivery arrived. At first, she was shocked by the huge bouquet.

And then, slowly, the despondent fog lifted for a second, making way for crystal-sharp vision. With a swift, angry gesture, she picked up the entire bouquet and threw it in the garbage.

CHAPTER 34

I
T WAS THE first Jeren monthly *melaveh malkah* since Yael had quit, and she'd been begging Ephraim all week to let her feign illness. But Ephraim wouldn't hear of it. The *melaveh malkah*s were sacrosanct—as she well knew. Rina had once shown up to one a mere hour after being discharged from the hospital with baby number four. And anything Rina did, of course, was the gold standard for the Jeren siblings.

Yet Yael couldn't shake the feeling that there was something else at play in Ephraim's insistence she come. That his obstinacy was, subconsciously, a form of punishing her. A way of saying, "you made your bed, go lie in it."

Though nearly four weeks had passed, her husband had still not gotten over it.

Her father-in-law was in a particularly expansive mood that night.

"*Nu*, how's the fashionista?" He turned to his eldest daughter. "I hear Ivanka's showing up to the inauguration in a Rina's exclusive."

Rina laughed. "Not quite, Tatty, but, *baruch Hashem*, the word's getting out in the right places. My designs are becoming crazy in demand."

Yael focused on her braised salmon. She knew from experience that Rina could keep up a conversation single-handedly for quite some time, and that was just perfect as far as Yael was concerned.

But after a few minutes, Rina got an emergency call from the babysitter, and Tatty Jeren, after smiling beneficently at the crowd, chose to zoom in on Yael.

"So, how's the clinic coming along?"

Yael reddened. Across from her, Ephraim gave her a slight shake of his head.

"Uh, fine," she stammered.

Her father-in-law grinned. "And the star OT, how is she doing? Getting lots of clients I bet, huh?"

"Oh, yeah," Yael said again. And she was. If you called the star OT Naomi.

She prayed silently for her father-in-law to move on to someone else—hey, hadn't Chayale gotten some sort of promotion recently?—but he seemed set on her.

"One of the best investments I've made," he said, leaning back, and Yael could tell he was trying to give her a big compliment. "Building that clinic—well, look how much good you all are doing."

Yael murmured some sort of assent. But something irked her about his words. Best investment he ever made—yeah, that was the one where he forced Aviva and Suri to give her a job. Where he decided to take her employment into his own hands, because apparently he didn't trust her to get a decent job herself. And no good Jeren should be without a good job.

But she didn't say a word of this, of course. Instead, she forced herself to smile, to throw out some vague line about all the children being helped, and to thank Tatty yet again for his generous donation to their center.

—

"HEY, I'M BACK! Missed me?"

Aviva, in the middle of cutting out paper dolls for her morning's first client, looked up, startled. Esti! Her mouth dropped open in horror. She'd completely forgotten today was the day her grad student came back. It had been such a nice, long break for finals and mid-semester vacation. Aviva tried furiously to remember just how long she'd agreed to do this mentoring for, anyway.

Esti bounced down on a beanbag. "So, what's been going on around here since I left?" She winked familiarly. "You've gotten bigger, obviously." Giggle. "It's any day now, right?"

Aviva glared. "Three months."

Another giggle. "Yeah? My sister, Sarah Leah, also has three months to go, but she looks..." She stopped herself almost in time. "Ah, well, I guess it's different if it's your first or your—what is it? Like, tenth? Eleventh?"

Aviva pursed her lips. She did not need this. Not this early in the morning. She turned back to her cutting without responding.

Esti jumped up. "Here, let me do that," she said. "Professor Feldbrand told us that this semester our hours should be much more hands-on."

She made a swipe at the scissors in Aviva's hand, resulting in the amputation of a carefully drawn paper doll leg.

Aviva closed her eyes, praying for patience.

"Oops, sorry about that! Let me tape it up." Esti scrambled up to search for scotch tape, as she continued her chatter.

"So I hear a lot's been going on since I've been gone. Fraidy tells me that Yael left. Gosh, *that* must've been quite a loss for you guys. I mean, her father-in-law donated the building and all! How long ago was this?"

Aviva swallowed. "About a month ago." Was she going to be forced to rehash every painful detail of the past month?

"Too bad. Though I heard the new OT's real good. Did Yael move to another job?"

"She…uh…decided she wanted to take some time to be home with her kids."

Esti nodded wisely as she carefully aligned the doll's leg to her skirt. "Makes sense. It's what we'd all do, if we had the money she does, right?"

Aviva wasn't quite sure what her honest answer was to that one, and she definitely did not want to think about it now. With a noncommittal grunt, she said, "Let me fill you in on our next client."

<hr />

AS MUCH AS Suri despised dramatics, she was very tempted to give her head a good *klop* against the wall. Dini Goldfeder had just left, and for the hundredth time Suri had tried and failed to wrap her head around the mystery of this girl. She'd suggested twice now that they drop speech and go try a psychologist instead, but Nechi refused outright. It was her money, of course, and Suri knew that the Goldfeders had enough to throw away on pointless therapy. Still, Suri didn't exactly enjoy doing pointless therapy.

She absently made her way down the hall, and almost bumped

into Naomi. "Oh, sorry." She blushed.

"No problem." Naomi flashed her a friendly smile, and Suri felt a pang of guilt. She'd been avoiding getting to know the new OT, had barely exchanged the barest of conversations with her since she'd come a month ago, and Suri knew she wasn't being fair. None of this had been Naomi's fault, after all, and if Suri still felt like crying each time she passed Yael's darkened OT room—the "We love therapy" drawings still arraying the walls back from Senator Pearl's visit—well, that was just something she would have to live with. She'd tried calling Yael several times over the past month, but Yael never returned her calls. Never even acknowledged the flowers they'd sent. It hurt, but if Yael was going to choose this method of coping, there was nothing Suri could do about it.

She made her way to the office. Empty. Zevi Heyman, surprise, surprise, was late again. She took off her glasses and wiped the sweat around her eyes. Yet another item on her list of uncomfortable to-dos. Zevi needed to be replaced with a full-timer, pronto, and she hoped Aviva would be okay with the news. She'd already hinted to her as much, and she'd kind of hoped Aviva would take the cue and do something about it on her own. (*Like what? Take the initiative and fire her husband?*) But Zevi was still clocking his three-hour days, and Suri, of course, was the one picking up the slack.

Sighing, she sat down at the desk.

"Anything I can help with?"

Startled, Suri looked up. She hadn't realized Naomi followed her in.

Be friendly. "Thanks. I'm just feeling stressed about a particular client. She's been coming for weeks, and I don't know, there's definitely something odd going on with her, but it's not the social-pragmatic issue her mom brought her in for, that's for sure."

Naomi sat down. "I know it's not my field, but if you want to fill me in, I'm happy to brainstorm with you. I firmly believe in collaboration between colleagues."

She said it with the type of confident conviction Suri could only muster for statements like, "I firmly believe there's a G-d."

So Suri told her all of Dini's history as she knew it, and she was surprised to find in Naomi a valuable, well, colleague—projecting the confident expertise of Aviva, but without that something that always made Suri squirm like a little girl.

Naomi listened quietly, and when Suri finished, she said, "Definitely sounds complicated. But—I have a thought." She turned to the computer and typed in a few words. She pulled up a page, then turned to Suri.

"Take a look at this. Does it sound like Dini?"

Suri moved over so that the screen was in view. Her mouth opened.

The heading on the page read, "Signs of bipolar disorder."

CHAPTER 35

HI, AVIVA! SURPRISE!"

Aviva, sitting in the office writing notes, looked up at the reception window and nearly fell off her chair.

"Naama!" She gripped the table hard, eyes rounding at the sight of her older sister. "What in the world are you doing here?"

Naama smoothed her perfectly set sheitel. "I happened to be in the neighborhood—an old friend of mine is making a *vort* tonight and she wanted my help with the setup—so I decided to stop by and finally see the famous clinic." She looked around at the colorful play area. "Nice, I love what you did with this space."

Despite herself, Aviva felt a glow spread over her cheeks. You'd think by her age she would stop needing her big sister's approval. "It wasn't me, we hired a decorator," she murmured.

"No shame in that," Naama said with a tinkly laugh. "Though you could've asked me. If I made the trip out for a friend, then of course for my sister—"

"Well, look who's here!"

The two women turned as Zevi walked in through the front door.

"Came to visit Aviva?" he asked, with a nod to his sister-in-law as he strode toward the office door.

She smiled. "I see I'm not the only one."

Zevi looked surprised for a moment, then laughed. Aviva narrowed her eyes, praying he would be smart enough to hold his tongue…

"Me? I ain't no visitor. I'm the secretary!"

Aviva closed her eyes as Naama laughed, clearly certain that this was a joke. But she opened them again to see Naama's expression flicker doubtfully as Zevi indeed made his way toward the reception desk.

"You're so funny, Zevi," Naama said. There was a question mark in her voice.

Aviva quickly stepped in. "Zevi has been working here for several months already as a clinic administrator. I don't know what we'd do without him."

"Ah, I didn't realize," Naama said delicately. "Administrator. Of course."

Zevi seemed on the verge of saying something more, and Aviva jumped up. "Can I give you the grand tour?"

"SO," ZEVI SAID, later, after Naama had blessedly left. "When did I get the promotion? I think I deserve a raise."

Aviva blushed. "You know Naama. I needed to say that."

Zevi stared at her for a moment, as Aviva felt her face grow redder. Finally, he said quietly, "Did you? I thought you got over it by now."

She sucked in her breath, stung. *Not fair,* she wanted to shout. *This is my family we're talking about, my perfect big sister.* But Zevi had never understood. Hailing from a big, warm, loving family himself, he'd never really grasped where she was coming from. Sure, he knew that a visit from her mother could throw her off-kilter for a week—but Zevi, with his laid-back, happy-go-lucky approach to life, couldn't possibly appreciate how deeply these family dynamics ran.

Instead of responding, she changed tacks. "By the way, while we're on the subject, I've been meaning to talk to you about this job." She forced her voice to sound steady, matter-of-fact; she wasn't quite sure how Zevi would take the news that they wanted to replace him. "All along this was supposed to be temporary, right? And Suri and I were discussing it the other day, we really need someone full-time, and—"

She faltered, taken aback by the way his expression suddenly hardened. "And, well, you've done so much, and we're so appreciative, but, *baruch Hashem* you're getting busier with your own business, and of course we can't expect you to give us so many hours, we figured it's high time we let you go back to doing what you're supposed to be doing, and we find ourselves a real secretary."

The words came out in a rush, and she looked at him anxiously. His face was impassive, though he flinched at her last two words.

"I see," he said, his eyes focused on the computer. Then he stood up abruptly. "You guys are on a roll, aren't you? First Yael, then me—replacing all the subpar staff..."

Aviva blanched. "Zevi, no, I didn't mean..."

He shrugged. "Sure you did. But it's fine. I never prided myself on my secretarial skills; I was just trying to help out."

She squinted at him. She'd often wondered why he'd jumped to take this on. "Is that really the reason?" she asked.

He raised his eyebrows. "What are you trying to imply?"

She shook her head mutely. She had no idea what she was trying to imply. Just that something about his eagerness to become their secretary had always seemed a bit fishy.

Zevi's cheeks were flushed. "Well, let me know when you find my replacement. Sorry for your sake that it didn't happen before Naama came and you had to suffer such a humiliation."

Aviva couldn't remember the last time Zevi had sounded so hurt. A terrible tightness gripped her inside. "Zevi," she pleaded in a small voice, "she's my sister." Couldn't he understand?

But he looked away, and she suddenly felt like crying, even as she tried to figure out what she'd said wrong.

———

SURI RUBBED HER eyes as she sat by her therapy table, nerves fluttering inside. It had been a long, long week. After her initial shock at Naomi's suggestion, she'd spent many hours researching bipolar disorder, including speaking to professionals, and she'd reluctantly come to the conclusion that Dini's symptoms aligned enough that it at least warranted further investigation. The psychiatrist she'd spoken to yesterday had been adamant that she encourage the Goldfeders to bring her in for an evaluation.

And now, Suri thought, her anxiety mounting as the clock ticked closer and closer to the Goldfeders' appointment, all that remained was for her to do just that.

She stood up, began pacing the room. She'd contemplated asking Aviva for advice, but had decided not to. First, because Aviva seemed kind of testy lately, and Suri blamed herself for that. She knew that Aviva had spoken to Zevi about leaving, and, picking up the vibes coming from both of them since that conversation, she felt terribly guilty about having made Aviva the bad guy. What had she been thinking, putting her in such a delicate *shalom bayis* position? Of course Suri should've been the one to tell him!

She caught a glimpse of herself in the full-length mirror on the opposite wall and made a face.

But it wasn't just that. No, she'd also been thinking of the last time she'd asked Aviva for similar advice—when her friend Tzippora had come in with little Ezzie and she'd suspected autism. At that time, Aviva had accused her, by implication at least, if not in so many words, of lack of confidence to do what's right.

And, Suri kept reminding herself, Aviva had been right. After all, look how that had turned out. Tzippora had been so grateful, Suri had come out looking smart and professional, and now, she'd recently heard, Ezzie was in a school for children with communication disorders and was thriving.

Maybe, a little voice inside her was whispering, *you can be the hero here once again.*

She started at the knock on the door. Heart racing, she ran back to her seat, calling, "Come in!"

Dini traipsed in. Today, Suri noted, she was back in her subdued Bais Yaakov mode. Nechi, who seemed to be in a better mood, perhaps because of this, stuck her head in with a little wave, and prepared to wait outside. But Suri called out to her.

"Just a minute! I...uh...wanted to talk to you about something."

With a slight raise of her eyebrows, Nechi walked inside. Suri hesitated, eyeing Dini. Though she hated asking her to leave, there was no way she could have this conversation in front of her. "Listen, Dini, I hope you don't mind, but I need to talk privately to your mother for a moment. Can you please wait outside?"

With a frown, Dini nodded and walked out.

Nechi crossed her legs and looked at Suri expectantly. "Is this another attempt to tell me what my daughter needs is not speech therapy?" She tried for a lighthearted smile as she said it.

Suri gripped her pen tightly. "Uh…yes. But this is something new. New information, that is."

She was finding it much more difficult to get this out than she'd anticipated.

"I…um…was talking the case over with a colleague, and she brought up a possibility that I hadn't thought of at all. And since then I've spent a long time researching this possibility, speaking to professionals in the field, and, well, they all feel that there may be something here."

Nechi blinked. "There may be *what* here?"

Just spit it out! She took a breath. "The suggestion was to get a psychiatric evaluation."

She stopped abruptly. Nechi had suddenly risen from her seat, her jaw clenched tightly.

"Oh no," she said. "No, no, no. I did not come here to hear this."

And with that, she stalked out of the room.

CHAPTER 36

SURI WAS DISAPPOINTED, but not surprised, when the Goldfeders failed to show up for their appointment this week. She had kind of been hoping that seven days' worth of reasoned contemplation would bring Nechi Goldfeder to her senses, or at least make her open to consider possibilities, but Shaul had laughed when she'd mentioned this hope (leaving out names, of course). Shaul, who was the most reasoned person she knew.

"People don't want to hear that a daughter of theirs has some messy psychiatric issue that will take a lot of effort to control and that they'll have to hide from their friends. Speech therapy is nice, polite. Safe. Everyone goes to speech therapy."

Suri reached across the table to clear his dinner plate. She had her seniors' group in another hour, though if it was up to her, she'd spend the evening curled up in bed. "Wasn't so long ago that even speech carried a stigma," she said as she stood up.

"Yeah, well, mental health problems have a much bigger stigma, and I can't see it going away so fast."

She sighed as she turned to face him. "You think I was wrong to bring it up?"

He raised an eyebrow. "Of course not. You needed to. If it's true, it could be *sakanas nefashos*. But—"

"I went about it the wrong way," she murmured, finishing the sentence he seemed unwilling to complete himself. "I should've eased it in a little more." She clenched her teeth as she began washing the dishes. "I messed up, didn't I?"

Shaul stood as well and walked over to the sink. "Why does your mind jump so quickly from analyzing a situation to taking full blame?"

Suri shook her head wordlessly, as she felt a lump forming in her throat. It was just too much, all these recent events back to back. Yael. Zevi Heyman. The Goldfeders. So many people angry or hurt, because of her.

She swallowed and blinked her eyes, as she whispered, "Maybe I should just go back to working at the Board of Ed. I never had all these problems there. I just did what I was supposed to, and everyone was happy with me."

Shaul took the dish from her trembling hand and began to dry it. "Hey, is that the goal here? To have everyone happy with you? Look how much good you've done with the clinic. Taking on a leadership role comes with responsibility, and not everyone's going to be happy with your choices. That doesn't mean you should stop."

She scrubbed a spoon silently for a moment, digesting this. "But what if they have a right to be upset? What if I made the wrong choice?"

"You mean, what if you're human?"

Despite herself, Suri gave a little smile. "So you think I shouldn't give up here, but should figure out the best way to convince them?"

Shaul placed the dried dish in the cabinet. "Sounds like a plan to me."

"Yeah." She sighed. "But first they have to agree to come back to see me."

AVIVA GLANCED AT Zevi from across the Shabbos table. Outwardly, nothing seemed wrong. He was singing the same exuberant, off-key *zemiros*, joking around with the kids as usual. He even complimented her on her blueberry kugel. (She wondered if he understood that she'd specifically made it for him; Zevi loved blueberries.)

Still, he'd never seemed so distant, and she sat at the table, staring glumly at her plate, until Chavi asked her what was wrong. "Nothing," she said, quickly perking up and trying to tune in to Zevi teasing Chaim into telling him what he'd learned that week in parashah.

Chaim, who'd struggled in school all his life, hated sharing anything school related, and no one but Zevi could manage to draw it out from him. Right now, Chaim was giggling, and Aviva knew that pretty soon he would agree to share his rebbe's *dvar Torah*.

An almost forgotten memory suddenly struck sharply. It was soon after they were married, and they had been invited to Naama's for Shabbos. Aviva had anxiously prepped Zevi for what he should expect and how he should prepare—much to Zevi's bewilderment. Above all, she'd insisted he come armed with a blow-their-socks-off *dvar Torah*—a *dvar Torah* worthy of the top-notch yeshivah bachur that he…wasn't. But that she desperately needed Naama to think he was. That, if she were honest, she herself desperately wanted him to be. Ashamed, she tried to convince herself that she had her future children in mind. *It's up to him to teach our sons Torah, to be their role model of a talmid chacham. So it's best he start now.*

Zevi tried valiantly that Shabbos, but whatever he'd prepared couldn't come close to Naama's brilliant *masmid* husband's Torah. Aviva had resolved never to accept a Shabbos invite from Naama again.

And now, after so many years, she was suddenly struck with an odd insight. Zevi's fun-loving, warm, and comfortable personality was doing a lot more for her sons' Torah learning than any brilliantly delivered *pilpul*. In fact, if Zevi had been that kind of father, Chaim would probably be too discouraged to open his mouth.

She swished a small piece of blueberry kugel around on her plate (she hated blueberries), as another odd thought arose: Was she…that kind of mother to her daughters? Worse—was she that kind of wife?

She sneaked another peek at Zevi. He'd barely alluded to their conversation the other day, other than to ask if she'd found a replacement secretary yet. She had placed an ad, she was scheduling interviews—but, unlike the OT hiring process, she realized that her heart was just not in it.

Maybe it was time to ask Suri to take over.

Maybe…

Her eyes suddenly popped open, and she gave a little jump in her chair. A contraction had hit out of the blue, full force.

Zevi stopped what he was saying, and looked at her curiously.

She shook her head, leaned back in her chair, wiped the sweat off her face. She'd never had that before, not in her seventh month.

She picked up her fork, tried to look normal as she waited for her heartrate to slow down.

And then—it happened again. She bit her lip, felt the sweat pouring out of her face. Zevi had gotten up, was walking over to her.

"What's wrong?"

She felt tears pricking her eyes, as fear rose up sharp and cold. "I…don't know. But I think maybe we need to go to the hospital."

SURI FELT A sense of déjà vu as she paced back and forth in her therapy room. It was Tuesday once again, and she felt even more anxious than she had two weeks ago, when she'd faced the big Goldfeder revelation. Now she had prepared once again to discuss the matter—but the big question was whether they would show at all. If they cancelled without notice two times in a row, she would have to assume that they were finished as clients. And then what should she do?

She jumped as she heard a knock on the door. No, it wasn't time yet for Dini's appointment. "Come in!" she called.

It was Esti, Aviva's grad student. "I'm sorry to bother you," she said, walking inside. "But I'm looking for Aviva. Has she come yet?"

Suri blinked. Oh no, they'd forgotten… "I'm so sorry, Esti, we should've called you. Aviva won't be coming in for a while. She's on bed rest."

"Oh!" Esti's eyes widened. "Oh, is everything okay? I mean, I guess it isn't if she's on bed rest, but, you know…uh…what happened?"

Suri shrugged. "She went into early labor over Shabbos. They managed to stop it, but now she's on bed rest until the end of her pregnancy."

Suri felt the same tightness rising up in her shoulders that she'd felt when she first heard the news. As if she didn't have enough stress right now, without having to single-handedly run the clinic.

"Poor Aviva," Esti said, shaking her head. "It must be so hard for her, not being able to move around." She brightened. "Hey, maybe I'll come over to her house to help out. I'm sure she could use extra hands right now!"

"That's very kind of you," said Suri, suppressing a smile. She doubted whether Aviva would welcome her grad student's help.

Esti waved a hand airily. "Oh, I love doing *chesed*!"

She left the room, and Suri resumed her pacing. Ten minutes passed, twenty, thirty, and Suri was just beginning to give up, when once again she heard a soft knock on the door.

Nechi Goldfeder entered, Dini trailing silently. "We came back," she said stiffly.

CHAPTER 37

NECHI SAT ACROSS from Suri, hands resting on the small therapy table. Dini sat next to her mother, hunched inside her hooded sweatshirt, staring at a spot on the wall to the right of Suri's head.

"...angry, I'll admit," Nechi was saying. "I mean, a psychiatrist, to treat a simple social issue! My husband..." She stopped, gave a slight grimace. "Well, you don't want to know what my husband said..." She paused for a moment, as if to allow time for Suri's imagination to conjure up the worst.

"But," she continued, "we decided to give you another chance. Dini enjoys coming..." She glanced over at her daughter, who squirmed slightly. "And, well," her voice softened, "at this point, you're our only hope."

Suri felt a tiny prick of pity at those words—but it barely registered compared to all the other emotions raging inside. She didn't get insulted easily, but this was beyond the pale. For a mother to sit across from her and say to her face that she considers her advice incompetent, but that they'll deign to give her another chance! She was so tempted to show her the door, to tell her she didn't need her favors, but she resisted. First, because Aviva's voice was screaming loudly in her head not to offend such an influential client. And second, because Dini's face hovered miserably before her, and she knew, even if the parents refused to admit it, that this was a girl in serious pain.

So she pasted on a smile, said, "I'm so glad you came back," and tried to pretend that her insides weren't steaming.

Nechi was still planted firmly in her seat. Suri raised an eyebrow at her. "Uh, shall we get started?" she hinted.

"Oh, yes, of course." Nechi looked flustered as she stood up.

I bet angry hubby warned her not to leave Dini alone with me, Suri thought, eyes narrowing. *Don't want any dangerous ideas suggested.*

But, if that were the case, Nechi didn't seem to know how to say this, so she hesitantly stepped outside. Suri took a breath and conjured up another bright smile.

"So," she said, turning to Dini. "How've you been?"

Dini finally shifted her eyes onto Suri's face. "Awful," she said. "You don't know what it's been like these last two weeks. All because of what you said."

Suri swallowed. How much criticism could she take in one morning? "I'm sorry," she murmured.

"They've been fighting something not normal," Dini continued. "Mommy saying that maybe it can't hurt to go see a doctor, and Tatty screaming that no daughter of his is gonna visit a shrink."

Suri nodded, not really knowing what to say. She felt like she was at one of her senior social groups, having all the ladies' life problems thrown at her as if she were supposed to have the answers.

Only here, she was the cause of the problem.

"I'm sorry I put you in such a difficult situation," she said again. "It must be tough, knowing they're fighting about you."

Dini shrugged. "Oh, they've been fighting about me for a long time, now. Ever since I started all my—you know, crazy behaviors."

Suri blinked. For all these weeks that she'd been treating Dini, their conversations had been safe and polite, sticking to neutral topics and never, ever alluding to the elephant in the room—even when that elephant was sitting across from her with pink hair and a nose ring. And now, suddenly, Suri's one misjudged recommendation seemed to move their relationship to a completely different plane.

"Ah, I see." *What do I say? I am not trained for this!*

But Dini didn't seem to need much encouragement. It was as if she'd been longing for this opportunity to finally open up. Her hands were twisting in her lap, and her eyes had shifted once more away from Suri's face, but still she kept talking.

"You don't know…it's been a nightmare, these past few months. Just…being me. And if you want to know why I've been acting so crazy…well, the craziest part of it is that I don't know. I just get these weird, wild moods and suddenly I want to, like, jump on the teacher's desk and pull off her sheitel. And the second an idea pops into my head, I'm doing it, just like that. My parents and teachers think I'm looking for attention. But what normal person wants attention like that?"

Dini's face was shadowed by her hood, but Suri saw her body trembling. Instinctively, she reached out and put a hand on the girl's shoulder.

"Do you…" Suri began hesitantly, trying to remember everything she'd researched about bipolar disorder. "Do you remember any specific incident that started this whole thing?"

Dini shrugged again. "No, everything's been normal. I mean… if you don't count the whole seminary thing, that's been really stressful, of course, everyone going nuts about where to go and will they get in. I was really nervous too…until, of course, I solved the whole thing by making sure I won't get accepted anywhere." Her mouth twisted sardonically.

Suri's heart melted… Poor, poor girl. And then her pity turned once more to anger. To think her parents were denying her the help she so desperately needed!

AVIVA STRETCHED OUT on her couch, magazine in hand. She gazed, bleary-eyed, at the article, rereading the same paragraph three times. Annoyed, she threw the publication on the floor. She'd never been a magazine person. She'd never been a lie-on-the-couch person either. She shifted restlessly.

Zevi, of course, had reacted Zevi-like to the doctor's instruction. "Six weeks of lying around doing nothing? Hey, Doc, can I go on bed rest too?"

He seemed to be viewing this as a big vacation, even stayed home a week from the office, to help her out, he said. But she didn't exactly see where the help was playing out. Zevi wasn't a cleaning-and-laundry type of person; true, he happily made dinner, but he didn't need to stay home all day for that. She suspected the real reason was that he didn't trust her to stick to her doctor's instructions.

Aviva shifted once more, drumming her fingers on the couch arm. Truthfully, she couldn't blame him.

She'd convinced him, after a week, to go back to work. "One

of us needs to be making money," she'd grumbled. And now, here she was, in a silent house, a house just begging to be put in order, and she was lying like a bump on the log. This morning, Chaim had shouted that there were no clean socks, and Kayla was wearing the same uniform shirt two days in a row. She would have to ask Chavi to put in some loads when she came home…but she did not relish seeing Chavi's expression at being given such a request. While she'd reacted blessedly maturely to the news of her mother's bed rest, Aviva knew it was only a matter of time before resentment reared its head.

She hated thinking of herself as that kind of mother.

Cautiously, she lifted herself off the couch. Just one quick load… How much could that hurt? Slowly, she stood up, took a tiny step, one, then another, imagining her baby hanging precariously inside, one false move and he or she would fall out. She took a few more steps, as she made her way downstairs to the laundry room. At least she'd had the foresight to ask Zevi to carry down the hampers. Now all she'd need to do is fill the machine and turn it on. How strenuous could that possibly be?

—

"AVIVA!"

It was several hours later, and Zevi had come home to find her once more lying innocently on the couch. After bringing her a drink and a slice of cake, he'd left the room…and apparently had an urge to head down to the laundry room, a place he visited maybe twice a year.

He stormed back up. "What happened to all the dirty laundry I brought down this morning?"

Aviva shrugged, tried to look nonchalant. "The kids were all out of clean clothes. I didn't want to put too much on Chavi. It wasn't a big deal." And, seeing the thunderclouds on his face, added, "I feel fine. Really."

"Aviva..." Zevi shook his head, but left the room without saying anything more. Relieved, she settled back on the couch. She'd gotten off surprisingly easy.

Until she got a phone call, twenty minutes later.

"What's this I hear about you being on bed rest?"

Aviva gaped at the receiver in horror. How had her mother found out?

"Zevi just called to ask if I could come help out for a while. Well, of course I'm happy to help, but why couldn't my own daughter be the one to ask?"

CHAPTER 38

BETRAYAL.

That was the precise and only word for what Aviva was feeling. She'd never felt so betrayed in her life—and to think it came about at the hands of her own husband.

She was reminded of that day Naama had dropped by the clinic. Zevi had never really understood about her family. He'd never fully appreciated how deeply her mother affected her, how much of who Aviva was had been shaped by the woman who would be walking through her door any minute.

That was the only possible justification she'd been able to muster for Zevi's epic act of betrayal. And it wasn't quite enough to get her to speak to him again for a very long time—at least until the baby was born. Or married.

Zevi, to his credit, had seemed to recognize at least a small portion of his mistake. The overwhelming panic that had taken hold of Aviva had been kind of hard to miss. And the fact that her instinctive reaction was to jump off her couch and race for her mop appeared to give him at least an inkling of how his scheme had backfired. With no choice, he'd grabbed the mop from her hands, and set to work cleaning himself.

Well, if it had been a miserable twenty-four hours for him, let that be just a fraction of penance for the misery he was about to inflict on her.

Mommy had not mentioned how long she was planning to stay, which sounded ominous. She was perfectly capable of moving in for the duration of the pregnancy—and weeks after, as well—if she suspected Aviva couldn't manage without her. Mommy didn't work; she'd spent the better part of her life being the perfect homemaker and mother. Once her children left, she had no career to fall back on, so she'd taken to volunteering instead. Aviva had often suspected that her mother regretted never having invested in a career. Someone with her energy level must find her quiet house stifling. That was probably why she'd encouraged her daughters so strongly in building their own careers.

Aviva glanced around the room. Zevi had certainly not done anywhere near the cleaning job she would have done, but it was at least passable. And it would have to do. Besides, she knew very well that the moment Mommy stepped through the door, she would have her gloves and apron on, polishing the house until it shone. Yes, she had no doubt her house would fare well over the next few weeks.

The question was whether she would survive.

"WHAT'S UP, MOMMY? You've been really out of it recently."

Suri stole a glance at Miri, sitting next to her in the car. Miri, her good girl, had willingly given up her afternoon off of school to go visit her grandfather. (The rest of the school was busy with last-minute production practice, but her daughter... Ah, but she wouldn't go there.)

Suri shrugged. No sense in pretending; Miri was too perceptive for that.

"I'm just preoccupied with a client of mine," she said. "Frustrated, really. I think she needs a different kind of treatment...from a different kind of professional...and her parents refuse to consider it."

"Why not?"

How did she explain that one? "I'm not really sure," she said carefully. "But sometimes, people are worried about how they appear to others. And they might not get the help or the diagnosis they need, because of the fear that others will find out."

Suri gave another quick glance to her right. Miri was shaking her head. "Aren't people ridiculous?" she said, with a world-weary sigh.

Despite herself, Suri couldn't help but smile. "Yes, they can be sometimes."

Miri twisted in her seat. "So, what are you going to do about it?"

"What can I do? I'm not her mother."

Miri was silent, and somehow, Suri had the impression that she was failing her daughter. That Miri had expected more of her, had expected her to fly out in a red cape and save the day.

You've got the wrong mother for that, honey, she thought. *I'm no superhero.* Just safe and steady, quiet Suri, doing her job, keeping the peace, making sure everyone's happy.

Except for Yael, of course. That incident had been far from peaceful. Though, now that the dust had settled, she was beginning to admit that it might have been for the best after all. Naomi was an excellent OT, and she was attracting many new clients. In fact, things were on such an upswing, they were even beginning to talk of expanding the clinic's services, bringing in a physical therapist, maybe some psychotherapies like art or music. And that was aside from their urgent need to hire a new speech therapist, to take over Aviva's caseload.

And then there was their new secretary. Aviva had asked Suri to take on the job of finding Zevi's replacement, and she had been only too happy to agree. "I should have been the one to deal with this from the beginning," was her awkward way of obliquely apologizing for causing friction between Aviva and her husband. And yes, it had been extremely uncomfortable informing Zevi that he was officially let go…but Shira, their new full-time secretary, was a gem. Her presence was changing the entire tone of the office, giving it a more professional feel, and also removing so much of the stress Suri hadn't even realized she'd been carrying around.

And, a small voice inside her was now saying, if those two examples of stretching beyond her comfort zone had proven correct in the end…maybe Hashem was sending her the message that it was time to try for a third?

"…are you even listening?"

Suri blinked. "What, sweetie? Um…sorry, were you saying something?"

Miri pursed her lips. "I was just suggesting that maybe there's someone else you can get involved who can help this girl. You know, like a *rav*, or a teacher, or someone like that. 'Cause you can't just leave this alone, Mommy. You can't do that to her."

Slowly, Suri nodded. "That might be an idea."

IT WAS AN idea that percolated for several days, until the next Goldfeder session arrived—the session that was quickly becoming the focal point, if not the obsession, of her week. But if Suri thought last week had brought surprise revelations, it was nothing to what was in store for her today.

"I have good news for you," Nechi began as she strode into the room.

Suri's mouth dropped open. "You mean you've decided—"

"—to give her something that can help her out, yes." While Nechi's voice was full of confidence, she wasn't quite meeting Suri's eyes.

Suri's brow wrinkled. "I'm afraid I don't understand. Something that can help her out?"

Nechi nodded briskly. "We've started Dini on Ritalin."

Suri stared at her. That was the last thing she'd expected her to say. "Ritalin? For what?"

"For her hyperactivity, of course. Isn't this what you've been going on about for months? That she needs some other kind of treatment? Well, here you go." Nechi's chin was tilted upward, as if to say, *Look what good parents we are.*

At a loss, Suri swiveled from her to Dini, trying to regain her footing in a conversation that seemed to have driven suddenly off course.

"Um, have you started the medication yet?" she asked Dini.

"Just yesterday. I'm still waiting to see if there's any effect."

Though Dini was taller than her mother, she always seemed diminished, somehow, when standing next to her. Now, however, she looked hopeful as well. Suri rubbed her eye under her glasses, frowning. There was something strange about this sudden shift... but, she supposed, if they'd done what they were supposed to...

"Well, then, great!" she said brightly. "Good for you for taking care of that. Which psychiatrist did you go to?" She wondered if it was one she had spoken to.

Nechi's shoulders stiffened. "We didn't go to a psychiatrist," she said coldly.

CHAPTER 39

AND THEN SHE tells me that they didn't go to a psychiatrist!"

There was a pause on the other end, and Aviva, cradling the phone by one ear as she rested her head on the arm of the couch, imagined Suri shaking her head in disbelief.

"I was so confused, I didn't know what to say. Was it a different doctor who prescribed it, then? I thought you needed a psychiatrist to diagnose—but I could be wrong, I have no experience…"

Aviva gave a sharp laugh, and her mother, hard at work polishing the *sefarim shrank*, turned to Aviva with a raised eyebrow. Blushing, Aviva turned her face and lowered her voice.

"Suri, don't be so naive. Nowadays there are ways to get Ritalin without a prescription."

The pause was even longer this time. Aviva pictured innocent Suri working to digest this.

"Without! But…but that's so dangerous!" Suri spluttered.

"Why would anyone be so irresponsible? To play around with her health!"

Aviva nodded grimly, though she knew Suri couldn't see her. "Scary what some people do to maintain an image."

"Maybe they researched it or something," Suri said. "Found that Ritalin could help exactly her set of symptoms."

Aviva's lips curled. "Ya think? Or maybe it's a lot safer to think your daughter has plain old ADHD, like half the world today, than to actually bring her to a doctor and risk getting a much scarier diagnosis."

Aviva chewed her lip. "It might be worth doing some research ourselves on this Ritalin business. Give me a sec, let me get my laptop."

She sat up and stretched across the couch to reach for the laptop lying on the coffee table.

"Don't you dare!"

Aviva jumped at her mother's voice, and sprang back onto the sofa. How in the world had Mommy even seen her, up on the stepladder with her back turned?

"You just sit where you're supposed to, young lady. If you need something, that's what I'm here for." She shook her head as she climbed down from the ladder and walked over to the table.

But Aviva had suddenly lost her appetite for the research project. "On second thought," she managed to squeeze out to Suri, through her constricted throat, "maybe you should look it up yourself."

YAEL STRETCHED HER arms out across the park bench and tilted her head back, enjoying the sunshine. Sruli was climbing up the slide yet again, while Simi was happily squishing sand through her fingers. She glanced at her watch. Ten more minutes, and then they'd head home. It was time to start on dinner.

The thought of dinner brought her husband to mind, and suddenly Yael's face clouded. These past few months that she'd been home had actually been idyllic—if you didn't count Ephraim's still bitter disappointment, and the fact that they hadn't had a normal conversation since she'd quit. Used to be, he'd ask her about her day, and be genuinely interested in what she was doing. Now, he immediately began speaking about himself, the latest news in the *kollel*, shul happenings, or—always—his family.

If Yael brought up what she'd done that day, it had to take the form of, "Listen to the adorable/brilliant thing our kids said." Never about the project she'd done with them, the cookies they'd baked together. What kind of accomplishments could she possibly boast of, just taking care of the children?

"Your mother was a stay-at-home mom all her life," she'd once blurted out.

Ephraim had stared at her, bemused. "My mother has always spent her time volunteering for organizations."

The crazy part was, he didn't even seem to realize he was acting any differently. The only time he actually brought up her job situation was before they visited his parents, when he felt the need to remind her, yet again, not to let on that she'd left the clinic. She wondered just how long they could keep playing this charade. Ephraim appeared to be wondering as well, as he became tenser with each visit.

Yael stretched again. Time to start gathering the troops. Just as she started to stand up, her phone rang. She glanced at the screen and her eyes widened. Fraidy, her old grad student? What in the world?

Putting on her peppiest voice, she said, "Hey! Long time no speak! How's it going?"

She closed her eyes as Fraidy's voice washed over her in response. She genuinely hoped the girl wasn't calling with a million OT questions about some project or other. She didn't think she had the strength.

But after going on for several minutes about how much she missed Yael, Fraidy finally came to the point.

"I was wondering if you could do me a favor. It's actually, well, regarding your mother."

SURI SAT AT her therapy table, head resting on her hands. She'd done some online investigating, as Aviva had recommended, and it turned out Aviva was right about the black market Ritalin trade. In fact, it seemed downright easy for anyone looking for a lift to get himself some pills.

But that wasn't the scariest part. No, what was rattling her up so much that she could barely walk straight, let alone think straight, was what she discovered after researching Ritalin and bipolar disorder. Not that she knew this was what Dini was suffering from—but just in case. And she read the results, her eyes widening in horror. *May have severe effects... During a manic state, taking Ritalin can bring on a psychotic episode...*

Trembling, she pictured poor Dini Goldfeder, taking the meds at her parents' insistence, so piteously hopeful that maybe this was the answer—and in reality she was very possibly playing with fire.

Suri lifted up her head and slammed a fist onto the table. "I could be dead wrong," she whispered to the silent room. "But I'd feel so much better if she was at least under psychiatric supervision."

She sighed, lowered her head once more. That brought her to the question of what to do. And she'd come to that decision late last night. Now, it was just a matter of working up the courage.

She'd considered consulting with Aviva again. But Suri didn't think it was fair to keep disturbing her bed rest. Look at how quickly Aviva had gotten off the phone yesterday, as if she'd tired herself out with the call. Besides, while Aviva was still definitely doing whatever she could remotely, Suri, as the only on-site partner, had suddenly taken over the role of calling the shots. It was not a role she would have ever imagined herself filling...but slowly, she was beginning to feel more comfortable in this position of authority. More than comfortable—she was even starting to relish it.

And if she, as clinic administrator, decided that it would be unconscionable to not do whatever she could to save Dini...well, then, it was up to her to act decisively and confidently, for once in her life, rather than running to Aviva for approval.

She stared at her phone, sitting on the table. *Just do it.* Picking it up, she dialed the number she had gotten off the school's website the night before.

"Can I please speak to Mrs. Savetsky?"

She'd expected to be told that now wasn't a good time, that the principal was busy, but to her surprise, within a few minutes she heard a warm, clear voice on the line asking, "How can I help you?"

"Uh, hello, this is Suri Taub. I'm a speech therapist at Big Bounce Therapy Center, and I'd like to speak to you about one of your students that I'm working with."

There was a slight pause. "Big Bounce?"

"Uh, yeah, we're a child development center located in—"

"I'm familiar with it, yes."

"Oh...um...good." Suri gave an awkward laugh. "Anyway, if you have a moment, I'd like to consult with you about a student in your school. Her name is Dini Goldfeder..."

The phone call was over in a matter of minutes, and Suri hung up feeling quite satisfied. The principal had certainly seemed to take her information seriously. They'd been banging their heads against the wall, at the school, over Dini's sudden behavior change. Suri hadn't quite intended to mention her suspicions, but somehow the word "bipolar" had emerged. She'd been impressed with Mrs. Savetsky's calm and intelligent handling of the call, and they'd ended with the principal agreeing to try to reach out to the parents, and promising to be in touch.

As she placed her phone back in her purse, Suri found herself smiling for the first time in days. *You might have just saved a life.*

CHAPTER 40

YAEL DRUMMED HER fingers on the kitchen table as she watched Ephraim, eating silently across from her. He had just finished updating her on the Jeren Pesach plans: Mommy Jeren decided she wanted to try out a new program in Italy, and Rina was all excited at this opportunity to bring her fashion line to the European market.

Yael frowned at her chicken. Italy sounded nice, but in her opinion, it had nothing to do with Pesach. And she was definitely not interested in enduring an entire week of avoiding questions about her job. Besides, he seemed to have forgotten that this was her parents' year.

Ephraim was humming softly as he chewed. Her eyes narrowed.

"So, how was your day, Yael? Oh, Ephraim, how lovely of you to ask. We went to the park, the kids had a fabulous time."

Ephraim lifted his head to stare at her, eyebrows puckered, mouth slightly ajar.

"Really? I'm so happy to hear you're taking such good care of our kids," she continued the one-sided dialogue relentlessly. "What other wonderful childcare activities did you do? Why, how sweet of you to notice! We also went to the library and read books together. Afterward they colored a picture. Sruli has real talent, I think."

Ephraim's mouth was still agape, and he was squinting as if trying to figure her out. Finally, he said, "Uh, how was your day? Or…did you answer that already?"

Yael sighed, but her lips twitched. Clueless. How could he be so clueless? "Actually, I got a phone call from Fraidy, my old grad student, of all the odd things."

"Yeah?" Anything to do with the clinic made him perk up. "What did she want?"

Yael shook her head. "Nothing to do with me. It was my mother she wanted. She went to Machon Bayla for high school, and wants me to put in a good word for her. For *shidduchim*," she added, at Ephraim's confused look. "People are going to call Mommy as a reference, but Fraidy's scared Mommy doesn't really know her well. And there was some silly thing about getting in trouble one year over a Purim prank… Didn't sound too dramatic to me, but she's convinced Mommy hates her over it." She rolled her eyes. "Mommy probably doesn't even *remember* it."

"Still, I guess you should make the call, if this girl asked you to," Ephraim said. "Why don't you do it now, before you forget?"

Yael's stomach tightened, as her mind translated: *Do it now, Yael, instead of procrastinating like you usually do. We Jerens understand that the mark of a successful businessman is taking care of jobs right away.*

Sourly, she picked up her phone and stalked out of the room.

"Hi, Mommy."

"Yael! Sweetie, I was just thinking of you. I spoke to someone the other day who mentioned your clinic."

"Oh, really?" Yael said, warily. She had told her mother in vague terms about her decision to leave the clinic. What kinds of things was her mother hearing now?

"Yes, it was about one of the therapy patients there, a student of ours. I know it's been two months since you left, but I wondered if you might be familiar with the case. It's a very delicate situation."

"I doubt it. I would've noticed if any of my clients were from Machon Bayla. Besides, I wouldn't be able to discuss it with you anyway, unless I had the parents' permission. Confidentiality, you know."

"Oh, of course." Her mother sounded a bit surprised, and was silent for a moment.

"Anyway, Mommy, I'm actually calling about another student of yours…"

AVIVA GNAWED ON a fingernail, as she listened, from her perch on the couch, to dinner taking place in the dining room. She hadn't chewed her nails since she was a kid, but since her mother had moved in, the old habit had suddenly returned.

Their weekday dinners were generally eaten in the kitchen, as the kids had tried insisting to their *bubby*. But Bubby was adamant that dinner was a formal affair, for the dining room, with china. She'd been horrified to hear that Aviva had slipped into using disposables during the week.

"Even for your *husband?*" she'd cried. Zevi, who had been in the room at the time, had made such a droll face behind her mother's back that Aviva had to hold herself back from laughing. Which was lucky, because, usually, her mother made her cry.

"You can't let her get to you so much," Zevi told her one night. "She means well. Just, you know, let those criticisms roll right off you."

Let the criticisms roll right off her? She'd stared at him in utter shock. Was he joking?

"You're just still feeling guilty for inflicting this on me," she'd said.

"You bet I am," he'd shot back, and, for the first time since her mother had arrived, Aviva had actually smiled.

But Zevi wasn't home right now to lighten the tension, and from what she could overhear, things were not going so well in the dining room.

"Chaim, we use a fork and knife, not our hands. Kayla, take your elbows off the table. Tzippy, here we eat everything on our plate, whether we like it or not. *Chaim!* What did you just call your sister?"

And, above all, were her comments directed at Chavi. "Chavi, go get some more napkins. Chavi, Tova needs help cutting her fish. Chavi, quick, go feed Kivi! He's trying to feed himself, and I don't want to think about what a big mess that will make!"

"Mommy lets Kivi feed himself," Aviva could just make out Chavi muttering. Which wasn't technically true; she only let Kivi feed himself when she was too worn-out to fight with him over it. Aviva could picture the scene perfectly: Chavi rolling her eyes mutinously, and Mommy pursing her lips, furious. It almost made Aviva want to rush in and rescue her children...but she didn't know what exactly she could do about it.

Besides, the thought of the barrage of criticism she herself would be subject to for doing that made her quail.

Instead, resolutely shutting the dinner conversation from her mind, she turned to her laptop. *Let's focus on a different worry*, she thought as she opened up the documents she'd been painstakingly cutting and pasting from her research. Down syndrome. There was a massive amount of literature out there on the disorder, and Aviva had set for herself a goal of reading it all. To be fully educated and equipped...just in case.

She soon became so absorbed in her reading, that she didn't hear the footsteps coming up behind her.

"Down syndrome?"

Aviva gave a little jump as she turned to find her mother standing there, a full plate in her hands.

"Here's your dinner." Mommy spread a placemat on the coffee table, and placed the dish on top of it. Then she put her hands on her hips. "Would you care to tell me why you are reading up on Down syndrome?"

SURI WALKED THROUGH the clinic hall with a bounce in her feet. Ever since she'd spoken to that principal, she'd felt so lighthearted, as if a huge weight had been removed. She'd done her job, passed on the information to someone who could help, and now, it was out of her hands. She still had the parents' reaction to deal with—oh yes, she knew there'd be a reaction, though she hoped Mrs. Savetsky would keep her word about not revealing their conversation. Nevertheless, she felt she'd done the right thing—as opposed to the easy thing—and she was so pleased with herself for that.

She'd even confessed uncharacteristically, in her senior social group last night, about how proud she was for having overcome her fear and taken a step that was difficult, and all the elderly women had been so supportive and complimentary that she'd come home glowing. Who knew how much of her newfound confidence was owing to those wonderful ladies?

Beaming, she stuck her head in the office. "How's it going, Shira?" she asked the new secretary. It was such a pleasure, having someone sitting at this desk that she could rely on to be on top of things. She always felt a pang of disloyalty toward Aviva when she thought that, but it was true nonetheless.

Shira looked up. "I have a message for you. From a Mr. Goldfeder."

Suri's heart started hammering. Here it came.

"He said he has something to tell you, and he wants to do it in person. He's coming by tomorrow afternoon."

Shira paused.

"And he didn't sound happy."

CHAPTER 41

THE DICE HOPPED on the table as Shayna Klein took her turn at the therapy game she and Suri were playing. The young girl moved her piece around the board and lifted a card, showing it to Suri.

"The opposite of 'quiet,'" Suri read. She furrowed her brow exaggeratedly. "Hmm…"

A knock on the door and Shira's head sticking in made Suri look up, startled. The secretary knew not to interrupt unless it was something urgent.

"Excuse me," she said. "But Mr. Goldfeder just arrived and he wants to speak with you."

Suri's stomach fluttered wildly, but she responded with a measured voice. "Tell him I'll see him after I finish with this client."

Shira's cheeks flushed. "I'm sorry, Suri, but I tried telling him that, and he…uh…*insisted* that you see him now."

Now Suri was annoyed. Who did he think he was? Sighing,

she put the game card down on the table. A man like him, he'd probably barge into the therapy room if he felt he was being kept waiting too long.

"I'll be back in a few minutes," she said to Shayna and her mother as she hurried out the door.

During the short walk down the hall, Suri tried to collect her confidence. She would be calm, cool, professional, no matter what he said. He was the one at fault here, willfully ignoring his daughter's needs. She had nothing to be ashamed of.

She stepped into the waiting area. Two mothers were sitting quietly, their children playing next to them. Where?

"Mrs. Taub."

She swiveled around to see a large man wearing a well-cut suit stride toward her.

"Hello, Mr. Goldfeder," she said quietly. "I'm in the middle of a therapy session right now, but if you could wait ten minutes…"

"No, I cannot wait even one minute," he said, his voice rumbling like an oncoming storm. "Believe it or not, Mrs. Taub, my time is very valuable. I would not have come out in the middle of a workday if the issue at hand weren't so burning."

She blinked. "Yes, of course," she said. "But, as someone who values time, I'm sure you can understand that to keep a client waiting, in the middle of a sess—"

He suddenly slammed his hand against the wall, and she stopped, eyes wide.

"Don't you stand there acting the good little professional with me!" His cheeks bulged as his voice rose ten notches. "After what you did to my daughter!"

Suri felt her face growing warm. She couldn't look at the mothers in the room, whom she was sure were listening avidly.

"Mr. Goldfeder, why don't we step into a room," she said quickly.

"Oh, suddenly you care about *privacy*," he sneered, his face purple. "Suddenly you worry about *confidentiality*! Didn't occur to you, did it, when you went spreading rumors about my daughter to her principal and teachers! Didn't stop and think, *Is what I'm doing ruining a girl's reputation? Am I ruining her life?*"

Suri's insides were crumbling fast, and she stood unmoving, eyes rooted on Mr. Goldfeder's face as he spewed forth his rant. *Defend yourself!* something in her brain was screaming. But she couldn't even move her lips, let alone think of words to say.

"Well, even if you don't care about my daughter, maybe you'll care about this!" He took a step toward her. "What you did, calling her principal, was not only inhumane and cruel—it was also illegal. Yes, Mrs. Speech Therapist, I should think you'd have known that. And don't think I'm going to let this rest."

He took out his phone, waved it in her face. "Mrs. Taub, one phone call. That's all it will take. One call to my lawyer. And I will sue you and your clinic for every penny you're worth."

Suri's breath caught in her throat, as he spun around and walked out the door.

SHE DIDN'T KNOW how she made it through the rest of the day, but somehow Suri stumbled through, not talking to anyone other than clients, not even catching anyone's eye, head down, speech therapy on autopilot, just finish, finish, until at last, blessedly, she found herself alone in her car. And she let herself breathe for the first time since Mr. Goldfeder's appearance.

Okay, Suri. She tried to pull out a thread of sanity through the cholent of thoughts swirling in her head. *He was bluffing. Obviously. He wouldn't really sue you for making an innocent mistake when you were trying to help his daughter.*

She pressed her forehead onto the steering wheel. *Sure didn't seem like he was bluffing. Nor that he thought she was trying to help.*

Deep breath. In, out. *He's a frum Jew. Would he really take another Yid to court? Destroy our business?*

She bit her lip. The way he acted today, she wouldn't put it past him. And suddenly rage rose inside, sharp and furious, rage at how he'd stalked in and humiliated her like that in front of everyone, rage at how he dared accuse her of ruining his daughter's life when it was *he*—and she didn't know if she was more angry at the thought of what such a powerful man could do, or more terrified.

She sat up abruptly and stuck the key in the ignition. What she did know was that she couldn't handle this alone. She was going to Aviva's.

Twenty minutes later, she was sitting in Aviva's living room, sipping the iced tea that Aviva's mother had brought her with a gracious smile. A thick slice of cinnamon cake was sitting on a pretty china dish on the table.

"Your mother's so sweet!" Suri exclaimed. "How nice that she's here to help you!"

Aviva gave her a rather strained smile. "My mother's a very good hostess," she said, and then changed the subject.

"It's so good to see you, Suri." The warmth in Aviva's voice took Suri by surprise, until she reminded herself that it must be lonely, stuck at home for so many weeks. Remorse flooded her. What kind of friend was she, not even thinking to come visit until she had a problem?

Suri tried to smile back, but the muscles in her face were

working funny. "Same here… I miss you. We all do." She realized suddenly how true that was.

She took a breath. "Aviva, I'm sorry I dropped in like this, but I need your advice. We had an…uh…unpleasant incident at the clinic today."

Aviva frowned. "What does that mean?"

Suri stared at the glass in her hands. How should she say this? "It means…" And before she knew it, words were tumbling out, the whole Goldfeder story, from beginning to miserable end, and it felt good, oh so good, to finally relieve herself of the crazy tension that had been building up for weeks, to know that she had someone to share her fears with.

Aviva was silent throughout the entire story, and remained silent for several moments even after she was done. Suri's eyes were still focused on her glass of iced tea, so it was only after the silence had stretched too long that she looked up and saw Aviva's expression.

She was glowering almost as much as Mr. Goldfeder.

"Suri," Aviva said, her lips white. "What have you done? My gosh, what have you done?"

Her voice was rising to a screech, and Aviva's mother called out from the kitchen, "Everything okay?"

"Fine, Mommy." She lowered her voice to a whisper, but it sounded even more deadly. "Suri, you understand what this means, don't you? We are ruined. Finished." Her hands were trembling.

If Suri had felt terrible before, it was nothing to how she was feeling now.

"Aviva," she tried squeaking out. "It's not the end of the world."

"Oh yes, it is!" Aviva glared at her. "Breach of confidentiality, Suri? That's, like, the ABCs of the therapy business. Once this gets out, no one will want to come to us." She raised a hand to her forehead. "We worked so hard, building this up, so hard…and now, with one stupid mistake…it's all over."

She looked at Suri, and the sharp glance was as good as words: *This is all your fault.*

———

YAEL TIPTOED OUT of her sleeping kids' room and picked up her phone. Before Ephraim came in, she would take advantage of the quiet moment to call Fraidy, tell her that she'd spoken to her mother just like she'd asked.

Look at you, Mrs. Super-on-Top-of-Things. She couldn't help smiling.

"Yael!" Fraidy squealed. "You called to get the scoop?"

Yael blinked. "Scoop? What are you talking about?"

Fraidy gasped. "You mean you haven't heard? It's, like, what everyone at the clinic has been talking about, all day! Listen to this…"

CHAPTER 42

AVIVA ACHED TO do something—run a marathon, cater a dinner for a thousand. Anything that involved getting off her stupid couch, out of this prison that her own home had become. And ever since Suri's news, the longing had become that much more desperate. Here her business was on the verge of collapse, and instead of marching forth to fight for it, she was stuck at home, impotent, worthless, with her mother breathing down her neck anytime she so much as scratched her nose.

She was texting Suri ten times an hour, but so far nothing more had come from Goldfeder's visit. As one day passed, and then another, she slowly allowed herself to hope that maybe the man really had been bluffing.

Which was a relief, to be sure—but she was still stuck in her jail cell.

She couldn't even continue her research project, not after that day her mother had discovered her reading up on Down syndrome.

She'd gotten away with the excuse that it was for a client, but she couldn't risk it again.

So now she was stuck with nothing at all to do. And facing endless weeks of more of the same.

She'd rather be in active labor.

"Aviva! Why in the world do you still have this clothing?" Her mother stalked into the room, several hangers' worth of dresses draped over her arm.

"Mommy!" Aviva spluttered. "What were you doing in my closet?"

"Getting started on your Pesach cleaning," she responded calmly. "From the looks of it, you haven't done this closet in years. Really, do you ever expect to be a size six again?" With a stern look, she folded the clothes into a box labeled "*Gemach.*"

Before Aviva could respond, the doorbell rang. She gasped. Suri. She'd come to show her the court summons in person. Heart thudding, she waited for her mother to answer the door, straining to listen.

The next second, she frowned. The high-pitched giggles she was hearing in her front hall were definitely not Suri's. Yet they seemed familiar, and were stirring up a vague feeling of irritation. As the voice came closer, her eyes widened. No. It couldn't be. Not in her very own house. But a moment later, Esti was bounding into the room, with a great big smile.

"Vivs! Surprise!!"

She did not just call me Vivs. Aviva closed her eyes, willing this to be a dream. But when she opened them, Esti was still there, beaming way too close to her face.

"Soon as I heard you were on bed rest, I told myself I'd come over to help you out. Took me a little while—life is just crazy busy, you know. Well, I guess not for you, right now, but, well, for the rest of us!" She winked and laughed.

Aviva wanted to punch her.

Instead she said, with whatever graciousness she could muster, "How thoughtful of you."

"Oh, it's nothing." Esti waved airily. "I love doing *chesed*. I was head of the *chesed* committee in twelfth grade, you know." She jumped up, looking around the room. "Hey, you too!" she cried, pausing by her mother's cardboard box. "What kind of *gemach* are you collecting for?"

"Clothing," Aviva's mother said smoothly, as Aviva was momentarily speechless. "I'm getting started on the Pesach cleaning."

"Really?" Esti's eyes brightened. "I love Pesach cleaning! Can I help?"

Aviva's mother smiled kindly at her. "If you don't mind, I'd appreciate the assistance."

This was just too bizarre. As the pair started walking off, Aviva quickly called out, "Not in my closet!"

⌐

"A LOVELY GIRL," Aviva's mother said. She was repeating the story of Esti's visit yet again, this time to Zevi, who was grinning bemusedly at his mother-in-law's enrapturement.

"She promised to come back tomorrow," her mother continued. "She said she'll come every day until we finish the bedrooms."

"Not *my* bedroom."

The adults turned as Chavi swept into the living room.

"I'm not having some strange girl go through my stuff." She picked up a magazine and plopped down onto the couch, next to Aviva.

Aviva's mother pursed her lips. "Did you finish washing the dinner dishes?"

Chavi groaned. "Soon, Bubby. It's been a long day and I need to relax." She turned a page of the magazine.

Aviva didn't need to look at her mother to see the expression on her face.

"I would also like to *relax*, but I understand that my responsibilities come first," her mother said in a clipped voice. And then, "It would be nice to see you mature a bit, Chava. Be like this Esti girl."

Aviva saw Chavi's face go red, and her heart constricted. She knew what it was to be on the receiving end of her mother's criticism.

And though she herself had expressed similar sentiments to Chavi many times in the past, anger suddenly arose out of nowhere—deep, rippling anger. *No! I will not let Mommy do to my daughter what she did to me!*

"That's not fair, Mommy," she said quietly, though she was quaking inside. "Chavi's a wonderful girl."

Her mother turned to her, eyebrows hitting the ceiling. "Oh? Or maybe you just don't want to admit where your *chinuch* failed?"

Aviva took a sharp breath, stung, as tears welled up. And then she felt a hand on her arm. It was Chavi.

Blinking hard, she covered Chavi's hand with her other one. "No, we haven't failed at all. I hope all my children turn out as beautifully as she has."

She smiled at her daughter, who gave her a wide smile back. Zevi—count on Zevi—began to clap and whistle. Her mother stormed out of the room.

SURI MESSED UP. *The clinic's in trouble.*

Ever since Yael had learned about the incident from Fraidy, her mind had been filled with little else. All she could see was this Mr. Goldfeder shouting at Suri in front of everyone, accusing her of—how had Fraidy put it?—ruining his daughter's reputation.

Suri messed up.

And though she felt bad for Suri, she truly did, she'd be lying if she didn't admit that a little voice inside was saying, *So I'm not the only one who fails.*

"...private beach. And close to Milano. High fashion central. Rina's going crazy, Mommy says."

"Mmmm." Yael blinked, trying to draw her mind back to the present, as she gave a quick glance at the hotel website Ephraim was showing her.

"...and Chayale and Zahava are both planning..."

"Ephraim. It's my parents' turn this year."

He stopped and looked at her. "I know. I was just saying..." He gave a wistful look at the screen.

"You said you love Pesach at my parents'."

He turned away. "Yeah. I do." He closed the website and sighed. "Anyway, who am I kidding," he murmured. "Spending an entire Pesach with my family would be torture right now." He stared down at the desktop. "Which reminds me... I...uh...about the *melaveh malkah* this Shabbos. Don't take this the wrong way, but it's probably easier if you don't go."

Yael's mouth dropped open.

Ephraim was scratching at a sticky spot on the stained wood desk. "I know I said it was better to keep pretending everything's normal, but as time goes by it's getting more awkward, you know? And it's simpler to just give an excuse why you couldn't come than to sit there fielding questions all night."

And to worry that I might say the wrong thing, Yael finished for him.

She narrowed her eyes. "How exactly are you expecting this to end? Are you waiting for me to just one day get my job back? Or will we keep on pretending until I'm ready to retire?"

Her husband shook his head slowly, his face strained. "I don't know," he whispered. He clenched his hand as he turned to look at her. "I…I know you think I'm being a baby about this," he said, and Yael sucked in her breath.

"But I don't think you get it. You can't get it, coming from a family like yours."

In all their years of marriage, Ephraim had never once spoken negatively about his upbringing. Yael gripped the handles of her chair.

"So explain," she said eagerly.

But he just shook his head. "I…can't explain it." His shoulders suddenly straightened, as if he was pulling himself back together after his unseemly moment of weakness. "Doesn't matter anyway," he said tersely. "All I know is, whatever it takes, we can't let them know we've failed."

Generous of him to use the *we*.

"Whatever it takes," he repeated, and that strained expression gripped his face once more.

Yael stared at him, felt that same tension taking hold of her—that same feeling of being utterly trapped. And, then, all at once, it came to her, in one glorious moment of inspiration.

The solution to all their problems.

CHAPTER 43

YAEL SAT AT her kitchen table, alone. In front of her was her phone and a bag of potato chips. Every half a minute, she picked up her phone, hesitated, and put it back down. Then she took another handful of potato chips.

Inside, the voices resumed their argument.

How could you?

How could you not?

You're a horrible person!

You're brilliant!

You're stuck, but good.

No arguing that one, buddy.

She'd been rehashing the same inner dialogue for the past half hour. The chip bag was almost empty.

Stuck but good. That, Yael knew, was the beginning and end of it. She was trapped, she and Ephraim, trapped in an untenable situation that she had placed them in and her husband saw no way out of. And, though he hadn't said it outright, she knew that he was deeply disappointed in her. It was that, more than any worry about her in-laws, that was driving her to carry out her plan. Her inspired stroke of genius. Her perfect way out. All it would take was one phone call.

So what if it was a low-down, nasty thing to do? Aviva and Suri hadn't acted the same toward her?

It's for shalom bayis, Yael. Isn't that one of the highest values?

She stuck her hand in the chip bag once more, but there was nothing left. She gritted her teeth and picked up the phone.

"Hi, Tatty? It's Yael speaking."

"Yael!" her father-in-law exclaimed, clearly surprised. She couldn't blame him; she could count on one hand the number of times she'd called him on her own. "Is everything okay? Why are you calling in the middle of the workday?"

Yael closed her eyes. "That's what I wanted to talk to you about. I wanted to...um...consult with you about something." She dug her fingernails into her hand. "There's been an...uh...incident going on, and...I've decided to leave the clinic." She spoke the words carefully. Technically, both statements were true.

"What are you talking about?" Tatty Jeren asked sharply.

"An incident which was unprofessional," she said vaguely.

"Unprofessional? Do you mean illegal?"

She should have known she wouldn't get away with vague.

"Um, no—I mean, well, yes, actually—but not, you know, illegal in, like, tax evasion or...or insurance fraud, or something you get hauled off to jail for. I think." She stopped, confused. Could you get thrown in jail for breach of confidentiality?

"Talk straight," he said. "Are you in trouble?"

"N-no, not me personally, it didn't involve me."

"Who, then?"

He was the consummate hard-nosed businessman, Zalman Jeren, and when he set out to achieve a goal, there was no escaping nor evading. Certainly not for his weak-willed, jelly-legged, insecure daughter-in-law.

And that was why, without ever intending to, she found herself relating the entire story as she'd heard it, down to every last name and detail.

"But how can I tell you the name of the client, if that was the whole problem?" she protested weakly.

"You said he came and shouted in front of the whole clinic. The story's public knowledge now."

By the time they hung up, her father-in-law was fuming at Aviva and Suri, particularly when it emerged that Goldfeder was a friend of his. ("Not another cent from me!" he shouted.) He also praised Yael highly for taking the high ground and knowing when it was time to get out. ("Always knew you had moral backbone," he said proudly. "Don't worry, there's plenty more places that'll be jumping to grab a star OT like you.")

After they hung up, Yael crinkled the chip bag into a tight ball and hurled it at the garbage can. Moral backbone, indeed.

EPHRAIM CAME HOME that day from *kollel* in a particularly good mood. And she didn't have to wait long to find out why.

"Yael! You did it!" he cried, and he drew out from behind his back an oversized bouquet of flowers.

Unbidden, the memory of another outlandish bouquet, and what she'd done with it, rose to her mind. But she forced a smile. *I did this for him. For us.*

"How beautiful! What's the occasion?" As if she didn't know.

"I spoke to Tatty today. He told me how proud he is of you, standing your moral ground, and that he perfectly agrees with the fact that you needed to leave that clinic environment. I couldn't make out all the details of what he was talking about, but it doesn't matter. The point is, you came up with some great story, and it worked!" His face was glowing, brimming with relief.

She tried to laugh naturally, to look as if she, too, were just bursting with joy. "Yeah, I came up with something."

"Whatever it is, it sure had Tatty all worked up. He said he was furious, that he would never support them again." Ephraim's face clouded momentarily. "I tried calming him down. I didn't want the others to suffer, you know, because of, well, whatever it was you said." He shook his head. "Then again, those two women certainly caused you to suffer."

"Did it work?" Yael asked hopefully. "Did you manage to calm him down?"

He shrugged. "Don't know. Was kind of hard, considering I was very in the dark about the story. And Tatty, not only was he upset, he said Mommy was even more upset. That she was planning on spreading the word around to everyone she knew, what an unprofessional place it was." He looked at her, his cheeks reddening. "Did you, um, totally make something up here?"

Yael quickly shook her head. "No, I didn't make anything up."

"Oh. Okay." He left it at that. Yael suddenly felt a surge of pride in her husband, who, unlike his father, had no interest in prying into someone else's scandalous story.

He was beaming once more. "I think this calls for a

celebration. How quickly can you get a babysitter?"

As Yael picked up her phone, she tried not to think about what it was they were celebrating.

—

SURI DREW A steeling breath before entering the clinic, just as she had every morning since the big Goldfeder outburst. *Just look straight ahead, walk, one foot in front of the other, pretend you don't see them, pretend all those mothers sitting in there aren't all looking at you, whispering, wondering.*

Even back in her lonely childhood days, before she'd learned how to make friends, she'd never felt this isolated. No one was on her side. Aviva's reaction had been a huge blow, and she'd come home in such an emotional state that she'd told Shaul she was ready to leave the clinic. If Aviva thought Suri had ruined everything, then, fine, Suri would step aside and let Aviva straighten it all out herself. She'd go back to working at the simple old Board of Ed.

But even as she'd said this, Shaul had raised a questioning eyebrow, and Suri had realized it would never happen. After having tasted what it was to run her own business, she couldn't just go back to being a regular employee.

So instead she'd forced herself to go back to work the next day, trying to convince herself of Shaul's reasonable words that it was only, after all, three or four people who had overheard the outburst. How far could this have spread?

As a few days went by and, it seemed, Mr. Goldfeder hadn't carried through on his threats, Suri began to admit that maybe Shaul was right. Maybe this was a one-time, highly humiliating incident which would die a natural, scandal-free death.

It didn't stop her from being paranoid each time she walked into the clinic, though.

She rubbed her eyes under her glasses as she entered her therapy room and closed the door. Home base. Safe. Now she could spend the rest of her day talking to lisping five-year-olds, and try to forget she had ever had a client named Goldfeder.

She jumped as the door opened.

"Hi, Suri, hope I'm not interrupting."

It was Shira.

"No problem. Come in."

Shira's face was puckered in a frown as she walked inside. "Have there been any new developments in that Goldfeder case?"

Heart hammering, Suri shook her head. "No, why?"

"Because this morning, all of a sudden, we've gotten a bunch of e-mails from clients wanting to know if the rumors they've been hearing about our clinic are true."

CHAPTER 44

I'M NOT GOING back. I mean it. Not. Going. Back."

Suri was holed up on her couch, wrapped in a blanket, as Shaul stood next to her, a helpless look on his face.

He had just come home from shul and broken the news that word was out. Men had come over to him, some he barely knew, and asked if it was true that the clinic was under threat of closing because of illegal activity.

"Illegal activity!" Suri's cheeks had paled. "They make it sound like we're trafficking drugs! This was a mistake, a simple mistake!"

"I told them not at all, and asked where they heard such a rumor. But they just said it's going around."

She'd groaned, and sat shakily down on the couch. This was in line with those e-mails Shira had received today. Somehow, word had gotten out. Had Goldfeder, who up until now had chosen to remain silent, decided it was time to go public?

And then Miri had walked into the house. "Hey, Mommy, is everything okay?"

"I'm fine," Suri had said. "Just feeling a bit tired."

Miri's eyebrows were creased. "No, I mean…well, I just heard some of our neighbors talking. Something about the clinic being in trouble."

That's when Suri had lost it. She'd cocooned herself on the couch, telling them all to leave her alone, and there she'd remained, all evening, until the kids were asleep and Shaul had now finally, tentatively, confronted her.

He watched her silently for a moment, listening to her emphatic declarations, until at last he said, "Do what you want, but you know that hiding is not the answer."

"Sure sounds like a good answer to me." Her voice was muffled from inside her blanket.

He settled himself next to her on the couch. "Well, it isn't. If you stay away, that will be feeding into all the rumors and then some. Everyone will assume they're all true, that the clinic really has been engaged in something terribly illegal."

"And isn't that what they think already?"

"No, they have no idea. It's simply more exciting to spread the most extreme scenarios. But your behavior over the next few days will prove or disprove whatever it is they're saying."

There were a few seconds of silence as Suri digested this. Slowly, she lifted her head out of the blanket. "And so I'm supposed to just walk into the clinic with my head high, pretend that everyone in the community *doesn't* think I'm some lowlife… lowlife cri-criminal—" The words were stuck in her throat, and suddenly, she was crying, tears dripping onto her blanket. How in the world had this happened? To her, of all people! Plain, quiet, unassuming Suri Taub, whose entire goal in life had always been to lie low and keep everyone happy?

"I'm not cut out for this," she mumbled, after her sobs had subsided. "Someone like Aviva, she could do it well. I can just see her sweeping through the crowd with total poise—but me? I can't, Shaul, I can't!" Tears were starting to spill out once more.

He turned to her. "You're a lot stronger than you think, Suri." He bent down to catch her eye. "I've been telling you that for years."

Tears were still leaking out, but quietly now. Suri rested her head against the armrest for several moments. It was Shaul's quiet confidence in her that ultimately won out.

"I'll do it," she said at last. "I'll go back."

IF SHE'D FELT uncomfortable entering the clinic yesterday, it was nothing to how she felt today. She half expected to find a horde of journalists waiting for her outside the building. And while, in reality, the outside of the clinic was just as quiet as usual, and the inner waiting room contained the same handful of mothers it always did, she was absolutely certain that those mothers were throwing her suspicious looks.

Let them stare, she told herself. *I've done nothing wrong, other than try to save a girl's life.*

But oh, was it hard to know people were staring!

Yet, as the morning wore on, she acknowledged that Shaul was right. It was far, far better coming to work and pretending nothing had happened than closeting herself in at home. She even found herself getting a secret pleasure out of each mother's discomfort as she walked into the room with her child, looking like she wanted to ask something but didn't know how. And as Suri smoothly moved right into the therapy session, she saw the mother's shoulders slowly sag, her face relax, and Suri knew she had scored a victory.

By her lunch break she was actually feeling quite good, and was able to smile at the mothers she passed in the waiting room on her way to the office.

"How's it going, Shira?" she asked brightly.

Shira was just hanging up the phone, and her face was dark. "That was Mr. Goldfeder's attorney. He just sent someone to the clinic, to deliver something."

Suri swallowed, as her good-mood bubble suddenly popped. "Deliver something?"

"I'm guessing it's not flowers," Shira said drily.

It was only fifteen minutes later—though it felt like hours—that they heard a sharp tap on their office door.

"Hello, I'm from the office of Benjamin Rothstein." The man gave a brisk nod to the two of them as he walked in. "We represent Mr. Samuel Goldfeder. I'm delivering this on his behalf to Mrs. Suri Taub. Which one of you…?" He looked between the two women.

For one wild moment, Suri was tempted to play dumb, to put on an accent and pretend she was the cleaner. But Shira gave her away by pointing in her direction.

"Mrs. Taub." He strode over and handed her a crisp, white, very legal-looking envelope.

"Have a good day," he said as he left.

"Good day. Ha, ha," Shira sneered at the closed door.

But Suri stood frozen to the spot, staring at the envelope.

ONCE MORE, SURI was standing outside Aviva's door. Once more, she would have to go in and give her bad news. But this time, she could not even look forward to sympathy and support, the way she'd hoped for the last time she'd come.

She wished more than anything she could just go home and pretend this was all a bad dream. She wished she didn't have to involve Aviva at all, that she didn't have to face her as Aviva accused her of ruining everything they had built.

And the worst was that this time, she'd be absolutely right.

But she had no choice, because the therapy center was listed as the defendant in this lawsuit, which meant that Aviva had as much of a stake here as she did. Which meant it was now Suri's distinct honor to walk into Aviva's home and announce to her that she was being sued.

She took a breath, gathered all the courage she could muster, and rang the bell.

To her surprise, it was Esti, Aviva's grad student, who answered.

"Hi Suri, nice to see you! Aviva's in the living room! Can I get you a drink?"

Suri blinked. What in the world was Esti doing playing housekeeper in Aviva's home? She could just imagine what *that* must be doing for Aviva's temper.

But, to her surprise, Aviva looked cheerful. "Thanks, Esti," she said, as Esti led Suri into the room and left. (She almost expected her to curtsy.)

"That girl was heaven-sent," Aviva said fervently.

Suri gave her an odd look. Had so many weeks on bed rest begun to affect her brain?

"You're…uh…happy she's here helping you?" Suri asked carefully.

Aviva grinned. "Because of her, my mother's starting to think about leaving. She actually trusts Esti to keep the place running here!" She laughed and, though Suri wasn't quite sure what she was referring to, she laughed along.

Then Aviva's smile died down. "What's happened?" she asked.

Suri took a breath. No use pushing it off with strained small talk. She pulled the envelope out of her purse and handed it to Aviva. Aviva grabbed it, quickly pulled out the papers and read them, her face turning white. Suri watched her, bracing for the onslaught, wondering what she could possibly say in her defense.

At last Aviva looked up, and suddenly Suri knew exactly what she could, and should, say.

"Aviva, I'm sorry. I messed up. And I know you're angry with me, and you have every right to be, but…I need your help here."

Aviva blinked a few times. Her lips were white, but slowly, as if it cost her an effort, she nodded and said, "Suri, you made a mistake. We…we all make mistakes. Don't worry. We're going to fight this and win. It'll be okay."

CHAPTER 45

"L ISTEN, I KNOW a good lawyer." Zevi had his phone out, and was scrolling through his contacts.

Aviva tried not to roll her eyes. "Some guy you schmooze with in the cubicle down the row? 'Cause I need someone tops, not some two-bit—"

"He's tops," Zevi said, touching his screen. "Here. Phil Handelman. Partner at Handelman and Associates, or something like that. Not a cubicle in sight at his firm, unless you're the copyboy."

Aviva was still suspicious. "How do you know about him?"

Zevi grinned. "Oh, I got my connections. Here, take a look."

He handed her his phone, which displayed a website for Handelman and Associates, specializing in medical malpractice. "See that landscape in the background? That's the view from his high-rise corner office. That good enough for you?"

Aviva couldn't help but laugh, despite the incredible stress she'd been under ever since Suri's visit. It had only slightly begun to dissipate once Zevi had arrived home. Warning him to brace himself for terrible news, she'd told him about the lawsuit. To her horror, he had actually laughed.

"Is that all?" he'd exclaimed. "I thought someone died or something!"

"All?" she'd cried, prepared to launch into a huffy tirade against people who cared so little about their own businesses that they couldn't appreciate when someone else's... But she'd stopped herself. Because, looking at Zevi, it had suddenly hit her: *He does care. He cares so much—about me—that he's trying to make me feel better by joking about it.*

And the realization had made her smile so broadly that, incredibly, she actually did feel a little better.

Now, she said, "But if he's such a hotshot, we'll go bankrupt just paying his fees, even if we win."

Zevi waved his hand in the air. "Liability insurance, my dear. This is what it's for."

Aviva's eyes widened. "You're sure legal fees are covered? Because if not..."

"Yeah, pretty sure. And if not, we'll take out a loan. Don't worry."

"Don't *worry*?" she spluttered. "A *loan*? Loans have to be paid back!"

"Not to bring up bad memories, but who paid back the entire *gemach* loan, way *before* it was due?" He thumped his chest.

She shook her head. "We're talking much more than a small *gemach* loan. If this isn't covered, we'll be paying it off the rest of our lives!"

"Aviva." Zevi held up his hand, as his expression suddenly

changed, softened. "You've put your life into this business. I'm getting you the best lawyer there is, and if it comes to it, I'll worry about the money."

Aviva stared at Zevi, as a hard-to-decipher emotion welled up inside. She was suddenly reminded of why she'd wanted to marry him, so many years ago.

She brushed the thought aside. This was no time for emotions; she needed cool business logic right now. She took a breath. "Okay, so you'll call this Phil Handelman, and ask him to take on our case? Make sure to check he's experienced with these kinds of lawsuits, because it's important to—"

"Lawsuit?"

Aviva's face whitened. She hadn't noticed her mother walk into the room.

"What's going on here? Is someone suing you?" Her mother's face was as white as her own, and she stood in the middle of the living room, hands on her hips, as if demanding answers.

Aviva gave a little shrug.

"Zevi!" her mother exclaimed, as the silence stretched on. "You tell me! Why are you talking about lawsuits? Something terrible's happened, I know it, and you two are deliberately keeping me in the dark!"

Zevi put on his most affable grin. "Don't worry about it, Ma. It's nothing, really. A client is suing the clinic, but it's nothing a good lawyer can't handle. This happens in every business."

"Every business?" She raised her eyebrows. "No, only the ones that fail. And from the sound of things, you're headed there. I heard you talking. A loan, that'll be staggering. You'll never be able to dig yourselves out from under such debt."

Aviva felt her entire body sag. Everything was buzzing around her, all she could see was her mother's cool white face, and her lips moving, and an angry buzzing cloud emanating from her, a cloud that was filling Aviva's lungs and making it so hard to draw air.

Her mother's lips pursed, and her eyes glinted in satisfaction, as if she had just given a lecture on the ways of the world to the children in front of her. Now, she sighed elaborately. "I suppose Tatty and I will have to bail you out. You'll probably be asking us at some point, so we might as well have it out now. How much?"

Dimly, Aviva saw Zevi's mouth open angrily, she saw him starting to rise from his chair, shaking his head vehemently, proudly— *We're fine, we don't need your help*—but Aviva raised her heavy hand to wave him back down. *She's right, Zevi. I'm a good-for-nothing, I hadn't thought, hadn't done anything properly, and now it's all self-imploding, and it's all because of me...* Every single mistake she'd made since opening the business flashed before her now, all the times she'd failed.

Her face was flushed, she felt her insides contracting, as she allowed the force of her mother's words to wash over her. Zevi was staring at her, eyes narrowed, and he was shaking his head... He was also disappointed in her, they all were... It was an actual, physical pain, and tears sprung to her eyes. All these years, when she'd tried to pretend that she was fine, she was perfect, that her mother's predictions were wrong—at last, the ruse was up. Her mother, her husband, and, soon, the entire world would know that Aviva Heyman was nothing more than a great big failure.

Her sheitel strands were growing damp from the sweat on her forehead, and the pain was becoming unbearable. Both of them, her mother and Zevi, seemed to be waiting for her to speak, but what should she say? What could she say?

She stole a quick glance at Zevi. He gave her a small, encouraging smile. She closed her eyes. That smile... She could almost hear his voice saying, *Don't let her get to you.* But how could she not, when her mother was only speaking aloud the words that were storming inside her own head? She put a hand to her temple, to try to quiet the noise.

And then she asked herself: Whose voice was that, whispering those menacing words inside her? And she realized: not her own… It was her mother's voice she was hearing, both inside and out. She listened again. What did her own voice have to say? What did she herself really think?

Aviva squeezed her eyes tight. She thought of the clinic, all their clients…of Zevi…the kids…Chavi…*failure*? She shook her head. And came up with: Aviva Heyman. Not perfect. But succeeding regardless.

She opened her eyes. And somehow, drawing on strength from deep, deep inside, from the very place where she was feeling her pain most intensely, she looked straight at her mother and said, "Thank you, Mommy, but we don't need your help. We're not failing. The clinic has been a success, *I've* been a success, and just because we're going through a rough spot right now doesn't mean we're finished. I'm strong enough to get through this and win and go on to do even better things." She took a breath and tried to steady herself—oh, how badly she needed her strength right now.

Her mother had a small, amused smile playing at her lips, as if delicately doubting everything Aviva was saying. Finally, she said, "Hmm. If you say so. It's nice to dream, of course. But, forgive me, you've always had your head in the clouds. Reality's important too."

Stung, Aviva looked at Zevi, whose fists were clenched, as if ready for a fight. Aviva took a breath—oh, how she wished this pain would go away!—and said, as calmly as possible, "I'm not saying I'm wiser than you, Mommy. Just that, maybe, it might be easier if you trust our judgment and leave us to take care of things on our own."

Her mother's cheeks suddenly flamed. "What are you saying? You don't want me around? That I should go home?"

Zevi spoke up. "We really appreciate all the help you've given us. But, yes, I think we're okay handling things on our own now."

It took several more moments of excruciating silence, but at last, her mother said, "Well, I'll go pack, then," and left.

Zevi gave Aviva a huge double thumbs-up. "You did it!"

She tried to smile back, but could only wince. "Zevi," she said quietly. "This is crazy, but I think I'm in labor."

CHAPTER 46

B EEP, BEEP, BEEP.
Noise, so much talking, screaming, shouting, questions, answers, more beeps, more screams—hers?—breathing in, out, in, out, past her endurance.

—

"A BEAUTIFUL LITTLE boy! Congratulations!"

Aviva, lying on her hospital bed, threw a quick glance at Zevi before nodding her thanks to the doctor who'd just entered her room. It was a mere few hours after delivery; the nurses hadn't even brought her baby back to her yet. She could read the question in her husband's eyes: *What was the pediatrician doing here?*

"Mind if I sit down?"

Now Zevi was raising an eyebrow back at Aviva, as he pulled out a chair for the doctor. He sat back down on his own chair, and began twisting his tzitzis around his finger—a sure sign he suspected what was coming. As for Aviva, she didn't suspect; she knew. Knew as soon as the doctor walked into the room. Really, she'd known even before that—known the minute the baby was born, from the way her obstetrician's mouth twisted as she gave Aviva a smile that did not quite reach her eyes; from the looks on the nurses' faces as they quickly removed the baby and whisked him away for cleaning. And all these long hours, as Aviva lay in her hospital room, resting, watching Zevi make gleeful phone calls to their family, she braced herself for the announcement she knew was sure to come.

Now here he was, Dr. Reimer, their longtime pediatrician, who had been there from their very first appointment with Chavi, when he'd patiently answered all Aviva's anxious questions about diaper rashes and burping and baby laundry detergents. He was shifting uncomfortably in his chair as he spoke. "Don't worry… thirty-six weeks…full term…he's small, but big enough…" When he reached the words "beautiful, adorable," he stopped and cleared his throat, and Aviva knew it was coming.

"I believe your OB had mentioned the, ahem, possibility, a while back, of the baby having trisomy 21."

Zevi's face puckered in momentary confusion, but Aviva nodded.

"Downs," she whispered to Zevi.

"Precisely," the doctor said. "You opted not to do further testing at the time." He cleared his throat again. "Your baby was born with clear physical indicators that he does, indeed, have Down syndrome. We'll do a blood test to confirm the diagnosis, but I think at this point we can be fairly certain." He stopped, and looked at the two of them.

Aviva felt the strangest sensation, as if she had left her body and was viewing this scene from somewhere near the ceiling, staring down at the players. Stage right, concerned doctor, leaning forward in chair. Stage left, mother in bed, eyes wide in horror. At her side, devastated father, speechless and trembling.

Zevi's face was white, whiter than she could ever remember, and he looked like he was struggling not to burst out in strong emotion. *Don't get angry, it's not the doctor's fault*, she wanted to tell him, but she couldn't speak, hovering up there outside of her body.

Then Zevi asked a question, and she realized it wasn't anger he was trying to suppress, but tears. And that rattled her so badly that her consciousness popped right back inside her head.

"It's okay," she said to him, pleading, because if there was one person she needed to be strong, it was her husband. "We knew all along, that this might happen. It's what Hashem wants."

Zevi's mouth opened in shock, and he turned away, as if he couldn't even look at her. *He blames me*, Aviva thought desperately. *He thinks it's my fault, that I should have done...something, I don't know. Should have wanted this baby more...* But there was no way in the world she could go there, and once again she felt herself rising up out of her body, into this new, blessedly calm, spectator state. She watched herself gather her wits, take a breath, turn to the doctor, eminently cool and in control—every inch Aviva Heyman.

"We'll need to start therapy right away. I've done research, I've already looked into which therapy approaches work best for children with Downs." She lifted her chin. "We're going to give him the best fighting chance possible."

Dr. Reimer blinked. "Uh, certainly, of course. All in good time. But first, it might be wise..." He hesitated, looking from Zevi, whose head was now down in his hands, to Aviva, sitting up straight in her hospital bed, though she was a mere several hours after birth.

The doctor stood up. "I'll have the social worker come in soon to speak to you. Any questions—and I'm sure you'll have plenty, once the dust settles—please don't hesitate to call." With a last look at the two of them, he left the room.

AVIVA HAD JUST finished feeding the baby when the curtains around her bed burst apart.

She looked up. "Mommy," she said, and for the first time since she'd heard the news, her heart began to flutter out of its state of calm.

Her mother strode over to the bassinet next to Aviva's bed, gave a short glance down at the baby sleeping inside, and then looked back at Aviva, an odd grimace on her face. "Is it true?" she asked. "Maybe the doctors are wrong? Ever since Zevi told us, I've been davening that there was a mistake."

Aviva shook her head. "The blood test results came back. There's no mistake."

She'd never seen her mother look so old and deflated. And then, to her utter shock, her mother came over and gave her a hug. "Oh, Aviva, how devastating. How totally devastating. I'm so sorry for you. What will you do?"

Aviva couldn't remember the last time her mother had hugged her—but right now, she didn't like it. Feeling annoyed, she gently pushed her mother away and said, "What do you mean, what will I do? I'll raise this baby like all my other children!"

Her mother shook her head disbelievingly. "Impossible. A child with such problems? What will his life be like?"

Aviva did not want to hear this. "It will be as great as I can make it," she said stubbornly, turning away.

"Hello?" A smiling head popped through the curtains. "Bad time?"

Aviva blinked. "Um, who…?"

"I'm Mandy, the lactation consultant."

Aviva's face cleared. "Oh, yes, I really wanted to speak with you. Can you come back in a little while?"

"No problem."

After her head popped back out, Aviva answered her mother's questioning glance. "Babies with Down syndrome have a harder time nursing, because of their low muscle tone."

Her mother's eyes squinted. "Trouble nursing… See, the problems are starting already… What does Zevi have to say about all this?"

Aviva's eyes clouded. She and Zevi hadn't spoken much since the big announcement, but she knew he was taking it hard. So hard, that he hadn't brought any of the kids to visit. "We need to process this first," he'd said.

If you hadn't been such a head-in-the-sand optimist when we first got the news, months ago, you wouldn't need so long to process it now, she'd wanted to tell him. But, instead, drawing on her newfound serenity, she'd said, "Of course, I understand. Take as much time as you need." For some reason, though, her response had angered him. He hadn't called at all this morning.

"Zevi's fine," she said now to her mother.

Her mother pursed her lips. "Oh, I'll bet." She sighed. "I want to ask you what I should tell my friends. Usually, I put a birth announcement in our shul bulletin, but of course, under the circumstances… Still, I can't hide it from my closer friends. What are you planning on saying?"

"Planning on saying?" Anger rose, sharp and swift, and Aviva lifted herself off her bed, grabbed her phone, and waved it at her mother. "I plan on sending out an e-mail to everyone we know, thanking Hashem for blessing us with a beautiful new baby boy who has Down syndrome!"

CHAPTER 47

SURI KNOCKED CAUTIOUSLY on the hospital door before walking inside. In her hand, she clutched a small, potted plant. Somehow, she wasn't sure why, it had seemed more appropriate than bright, airy balloons.

"Aviva?" She felt almost as nervous as she had that day she'd stood in Aviva's living room and broke the news that Goldfeder was suing. What did one say to a new mother of a baby born with special needs? Especially when that mother was perfect Aviva Heyman?

She's no stranger to children with disorders, Suri tried to tell herself. *She works with them every day.* Still, it had to be different when it was your own... And, for the first time, Suri felt pangs for the jealousy she'd been harboring just below the surface, a low-level undercurrent that had run through all her interactions with Aviva ever since she'd found out about the pregnancy.

"Suri! So sweet of you to visit! Come look at my gorgeous little *tzaddik'l*."

Suri was caught up short as Aviva, wearing a sheitel and velvet robe, swooped down on her (shouldn't she be in bed?) and kissed her on each cheek.

I needn't have worried, Suri realized. Perfect Aviva Heyman's reaction was, obviously...perfect.

Suri looked down at her hands, awkwardly balancing her plant. "Mazel tov," she said. "I brought you a gift." Her voice sounded so unnaturally stiff. Could Aviva tell how uncomfortable she felt?

"Thanks so much! I love orchids!" Aviva made a production of moving the nightstand next to the window and positioning the flowerpot just so. "They need lots of sunlight." Her own smile was bright and sunny, and she laughed off Suri's protestations that a *kimpeturin* shouldn't be moving furniture. "I feel great! More than great! After all, I have a sweet new baby. What can be better?"

Suri stared at her. Aviva was using her peppy, let's-welcome-all-our-parents-to-the-therapy-clinic voice. "Um," she tried, wondering if she dared broach the topic of the baby's disorder. But, she reasoned, with Aviva's grand announcement to the world, she wasn't exactly begging for secrecy. "How did it feel... I mean, did you have any idea, that the baby would have, you know, Down syndrome?"

Suri's cheeks burned, but Aviva appeared unruffled. She sat down on her bed. "Yeah, we had some warning. Nothing definitive. But enough to give me time to prepare." She glanced at the baby, lying peacefully in his bassinet. "I've been reading up on oral-motor therapy approaches. I never worked with newborns before. Fascinating stuff!"

Suri looked down at the baby. She reached out and stroked his cheek and gave a little smile at the way he began to suck in his sleep. It had been so long since she'd been around a newborn.

"How have your children taken the news?"

Aviva shrugged. Her oversized smile trembled slightly. "Well, they need some time to process it." Her voice wavered ever so slightly at the word "process." "It's an adjustment, of course. It'll be an adjustment for all of us. But they say a child with special needs brings such *berachah* into the home!" It was back again, that megawatt *tzaddeikes* smile.

Suri turned away for a moment to hide her expression. She'd known Aviva for many years now, and she'd never seen her self-possession so obviously put on. The question she was scared to answer was, just who was Aviva trying to fool?

YAEL'S MOTHER-IN-LAW FINGERED the soft cashmere silk of the little girl's dress on the hanger. "Libby Cooper's grand-daughter wore something similar at their recent *simchah*. Wouldn't Simi look darling in it?"

Yael was having a hard time getting past the price tag to see the dress. She would never, in a million years, spend half this much money on her *own* clothing. And to spend it on an almost two-year-old, who would probably drip ketchup on it the very first minute! And dry-clean only, naturally!

"Um, thank you, Mommy," she choked out. "But I don't think Simi needs something quite so...um...elegant."

Her mother-in-law pursed her lips. "You mean because you'll be spending Pesach by your family? I understand. Now, if you were coming with us to Italy, that would be different, of course..." She let out a delicate breath of air, and turned to the next rack. "How about this? Sophisticated but understated."

Yael cringed. This whole thing was a joke, her even setting foot in such a store, but how could she have turned down her mother-in-law's generous offer to go shopping for *yom tov* clothing for the kids? Particularly gracious, as Ephraim had pointed out more than once, because she was still getting over the fact that Ephraim and Yael would not be joining the extended Jeren clan for any of the holiday.

Yael swallowed. "Uh, yeah, looks beautiful." She tried to picture her sisters' faces as they'd take in little Simi swathed in such fabrics. The price calculations would be whirring in their heads loud enough to be heard.

She turned away, and brushed against a display of newborn clothing. Absently, she touched a soft wool baby boy's suit. Hmmm... Should she buy it? Insane amount of money, but really, it would be just the thing.

Her mother-in-law had noticed her interest in the baby clothing, and was turning questioning eyes in her direction. Yael blushed, and quickly said, "I need to get a baby gift for a friend. Something special. What do you think?"

In a matter of minutes, the Jeren credit card was swiped, and Yael was holding a shamefully expensive *yom tov* dress that she wondered if she'd have the guts to put on her daughter—and an extravagantly wrapped present that Yael planned on sending to the Heyman home.

Ever since she'd received the e-mail about Aviva's baby, she'd been wild to do something to show that she felt for what Aviva was going through, to demonstrate that she still cared, that she was ready to forgive and move on. While all the while, she was painfully aware—every moment of every day—that the game had changed, and that it was she who needed forgiveness.

She'd thought that time would dissipate her guilt, that she'd come to understand that in this case, the end really did justify the means. But with each passing day, her sense of shame grew heavier and heavier. How could she have done such a thing as pass on such damaging gossip? Who in the world had she become?

Yael looked down at the gold lace bow wrapped around the gift box. This was exactly the type of present that Aviva would delight in. Maybe, in some small way, it would compensate for everything else?

"SO YOU BROKE confidentiality and called her principal."

Suri, sitting across from Phil Handelman, nodded nervously. She felt like she herself was sitting in the principal's office right now.

"And you felt it was a life-threatening situation."

She nodded nervously again, then reconsidered. "Well, I mean, I don't know what you call *life*-threatening…but yeah, well, it's serious stuff, a potential psychiatric disorder. I didn't think it was something I could just sit back and let the parents ignore."

She reddened, under the scrutiny of the eminent attorney at law. How she wished Aviva were there with her. She even wished she'd taken Shaul up on his offer to come for moral support. "It's okay, I'm a big girl," she'd told him. Little had she known she'd be sitting there feeling like a ten-year-old.

But there was no choice. Aviva's giving birth four weeks early would not push off their date in court. Suri had gotten them into this mess, and it would fall to her to get them out of it.

Handelman nodded. "Tell me everything about your relationship with Goldfeder, from the very beginning." He leaned back in his chair. "Don't leave out any detail."

An hour later, totally drained, Suri walked back into the clinic. "How'd the big meeting go?" Shira looked up from her computer.

Naomi, sitting at the desk next to Shira, raised her eyebrows. "Meeting?"

"With the lawyer," Suri explained, reddening a little. She'd only shared vague details about the case with Naomi. The lady struck her as so highly professional, Suri was embarrassed to admit her giant flop to her.

Now she said carefully, "He definitely thinks we have a good chance of winning. He said it's hard to prove monetary damages in such a case, anyway. But I still might…"

Her voice caught in her throat, as she remembered the lawyer's words. *This man doesn't need your money. He's clearly after your reputation. And if he wants to go that route, he actually has a much better case for convincing the speech licensing authority to strip you of your license.*

CHAPTER 48

THE "WELCOME HOME, Mommy and Baby!" sign was bright and colorful, drawn by eager little hands that hadn't yet been told there was something wrong with their little brother. The older children, on the other hand, hung back, slightly scared, as Aviva made her grand entrance with baby in tow.

The little ones ran up to her immediately. "Mommy! Mommy!" But the bigger ones seemed to be waiting, to take their cue from her.

Aviva, it's all up to you. How you act right now will determine their relationship with their little brother for years to come.

She shook her head slightly at herself—even she knew that was ridiculous—but nevertheless she put on the widest smile she owned and cried, "Mazel tov!"

Relieved, they all rushed to crowd around the baby, sleeping in his infant seat.

Zevi was standing off to the side, car keys still in his hand.

Aviva glanced at him uncertainly. The ride home had been full of unnatural conversation and even more unnatural silences. After so many days apart—the hospital had kept the baby a while for testing—Aviva felt almost shy around her husband, who suddenly seemed closed off to her. Outgoing, talkative Zevi, who'd always been as open as a book—unlike her own complicated self. She longed to ask him what he was feeling, but she didn't know how, and some part of her was afraid of the answer.

Now Zevi walked slowly over to the small group clustered around the baby. With a strained smile, he put a hand on Chaim's shoulder, moved him gently aside, and looked down at the sleeping baby. Aviva watched as, hesitantly, he reached out a hand to stroke the baby's cheek; watched as his gaze softened, and as, blinking, he turned away.

With forced cheeriness, he turned to the crew and called out, "*Nu, chevrah*, who does the baby look like?" Amidst the laughing and clamoring, he looked at Aviva and said, "Go get some rest. Didn't you just give birth or something?"

It was almost the old Zevi, minus the sparkle.

Nodding, Aviva made her way upstairs, surprised to find how weary she really was. Was this what having a baby in your old age did? She chuckled to herself at that as she snuggled deliciously under her covers, closing her eyes…

She'd barely begun to doze when she was awakened by some little voices at her door. Opening her eyes with a start, she was aware of a vague feeling of disappointment, as if she'd been dreaming something achingly pleasant. Wincing as she stretched—body not back to itself yet—she called out, "What is it, Tovaleh?"

"Tatty said to tell you the baby's hungry."

Baby…hungry…oh. That lingering feeling of well-being from her brief sleep dissipated like a puff of smoke, as something hard and cold clunked into place in her brain.

She'd been dreaming that she had no baby.

"WOW, MA, TAKE a look at this!"

Chavi had just answered the doorbell, and now she was walking into the living room bearing an elaborately wrapped present. She whistled as she saw the store name embossed on the box. "Who do you know who shops at Laura's Lace?"

Aviva raised her eyebrows as she reached for the gift, carefully untying the gold lace bow. She sucked in her breath as she lifted the cover.

"No way!" cried Chavi. "Someone bought Dolce & Gabbana for a *baby*? That has to cost, like, hundreds of dollars!" She reached out to touch the soft material of the tiny suit.

Aviva opened up the card—not that she couldn't already guess who this was from. There was only one person she knew who could afford such a gift. She crinkled her eyes as she read the note—warm, polite, brief. The question was…why?

Chavi was peering over her shoulder. "Yael Jeren? Isn't she the one who used to work with you? Filthy rich?" She laughed. "Hey, maybe you can ask her to buy *me* a Dolce & Gabbana? I'd take a nice handbag, tell her it's my birthday soon."

Aviva smiled, even as she wondered what on earth such an extravagant present could mean…

"…probably just her way of saying she's over what happened." Zevi, when he'd gotten home, had not been as taken with the mystery of the gift as Aviva had been. He'd shaken his head over it ("Designer clothing for a baby?! Do you know how many chili dogs that would buy?"), but hadn't seemed too interested in delving into its layers of meaning.

Aviva shook her head in wonder. "Why would she spend so much money just to say that? Any simple gift could have done."

"Maybe for her that *is* a simple gift."

She rolled her eyes. "You know what I think?"

He smirked. "Dying to know."

"I think she feels bad for me, because of, you know, the baby."

That wiped the smile off Zevi's face. "So you're saying we can expect such fancy gifts from all our friends? Maybe I won't have to go into debt for Pesach this year."

"Zevi, be serious."

He paused. "You really want me to be serious?"

Aviva was suddenly frightened by the look he gave her.

"Here's a serious question, then. Do you feel bad for *yourself*?"

Aviva's eyes widened. "Feel *bad*? Of…of course not!" she stammered. "I mean, Hashem *chose* us, didn't He? He gave us this precious *neshamah*, and He *davka* set us up to be the perfect family for him, right? With me being a speech therapist, and knowing just the right way to care for him and help him develop. And I've already started on some oral-motor techniques I've learned, and I'm really excited with how he's responding."

Zevi stared at her for a moment. At last, he said, "You didn't answer my question."

SURI WAITED UNTIL she heard the door click closed behind her client before putting her head down on the table. She was tired, so desperately tired, and she almost didn't mind that her last two clients of the day had canceled.

Almost. If only it hadn't been part of an epidemic of cancellations. If only Suri hadn't understood only too well why people were suddenly wary of coming to the speech therapist being sued for professional misconduct.

She pressed her head harder against the cold wooden tabletop.

"You okay?"

Suri looked up to see Naomi standing in the doorway.

"Just tired," she answered. *Tired? Hah! Try emotionally depleted, depressed, and frightened out of my mind.*

"Well, not so surprising, considering what you're going through."

The older lady stepped inside the room and closed the door behind her.

"Maybe I can help?"

Suri considered. She hadn't really gotten to know Naomi too well. Aside from her help with the bipolar diagnosis a while back, their interactions hadn't consisted of much more than basic greetings. First, there had been the uncomfortable circumstances surrounding her hiring. And in recent months, Suri had been so busy, what with Aviva gone and a whole new clinic staff around, including a physical therapist, a second part-time OT, and an additional speech therapist who'd been hired to replace Aviva, but was probably going to stay on after Aviva returned, assuming their current rate of growth continued... Assuming Suri didn't drag the clinic down with her own toxic reputation.

Tears pricked at her eyes. Alone. She felt so alone. With Aviva out of the picture and Yael long gone, she was the only one left to shoulder all the responsibility. The stress was killing her.

She gave a small smile to Naomi. "I would love some help, actually."

Naomi sat down on the kiddie chair opposite her. "Fill me in."

Naomi turned out to be a great listener, to Suri's surprise (though why she was surprised, she didn't know). She frowned as she listened to the details, nodding slowly, as if processing everything inside her eminently levelheaded, sensible brain. At last she said, "And where does the Ritalin fall into the story?"

Suri squinted. "Ritalin? I told you, the parents said they were putting her on Ritalin, but I thought they had missed the boat, and so I decided to go above their heads…"

Naomi shook her head impatiently. "No, I mean where does the fact that they acquired Ritalin *illegally* fall into the story? Did you tell that part to the lawyer?"

Suri rubbed her forehead. "I didn't…I mean, I don't know for sure it was illegal. They never said. Maybe they did get a prescription."

"Yes, maybe they did." Naomi raised her eyebrow. "We don't know. But we don't have to. Not if it's reputations we're talking about here…"

Suri stared as Naomi gave a smile. Slowly, Suri smiled back.

CHAPTER 49

YAEL GIGGLED AS she walked up the boulevard next to Ephraim, sipping a milkshake.

"I feel like we're dating," she said.

Ephraim wiggled his eyebrow. "The fun is just beginning."

It had been a total surprise when he'd told her, this first morning of *bein hazmanim*, to get the kids packed up and ready to be dropped off at his mother's.

"Why?" she'd asked, startled.

He'd smiled. "I've planned a day for just the two of us. It's been a long winter."

There was no arguing with that one. Yael was so touched that he'd made the effort to plan such a day. And it was done in perfect Ephraim style. Or was it Jeren style? First, they'd gone to a pottery painting studio, where she'd laughed her way through Ephraim's sorry attempts at decorating his ceramic bowl. Then they'd stopped off for lunch at a local café. Next stop, he'd just informed her, was Manhattan, for Chelsea Piers and dinner.

She couldn't help but giggle. It really did remind her of their dating days, when he would routinely surprise her with such elaborate outings. At the time, she'd been astounded at the idea of throwing around money on one expensive activity after another without a moment's thought—and heady with the knowledge that such unimaginable wealth might actually soon be hers. It was too insane a concept to properly wrap her mind around, but she knew with certainty that, undeserving as she was, Hashem had chosen to gift her with every blessing this world could possibly offer.

And now? As she strolled down the shopping strip, she pondered the fact that, several years older and wiser, she had come to learn that wealth was not necessarily a blessing.

"Hey, look! Rina's Racks! Whaddaya know?" Ephraim had suddenly stopped in front of the familiar—to Yael—storefront on this posh row of boutiques.

Yael gave a little shrug, as her high spirits sank abruptly. "Yeah, I knew it was on this street."

Ephraim gave the chic window display an appraising look. "Impressively Rina. Wanna go in and say hi?"

Not particularly. But Yael couldn't say that, couldn't say anything about his family without souring the day, so she sufficed with another shrug.

Ephraim took that as an enthusiastic yes.

"Hey, sis! Surprise!"

Rina was in the middle of discussing summer styles with a customer and her teenage daughter. Her mouth dropped open as she saw the two of them.

"Ephraim! My goodness, to what do I owe this honor? Hold

on a sec." She turned to the customer. "That's my baby brother who just walked in."

Yael saw Ephraim's eyebrows crinkle in a fleeting frown at the "baby brother." He turned away, staring around the lavishly decorated store. "Quite some business," he said, and Yael could hear the jealousy dripping from his voice. "Are all these your own designs?" He waved vaguely around the floor display.

Rina shrugged modestly. "Not *all* of them. But mine are being grabbed up fast, by everyone who's anyone."

He nodded. "Always the success," he said, and Rina beamed.

"So, what brings you two here?" she asked.

Ephraim gave Yael a wink. "Taking advantage of *bein hazmanim* to spend some time together."

"Really?" Rina exclaimed. "That sounds so...nice."

Yael glanced at her in surprise. Was it her imagination...or was it her sister-in-law who now sounded jealous?

SURI HUNG UP the phone slowly. The conversation with her lawyer had been much more positive than previous ones; he'd found the new information about the Ritalin interesting. "I can see the potential" was the way he put it.

"Knock, knock. You ready for us?"

Suri looked up. Her next client was here. She pasted on a smile and called out in a hearty voice, "Come in! How are you, Faigele?"

She winced at the fakeness of her tone; it had been like that ever since the Goldfeder debacle broke. When she'd started having to pretend enthusiasm for playing dolls or Candy Land with her little clients, when really all she wanted to do was curl up and cry. *Am I doomed to be a hearty-sounding speech therapist for the rest of my career?* she wondered. And then remembered: The rest of her career might not be very long.

The thought did not help matters.

Suri grimaced as she pulled a game of Memory off the shelf. She couldn't go on like this. Maybe her lawyer was right in what he was suggesting she do. Maybe this was the only way.

"Hey, I heard you're a Memory champ!" she said brightly as she set the game on the table. "Is that true?"

The little girl giggled, but Suri cringed inside at the saccharine cheeriness in her voice. So not her. *Fake! Fake!*

She clenched her teeth, as she started selecting picture pairs. She couldn't go on like this.

"I FEEL AWFUL bothering you…" Suri sat perched on the edge of Aviva's couch, feeling a strong sense of déjà vu. Was it just a few weeks ago that she had sat there and informed Aviva of the lawsuit? And now here they were, Aviva with a baby, dealing with all the implications of Down syndrome, and Suri…where, exactly, was Suri holding?

"No problem," Aviva said. "What's going on?"

She twisted her hands. "I want to consult with you about a potential development in our case. I…" She hesitated. "I feel so bad, I'm sure you don't have the headspace for this right now, with everything on your plate. How's the baby doing?"

"Wonderful! So adorable!" Aviva said brightly. "He's really advancing. *Baruch Hashem*, the doctors haven't found any heart issues, which are fairly common in this population, I'm sure you know."

This population? Aviva sounded like she was talking about a medical study, not her baby. Suri gave her a quick quizzical glance, before nodding.

"And they say that, if he continues doing well with his feeding, we can even do the bris soon. I'm planning on throwing the biggest bash for my little *tzaddik'l*."

Suri was suddenly reminded irresistibly of her own hearty voice in the therapy session. *Fake! Fake!*

"So happy to hear. Let me know if you need any help with the planning."

Aviva gave her a wry smile. "Thanks, but I think you're the one with a lot on your plate right now. Tell me the latest developments."

Suri ran a finger against the cold leather couch arm. "I spoke to the lawyer this morning. I—Naomi, actually, advised me to, she thought it would help if I tell him the stuff about the Ritalin, that we suspect they bought it illegally and that's why I decided to go over their heads and speak to the principal. I wasn't so sure about it; I mean, I have nothing to go on…" She paused, doubtfully, as Aviva nodded her head vigorously.

"Suri, you're ridiculous, of course you needed to tell him this! It's so important! And please, nothing to go on? I'd bet the entire Goldfeder fortune that the stuff wasn't kosher."

Confidence, Suri, it's all in the confidence.

"Anyway," Suri continued. "Like I said, he found it interesting, but he said there wasn't so much we could do without proof. He wants to start issuing subpoenas, demanding documents so we can see what exactly was going on with the meds."

Aviva smirked. "So, things are heating up, hmm?"

"I guess you could say that." Suri squirmed in her seat.

Aviva squinted at her. "So, what did you want to consult about?

Wait, I know! You want advice about how we can get this proof on our own. A plan, we need a plan!"

Suri watched in fascination as, within the space of a moment, Aviva's face suddenly came back alive, as if she had shed her mask.

"Okay, so here's what we do. We set up a stakeout, video the exchange of goods. Mr. Goldfeder will probably be wearing a baseball cap and sunglasses, but he'll still be recognizable..." Her eyes danced.

"Aviva!" Suri burst out laughing. "You're not serious!"

Aviva giggled. "No, of course not. Though admit it, how fun would that be? No, here's my real plan. You set up a meeting with Dini, try to draw her out somehow, heart to heart, and get her to tell you the real story. Maybe even use a hidden recorder..." She paused, considering. "I don't know, might not be legal, we should check with Handelman. I can call him." She looked at Suri, her face all animated. "What do you think?"

Suri bit her lip. "Might work..." she said slowly. "But I think I like the stakeout idea better."

CHAPTER 50

S URI GLARED AT herself in the mirror, as she gave a tug at her sheitel, which had somehow gone on lopsided. She had only fifteen minutes until the senior social group began, and the women got nervous when she came late.

She'd been so tempted to cancel this month's meeting, with all that was going on, but she knew how much it meant to the women and, with Pesach coming up, it would be a long time until they could meet again. As she got ready, her ever-present worries replayed themselves once again in her head. Ever since leaving Aviva's house, Suri had felt vaguely disappointed in herself. Here Aviva had gotten all excited about this new legal angle, and had been ready and willing to use all her creative energies in pursuing it, while all Suri could do—she whose neck was actually on the line—was to give halfhearted assents or protests to some of Aviva's wackier ideas. What was wrong with her?

It was during the short drive to the shul social hall that she asked herself what exactly it was that she'd come to consult Aviva about in the first place. Had she really wanted ideas for playing amateur detective? If so, why had she found Aviva's enthusiasm so off-putting?

She walked into the room, where she was greeted by the women, most of whom were already gathered. It took several moments to register the change in her inner state—the way her shoulders loosened, her neck muscles relaxed. As she took her seat in the circle, it hit her: Everyone in the room was smiling at her, was treating her with the same warmth they always had. As if she weren't a professional pariah. *They don't know, that's all*, Suri told herself. But, somehow, as she looked around, the tension of the past month draining blessedly away, she had a feeling that, even were they to know, these ladies—with their sense born of years of life experience—wouldn't care at all.

Suri, we know you, she could almost hear Mrs. Lieberman saying.

Whatever mistake you made, it must have been for a good reason, Mrs. Sussman would chime in.

You have a heart of gold, Mrs. Mandel would add, and all the women around the circle would nod fondly.

A lump rose to Suri's throat, and for a second she was tempted to actually reveal her sorry story to the beautiful women sitting around her. But, she realized, it wasn't necessary. She had already gotten the answer she needed, just from being there.

She had never really intended to ask Aviva's advice about how to go about digging for dirt on the Goldfeders. No, she'd wanted to ask whether she should tell the lawyer to drop that line altogether. Whether, just because the parents were out for Suri's reputation, she should turn it around on Dini.

It was what any sensible person would do, obviously. Certainly, her lawyer wouldn't even understand the question. Aviva might not either. But—drawing warmth from the expectant smiles around her as the ladies waited for her to begin—she knew that these women would. And she could even hear their answers.

Do what you think is right.

Be true to yourself.

What seems like such an urgent need right now won't mean a thing years from now.

With a wide grin, and a feeling of peace and inner conviction she hadn't felt in weeks—weeks? decades, actually!—she began the evening's program.

YAEL GRABBED HER ringing phone while stirring the pot on the stove. Meatballs seemed a bit of a letdown after last night's steakhouse dinner, but—she'd amused herself by philosophizing as she'd put up the pot—life couldn't be all steak, medium rare, all the time. It had to have its meatball moments too.

And, face it, Yael, she'd thought, the grin suddenly fading from her face, *you've been quite the meatball, lately.*

That's when the phone rang. She glanced at the screen. Fraidy. Just the person to lift her spirits.

"Hey, Fraidy! So great to hear from you! What's up?"

Surprise, surprise, Fraidy wasn't really calling for her. She was calling for her mother.

"I'm finding this whole *shidduch* thing so *confusing*, and I just need someone to talk to. And Mrs. Savetsky, well, she was always so wise, and so inspiring, but I'm sure she's so crazy busy, would she even have time to talk to me? And, of course, there was that Purim incident, I'm still so embarrassed..."

Yael rolled her eyes. "You want me to ask her if you can call?"

"Oh, Yael, *would* you?" she squealed.

After hanging up, a funny thought occurred. Here, all these girls were falling over their feet to get an appointment with her mother. So why hadn't she thought to ask Mommy's advice?

"Mommy? It's Yael. Do you have a few minutes?"

It was after dinner, Ephraim had gone out to night *seder*, and Yael, curled up on the couch, felt tears prick her eyes as she heard her mother's response.

"For you, sweetie? I have all the time in the world!"

Her mother. Her family. She missed them so much. How had this happened, that she'd gotten so caught up in the world of Jeren that she'd cut herself off from her own family? Not literally, of course, but emotionally. There was a time when her first instinct would be to turn to her mother with any problem. And now... *Why, Yael? Is it because you feel, on a certain level, that you've turned your back on them by marrying "up"?*

Or maybe—and her eyes widened—it was the opposite. That she felt it was they who'd turned their backs on her by letting her go through with such a *shidduch*, completely naive to all the ramifications of marrying into a family so different from her own.

She took a breath. Whatever it was, it was high time she got over it.

"Mommy, I've messed up big, I said something I never should have, and I don't know what to do..."

"GOOD NEWS!" AVIVA cried as she walked through the door. While the house seemed empty, she was sure Zevi would materialize out of one of the rooms. His newfound work ethic of the past few months had suddenly dissipated with the baby's birth. Instead he spent his time moping around the house.

Not moping, she reminded herself with a frown. *Helping*. He was staying home helping her, he said, to avoid having her mother make a repeat visit. But the way he kept sighing over the baby every time he held him was starting to grate on her nerves. She wished he'd go back to the office already; she was managing at home just fine.

"What is it?" Sure enough, Zevi popped his head out of the kitchen, a donut in his hand.

"Dr. Reimer said *tzaddik'l*'s weight has gone up enough that he expects him to be ready for a bris by next week."

Zevi grinned. "Next week? So soon?" He came over and gently stroked the head in the infant car seat. "Hey, kiddo, you're a fighter, aren't you?"

That bittersweet look crossed his face again, and Aviva found herself growing annoyed. "Of course he's a fighter," she said briskly. "Why wouldn't he be?"

"Like mother, like son, eh?" Zevi raised an eyebrow.

Aviva nodded. "Exactly. Together, we'll do great. But we have a lot of work to do." She sat down on the couch. "Next week is really soon. There's so much to plan for the bris."

"You're right, people usually have much more time to plan these things."

She pursed her lips. "Very funny. This bris needs to be something special. You know, to introduce our special baby to the world." Aviva pulled a pen and notebook out of her purse. "I should speak to Naama, she's great at these things. Maybe she'll even offer to come help." She began scribbling.

A high-pitched wail interrupted her. Without glancing up

from her notebook, she said, "Pick up the baby, will you?"

Zevi dutifully unbuckled the baby from his infant carrier. "What's up, little guy? Hungry, are we? Guess you're like your Tatty there."

He brought the baby over to Aviva. "Can you take a break from bris planning? I think he wants his mother."

A small crease appeared between Aviva's eyes. "Can't you hold him a little while longer? I just want to get this down before I forget."

Zevi was silent, and after a second, she looked up. He was biting his lip, as if trying to hold himself back from saying something.

And then, a moment later: "Aviva, can I ask you something? Why don't you like holding the baby?"

CHAPTER 51

THE DAY WAS a bustle of visitors arriving, and Aviva smiled and simpered and graciously accepted compliments: "You look amazing! I'd never believe you just gave birth!" "Your home is so stunningly neat. As if you didn't have a newborn and eight other kids to take care of!" "Where in the world did you find time to bake like this for the *vach nacht*?"

Aviva flung her newly set sheitel over her shoulder and smiled, smiled, smiled. The compliments had never been so well deserved. And though she made sure to demur modestly, to pat Chavi on the shoulder and insist her eldest daughter deserves much of the credit, she knew, her whole family knew, that it was all her hard work, her efforts fueled by sheer, sleepless determination—her utter insanity, as Zevi called it (and she privately agreed)—that had created this glistening, glamorous welcome for all of their arriving family that was, even according to Aviva's standards, perfection itself.

With both their families from out of town, everyone had

arrived early to be there for the big event. The "Circumcision of the Century," as Zevi had dubbed it when informing his friends and family (but not, thank goodness, hers). He had shaken his head and stayed pointedly out of the endless discussions about bris decor and menu taking place between Aviva and Naama, with Chavi's occasional input.

Now, finally, everyone had arrived, the *vach nacht* was tonight, and everything was perfectly in place. With a heavy dose of makeup, and an even heavier dose of caffeine, Aviva had managed to disguise the damage of sleep deprivation. Little *tzaddik'l*, of course, was decked in his pre-bris best, currently being fussed over by Zevi's mother and sisters.

Aviva's mother-in-law had given her a warm hug, eyes brimming with tears as she wished her "all the *nachas* in the world" from the baby, and, after exclaiming over how thin she was so soon after giving birth and hoping she was taking it easy, she ran over to the baby, virtually ignoring the spotless home, carefully placed bouquets, and buffet of sandwich wraps and crepes laid out on the dining room table.

But that was okay. Aviva hadn't put in all this effort for Zevi's family. It was Naama's whistle when she stepped through the door, her other sister Chumi's murmur of "I'm impressed" as she sampled a crepe, and, most of all, her mother's curt nod of approval as her sharp eyes glanced around the room, the look that said, "I see you finally got it together," that made Aviva know it had all been worth it.

Now they were all standing around, eating, chatting, enjoying the party Aviva the *kimpeturin* had thrown. At a certain point her mother-in-law whisked her away, telling her the baby needed to eat. Aviva dutifully went up to her room, ignoring the twinge of resentment, and it was only when she rested her head against her nursing glider that she suddenly realized how exhausted she was.

She awoke with a start two hours later, the baby asleep in her arms. Two whole hours! They all must be wondering what happened to her! Carefully, she laid the baby down in his bassinet and walked downstairs. Her in-laws, she saw, had left, and her own children had scattered, but her parents and sisters were sitting in a tight group in the living room.

"Don't understand her," her mother was saying, and Aviva's breath caught in her throat, sure she knew who that "her" was. "All this fuss, for a baby with Down syndrome? Why doesn't she do it all low scale, hush things up a little for heaven's sake? If she had any sense, she'd have done the bris right here, just the family, instead of screaming it out to the world."

Aviva, whose heart had stopped beating, stood still on the stairway as she contemplated turning right around and going back upstairs. Then she heard Naama's voice.

"Mommy, how can you say that? Nowadays, people don't 'hush up' babies with problems like they did in your day. I think Aviva's handling this beautifully. You should be really proud of her."

―

"AVIVA! COME TAKE a peek before it starts!"

Aviva had just walked into the hall, with the baby and all her girls in tow. The boys had gone earlier with Zevi to daven *shacharis*. Aviva had nearly blown up when Kayla had shrieked that her outfit was stained, and Chavi had taken her sweet time doing her hair, but somehow she'd remained calm, shepherding the family out and arriving at the shul only a few minutes later than planned, where Naama had instantly grabbed her.

"You gotta see the setup! It's out of this world!"

Naama had been there since six in the morning, directing the caterer and adding her own expert touches. As Aviva walked into the hall, she gasped and clutched her sister's arm. "Oh, it's stunning! You worked so hard. How can I thank you?"

Naama gave her a hug. "Anything for my little sis. And don't you talk to me about working hard. You're the one who does too much for one human being."

Aviva couldn't remember the last time she'd hugged her sister like that, and when they parted, she felt tears pricking her eyes. Naama patted her back.

"Now they're all waiting for the little guest of honor."

Aviva nodded, but the lump in her throat was still there minutes later as she greeted the mohel and handed him the baby. It was there as she nodded along at his instructions, her mind in a fog. And when she handed little *tzaddik'l*, swathed in his bris outfit, over to Zevi's newly married sister, the *kvatterin*, the lump in her throat suddenly grew so big it threatened to burst.

"Aviva? Over here." Naama was whispering to her, ushering her over to the women's section, and, through her haze, she saw rows of her friends all smiling at her. There was Suri, and, next to her, Yael (the fact that Yael had come just barely registered), as she walked to the front, right next to the *mechitzah*, and parted the curtains to peek through.

The baby had already been handed off to Zevi, and now her husband was clutching him, whispering something as he laid him gently on the lap of the sandek. It was Rav Biederman, the *rav* Zevi had consulted with so many months before, who had told them not to do any further testing, who had said there's no *toeles* in finding out for sure…that nothing's ever for sure…

And suddenly, without warning, a great, gaping hole burst open inside Aviva, and a raging river of tears began gushing out—boiling-hot tears that streamed down her cheeks and made her entire body shake. *But the doctors were right, Rav Biederman! My baby does have Downs, and while nothing in life is for sure, what is for sure is that my life will never, never be the same again.*

Through her burning eyes, she saw the mohel bend over her baby, heard the piercing wail… Her baby, her little *tzaddik'l*, who would never be normal, never grow to be a regular kid, and everyone who was standing there right now was pitying the baby, pitying her, and they were so right to do so. Now there was her father-in-law, standing by the *bimah*, doing the *Krias Sheim*, bending down to listen to Zevi, calling out: "Yerachmiel ben Yehuda Zev." Yerachmiel, because their little boy needed Hashem's *rachamim* so badly, and she could hear the women behind her murmuring, no doubt thinking the same.

"*Kesheim shenichnas labris, kein yikaneis leTorah u'lechuppah u'lemaasim tovim!*" cried her father-in-law, and as everyone present chanted in response, everyone blessed her little Yerachmiel to grow to be a *talmid chacham*, to get married…and that's when Aviva lost it.

"Excuse me," she tried to whisper, but she wasn't sure if her voice was working. Yet her feet were, and they were carrying her out of the *ezras nashim*, quickly, quickly, and she was dimly aware of someone calling her name, of someone else trying to grab her, but she shook them off and kept walking. She reached the rabbi's study, where the bris preparations had taken place, and she quickly closed the door. She couldn't face any of them; she would stay put right there, until it was all over, until all the crowds had left.

They would find her there, they would know to bring the baby back to her—her little Yerachmiel. Such a pure *neshamah*, such a world of hardship ahead of him… *Yeracheim Hashem!* Why? Why do this to such an innocent little baby? She rocked back and forth, her heart bleeding tears, and soon enough there was a knock on the door, and she heard her mother saying, "Here she is, just ran out in the middle, never seen anything like it," and Zevi whispering her name: "Aviva? Are you ready to take the baby?"

And she nodded, reaching out convulsively for her baby, and held him close and fiercely, as if to shield him from the world.

CHAPTER 52

YAEL HAD THE door open before her mother could even knock. It wasn't so often that her parents could take time from their packed schedules to make the trip out to her house. But Simi's second birthday party was a good enough excuse, and her whole family had come out for the occasion.

"Yael! You look great! Is that a new sheitel?" Her mother gave her a hug, then walked inside. One by one, each of her family members followed, and she couldn't help but notice that they all did the same eye movement as they came in, a quick ocular dance that took in the elaborately decorated foyer and living room, and flashed the same wondering look: *Does she really live here?* It happened without fail, every time they came.

Yael patted her sheitel self-consciously. "Uh, yeah, it is. A Pesach gift from my mother-in-law."

Her mother nodded, eyes swiveling to the Jerens, who were already ensconced in the living room. Yael knew that her mother hadn't bought herself a new sheitel in over a decade.

Her mother turned back to Yael, lowered her voice confidentially. "So, how was the bris? Did you manage to speak to them?"

Her mother had suggested, during their long phone conversation a few days ago, that Aviva's bris would be the perfect, non-professional setting to try to patch things up.

"You mean apologize?" she'd asked.

"To reveal that you spoke *lashon hara*? That's a halachic *shailah*. Better to discuss it with Tatty." She'd paused, and then asked, with her unerring perception, "But that's not your real question, is it?"

That's when Yael had started sobbing like a little girl. "What in the world's happened to me? How could I have done such a horrible thing? It's so completely not me, to spread such vicious rumors, to take revenge like that! I feel like I've become someone else, these past few months, and whoever she is, I really don't like her..."

A long conversation had followed, and for the first time in years Yael thought about what she really wanted in life. Somewhere along the way they veered off into the territory of values and money, about her priorities as a wife, and the vast cultural divide between her and her in-laws.

At the end, Yael had said, sniffling, "You know what, Mommy? I feel like we should have had this conversation years ago, before I got married."

Her mother had been silent for a moment, and then she'd said, "Yes, we should have. I don't think I realized how much of an adjustment it would be for you. But that's no excuse. I should have realized, and I should have guided you then, instead of leaving you to struggle on your own for so long."

Now, in response to her mother's question, Yael replied in a low voice, "I went to the bris, and I sat next to Suri. It was awkward, really awkward, but I forced myself, and once we got past the weird beginning, we started chatting almost normally. Suri and I had always gotten along," she added.

"And Aviva? I'm sure she was preoccupied, of course."

Yael raked a hand through her new sheitel uncomfortably. "Aviva wasn't there."

"Wasn't there? The mother of the baby?"

Yael shrugged. "She was there for the bris, and then, just as it was finishing, she, uh, scooted out really fast. No one saw her after that."

Her mother's eyebrows had shot up, but Yael turned away. She wasn't interested in discussing Aviva right now. "Let's go say hello to my mother-in-law," she said.

It wasn't so often that her parents and in-laws had a chance to interact. Now, as her family made their way into the living room where the Jerens were sitting and talking, she saw her father-in-law immediately rise from his seat.

"Rav Savetsky," he said, extending a hand, and Yael noted with what respect her father-in-law quickly pulled out a chair, and remained standing until her father was seated.

"How lovely to see you." Mrs. Jeren smiled at Yael's mother. "So sweet of Yael to throw this little get-together."

Yael hid a smile, as her eyes caught Ephraim's. She knew that his mother had been disappointed and outright bewildered that she'd decided to go with an understated "little get-together" for Simi's birthday rather than the circus in a tent for all the neighborhood children that she had suggested.

"It's a nice excuse to get a break from the Pesach cleaning," Yael's mother said.

Once again, Yael had to stifle a giggle, as she saw her

mother-in-law's uncomfortable expression. Yael knew she was deliberating whether to delicately reply that they were going away for the holiday, but oh how she could sympathize with the rough Pesach cleaning (which she couldn't, of course—not with the housekeeping staff she kept), or whether to commiserate by relating all of her packing woes. Momentarily confused, she settled with a little cough, as Yael's mother continued pleasantly, "But of course, you're going away for Pesach. France, is it? Or Italy? It must be beautiful there, but, I confess, there's nothing like Pesach at home. Don't you agree?"

She gave a wink to Yael as Mrs. Jeren murmured something polite and noncommittal.

Yael looked around, wondering if she should officially start the ceremonies. Everyone seemed to be there. Wait a second, where was…?

The doorbell rang just then, and, after a moment, Rina sailed in. "Sorry I'm late," she said breathlessly. "The store, it's just crazy now in this pre-Pesach season."

Yael felt bad that her sister-in-law had felt the need to take off of work to come to a little birthday party, but she knew it wasn't for her sake that she'd come.

Yael jumped up, realizing it was time to play hostess. "Adults in the dining room," she called. "There's lunch set up there. And children follow me into the playroom. That's where the *real* fun is!"

Her nieces and nephews and young siblings all trailed after her, giggling. She had set up art supplies on the small plastic tables, and they all eagerly took seats. Ephraim came along, to see if she needed help, and to her surprise, Rina followed him.

"Mind if I join the kids?" she asked with a smile.

Rina leaned against the wall, watching as Yael described the tissue paper flowers they would be making. Yael glanced at her, and once again caught that wistful expression she had seen on Rina's face the other day, in her store.

Now, Rina turned to Ephraim and said, "You don't know what a gem you have for a wife. Look at how incredible she is with the kids. I hope you appreciate how lucky you are."

***

SURI LEANED BACK in the recliner and wiped her forehead. Five bookshelves down, five more to go. And then the breakfront, the desk drawers, and the couch cushions. She closed her eyes briefly. It would be a long night.

The urgent knock on the door made her eyes fly open. Who would be knocking like that at this time of night? Heart pounding, she stood on tiptoes to see out the peephole. Her mouth dropped open as she quickly opened the door.

Dini Goldfeder fell inside.

"Sureeee! Help me! You gotta help!"

She staggered into the living room, wildly off balance, and began racing from one side of the room to the other. Alarmed, Suri rushed over and grabbed her by the shoulders.

"Dini, what happened?" she cried.

Dini clutched Suri's shirt. "They're after me, they're coming after me right now, and if you don't help me they'll lock me up for the rest of my life!"

Suri's face whitened, as she tried to make sense of the girl's words. "Who? Your parents?"

Dini tightened her hold. "All of them! They have knives and guns, and they're right behind me!" She twisted around wildly.

Suddenly, she let out a scream and, releasing Suri, raced down the hall, toward the kitchen.

Suri ran after her. "Dini?"

Dini was already opening up drawers in the kitchen. "Knife, need a weapon," she muttered frantically.

"No!" Suri cried, so loudly that Dini jumped.

"I do!" she shouted. "They're coming!"

Suri reached out and arrested her hands. Dini's eyes were darting from side to side. Suri had never seen her like this. She sucked in her breath, as things suddenly clicked in place.

"Come with me, Dini," she said, keeping firm hold of the girl. "I'm taking you someplace safe. Give me your phone, please."

Wordlessly, the girl dug into her pocket and handed it to her. Quickly scrolling the contacts, Suri found the number she was looking for. *Mommy*. Guiding Dini away from the kitchen, Suri called Mrs. Goldfeder.

CHAPTER 53

DINI PACED SURI'S living room frantically while Suri kept a close eye on her. The minutes dragged on, and Suri began to wonder if the Goldfeders had decided not to come after all. It had been a short and terse phone call: "Mrs. Goldfeder? Suri Taub speaking. Dini just showed up on my doorstep. She's not in a good state at all. I think you should come over right now and take her to the emergency room."

Nechi had barely spoken. She'd gasped, cried out, and asked for Suri's address. Then she'd hung up. Twenty long minutes later, and Suri began to wonder. She pictured to herself what must be taking place in the Goldfeder home. How Nechi would have surely told her husband about the alarming phone call, and how Mr. Goldfeder would have angrily dismissed the whole thing as a hoax, designed to get them to drop the lawsuit. How Nechi would have wavered, wondering if she dared risk ignoring the call, but ultimately, her husband's forcefulness would be too much for her...

The timid knock on the door interrupted her thoughts. Suri quickly opened it to find Nechi standing there, dressed impeccably as usual—even at midnight—but with a caught-in-the-headlights expression.

"She's here?" Nechi asked. Suri noticed that she was avoiding her eyes.

Suri gestured toward the living room. Any attempt at conversation would be beyond awkward, and in this circumstance, Dini's behavior clearly spoke for itself.

"Mommeee!" Dini nearly jumped a mile when she saw her mother standing in the living room. Racing over, she cried, "Take me out of here, quick! They're coming, they're after me, really! Suri won't let me stay, I mean she won't let me leave, she's keeping me here and she won't let me fight, she wants them to catch me, she wants me in jail, you have to help me!"

Suri caught Nechi's sidelong glance at her, as if not sure whether to take her daughter seriously. As if wondering fleetingly whether Suri did, indeed, want to throw Dini in jail.

Impatient, Suri said, "Dini showed up at my doorstep half an hour ago. How or why she got here I don't know, but she was yelling that people were after her, chasing her with guns and stuff. She ran into my kitchen and started searching through drawers for my knives. I was able to stop her, *baruch Hashem*. I don't want to think about what she might have done with a knife in this state."

Nechi was staring at Dini in horror.

"Has she ever been like this before?" Suri pressed.

Nechi shook her head slowly. "Not…like this," she whispered. "She's been very, uh, hyper before, but this sounds…psychotic." Her face was white.

Dini had resumed running around the living room. She paused

in front of the breakfront, gazing at it intently. Suddenly, she whipped open one of the glass doors so fast, it banged into the bookshelves next to it and the glass shattered.

"Oh my!" Nechi gasped. "Dini! What's gotten into you?"

Oblivious, Dini reached into the breakfront. Suri wasn't sure what she was going for, but she didn't want to wait to find out. "Stop!" she cried, sprinting over to grab her.

"Care to help?" she called out, panting, to Nechi, who seemed dumbstruck. Slowly, Nechi walked over and took Dini's hand. "Come with me, Dinaleh." Her voice broke.

At her mother's touch, Dini calmed. Clutching Nechi's hand, she gave a shudder that shook her entire body, and then slowly began walking after her mother. As they neared the door, Nechi turned back uncertainly.

"Suri, I have no right to ask this of you, I know..." She hesitated, as Suri braced herself for what was coming. *Please keep this whole episode a secret. Even though it might be your ticket to winning the court case.*

Nechi's eyes were pleading. "Do you think you can come with us to the emergency room?"

"I'M SORRY FOR dragging you out like this in the middle of the night, I just don't think I'm up to going alone," Nechi had said by way of apology on the way to the hospital. Mr. Goldfeder, Suri was given to understand, was currently out of town, though Nechi had texted him immediately upon receiving Suri's phone call. (She didn't say what her husband had texted back, but from the way Nechi's car swerved as she mentioned it, Suri could take a lucky guess.)

Dini was much calmer by the time they reached the ER, calm enough that they were left to wait for almost two hours before they were taken in.

"If my husband were here…" Nechi muttered more than once, shaking her head each time one of her entreaties to the nurses was answered with a condescending, "Any minute now, ma'am."

Just as Nechi was beginning to decide that this was all a waste of time, that they'd gotten hysterical over nothing ("Look, she's completely fine now!"), Dini's name was called.

They were directed into a small office with sterile, cream-colored walls, where a Dr. Mann introduced himself as a psychiatrist. Suri wavered by the doorway, not sure if she belonged inside, but Nechi pulled her in, instructing her to tell the doctor what had occurred.

Dr. Mann listened intently, asking a lot of questions, initially to Suri, but eventually directed at Dini and her mother. It emerged that Dini hadn't slept at all in the past forty-eight hours. It also became clear that she had undergone a number of what the doctor termed manic episodes over the past year, including some of the incidents that Nechi had described to Suri long ago, when Dini had first started coming to the clinic. But none of them, Nechi stated emphatically, had been anywhere near as drastic as this one.

The doctor furrowed his eyebrows. "Has anything happened recently, any environmental trigger? A stressful life event? Recent illness?" He glanced at Dini, as Nechi shook her head. "Alcohol or substance abuse?"

"No!" Nechi said quickly.

"Is she on any medication?"

"No…um," Nechi stumbled. Suri gave her a sharp glance. So did the doctor.

Dini spoke up. "Ritalin."

The doctor paused. "You're taking Ritalin?"

She nodded.

"For how long?"

Dini looked at her mother. "A few months?"

"And have you ever experienced side effects before?"

Nechi shook her head, while Dini shrugged. "I dunno," she mumbled. Her eyes were glazed and her head was starting to droop—not surprising, Suri thought, considering she hadn't slept for the past two nights. Three, counting now.

"And you've been taking it regularly?" the doctor persisted. "Any recent changes in prescription?"

Nechi shifted uncomfortably. Dini said, "Well, I did take extra the other night. I'm having exams right now, it's ridiculous that our teachers give us tests so close to Pesach all my friends say, but whatever, I have them now and I needed, like, some extra focus, that's why I take the Ritalin, my mom says, to stop acting so crazy, you know? So I took extra and since then" —she giggled—"it's been wild, Doc!"

Dr. Mann was frowning. "Ritalin can have severe side effects on bipolar disorder. There's a known risk of triggering psychotic episodes—which it seems your daughter experienced. Who's the prescribing doctor?"

Nechi, who had blanched at the words "bipolar disorder," was positively ashen now. "Um...well...my husband..." she stammered.

She looked like she wanted to bolt. Dr. Mann's eyebrows were raised to the ceiling. Even Suri was digging her fingernails into her palms. At that moment, the door to the office burst open. "Where's my daughter?" demanded an all-too-familiar voice, as Mr. Goldfeder strode inside.

"Hello, Doctor, I'm this young lady's father. I came as fast as I can, was out in Philly." Indeed, his face was ruddy, as if he had sprinted the entire way.

Dr. Mann nodded politely. "We were just discussing—"

But Goldfeder interrupted him, as his eyes suddenly focused on Suri. "What's she doing here?" he asked, his voice low and rumbling.

"Shmuel, don't, Suri's the one who—" Nechi started, but her husband brushed her aside.

"My lawyers will hear about this!" he yelled, pointing a finger at Suri as his voice rose and his eyes bugged out. "It's not enough that you spread these rumors to her school administration—now you're doing it to the medical men too!"

"Please, Shmuel," Nechi tried, but Dr. Mann had risen from his seat.

"I don't know what delusions you are under, sir," he said. "But you owe this woman a debt of gratitude. She may have saved your daughter's life tonight."

CHAPTER 54

"SHABBOS HAGADOL AT a hotel!" Aviva arched her head disbelievingly as she looked around at the lobby full of people milling around after shul Friday night. Zevi had just walked up to the quiet corner she'd found for herself, where for the past hour she'd been resting on an armchair, gently rocking Yerachmiel in his stroller as she enjoyed the view. She knew no one, and she found she was not even tempted to introduce herself to the cluster of ladies sitting nearby. When she considered how her younger self would have been the center of the group within minutes, she could only shake her head and wonder why it had taken her so long to discover the magic of just being.

She nodded now toward the scene in front of them. "I know why *I'm* here, but what in the world are they all doing here a few days before Pesach?"

Zevi sat down in the armchair opposite her. "And why are you here?"

She raised her eyebrow. "Because my husband kidnapped me."

He nodded seriously. "Maybe these women all have the same excuse. Gotta be *dan lechaf zechus*, ma'am."

"Or maybe they've all been working *really hard* for the past few weeks. Unlike me," she murmured.

Zevi had insisted on hiring help to do all the Pesach cleaning. Insisted wasn't even the word; he had done it behind her back. One morning a few days after the bris, just as she'd begun waking out of her self-pitying haze to realize Pesach was frightfully soon, Aviva had opened the door to find four eager bachurim standing there. She'd thought they were collecting for their yeshivah, but Zevi had quickly pushed her aside.

"Ah, *chevrah*, you're here!" And, ushering them past a bemused Aviva, he'd proceeded to give them instructions. "Helfgot, you take the *sefarim shrank*. Rosen and Lichter, the kitchen cabinets—and watch the china, my wife'll kill me if it breaks. Markowitz, start on the fridge. Help yourself to anything in there but my buffalo wings."

He had then forced Aviva up to her bed, assuring her that he had everything under control.

"Give these men two days and a couple pies of pizza, and the place'll be Pesach perfect."

Aviva didn't know how she'd allowed herself to be convinced; she had never before relinquished control of her Pesach cleaning. As the hours had passed and she'd found herself straining her ears to listen for suspicious crashes above the blasting Shwekey music, she'd begun to formulate plans of sneaking downstairs in the middle of the night to redo all of their work. Just in case.

She'd been dozing when Zevi came to check on her, waking with a start, and blushing out of a vague sense of guilt. How utterly decadent, taking a nap a week before Pesach! Zevi, on the other hand, was all hyped up, and seemed to be having the time of his life.

"You don't usually get this excited about Pesach cleaning," she'd grumbled.

But her real concern was how they were affording all this help. Without directly answering her, he'd announced that, what was more, he was also taking her away for Shabbos HaGadol. It was all arranged, he'd even reserved the grandparents to babysit. (His parents, not hers, he'd hastily assured her.)

"And how...?" she'd tried again, but he'd waved her off.

"That's for me to worry about."

And so here they were, a whole Shabbos with just the two of them and the baby, and someone else doing the cooking and cleaning.

"I could get used to this," she said later that night, as they went for a walk around the lit-up grounds.

"I don't remember the last time I've seen you this relaxed," Zevi said.

Aviva laughed. "Can't say the same for you."

"Yeah, well, that's me, always chilled." An odd shadow passed over his face, and Aviva glanced at him.

"You know," she said, after a pause, "sometimes I'm jealous. I wish I could be more like you."

He snorted. "No, you don't."

She was surprised by his vehemence. "Why do you say that?"

"We've been married way too long for fake politeness." He stopped next to a bench and motioned for her to sit down. "You really wish I could be more like you. Mr. Type A Intenso-Man, who has some business where I'm never home but making piles of money, so that you wouldn't have to work and could afford full-time cleaning help, but would still work and clean anyway, of course, because you wouldn't know what to do with yourself otherwise."

Aviva would have smiled at the spot-on description, but somehow didn't feel like it. What hurt the most was the fact that it *was* so accurate—and that Zevi must have been sensing some underlying disappointment all these years. Whereas, all along, it was she who had been so, so incredibly stupid.

"Zevi," she said quietly. "If I'd been married to a Mr. Intenso-Man"—her lips twitched at the term—"I...I don't think I would have survived these past few weeks. Literally." She watched Yerachmiel, lying in his stroller. He was starting to make sucking motions in his sleep, and she knew they didn't have much time left outside.

"I thought you were the one with the poor coping skills," she continued, still staring at the baby, "in denial all along about the possibility the doctor had mentioned, while I was being so realistic and sensible. But it was my coping skills that were off. Guess they've always been," she added, suddenly struck with the realization. "My answer to everything is to work harder, to force everything to be perfect. Only, suddenly, we had this gorgeous little baby, who will never be perfect, no matter what I do."

She looked up at Zevi, her eyes moist. "And I always thought you were the crazy one." She gave a short laugh, her lips trembling. "Just picture how messed up our kids would be if you were as crazy as me."

"Wackos, both of us," Zevi said. Through the darkness, she could see his eyes shining.

They were both silent for a while, listening to the wind rustle the leaves in the tree next to them. At last, he said, "Ever since I've known you, you've always been Superwoman. You did everything yourself, and did it much better than I ever could. There was nothing you needed, nothing I could give you…except for one thing. You needed someone to take care of *you*."

Aviva stared at Zevi sharply, as something suddenly clicked in place. "Is that why you wanted to become the secretary at the clinic? I'd always wondered."

Zevi shrugged apologetically. "Dunno, maybe. Yeah, I guess so." He shifted his legs. "Or maybe it was to tap into my inner Organizer. My plan was to take the administrative assistant world by storm with all my heretofore unrevealed talents. I was even gonna put my name down for the Secretary of the Century award. Still think I could've won, if *someone* had given me the chance."

Aviva was glad he was back to joking. Still, she needed to say it.

"Zevi, what you just told me now. That's…that's…" Turned out, there weren't really any words. "Thank you," she whispered.

‎——

SURI HAD SPENT the whole Shabbos deliberating.

She hadn't heard from the Goldfeders since their meeting in the hospital. She still found herself chuckling as she remembered the look on Mr. Goldfeder's face after being told off by the doctor. But she had excused herself soon after, thinking it both unwise and inconsiderate to stay around. So, she didn't know how they had gotten themselves out of the Ritalin hole, nor what had been decided for Dini in the end. And though she was curious like anything, she knew, as Shaul kept reminding her, that neither of those issues were her business.

What *was* her business was the lawsuit hanging over her, and the fact that she was suddenly in possession of a whole lot of damaging information. She could just picture the look of glee on her lawyer's face when she told him.

If she told him.

She'd spent the whole Shabbos deliberating about that.

It had fallen into her lap, a literal gift from Heaven, this simple way to end the entire thing. Of course, she'd been hoping that the Goldfeders would decide on their own to drop the lawsuit, once they realized she'd been right all along. But there'd been no communication from the other side over the past few days, and from the glare Mr. Goldfeder had shot her as she'd left—all the more venomous after he'd been humiliated by the doctor—Suri had realized that hope was unrealistically optimistic. And so, she was left with only one choice: to have her lawyer relay the whole sorry incident in court. It was the only option, she told herself.

Or maybe not.

CHAPTER 55

SURI GLANCED AT the house in front of her dubiously. If she'd been intimidated by Yael's sprawling home, that was nothing compared to the Goldfeder mansion.

She hesitated by the imposing wooden door. This was a mistake, a crazy mistake. She should have done the sensible thing and gone to her lawyer. Wasn't she paying him the big bucks because he knew just what to do with the sort of information she held in her pocket? Instead, she'd chosen to take a trip into the lion's den.

The doorbell reverberated as if through a cavernous hall. A moment later, the door opened, and a lady who was clearly the housekeeper ushered her inside. Each step through the marble, art-lined hallway served to drive home the message more sharply: These people were in a totally different league. Attempting to fight them was like a mouse trying to nip at the heels of an elephant.

But then again, that's why she was there. Because she wasn't interested in fighting.

"Suri, what a pleasant surprise!" Nechi was her usual smooth self, a far cry from the other night. All gracious politeness, though it was clear she did not find anything pleasant about this surprise. Suri had considered calling them in advance, but she thought it likely they would tell her not to come.

"I know it's an inconvenient time for visitors, just a few days before Pesach," Suri began awkwardly, as she sat down on the embroidered armchair—surprisingly comfortable for something that looked like it was meant to be hanging on a wall.

Nechi waved her apology away. "I just have a bit of last-minute packing left. We're flying tomorrow."

Flying tomorrow. Of course. How silly of her to imagine people like the Goldfeders made Pesach. Indeed, a minute later, a china platter of very *chametzdik* biscotti appeared, along with two plates and linen napkins. *Must be nice to have a kitchen staff.*

Suri cleared her throat. "I...um...wanted to see how Dini was doing."

Nechi's smile tightened slightly. "She's doing well, thank G-d. She gave us quite a scare. Thank you again for your help. Dini's not home right now, otherwise she would thank you herself."

Suri longed to ask what steps were being taken to help Dini, but she knew the question would be way out of bounds even if they didn't have a lawsuit hanging between them. She took a biscotti, to buy herself time as she thought of how to phrase what she wanted to say next.

"Nechi!"

Suri gave a little jump at the sound of his voice. Why, oh why was Mr. Goldfeder always so *present?* she wondered as her heart sank. She had hoped to have this little conversation alone with Nechi.

Nechi also looked vaguely alarmed, and called out quickly, "What do you want?"

"My machzor! Where is it?"

"Coming, Shmuel." Nechi was on the verge of getting out of her seat when Mr. Goldfeder walked into the room. And stopped short.

"You again?" he cried.

"She came to see how Dini's doing," Nechi said quickly.

"I'll bet." His eyes narrowed. "Thought to do some snooping around, Mrs. Taub?"

Snooping around? Really! And as her indignation rose, she suddenly regained her confidence.

Looking him in the eye, she said quietly, "I have no need to 'snoop around,' Mr. Goldfeder, even if I were the type to do so. You and I both know that. After what happened the other night, I think I have all I need to win my case—or at least to bring up certain uncomfortable things that you'd probably prefer not be aired in court. Isn't that right?"

She paused long enough to see him wince, while Nechi's face was white and terrified.

"But that's not why I came today." She took a breath. "I came to apologize."

"A-apologize?" Nechi looked startled, and even her husband blinked.

Suri felt her face burning, but her voice remained steady. "I was wrong to go over your heads and speak to the principal. I wanted so badly to help Dini, and I believed, for whatever reason, she wasn't getting the help she needed." She paused, leaving the obvious—that she had been right to believe so—unstated. "But that doesn't really matter. Because whether the court in the end decides I did the right thing or the wrong thing, I've come to understand that I went about it the wrong way, and by forcing you into a corner, it probably did Dini more harm. So, for that, I want to say I'm sorry."

There was utter silence in the room, and then Nechi reached her hand across the table and squeezed Suri's. "It takes a lot of courage to come here and say what you did. We—my husband and I—appreciate that."

She threw a glance at her husband, who, after a moment's hesitation, gave a brief, jerky nod.

YAEL WIPED HER forehead as she zipped the duffel bag. There, the children's clothes were packed. Now it was onto her own clothing. She glanced at the clock. Ephraim wouldn't be happy if they left too late for her parents'.

"Almost finished?" Ephraim walked into the room. "Simi's ready for a nap, didn't know if I should put her in now or let her sleep in the car."

"Yeah, just about finished," Yael said, as she took a dress out of the closet.

"Is that new?" Ephraim asked.

Yael nodded. "Rina's Racks exclusive!" She grinned as she wrapped it in a garment bag. "Your sister is so sweet, the way she keeps giving me outfits from her store."

Yael wasn't sure why the offer hadn't bothered her this time. When Rina had pulled her over at Simi's birthday party and insisted she come into the store to choose a Pesach outfit, Yael had not felt the same queasiness she'd felt the first time, that sense that she just wasn't good enough, and Rina was trying to make her over in the Jeren model. This time, somehow, it had come off differently—as a simple desire to do a favor for a sister-in-law. She wondered if it was Rina's attitude that had changed, or her own.

"Rina thinks so highly of you," Ephraim said. "She's always going on about what a great mother you are… Sometimes I think she's jealous."

"Jealous of me? What a joke." Yael pursed her lips as she struggled with the zipper of her garment bag, which had gotten stuck. "When she's like, high-powered, super-successful Businesswoman of the Year?"

Ephraim shrugged, as he took the bag from her. "Maybe I just imagined it."

They were silent for a moment, and then Yael said slowly, "Can I ask you something? Do you think that there *is* something to be jealous of?"

She blushed as he raised his eyebrows, and said quickly, "I don't mean of *me* specifically, but I mean…" She knew what she wanted to say, and hoped it would come out the way she meant it. "Well, do you think a woman who's so invested in her job that she's rarely home would have what to be jealous of a mother like me, who's home all day with her kids?"

Ephraim was silent for a while as he tugged at the zipper. Finally, with a yank, he freed it. He looked up. "Yeah, I guess she would. I mean, I think so."

"You sound very sure of yourself," Yael said drily.

Ephraim's eyes widened. "No, I mean it. Being a mother's the most important job there is, right?"

"How *frum* of you."

He seemed to fear he'd offended her. "Seriously! And you…

well, Rina's right. You do a super job at being a mother."

She gave a short laugh. "Unlike an OT."

He scratched his beard uncomfortably. "Yeah, well…we can't be good at everything, right?"

"And if you had to choose…?"

Ephraim gave her a small smile. "What kind of question is that? I'd much rather you be a good mother than a good career woman!"

Yael's heart beat faster. "So you're not disappointed in me?"

"Disappointed? N—" He stopped, as if wavering between saying what he knew he was supposed to say and his innate honesty.

Honesty won. "Okay, so I won't pretend I wasn't disappointed. But, *nu*, so it happened, and now you're at home, and I will say I've noticed how much happier you've been." He threw her an anxious grin. "And hey, for me, having a happy wife is the *most* important thing."

Yael felt almost giddy from the wonderful relief that flooded her. Placing the garment bag on top of her closed suitcase, she decided to press her luck just a bit further. "So now that you've come to this realization—do you think it's time to tell your parents?"

CHAPTER 56

THERE WAS SOMETHING so magical about Seder night, Yael reflected, as she leaned back in her seat and drank in the atmosphere. Everything in the house—the windows, the glass goblets, the normally tarnished silver—was polished and buffed to a shine. But, more than the elegant physical accoutrements of the usually *heimishe* household, it was her family itself that shone. Like the perfect setting for a diamond, Pesach night brought out all that was beautiful and right about her family.

Getting poetic in our old age, are we? She smiled at herself. Her mother, catching her smile, said, "I'm so happy you're here, Yael. I love having the whole family together."

Yael couldn't agree more. And to think she might have been halfway across the world sitting in some swanky hotel in Italy right now, instead of right here, home with her family, where she belonged...

They had just served the meal, and her father and brothers were now trading *divrei Torah*. Yael studied her mother, who was listening carefully, occasionally throwing in a question or comment of her own. Her sheitel was freshly set, but nothing compared to Yael's own new Shevy, and she knew that her mother-in-law would be horrified at Yael's mother's idea of appropriate Seder night attire—but, nevertheless, Mommy gave off a regalness that Yael wondered if she could ever attain.

This was her mother's night, Yael realized. As successful as Mommy was in her own career, tonight she was glowing from the *nachas* of the family she'd created. Basking in the Torah of her husband, of the joint mission the two of them had taken on in passing that Torah down to future generations—both their own children, and all of their *talmidim* and *talmidos*.

Yael adjusted Simi, whose head was drooping on her shoulder. Would she and Ephraim, for all their outer material trappings, ever merit the true spiritual accomplishments of her parents?

As she looked over at Ephraim, who was now sharing his own piece of Torah, the question pricked deeper: Did her husband even want that?

—

"YAEL, I'VE BEEN meaning to ask you something. Do you have a minute?"

Yael looked up as her mother stuck her head into her room. It was the first day of *chol hamoed*, and Yael was busy packing up her family for an outing to the zoo. She glanced briefly at Ephraim, who was, she knew, itching to get out of the house. "Not that I don't love your family," he'd told her that morning. "But, you know, two days of being on top of each other..."

That was just one more of their many cultural differences. She, who'd grown up with a big family and small house, loved the sense of family togetherness during *yom tov*. The fact that she, Ephraim, and the two kids were all squeezed into her former bedroom (her sisters graciously piling together into the second girls' room), in her mind just added to the fun. But Ephraim, used to having all the space a human could possibly need, didn't quite see the enjoyment in this slumber party atmosphere.

"Be back in a second," she told Ephraim, following her mother into the hall.

"We got a *shidduch* suggestion for Raizy," Mommy said, after glancing to make sure no one was around. "And I wanted to ask your opinion."

"It's someone I know?" Yael asked, eyes dancing.

Her mother tilted her head. "I'm not sure, but they're friends of your in-laws."

Yael's blood suddenly ran cold. No, no, no. What was her mother thinking, wanting to repeat the same mistake?

"Don't do it," she urged, lowering her voice.

Her mother's eyebrows shot up. "I didn't even tell you the name yet."

"Doesn't matter. If they're in the same set as my in-laws, it's not for Raizy."

Her mother stared at her for a moment too long. Finally, she said, "That, actually, was what I wanted to ask you." She let the unspoken question hang heavily between them for several seconds before continuing delicately. "He's a wonderful man, your husband. Every time I see him, I'm more impressed. Considering his background, he's so modest and refined." She paused again, to let that sink in. "We checked into that, Tatty and I. That was what concerned us most when we first heard about him—that he shouldn't be one of these spoiled, self-entitled rich boys. But everyone across the board vouched for his beautiful *middos*."

Yael looked at her mother in wonder. What an idiot she had been. *Of course* her parents would have thought out the potential pitfalls of marrying into wealth, and would have done their best to ensure her happiness. And it was true. Ephraim *was* modest and unassuming. She'd never before appreciated how unusual that was, coming from the family he did. But still…

"Mommy, I'm not *chas veshalom* complaining about Ephraim. He's a wonderful husband." She swallowed, thinking of all the times this past year she'd been scared to reveal her true feelings to him, the fact that she'd tried to twist herself into something she wasn't, just to fit into his and his family's perception of success. But that didn't mean they had a bad marriage, she realized. That just meant they had a…marriage. With its ups and downs and trying to adjust to each other's cultures and individual personalities and all the other million things that went into making a person who they were.

Still, her parents had to realize that it wasn't only about *middos*.

"But," she continued, "it's been hard. Really hard. And, like we spoke about that time on the phone, there've been times I've felt like who I used to be has gotten totally swallowed up in this huge, domineering new force in my life. And then I come back here, and I remember what my life used to be like, and I wonder… what if I would've married some struggling *kollel* husband like I'd always expected? Would my life be less complicated? Or more spiritual?"

Yael felt her face getting red. She had never articulated these thoughts, even to herself, but suddenly, talking to her mother, she understood that they had always been lurking there in her subconscious. Horrified at herself, she quickly said, "That sounded terrible! And here I have everything, all the money I could ever want, and my in-laws really are so generous, and it's not like my husband isn't into his learning, and—what's wrong with me?"

She heard Ephraim's voice just then, admonishing Sruli about something, and she startled. She hadn't realized how close she was standing to their bedroom. Paling at the possibility that she may have been overheard, she quickly mumbled, "Anyway, just some things to think about. *Hatzlachah* with Raizy."

As she turned to return to her room, her mother reached out to stroke her cheek. "There's nothing wrong with you, sweetie. But, if I may—you might be underestimating your husband."

"THIS IS NICE," Ephraim said, breathing deeply as they settled down on a grassy hill for a matzah-pizza picnic at the zoo. "Let's do this tomorrow, also. And leave the kids home with your parents," he added, as he pulled Sruli back from rolling down the hill.

Yael watched him curiously. "This is the first time all *yom tov* that you look relaxed."

"Your family's great, but they can get pretty intense," he said.

"Intense?"

"Yeah, you know, everything's all Torah, all the time."

Yael felt her heart thudding, as she said carefully, "And that bothers you?"

Ephraim was picking at a blade of grass, not looking at her. "Well, no, obviously. That's actually what I love about your family. Right from the start, when we first met, that's what struck me about them—how authentic they were. In your parents' house, Yiddishkeit is lived and breathed, you know what I mean?"

"I sure do. And…" she looked at him anxiously, "isn't that the kind of family we want, also?"

"Absolutely," he said, with such conviction that she felt herself breathing freely again. "But…I don't know if you can understand this, but it was, well, a culture shock for me, marrying into your family. I grew up differently. In my house, we spoke about politics at the Shabbos table. We went ice skating on Sundays. Not to say my parents aren't good, *frum* Jews, but, it was looser. You know?

"As I got older and into learning, I decided I wanted something more intense for my own life, more spiritually focused, and I told my parents I wanted to look for a girl from that kind of background." He winked at Yael. "And that's what I got, *baruch Hashem*. And it still is my *she'ifah* in life. But I don't think I quite appreciated what such a lifestyle entails. The whole breadth and scope of it. It's an adjustment for me."

He threw her a quick look, and she was almost positive she caught a twinkle in his eye. "Can you understand that?"

She kept her expression as serious as his own as she answered, "Perfectly."

CHAPTER 57

SURI WAS IN the middle of a therapy session, the first day back at work after Pesach, when the phone call came.

"Goldfeder's lawyer," Shira mouthed, when Suri raised her eyebrows at the interruption.

Suri was tempted—oh so tempted—to send a message that she was busy, that he should call back in a half hour. She really did not have the stomach to deal with whatever Goldfeder's lawyer had to say. But she decided it was unwise to play the arrogant professional to the other side's legal team. So, with a hasty apology to her client and her mother, she took the call.

She returned five minutes later, a wide smile on her face.

*

"WAIT, WAIT, START from the beginning! I want to hear *every* detail!"

Aviva leaned forward on her couch, looking more animated

than Suri could remember seeing her in a long time. No, she thought, animated wasn't the word. Aviva was often excited, but now, Suri realized, as she watched Aviva stroke little Yerachmiel, who was sleeping in her arms, there was something else there as well. She looked at peace with herself.

Suri thought back to the last time she'd seen Aviva, at the bris. She'd been nervous to contact her, realizing Aviva clearly needed space. But now, a few weeks later…it was obvious that some sort of change had taken place.

Meanwhile, Aviva was eagerly digesting Suri's news. "So, you actually went to their house and apologized? I could never have done that!"

"What are you talking about? You would've been much more confident walking into their house than I was. I'm telling you, I nearly ran away!"

Aviva waved her hand. "I meant I could never have apologized. That must have taken a lot of *avodas hamiddos*."

Suri was not used to that look of undisguised admiration coming from Aviva, and she adjusted her glasses uncomfortably.

"Yeah, well, I wasn't really sure how it went over. Nechi was all gracious about accepting my apology, of course. Accepting!" She shook her head. "Didn't even occur to her that maybe I deserved one also. And her husband, forget about it. He still looked like he wanted to throttle me when I left."

Suri's eyes twinkled. "And now, today, I get this call. 'My clients have decided to drop all charges.' I nearly fainted!"

Aviva laughed in delight. "Unbelievable! Your apology really did do the trick after all. Or maybe it was the fact that you saved their daughter's life?" That look of admiration was back. "Suri, you did it. I know I wasn't as involved as I should have been. You took care of this all on your own."

Suri squirmed. "Yeah, well, I got us into this mess all on my own too."

Aviva ignored that. "So, how are things going at the clinic? Are people still scared away?"

Suri grinned. Yet another thing that had gone right today. "Shira actually told me that she's been swamped with phone calls. You know it always gets busy right after Pesach. *Baruch Hashem*, there was no lasting damage, it seems."

Aviva shifted Yerachmiel to her other arm. "Gosh, I can't wait to get back! It's been forever!" She looked down at the baby, a wry smile flitting across her face. "He's the sweetest little baby, but am I a terrible mother for admitting I'm desperate to get back to work? I'm even thinking of cutting my maternity leave short."

Suri was conscious of a sudden clenching inside, and that old nasally voice saying, *Here she goes again with all her kvetching, totally oblivious to the fact that there are women who would give anything to be home on maternity leave.*

But would you, Suri? she suddenly shot back. *Under her circumstances? Would you give anything to have a handicapped baby?*

It was a question she wouldn't dare to answer. Watching Aviva now, it hit her that Aviva *had* dared. That she'd chosen to come face to face with her fears rather than live in denial. An overwhelming fondness for the old friend sitting across from her suddenly bubbled up inside.

"Aviva Heyman. You are probably the only woman in the world who would actually come back to work before her maternity leave is up."

Aviva waved her off. "Please. If you were stuck for months on a couch… Anyway," she said brightly. "I think this calls for a celebration, don't you? Let's go out to eat, just the two of us. Or… uh…three of us," she added, with a nod to the baby.

Suri bit her lip. There was one more topic she wanted to bring up, something that had been niggling at her for a long while. A piece of unfinished business it was high time they took care of.

"Sounds great," she said. "But do you mind if we make a stop somewhere else first?"

YAEL HUMMED AS she folded and put away the kids' *yom tov* clothing. It had been wonderful being with her family, but she had to admit, Ephraim wasn't the only one who'd sighed with relief when they'd walked back into their house *motza'ei yom tov*. It was the first time that she could remember that, leaving her family to come back to their palatial residence, she had the sense of coming home. To the home and family that she and Ephraim were building. It was different than the family her parents had built, and also than the one his parents had built. And that was okay, because this was their own.

She didn't know if Ephraim had sensed any change as well, but, whatever the reason, when she'd remarked this morning that his parents were due back from Italy tomorrow, he'd responded casually, "Yeah. I was thinking we should let them settle a bit, and then have a talk with them. About, you know, our decision that you won't be looking for a new job, that you'll be a stay-at-home mom."

Our decision. She didn't know how that talk would go, but as she hummed to herself, she found that she didn't care. Well, not much, at least.

The doorbell rang, causing Yael's eyebrows to shoot up. She

wasn't expecting anyone. Hoping that the peal hadn't woken her napping children, she ran quickly to the door.

Standing on her doorstep were the last two people she would have expected.

"Aviva! Suri! What in the world brings you here?"

"Surprise," said Aviva, with a slightly awkward smile. "Mind if we come in?"

As Yael led them through her hall, and caught them sneaking the same amazed looks as they had the last time they'd come, it was impossible not to have a sense of déjà vu. Yet, so much had happened since that time. Then, she was filled with bitterness and shame. A short while later, she'd done her own grand act of betrayal, and the shame was directed at herself. But now, today, she finally felt that she'd risen above both of those feelings, that she'd brought herself to a much healthier emotional place.

Suri twisted her hands in her lap as she sat facing Yael, and even Aviva was tapping her foot ever so slightly on the carpet as she gently bounced Yerachmiel. Yael threw out some remarks about how cute the baby was, all the while wondering.

"So, you want to know why we came," Aviva began, with a small smile.

Yael's lips twitched. "Nah, not even remotely curious."

Suri laughed, but stayed silent. Apparently, this was Aviva's show.

"I came," Aviva said, with a small glance at Suri, "to apologize." She took a breath. "For real. I didn't treat you the way I should have, a few months back. I was so concerned about the clinic that I forgot to be concerned about you and your feelings. Which are obviously much more important."

Yael didn't think she'd ever seen Aviva blush before. "Uh, thanks for saying that. I appreciate it." And she meant it. "But, why now?"

Aviva absently smoothed the soft hair on Yerachmiel's head. "I don't know. Maybe…I don't think I was ready until now to understand that I'd done something wrong." She blinked, and Yael, imagining just how hard an admission that must be for someone like Aviva, was touched.

"It's okay," she said. "I don't think I was ready until now to hear your apology." She smiled. "But I can tell you now that I truly, truly forgive you. And wish you only the best with the clinic."

She had the urge to get up and give Aviva a hug—it seemed like such a hug moment—but something told her Aviva didn't do hugs. Wrapping her arms around herself in absentia, she rocked slightly as a voice inside began screaming, *You, too, have something to apologize for!*

But Tatty had told her that revealing her part in the whole story would just make things worse. Besides…

"Speaking of the clinic, we actually have some good news," Suri said. Her face was beaming. "I don't know, I assume you heard about the lawsuit against us?"

Yael nodded, squirming in her chair.

"Well, *baruch Hashem*, we got a phone call this morning from their lawyer. They've decided to drop all charges! Isn't that incredible?"

Yael broke out into a smile. "What wonderful news! I'm so happy for you!"

"Yes, we're very relieved," Aviva said. "We're actually on our way now for a celebratory lunch." She paused. "Up for coming?"

Startled, Yael said, "Uh, really? But, I didn't…um, really? You sure you want me?"

Both Aviva and Suri were nodding now. Elation rising inside, Yael jumped up. "I'll need to get a babysitter. Unless you want to celebrate here? Order in? Hey!" she added, as it hit her suddenly, spectacularly—what in the world did she have to be ashamed about the fact that she had money?—"It'll be my treat!"

She ran away to get her phone before her two former partners had a chance to protest. As she left the room, she couldn't help laughing aloud. What they didn't realize was just how much she belonged at this celebration.

Over Pesach, she'd had a long talk with her mother about the whole Goldfeder saga, and the strong guilt she still felt.

"Well, I'm partly to blame, I suppose," her mother had said. "I played a role in this too."

"Isn't there something you can do?" Yael had beseeched.

And her mother, who could do anything in the world, had said calmly, "Yes, actually, I think I can. I'm going to have a chat with the Goldfeders."

ONE MONTH LATER

Aviva surveyed the buffet tables set up along the wall of the clinic's large waiting area. Chavi had been hard at work all afternoon; she'd been taking some little after-school course on food arrangement, and was eager to show off what she'd learned. Naama had offered to do the setup for this evening, but Aviva, despite her misgivings—Naama, after all, had magical hands, while Chavi, who knew what she'd come up with?—had said no. Chavi would be in charge, she'd decided, and, though it had meant literally sitting on her hands several times today to stop them from rearranging things, she'd stuck to her resolution, giving Chavi free rein.

"Looks stunning, sweetie," she said, for the hundredth time.

(How many more until she would start believing it?) "You really have talent!"

Chavi beamed, and from the way she held her head higher as she walked away, Aviva knew that all her self-control had been worth it.

Suri's family was first to arrive. Aviva saw Suri's daughter give Chavi a shy compliment on the tables, and she swelled with pride for her daughter. Her parents came in soon after; her mother raised an eyebrow at Chavi's design, and, saying nothing, she turned toward Aviva. "I don't understand what this is all about, but here we are. Where should we sit?"

Her sisters came soon after with their families, followed by Zevi's family, and, last of all, Yael and her husband.

"Mazel tov, thanks for inviting us," Yael said, squeezing Aviva's hand.

Soon enough, everyone was more or less seated, and looking at her expectantly. Aviva glanced at Zevi. She was used to speaking in front of crowds, but, somehow, the prospect of speaking in front of this audience of their family and close friends made her nerves rise into her throat. She was not one to chicken out, but the look she threw at her husband clearly said, *Can't you do it?*

Zevi walked over to her side and whispered, "You'll be awesome. Just speak from your heart."

Taking a breath, Aviva said, "Thanks, everyone, for coming. As you know, the past few months have been quite a roller coaster ride, first with my bed rest, and then Yerachmiel's birth. And of course, with everything going on concurrently at the clinic." She paused. "Sometimes, we think we're in control, that we know exactly what's best for us...and then Hashem throws us a curveball, as if to remind us that only He's in control. It took me a while, I admit, to come to terms with that."

She threw a side glance at her husband. "We want to thank you all for the support you've given us during this time. I know that we have a long road ahead of us, raising Yerachmiel. But with every passing day, Zevi and I appreciate more and more the *berachah* that we have in our lives—not just in Yerachmiel, but so much more."

She looked around at the audience, at Yael and Suri sitting next to each other at one table, at her mother frowning in concentration, at Chavi who was busy hushing little Kivi. "All of you are a part of that *berachah*. And so Zevi and I decided we wanted to throw a *seudas hodaah* of sorts, to thank Hashem for all the good we have in our lives." She lowered her eyes. What she didn't say was that she'd been eating herself up over her embarrassing scene at the bris, and that Zevi had suggested this little gathering as a kind of second chance. Her husband, who understood her so much better than she understood herself.

Looking back at the audience, she concluded, "Thank you."

EPILOGUE

SURI STUCK HER head into the waiting area on her way from the office to her therapy room, and gave a quick nod to the mothers sitting there schmoozing. There was a buzz in the room that followed her down the hall, the hum of multiple conversations being carried on simultaneously, mingled with the squeals of children jumping on bouncy balls as they waited. As she walked toward her therapy room—passing five more rooms on the way, all of them occupied—she reflected for a moment on how far the clinic had come in the past three years since it opened. It hadn't been so long ago when there would be only one mother sitting in the waiting area, and when Suri would feel the need to make forced conversation as she passed. Today, with a growing staff of therapists, the clinic was usually bustling, especially at peak hours.

"Taking a break, Suri?" Naomi greeted her as Suri passed her open door.

"Just for a bit. I've been going straight for the past four hours."

Naomi shook her head in commiseration, and Suri waved and

walked by. Her next four hours would be packed as well, including her new client—the one that she'd been dreading ever since she heard about him.

"It was a mistake," she whispered to herself, yet again. "I should never have agreed to take him on. What was I thinking?"

But the deed had been done, and all she could hope for now was that she wouldn't be kicking herself over it for the next five months. Or years.

Resisting the urge to go over his file yet again—she knew it by heart already—she instead began typing up her session notes, when she heard a knock on the door.

"Hey, stranger, got a minute?"

Suri looked up and broke into a smile. "Yael! What are you doing here so early?"

In the past few months, Yael had started giving therapeutic art workshops for kids at the clinic. They'd become quite popular, and Suri got real pleasure seeing Yael so clearly in her element. But the groups took place during after-school hours, and Suri rarely got a chance to exchange more than a few words with Yael.

"I wanted to speak with you about something." Yael pulled out a chair, as Suri glanced at her watch.

"I have about fifteen minutes till my next client," she warned. From the way Yael was leaning back in her chair, it looked like she was settling in for the long haul.

"No problem, if I go on too long, feel free to throw me out." She winked, and then opened her handbag—Luis Vuitton, not that Suri was noticing—and took out a folded scrap of paper.

"I ran into someone the other day, who wanted to say hello to you." Yael's eyes were twinkling as she handed Suri the paper.

Wondering, Suri unfolded the note. Her mouth dropped open as she saw the name on the bottom. "Dini Goldfeder! Where in the world did you see her?" It had been nearly a year since she'd gone to the Goldfeders' house to apologize, and she hadn't seen or heard from any of them since. She'd been dying to know what had become of Dini.

Yael's chin was lifted proudly. "Worth giving up your lunch break for, huh?"

Suri gripped the table. "How? When? Why? Tell me everything!"

"Ah, I was volunteering in the psych ward of the local hospital when suddenly this girl comes flying into me, about to take her life, and at the last second I—no, just joking." Yael gave a self-conscious laugh. "As usual, it had nothing to do with me, it was because of my family."

Oh, right. How could Suri have forgotten that the Jerens were good friends with the Goldfeders? Yael had let that little tidbit slip, during the celebratory meal that the three of them had shared after learning that the lawsuit was dropped, and Suri had not been surprised. Of course, it made so much sense, how could they not travel in the same circles? The Jerens and Goldfeders had probably met up recently at some elegant little luncheon, all the ladies with their Luis Vuitton bags and Chanel dresses…

"…my mother."

Suri blinked. "What? What does your mother have to do with this?"

Yael looked momentarily flummoxed. "Didn't you know? Oh, no, you…uh…didn't." She blinked rapidly, as her fingers began playing with the clasp of her bag.

"My mother…um…well, you see, she's the principal of Dini's

school. You know, the one you spoke to, that started the whole story."

Suri stared at Yael. "You're not serious? Mrs. Savetsky, the principal of Machon Bayla? That's your *mother*?"

Suri didn't know why that information should have, could have made any bit of difference, but somehow, she had an instant, crazy sense of feeling betrayed, for not having been told this vital information. Her eyes narrowed as she watched Yael, who seemed unable to make eye contact. And she asked herself: Who, exactly, should have let her in on this secret? Yael, who had been sitting at home at the time, after being pushed out of the clinic? Mrs. Savetsky, probably feeling bitter toward an unknowing Suri, but speaking graciously all the same?

Suri closed her eyes briefly. No, it was not worth it to go there. The whole incident was, *baruch Hashem*, in the past, and it deserved to firmly stay there.

She opened her eyes to find Yael looking at her anxiously. "Life can be funny sometimes, huh?" she said lightly, and Yael's forehead smoothed.

"Funny, yeah. Anyway, ever since the whole episode, my mother's been in close touch with Dini and her mother, even after she graduated. Dini's living at home this year, and going to a local seminary. Her father, apparently, still wanted to get her in to a top seminary in Eretz Yisrael, but my mother thought sending her away was insane, and it seems Dini's mom agreed."

And, even more impressively, stood up to her husband, Suri added to herself.

"So, the other day, I was visiting my parents when Dini dropped by. My mother introduced us, and when Dini realized we work together, she got all excited and begged me to say hello to you. Then she decided she would do it herself, and wrote you this note."

Suri leaned forward. "How's she doing? Has she gotten treatment?"

Yael shrugged. "Dunno. I couldn't exactly ask her that."

"But your mother must know!"

Yael raised an eyebrow. "Even if she did, she wouldn't tell me. Right?"

Suri blushed. "Uh, right."

"But she looked good, if that means anything."

It didn't mean a whole lot, but still, Suri peered at the handwriting on the paper in front of her, as if the curly purple ink could somehow reveal the answer to her question.

"*Nu*, what did she write?" Yael asked.

Suri read aloud. "'Hi Suri, it's Dini Goldfeder. It's been a while, don't know if you remember me. Ha, ha, just joking! I'm so excited to have the chance to say hi, even if it's not in person, and to tell you that you're amazing and that you totally saved my life and that one day, I'm gonna invite you to my wedding, *im yirtzeh Hashem*! Even if my parents refuse.'"

Suri grimaced. "Oops, sorry, bad joke again. But seriously, what I really want to say is, you're the best and I can't thank you enough.'"

Suri looked up to see Yael beaming.

"Nice, huh?"

Suri nodded slowly. Dini sounded different now—sounded, if Suri wanted to put her finger on it—like a typical seminary-age girl. She didn't know how meaningful it was being told by a teenage girl that she's "amazing and totally saved her life." But perhaps the fact that Dini sounded so age-appropriately normal was actually the biggest thank-you of all.

"ALL READY, *TZADDIK'L*?" Aviva asked brightly, as she slipped a sweater over Yerachmiel's outfit. It might have been overkill, dressing him in Dolce & Gabbana for a little outing, but he'd finally grown into Yael's baby gift, and Aviva wanted to make the most of it.

"Hey, first impressions count for something, no?" She smiled as Yerachmiel babbled back at her, as if in agreement.

"You bet. That's why I always try to be so charming to strangers."

Aviva turned around, as Zevi walked through the front door. "What are you doing home?" she asked. She tried to keep the judgment out of her voice as she said it, but it might not have worked, because Zevi stepped back in mock hurt.

"I rushed out of the office, leaving five clients yelling after me, just to get home in time to give the little guy the big send-off, and you ask me what I'm doing home?"

Aviva bit her lip, trying to decide if he was really offended, and also if he could possibly be serious. On the one hand, Zevi was totally nuts about Yerachmiel. Still, even Zevi couldn't possibly leave work in the middle of the day just to—

"Nah, I'm actually meeting up with the *chevrah* right now. Special event, Danny's birthday, they wanted me to come."

Aviva wasn't quite sure how it had happened, but somehow, Zevi's stint with his Pesach cleaning crew was such a hit that he ended up befriending the bachurim, and, one thing leading to another, he somehow got connected to a group of at-risk teenagers. They now met once a week to play basketball, eat, and schmooze, in what Zevi called Hoops 'n Heroes, and Aviva had to admit that if anyone could reach these boys, it was her husband.

The thought made her proud.

"Okay, enjoy."

"You too," he said, giving Yerachmiel a rub of the head that made the boy giggle and grab his father's arm. "Good luck, kiddo," Zevi added. "Show 'em what you got."

Aviva glanced at her watch as she strapped Yerachmiel into his car seat. How embarrassing if she were to come late. Luckily, there was no traffic, and she pushed the baby's stroller through the familiar doors just on time for the appointment.

"Great, you're here!" Shira said, with a smile at Yerachmiel. "Go right in, she's waiting for you."

Aviva turned down the hall, toward Suri's therapy room. It wasn't without misgivings that she'd decided to give over Yerachmiel's speech care to someone else, but she knew that treating her own son wasn't the ideal setup, and it was time to hand over the reins. Much as she hated handing over reins.

"Knock, knock!" Aviva said brightly as she carried Yerachmiel inside Suri's room.

Suri smiled. "Hi, Yerachmiel!" But her smile was strained, and she looked a little tense as she told Aviva to sit down.

"You going to explain to me the therapy procedures?" Aviva asked with a grin.

Suri took a breath. "Listen, this is weird. And we both know it. So, I was thinking about it, and I decided it's best to discuss this from the start."

Aviva hesitated, then nodded. "Agreed. Discuss away."

Suri continued, "I'll tell you what's worrying me. You're my good friend, and you're also the best speech therapist I know. And you're—okay, how can I put this delicately?—um...you can sometimes be a bit of a perfectionist."

Aviva burst out laughing. "Ya think?"

Suri bit her lip. "So you see why I'm worried here? You're going to be sitting in on my sessions, and I'm going to be on eggshells the whole time, all self-conscious that maybe I'm making a mistake, and you're going to catch me on it and be disappointed by the quality of Yerachmiel's treatment, and it's going to come between us."

Aviva ran a hand through her sheitel and then she shook her head impatiently. "Suri, I'm totally offended." Suri's eyes opened wide, and Aviva smiled. "Did you really think I hadn't thought of exactly this issue? That's why I've decided that if I'm putting him in your care, that means I'm going to step back. I'm going to stay out of the room, I'll watch from outside, and if I feel tempted to say something, only the walls of the hallway will hear it. I can't promise that I won't want to have a hand in deciding his therapy goals and which treatment to use, but we will sit and work that out together and I will try my hardest not to pretend to be a know-it-all." She paused and looked at Suri. "Does that satisfy you?"

Suri's shoulders relaxed as she nodded. "Yes, it does. Thank you for understanding."

Aviva shook her head. "No, thank you. And...I hope you realize one thing. I wouldn't just choose anyone to treat my precious son. Even if she is my good friend. The reason I chose you was because you're a super therapist."

Aviva couldn't remember ever seeing Suri glow like that before. Her whole face was suddenly shining, as she turned to Yerachmiel and said, "Okay, let's begin."

ABOUT THE AUTHOR

GILA ARNOLD HAS been filling up notebooks with stories for as long as she can remember, and if you take a trip to her childhood home in Queens, you may still find some in her old desks and night table drawers that, to her parents' chagrin, she never got around to cleaning out. These days, she's moved up from notebooks to computers, and from New York/New Jersey to Ramat Beit Shemesh, but she's still writing away.

Gila has been published in numerous Jewish publications, and is a regular contributor to *Mishpacha* magazine and the *Jewish Press*. A multi-genre writer, she also works as a copywriter and translator. She enjoys crafting language, and also enjoys helping others develop their own innate language gifts, through her work as a speech therapist. But most of all, she loves being a wife and mother, and when she's not at work, she can frequently be found trying her hardest to provide her family with dinner and clean socks.